THE LEPER COLONY

Ron McKay grew up in Glasgow and lives in a very well-defended refuge outside the city. He has worked for several broadsheet newspapers, covered many wars – some of them abroad – and he now writes a weekly column for *Scotland on Sunday*. *The Leper Colony* is his fourth novel.

By the same author

THE CATALYST
THE PROPHET
MEAN CITY

RON McKAY

The Leper Colony

VICTOR GOLLANCZ
LONDON

First published in Great Britain 1997
by Victor Gollancz
An imprint of the Cassell Group
Wellington House, 125 Strand, London WC2R 0BB

A Gollancz Paperback Original

A catalogue record for this book is
available from the British Library.

ISBN 0 575 06474 9

Lines on page 72 quoted from 'You Don't Know What You've Got
(Until You Lose It)' by Paul Hampton and George Burton.

Typeset by SetSystems Ltd, Saffron Walden
Printed and bound in Great Britain by
The Guernsey Press Co Ltd, Guernsey, Channel Isles

97 98 99   5 4 3 2 1

For Caitlin

Part One

1

It's not easy performing a clean amputation on a cadaver using only household utensils. Not only does it require a high degree of ingenuity and lateral thinking, it works up a fair sweat. It isn't the kind of thing they teach you in first aid, or the Special Forces, which is more to do with creative presentation of the corpse than butchering it into component pieces, although the latter can sometimes follow the former, depending on the method used.

I looked around the small room, the dull paint, muddy wallpaper, pictures askew on the walls – hopelessly romantic views of hills and glens and noble stags grimed over by years of smoke and dirt and microscopic flakes of skin from the bodies which had moved through it. Walking across to the lumpy stone and cement fireplace, the soles of my shoes seeming to pull like Velcro from the matted carpet, I stretched up and ran my right index finger along the top of the white plastic frame holding a print of something by Landseer, or one of his sad and tweedy disciples, and drew it back. The whorls on my finger were greasy and smeared with what looked like sticky fingerprinting ink. How much of me, I wondered, was in the dirt, the accumulated and congealed fragments of skin and household dust? I wiped the finger on the pocket of my jeans, which had seen better days, and not just on me.

Slowly I turned away and walked over to the front window with its mucky net curtains and the fog beyond them, the blurry outlines of buildings and, above them what I presumed, from the uniform grey, was the sky. With the same stained finger I rubbed a hole in the fogged glass, wiped it on my pocket again and peered out. Trying not to remember how many times I had looked out from here, barely able to recall, everything blending into one long view from the other side of the glass of a despairing kid looking out on an uncaring world. I chided myself: whatever I had lost, it was not my capacity for self-pity. Now there seemed to be glittering jewels on the ground out there, but when I used the heel of my hand to create a larger porthole in the greasy film of condensation, I saw that it was only the low winter sun catching the shards of broken glass and discarded beer cans in the tiny front yard.

I shivered, whether in disgust or from the chill I wasn't sure, remembering my mother on her knees inside the small fence, shattered and rotten now, just a few upright brown wooden teeth sticking from the ground, digging away at the shallow earth with a trowel, bedding in the scraps of plants which almost never survived the detritus, the scuffling feet and my father's scorn. Almost nothing survived that. I could envisage her now, her skinny back hunched, wrapped in a lurid fluorescent training suit, some meaningless decal on the chest like *jogging* or *power*, trowelling and hoeing away at the earth, occasionally wiping her brow and then going back at it in what I now like to think was some silent and indefatigable protest against her state. That was probably too fanciful. It just got her out of the house for a while and away from *him*. I shook my head: anyway, it didn't matter now.

A couple of kids in baseball caps, black, about thirteen, were hovering in the orbit of the rental car. Instantly suspicious. Then, *who gives a fuck*? I said to myself, shaking my head and picturing the car without wheels, of being trapped there; then a flicker of irrational panic ran through me, so I rapped the glass hard a couple of times, watched as they

10

broke away from their gravitational intent, smiled and turned back into the room.

The coffin was perched on the seats of four kitchen chairs. Someone, from the mortician's, or the welfare, or one of the neighbouring houses, had dragged a small table to the head of the box, draped it in kitchen roll and stuck a couple of candles into two flowerpots, the shrivelled leaves of the dead plants like petrified wreaths around them. There was an envelope and a photograph, one I didn't remember ever seeing, in an ornate wooden frame, clean and cared-for. I picked up the dun envelope, slapped it against the palm of my other hand, felt something sliding about inside. Well, it wouldn't be a will, or a treasure map, or tickets to a better life. The undertaker's bill, probably. Folding it, I slipped it into an outside pocket of my quilted combat jacket.

Then I looked again at the picture in the frame, which stood at an angle, one of those cardboard props that fold out behind holding it in place. The image was surprisingly vivid, as if it had been kept away, out of the light, for years: two young people, a man and a woman I guessed must be my parents – peering closer, I was sure it was them – an unfamiliar backdrop of what looked like a tenement building, and the woman, Ma, smiling and proud, holding a baby in a shawl. Me, I suppose. I picked it up with my right hand, my still soiled index finger leaving a clear, mucky print on the glass. Breathing on the surface, wiping it on my jacket, I transferred it to my other hand, licked the smudgy finger once more and then wiped it down my pants.

I was standing over the coffin, looking down at the husk of what had been my father, my mouth in a twisted grimace, thinking, *You don't know how often I've looked forward to this, Da*. But there was no heat in the pleasure, I suppose because he was unaware of it. Despite the irrefutable evidence before me, the certificates and intimations, I passed the glass surface of the picture frame over his mouth, which clearly hadn't

11

been properly fixed or wired shut and had fallen open, presumably once rigor mortis had passed, and the slight incline of the head on the satinet pillow had caused it to yaw and drop. I looked for moisture on the glass. Nothing, of course. Good to be sure, though. But the ghoulish thought occurred: vampires and the undead don't give off vapours, do they?

I looked once more at the picture, caught a dull reflection of my grown self swimming through the old characters, then looked back at the coffin. His face seemed caved-in, fleshless, with sagging skin which had been made-up in some way, the cheeks flushed, the eyelashes blackened, the sight of which raised a sneer. Why do they do that? I wondered. To cosmeticize the painful reality for relatives? For me, all it did was make death into a powdered farce.

I had wanted to enjoy the reality of that place, as I never had all the times before. I thought of *The Scream* by Munch for some reason, considered that a print of it would have been much more appropriate on the walls all these years, rather than the bucolic scenes of the old country; then, vaguely, I considered whether to attempt to pull the eyelids apart, just to render the illusion in the coffin more complete.

'Probably glued them together,' I said out loud, breath misting in the cold atmosphere like a small cloud over my father's face. Then to myself: they would do it just so's his baleful, miserly stare doesn't disturb the fun of the funeral drinks party, as if he was lying there totting up how much his going had cost him. But had there been anyone to mourn him over a glass? Doubtful. He was not a man to encourage neighbours, casual friendliness or lasting regard.

Still holding the photograph, I rummaged around in pockets for matches, having decided that I might as well light the candles. What was a wake without the smell of tallow? Laying the picture face down on the kitchen roll, which I now saw had a tiny motif of green bears threading across it, I struck a

12

match and lit the two candles. When they burn down, I mused, they'll set off the foliage, which will spark on to the paper, set the mourning table alight and, with judicious neglect, cremate the corpse and save time and money on the funeral. Even in death I wanted to get something back at him.

It was strange he hadn't left a demand to be shipped back to the old country, so often had he gone on about it. But perhaps he had – it was just that nobody wanted to honour it. Get back at the old bastard posthumously. Inter him for perpetuity in an alien land, his soul lost, with only an exit map from Govan.

Then I realized I was beginning to shiver, chittering as Ma would have called it, my teeth beginning a staccato. I turned the gas fire's cracked bakelite knob, heard a hiss and clicking followed by the grind and whump of a small explosion as the spark set the fake coals flickering and reddening. This was one of those old fires which rely on a grindstone, or a couple of vigorously rubbed twigs, to ignite them.

I was surprised the gas hadn't been cut off, like the electricity, as I crouched over the growing flames, rubbing my hands. But although the heat of the sputtering fire was beginning to colour my face, I was still shivering. I had spent my early childhood cowering, and now here I was, as adult as I guessed I'd ever get, and I was still shaking like a victim. I took out the tobacco tin, reached over for the photograph and squatted down with both hands between my legs in a wide lotus position. My thumb, in its usual practised way, flipped the lid off the tin; I spilled the crystals across the happy family scene, and then slid my right hand inside the lining of my combat jacket and pulled out an army knife, opened the keened main blade and began slicing the crystals to powder.

It tasted familiarly metallic at the back of my throat as it froze its way to my lungs and then into the bloodstream. I wiped the smeared knife on my left index finger and licked the finger for any residue. By now I could feel my heart beating, although, of course, it made no difference to my emotions. All I seem to have left now are anger and a lack of it. Apart from that there is nothing within me, except a vague self-preservation instinct. Nothing much without, either.

The ten-dollar bill on the floor between my legs was one of the few remaining. By the end of the week I'd be on welfare, or at war. And, since I don't suppose I qualify for the former, it would be back to unleashing the latter.

On arriving I had gone over the whole house, but there was nothing of value – not just nothing of value, there was absolutely nothing of the past, apart from the household dross, pans, crockery, old dried-up cloths and dead spiders. I thought of Ma again, slumped, humbled, prematurely aged and dried-out. Everything except the photograph in the cheap frame – and the cheap corpse in the other wooden one – seemed to have been removed, destroyed or stored somewhere I couldn't begin to imagine. There were no mementoes of memories. I suppose I had been hoping for something – old pictures, letters, cuttings? – to jog a few of my own. But the house had been stripped as clean as my own past. I imagined my old man, coughing and wheezing, but cackling grimly nonetheless, out in the back yard burning everything that would provide a record, denying me even my own remembrances.

The army shrink had said that either I was in denial or I was a bare-faced fucking liar.

'Absolutely. I'm sure you can be both,' I had replied, shrugging, looking down at the prison fatigues, then glared challengingly at her: 'Both. It's what I've been trained for, after all. Took the oath for. They're the twin doctrines, or maybe the successive, of denial – and denial. Nothing happened. Even if it did, I wasn't there. Or if I was – and I'll need the tape or the transcript to confirm it – I was looking the other way, or taking a leak.

'You know the routine, throw me at a congressional committee, bind my pulse and measure my heart rate, shoot my veins full of Sodium Pentothal or hypnotize me and still – a blank. It's what one of my instructors called the Bruce Doctrine – that'd be Lenny, I think, not Willis or Robert The, who's an icon you probably wouldn't be familiar with, being a Scottish legend from my folks' past – which holds that even if you're caught *in flagrante* with your cock up a chicken you deny it, or blame it on a trick of the light.'

I realized that I was mumbling to myself, always a telltale sign, so I shook my head and got up, clasping the knife and waving it in front of me like a prod, or perhaps, a lightning conductor. It had become noticeably duller, in spite of the fire's circle of broiling light, and the sun, which must have been at its lowest point, was streaming in a rough circle through the clean patch of glass and casting a milky circle on the dark carpeting. Spooky. Through the window I could see that the black kids were back so I battered the glass again and shouted, 'Fuck off', aware my voice sounded damp and muffled in my ears. On the path to heightened perception lies the jungle of sensory deception, I told myself. That's another telltale effect, internal garrulousness and pathetic sub-Wildean attempts at ironic humour.

There was condensation on the glass now, droplets, tears, forming and dribbling slowly down. I saw my bleary reflection through the water, felt nothing but a chemical sense of well-being shot through with mild disgust. Well, it beat the usual full-scale self-loathing. A wake, no one of my own flesh and blood left alive that I knew of and, despite the betraying image of mourning I saw in the glass, my teary visage, there was no other feeling.

Then, possibly as a result of the chemical jump-start, I sensed my old man looking at my back. I ignored it. Call it habituation. Instead, with the point of the knife I probed the jagged scar beside my left eye where he had caught me with

15

his closed fist, the diamond in the ring cutting through my skin and bruising the bone as my head shot back in a spray of blood.

About now I should be feeling something, even hate, I told myself as I toyed with the knife along the scar and down on to the cheek below my eye. Skinheads used to tattoo tears on their cheeks, perhaps still do, although what it signifies, apart from a stupid pseudo-hardness, I don't understand. Then, carefully, on the ridge of bone under the eye, I made a small downward incision.

I felt a blob of blood well up and then trickle down my face. I wiped the glass with my forearm and saw myself again with the dark, single tear. 'There you are, Da, pain, remorse and regret.' And the words turned to condensation on the glass and blotted out my face.

The candles had burned half-way down, the flames giving off tendrils of dark smoke. Cheap, I thought. My nose was running like a torrent now, which I wiped continually on the back of my sleeve. Still, no one around to tell me off for it. Why had I come? I asked myself again. To make sure it was all over, that there were no remaining undead, was the best reason I could come up with, best on myself. There was also a substantial element of perverse pleasure in it, and no gainsaying. And so, finally, what now?

I moved round the coffin and picked up one of the candles, tearing away the dead leaves, moving the stuttering light across my father's body in the casket, the wasted form packed into a dark blue double-breasted suit which gave off a faint shine in the candlelight. The arms were down by the side of the body. Don't they usually fold them across the chest? Probably couldn't prise them away from their death grip on his pockets. And then I noticed a quick blue flicker and brought the candle back, over the right hand. It was still there. The diamond set in gold. My eyebrows must have gone up.

Why hadn't it been taken, it being about the only thing of value in the whole place? Then, holding the candle with my left hand, I began to tug at the ring. Wouldn't move. The old man's finger within it felt like a sliver of ice. Why wouldn't it come? He had lost maybe half his weight, his fingers like shrivelled talons; and then I remembered his fighter's hands, the broken and re-broken knuckles, the swollen rolls of knotted gristle and scar tissue. The impact of them.

Couldn't get it, eh? I imagined the undertaker wrestling with the ring, the body sliding around the slab, the old bones refusing to give it up, the debate about whether to chop it off at the wrist. I suppose that's what put it into my mind, although that's probably an excuse. It was always my intention.

With the candle flicking a sputtering, changing view of the room in the mellow darkness, the flames of the gas fire roaring like the hell to come, I moved from the living room into the dank kitchen and, placing the candle on the draining board, I hunted around for soap, found none, then opened the cupboard below and pulled out a jar of plumbing sealant. Unscrewing it, I plunged my fingers in. It was oily and thick. Slimy. Grabbing the candle again I went back into the living room, dribbled some candle-grease slowly on to the edge of the coffin nearest to the hand and, carefully, my right hand glistening with the gunk, put the candle into the firming splat of grease. It held. I leaned over and picked his frail hand up by the sleeve with my left and smeared on the jelly. Then I began tugging at the ring, but although it would move up towards the knuckle of the punching part, I couldn't get it downwards over the thickened bridge, no matter how I turned and pulled at it.

Defiant even in death, I thought.

As I stood up and back I felt a crunching underfoot, looked down. The photograph! Shit. I bent down and scrabbled for it, feeling a prick on my right index finger as a piece of glass nicked it. Carefully I pulled up the damaged frame, flicked out the broken pieces of glass and, before taking out the photograph, licked the bloody, sour finger so that it would not smear the print, then pushed it into an inside pocket.

I turned back to the body. The candle had slipped and settled at an angle so that the light was throwing deep shadows and valleys across my father's face, the mouth like a gaping black hole. The harsh contrast reminded me of Harry Lime and Orson Welles, looking down on the city. Back came the memory, roaring in light, as if a switch had been flicked. I remembered it being Christmas, the black and white film on the TV, and him giving me one of his two-handed beatings with a belt, that jangling, jaunty harmonium the accompaniment. And now one of the ants had ceased moving, and did it matter? Not at all. Not to me. And there was no one else.

I asked myself: why exactly did I want the fucking ring? It wasn't all that valuable. How much would a small diamond and a hunk of gold fetch? A couple of hundred bucks at most probably. Not that I was going to sell it. But, somehow, I was going to get it. I mean, hadn't I been taught to finish everything I started, on penalty of pain?

I sucked my finger again. It tasted like the lees of a sump. Why did I want the ring? A keepsake? Hardly. I thought about it while the shadows shifted and settled across the face. Maybe it's just so as he can't take it with him! It was stupid, but it would have to do. I grinned, thinking that if there is an observational elsewhere, a grand seat looking down on events, he'll now be squirming in it.

If I was going to take the ring, there was only one way to do it. The finger would have to come off. The challenge was how to do it. The implements. What would there be in the kitchen or the tool cupboard in the hall? Cleaver? Saw? Perhaps. But when I considered it, taking the hand off at the wrist seemed a little extreme because, given the constraints of space, the proximity of the other digits and the crude

18

approach, there seemed no way of neatly lopping the finger off without taking most of the rest of the hand. Even to do that I would probably have to drag the old man out of the coffin and into the kitchen, lie him on the floor, put a block under the arm and then give it several mighty, meaty whacks with the cleaver, which would certainly be a quicker, if a less clean, job than sawing through.

But then I'd have to deal with the finger, put the body back, make him look the way he was before, was now – well, minus the hand, of course – which might just be noticed when the undertaker finally screwed down the lid, or maybe, for this cheap-jack affair, knocked in a few brass nails. Shit, I could always pull the sleeve of the jacket down over the stump or strew a camouflage of flowers across the lower section of the body.

'Wouldn't surprise me if they have the suit off at the last minute and sell it to a thrift store,' I said down to him. 'Mind you, if anything can scare the bejesus out of a blasé mortician, it'd be a suddenly handless corpse which was entirely whole before.' I was giggling and shivering. Clearly in need of a spot more of the pacifying powder. Later, I told myself. Deferred gratification.

Thinking about it, there was only one obvious and unobtrusive way to do this. It'd have to be the finger alone. Sawing through the bone would take forever and I'd have to use the saw blade of my army knife, which would be awkward, but anyway, I wasn't sure the steel was up to it – Swiss, tempered and tungstened or whatever it was. The clever way was just to dislocate the finger, open up a channel in the knuckle so that all that was holding it on was gristle and cartilage, then whip the knife through the gap like a scalpel. A couple of quick strokes and it'd be free. In theory.

For surgical precision I needed all the light I could get, so I disentangled the other candle from its dead foliage – it looked vaguely phallic, surrounded by the dried, pubic forest – made a puddle on the other edge of the coffin and stuck the base of the candle in the congealing wax, 'No need to scrub up for this one,' on my breath as I pulled out the knife, opened it and laid it on Da's chest. Then, shuffling round the perimeter of the box so that I was slightly behind the body, I grasped the cold hand with mine (it felt like something you would find underground, I thought, and then remembered that this was exactly where it soon would be), bent back the other fingers letting the target finger come out between the clench of my fist, then wrapped my other hand round it. I took a deep breath and with all my not inconsiderable strength jerked upwards and outwards.

The bones made a resistant grinding sound, which set my teeth on edge, exactly like the remembered sound of a cold roast chicken leg coming off in the kitchen, or more recently, ball and socket injuries. The finger was distended and loose, not at all human-looking. Standing back I picked up the knife. How do I feel, I thought? Foolish. And shouldn't there be some music to go with this? Maybe the Saw Doctors? Oh, I can be gruesomely funny.

Breathing in, concentrating, aiming the knife, I made a deep V-shaped incision around the top knuckle of the hand. The flesh peeled back like old canvas, revealing the bloodless string of membrane below. I stuck the point of the blade in and sawed deeply, and after five or six vigorous back-and-forths the finger dropped off and plopped down into the folds of his suit. Textbook stuff.

How did I feel now? Even more foolish. The only sound in the house was the hissing of the fire and in my ears the rushing of wild blood.

The ring had come off so easily and now I toyed with it in my fingers, crouching down in front of the fire. Scrabbling around in a kitchen drawer I had found a roll of sticky masking tape and wrapped some round the hand and the finger, reassembling it in some kind of rough order in a swathe of plastic bandaging (if I could have found needle and thread I would have surgically reattached it, so pleased was I with myself!), the hand now looking as if it had suffered some pre-death injury trauma.

The diamond sparkled in the moving firelight. Occasionally I touched my fingers to the scar, then ran the cold face of the ring across it. Musing. And then I remembered the picture inside my coat, shuffled into a more comfortable crouch and pulled it out, wondering whether I could see the ring on the old man's finger in the snap. I peered closely, holding it towards the fire to catch the warm light, but I was disappointed to notice that the hand in question was concealed by the baby's shawl – *my* shawl?

I dropped the fading black and white photograph and rubbed at the inside of the ring. There was an inscription which I could just pick out. What looked like a date, 26/6/60. And some lettering. *To T. L. K?* I licked a finger and rubbed at the senseless inscription. It was definitely 'To' and, running a nail around the cut letters and then holding the ring close to my eyes, I was sure that the other letters were T, L and K. What kind of initials were they?

I leaned back against the battered armchair, toying with the ring. *To T. L. K..* Maybe the L stood for *love*? Couldn't be. And who were T and K? Why would you wear a ring with those initials cut into it when your name was Eddie? Why had my father worn someone else's ring?

Then it occurred to me that perhaps it had been a gift, or stolen, or bought from the pawn, the inscription never erased. Or some reclaimed gambling debt, maybe? Or perhaps he had even acquired it in the same way as I just had? I shook my head slowly. You wouldn't wear a ring inscribed with other people's initials or love pledges. Would you? Only if you were completely perverse. Which he was, my old man. But to *that* extent?

I looked down to where the photograph lay, a sheen of fire playing across the surface, dancing, illuminating, as if intimating something of importance. So I reached for it, with a peculiar sense of foreboding, knowing that I was about to learn something I didn't want to know.

But nothing had changed with the figures in the composition. The same fixed smiles, the grey, puzzling backdrop which I knew must be Glasgow, and then eventually, naturally, I turned it over and there it was, Ma's handwriting for sure, the familiar neat characters, the concentrated lettering of someone ill at ease with her hand, a wavy blue underline. All it said was *Christening, August 3rd, 1964. Tom, Kathy and Tom Jnr*. A photograph with an inexplicable legend in one hand and a ring with a mis-directed dedication in the other, but both consistent. An unknown date. Three unknown names. I threw my head back, looking up at the narrowing hollow of red light above, then back at the fire. My body felt hot, my back and my ribs stinging with welts, old scars. Nothing else in my mind but hidden memories burning in old wounds. I could hear the whistle of the leather belt in the air, a low moan, the rush of displaced air and then the sharp crack or the muffled jangle, depending on which end I was being hit with. Afterwards, my mother tending them. My mother. Jean!

Shivering, scrambling sorely to my feet, I pushed the photograph and the ring into my side pockets, knowing that all of this was some last, ghastly violation of me from beyond the grave. My fingers in the right-hand pocket felt the envelope, pulled it out, the hand trembling as I held it. What else? Tearing open the seal, I pulled out a small, thin, shiny book, a passbook. Riffling the pages, turning away from the fire so that the light cast a magenta blush on the stiff paper, fingering to the page with the last entry, and there, running a finger down the column: fifty-thousand and some dollars. Credit. I held it like a child with his first schoolbook, or a missal, turned the front cover towards me, read the name of the holder in the oblong window. John Downe.

It took a second to happen. The room seemed to palpitate, bile boiled in my gullet, heart pounding like drum roll, cheeks broiling, thoughts forming and exploding like bubbles in my brain. Re-scanning my name, I moved towards the door, rocking the coffin on the table as I went, dropping the passbook, trying to get away. My hand shook on the Yale lock as I turned the handle; a cool wash of air rushed over me as I stood looking out, trembling, the sky bright with stars, streetlights casting a mucky yellow glow on the neighbouring houses, the cars in rows along the kerb, most of them scuffed, bashed and worn, Pontiacs, Chryslers, a Ford pick-up, the hired Pinto, the only newish one, the only one with a reflective glow from the polished bodywork. Caught a glitter in the glass as a couple of shapes moved behind the windshield, fancied immediately that it must be the two black kids from earlier, conflicting thoughts about what to do (had to get away, but didn't want any involvement), opened my mouth while considering whether to shout, watched the car cough and choke as the engine turned, and then it caught, stuttered and moved.

There seemed to be two explosions. The first ruptured the bonnet, blew out the glass, knocked the car down at the front like in a Keystone Kops clip, and then the second, when the charge ripped into the gas tank, causing the mushrooming fireball. Somewhere between the two I instinctively whirled away and threw myself headlong back into the hall, the night hot, flaming and fuming behind, shards of glass and metal, white, red and molten, spraying, impaling, tossing and falling, the road alight, windows blowing in, streetlamps going out, the paintwork and tyres on nearby cars starting to burn.

When I came out of my protective sprawl I looked back, first to the pain in my right leg where the denim had been

23

torn away and the dark slick to the flesh told me I had been caught there by the blast. A burning in the leg, probably glass or metal. Then I looked up and back to the two in the car, or what was left of them and it, just a burning chassis and a bundle of broiling meat in the passenger seat, and in the driver's place what was left of the young get-away guy, who seemed to have a charred hand up and was waving, although I told myself that could only be the effect of refraction, as I watched him greeting and beckoning me through the hell of heat and smoke and wavering fire.

The silence was absolute, even when the pieces of metal and flesh from farthest away, nearest the epicentre, came sprinkling back to earth. I held my leg, realized that the noise of the explosion had deafened me, and when I looked slowly around I saw that a finger of burning petrol was running and pointing at the house, that the window had been blown in and that the curtains were in flames. I stumbled to my feet and rushed back inside, crunching over glass, not even thinking about it but impelled to retrieve the fallen passbook, my bloody inheritance, barely noticing that the waves and reverberations of the blast had collapsed the funereal plinth, turned over the coffin and spilled out my father, who lay face down on the smouldering carpet.

2

'Why don't you ever take the tee shirt off?'

I looked up, squinting against the sun, trying painfully to focus on a silhouette against it, clearly a woman by the voice, although the usually distinctive shape was somewhat unclear due to the flaring in my eyes. I cupped my right hand over them, trying to blot out the glare, which reminded me uncomfortably of a salute, then scrabbled around for sunglasses. 'Sorry, I hadn't realized I was being regularly spied on or I would have changed it more often.' The glasses were under the apex of the opened book and I slipped them on and sat up, feeling grains of sand dribbling down my nose rather undignifiedly.

'It's just curious, that's all. And you haven't answered.'

'You're very direct,' I said. 'I didn't realize that going topless was mandatory on this beach. Look at you, for instance, you're not observing the dress code.' I could see now that the girl looked about sixteen, she was wearing a down jacket, open all the way, over a two-piece costume. There was a patch of damp sand around her navel. She was still standing against the sun and despite the army-issue shades designed to survive a nuclear holocaust (who'd be around to wear them, except mutants?), she was still bleary and monochrome against a flaring aura. I shuffled around on my bum, the backs of my legs hitting the hot sand, so that the sun was coming at me over my right shoulder. Now that I could see her more easily, she looked a little older than my first estimate, but not much. I could also now pick out that the open jacket was navy and fleecy, with some sort of decal on the left breast, and that the costume below was light blue. Costume? It looked more like a hasty cover-up with a felt-tip pen than a swimming suit.

She was tanned, hair down to her shoulders, which looked chestnutty, with sun streaks. A pair of aviators stuck midway up her crown kept the hair off her face. A typical Bondi surf bunny, I said to myself. And then, what is this all about and what's my part in it?

'Well?' she said.

'You're always this pushy.' It wasn't a question. She said nothing. I noticed a group of kids about her own age were hanging back about ten yards behind her, surfers, all tangled long hair, fluorescent clothes and multicoloured boards.

'It's a nice tee shirt,' she came back. It was plain, actually, white, regulation netherwear, with a couple of snags around the stomach, hardly anything to remark about. 'The body underneath might be too. But who knows? My bet is it's either covered in a pelt of bear's hair or a frieze of tattoos of pneumatic girls, beach balls and seals, with "mother" intertwined in a rope of hearts.'

'That,' I nodded, 'and "gay pride".' It came out from behind a grin. She didn't respond, just kept on staring. 'So, do you win the bet if you get me to take it off?' With my right forefinger I wiped the sweat from my brow.

'It's a dare more than a bet. And you're not gay.' She tried to look wise and mature. 'I can always tell.'

'See,' I rubbed the sand residue from my face, unsure where this verbal shuffle in the sand was going, 'what's wrong with young people today is an unhealthy obsession with looks, and sexual excitement. Don't you get enough excitement out there?' I motioned with my head towards the ocean.

'They think—' she sat down cross-legged in front of me,

26

leaned forward, peered into my glasses, rubbed her nose and nodded over her shoulder. 'You're older than I thought.'

'Really? I'll try not to decompose too alarmingly in front of you.'

She ran her hands through the sand, looking down at them as they moved around under the surface like cruising predators. A strange gesture I put down to discomfiture. But I'm hopeless on body language. Behind her I could see the lipping waves, the disconnected dots of surfers, the churning froth of the boiling water on the foreshore, which reminded me somewhat bizarrely of the desert and the absence of beer. 'Not that old. And I'm older than I look—'

'I'll bet.'

'Twenty – well, almost. Actually,' she pulled a hand from under the surface of the sand and rubbed her nose with the back of it, 'when I said it was a dare I neglected to mention—' She shook her head and went back to sifting sand. I looked past her at the semi-circle of surfer geeks still waiting. Jesus, there was a certain sense of imagination missing here. For me, at that age, dares had involved railway lines, hanging from ledges or throwing back booze and popping pills. '—That I was ripped, totally stoned.' She had her hand over her mouth, tittering behind it.

Imagination, did I say? Substitute replication. 'I'm going to sound a little decrepit here, but is that not a bit dangerous—' I pushed the glasses back on the bridge of my nose, the sweat was beginning to slick my face, '—when you're hanging five, or whatever it is you do out there?'

'Sure. That's what it's all about. Heightened pleasure.'

'Danger is pleasurable? I hadn't realized.' A small lie, but the first of many.

'Mostly I just hang about the beach. You know, as an unattainable object. Siren of the shore. You hadn't noticed?'

I shook my head. 'Sorry. So many sirens to avoid, you

must just have seemed like one of the gallery.' Her mates were looking bored and one or two had broken away.

'You're American.' My cadences had evidently seeped slowly through her befuddled state. 'On holiday?'

'Sort of . . . Well, I'm working around here.' If you could call Indonesia the neighbourhood. 'So,' I looked around, trying to steer the conversation away from geography and intent, 'do you win or lose?'

'You're not taking the shirt off?'

'That's right, I'm not.'

'Please.' Slowly I shook my head. 'Why?'

'Put it down to shyness. Or not wanting to be shown up by the steroid brigade.' They were all around, like slow-moving, slicked behemoths, all body oil and pumped veins. It was like sitting in the middle of some bizarre un-nature park.

'Here?' She shook her head so that the hair swirled as if it was under water. 'The body sculptures?' I nodded. 'I don't believe you.'

'Whatever.' The sweat was trickling from my armpits down both sides of my body, tickling, causing me to shiver involuntarily. At least that's what I thought it was. 'Well?'

'So I lose my dare.' She leaned forward, seemed to think about it, then kissed me lightly on the lips, sat back, pulled her glasses down, wiped the sand from her legs and stood up.

'Was that another part of it? The dare?'

She shook her head. 'Remember . . .?' Tapped her right forefinger to her lips. 'Stoned. I'm not properly in control of my senses and emotions. I have licence.'

'Yeah? Well just make sure the driving one doesn't get pulled,' I returned.

I had been coming to the beach for the best part of a week, but I hadn't noticed her – at least if I had she was just one overlooked, under-clothed item in the panoply of female gorgeousness – and all of this, even taking into account her infusion of chemicals, seemed more than slightly weird. In my experience strange young women did not normally lean over, a few sentences after not being introduced, and kiss you. Sadly. Unless, of course, you had paid them first. 'So, why did you do that?' I was squinting at her. By now she was lowering over me, giving an elongated view of her stomach and breasts before she turned away.

'Sort of stoned intuition. *In narcosis veritas*, or something. You looked vulnerable, somehow.'

'Vulnerable? So *that's* what hallucinogens do.' I started to laugh, caught myself. 'Can we start all this again?'

She had taken a couple of steps back towards what was left of her knot of friends, a couple of guys, probably contestants for her. 'Will you take off your shirt?'

'You're persistent.' I got up, unreasonable anger flaring, as ever, wanting to shock. 'Ladies first,' spitting the words out. She looked at me for a few seconds, smiled rather resignedly, then dropped the fleecy jacket from her shoulders on to the sand, put her hands behind her to the catch on her swimming suit, which is when I stepped in, not out of any sense of prudishness, embarrassment or perceived gentlemanly behaviour, but because I didn't want her to have the high ground. I pulled her hands back in front of her, then whipped the cotton shirt over my head until it was around my elbows, sending the glasses spinning into the sand. 'OK?' I turned round in the sand quickly, showing my back as well. 'All right?'

'Jesus!'

'He only had the hands and the side. So there you go.' Quickly I slipped the shirt back over my head and then squatted back down, rummaging for the sunglasses, blew sand from the lenses and put them back on. 'So you won. Now fuck off.'

I heard her snort and the slapping, soughing sounds of her feet moving away. 'You're right,' I just caught, 'you are shy. Christ, at last I've met one.'

*

Counting as I ran – *one, two, three, four* – metronomically, keeping the timing precise, forcing the legs to strike in harmony. My feet were slapping the wet sand, like a hand on a bare backside, I thought rather alarmingly as I set out, but now all I could hear was the panting of my own breath, and the harsh counting of time. I wanted to run myself into a trance until all the anger was spent and all that mattered was pleasing the timekeeper. What had all that been about? Why me? Had it just been a bizarre bet? Or was it a come-on? A come-on? I'm not sure I'd recognize one any more.

Occasionally I was having to dodge bodies on the edge of the surf, or make detours around joggers in lurid costumes and hats, waterproof Walkmans clamped to their ears, but mostly, I suppose, people saw the determination in my gait, or picked up on the suppressed anger, heard the slapping of my approach and moved out of the way. The beach wasn't too busy anyway, it was out of season, but pleasantly hot nevertheless, without having that broiling edge. My skin can't really take the sun, something to do with my north European pedigree. *One, two, three, four.* Blind obedience to the internal timekeeper. I thought: if it took the Jesuits eight years, or whatever it was, to have a boy for ever, the army can manage it in the same number of months. It's just a different brand of religion.

When I reached the tip of the crescent of the bay I stopped, caught my breath for a few seconds, touched my toes half a dozen times, turned round and headed back, the metronome automatically clicking into gear. There was a slight breeze against me which pinned the shirt to my chest. It was darkly sweat-stained, the colour of boiled meat. I have seen a lot of boiled meat, and some of it was even animal. My legs, lightly out of condition, ached as I ran: I seemed able to feel the strain and interaction of every individual muscle and, when I thought about it, I could envisage those bloodless peeled-back physiology drawings of the body in medical textbooks (and a few from real life), the cross-section of the heart, which in my chest felt as if it had been inflated by a pump and was bumping against the ribbing of the cavity. *One, two, three, four.*

I had expected the beach to be much bigger, something like one of those endless Californian or Mediterranean strips with mile after mile of sand, but it swept in a graceful arc – how long, maybe two or three miles? – against a jostle of hotels, gaudy bars and surf shops, low-level, even planned, in a haphazard way. High summer and it would be choked, but now it was for the inveterates and the unacclimatized, who, when I encountered them and cut through, broke apart before me and spilled behind like a wake.

The timekeeper was becoming breathless, a wheezing bark in my ears. I allowed him to slow down and my legs to follow as I settled into a wind-down jog as I neared the towel and book. I was walking by the time I came up to my little scrap, my undefended cotton island on the sand, where my eye was immediately caught by a damp area just above where I had left the book, a James Crumley, refreshingly and predictably full of alcohol and extreme violence. Cut into the sand was a finger-drawing of a large-budded flower, with a number below it, obviously a telephone number. No message apart from that, and no name.

Where did the water come from to wet the sand? I thought about it because the sea was a good hundred yards away. Perhaps she slopped beer or pissed on it. I looked about, but there was no sign of her. I thought about wiping the sole of my foot over the message, although not for long. Then I told myself that dares were meant to be fulfilled, shook my head at my juvenile mind, sat down and caught Crumley in mid-swallow.

3

I felt deeply embarrassed to be a victim. What are you expected to do, other than mill about, moaning and wailing, until help arrives? The street was full of people screaming and fussing, trying to look either efficient or officious, others genuinely shocked, crying and shaking, or else that dumb-struck, vacant, zombie-look you get at the periphery of serious calamity. A knot of rubber-neckers were clustered round the burned-out Pinto, tutting and cooing. The grass had gone out, a number of the less seriously affected had beaten out the flames with feet, jackets and brushes, but the old family home was nicely alight. If it had been my father's wish that he be buried, I was glad it wasn't going to be realized.

I had limped a little way from the general bedlam and was sitting on the sidewalk, under a functioning streetlamp, trying to assess the damage. With the Swiss army knife I cut away the leg of my jeans (it comes with a handy little pair of scissors which are tickety-boo for the job), and with the surplus gory material I was trying to wipe away the blood to see what was going on there. But it was too dull to see much, other than a long, seemingly deep laceration. So, what to do apart from wait and try to effect a temporary repair, given that the car had gone and the prospect of a smoke-stained gimp with half a trouser leg and a dousing of blood hitching a lift out wasn't too likely?

I folded the torn denim into a pad, pressed it against the

wound, whipped off my belt and wrapped it around the leg in a makeshift bandage, when the night became intensely bright and I heard a beating overhead of an emergency services helicopter. As it came nearer, the down-draught grew wild, whipping up the fire in the house. Someone on board must have deduced that this was not a clever manoeuvre, because the chopper went up to a wind-free height and continued to play the searchlight over the scene. It felt like something from a Spielberg movie.

After a few more minutes, the sound of sirens could be heard above the hum of the rotors, and a fire engine slewed round the corner, followed by two cop cars. After the personnel tumbled out and ran around shouting and hooking up to hydrants, a large armoured truck also drew up. That'll be the bomb squad, I told myself, trying to concentrate on blending in with the general hysteria. Fat chance. As the jet of water began to turn on to the house and the police got on with clearing people away and putting up tapes, I felt a tap on the shoulder.

'Sir?' It was a paramedic, a black guy in his thirties. I hadn't even seen an ambulance arrive. 'You're injured, sir?'

I looked at him and then back at my bare, bound leg, shook my head in wonderment at his acuity, wanting to say that it was nothing to worry about, just a trivial Masonic initiation ritual, but it hurt like hell so I nodded. Looking back past him I could see nothing but official cars and trucks, lights whirling, colour strobing across the tarmac. The helicopter, I realized, had now moved off. 'Shrapnel, probably.'

'Stay there,' he said, patting me on the shoulder.

Where else would I be going? When he came back he had a cop with him. One of those been there, done it kind of guys who wasn't going to get overheated about a mere random and unspecific bombing in a city suburb.

'That your car, by any chance?'

Cops always ask a question when they know the answer.

33

At least it's best to assume that, otherwise you get caught in a lie straight off, when it's better to be strategic about your untruths. 'Yeah . . . well, Avis's.'

He nodded, hunkering down beside me as the paramedic started undressing my wound again. 'You know what happened?' He had a bulbous face, a fleshy nose and a slight tic in his left eye. His shirt looked tight in the collar, like he had recently put on some beef.

I was wincing because the paramedic was cleaning the cut with something astringent. 'A couple of kids, black maybe, tried to heist the car. It seemed to go about a yard or so and exploded. A bomb.' Obvious conclusion.

Just for a second I could see a slight flash of doubt in his immutable cool. 'A bomb, you say. What makes you think that?'

I snorted with pain and derision, and looked him straight in the face. 'You think maybe it was spontaneous combustion, or perhaps some intrinsic Ford design flaw, something Ralph Nader should know about?' His mouth tightened. 'Obviously, it was a bomb.'

'Well, maybe. You're pretty certain about that. You got some specialist knowledge?'

'Not if you mean, did I make it, was I carrying it about – not that kind.'

'No? So, if you're so sure, maybe you know who put it there?'

'Sorry,' I shook my head. The paramedic had swabbed the leg and put a temporary dressing on it. 'Can't help. Don't have an enemy in the world.' I thought about it. 'Well, the only one I could think of who might do something like this is cooking away in the house over there.'

The cop got up quickly, turned to the fire. 'There's someone in there?' he shouted back over his shoulder at me, beginning to stumble off, clearly to find a superior.

'Not exactly,' I called out. 'He's been dead for several days.'

Gone to a place even hotter, I hoped. 'The funeral should have been tomorrow.'

The cop turned back, and there was no disguising that his sang-froid was fried. 'Smart-ass, we're certainly gonna want to talk to you,' he shouted, turning back now and motioning at me.

'We're going to have to take a look at this,' the paramedic was saying into my ear, putting his hand under my elbow to encourage me to get up. 'There could be metal in there and it's a pretty big cut; it'll need some stitching.'

'Well, just take me to your cheapest—' I started to say, and then I remembered the passbook and hopped on one leg when a little twinge of doubt and realization sparked in me. Maybe it was the old man's idea of a post-mortem joke and there was no money in the account? Well, what the hell, I told myself, if the suits in casualty start sniffing around for cash or insurance cover I'll just lapse into post-traumatic shock.

And then a second realization, which came to me in a rush, was that I would have to quickly and surreptitiously dispose of the crystals before the police started to interview me in earnest.

Lying in a booth in ER being stitched, under local anaesthetic, I seemed to be the only casualty, other than the fatalities, so the gravitational pull of the investigation was inevitably moving towards me. From outside the curtain I could hear the activity, the whisperings, occasionally my name bleeding out. Even the doctor, an agreeable young woman with short-cut blonde hair and a winning smile – at least I liked to think it was, judging from the outline of it through her mask – had been pulled out for a muttered conversation and had come back looking both angry and flustered.

'They think it was me,' I said to her confidently. 'Leap to an immediate conclusion, saves time and money investigating. Everyone's happy, except the innocent.'

She was bent over my leg, sewing away. The badge on her uniform said Dr Corinne LaTour. Clearly, French antecedents. 'What they want,' she was talking slowly, concentrating on the needlework, 'is to talk to you. Right away.' She looked up, pulled down the mask (and her smile, when it came, was indeed truly winning). 'Do you feel up to it?'

'Sure.' She knotted off the final stitch – there looked to be about a dozen – and cut the thread. It seemed to free me from the obligation of being a patient so, nothing ventured, I asked, 'What about getting something to eat when you get off? With me? The sight of all that raw meat's probably given you a raging appetite.'

She was pulling off her rubber gloves and binning them. 'I don't know when that'll be,' turning towards me, the trace of a smile. 'It's the middle of the night now, anyway.'

'I don't know when I'll get off either. You could ask the guys outside. And then we could celebrate. Vegetarian if you like.'

'You should be resting that leg.' She was definitely smiling now.

'Look, do I have to say this? It wasn't me. The car. Honest. I have an alibi.' I shrugged my shoulders. 'Unfortunately my principal witness – is dead. My father.' She looked at me oddly, before turning to the sink and running the water to wash her hands. 'I was holding a wake when it happened,' I tried to explain to her back. 'My father, sadly but understandably, if you knew him, was not a popular man, so it was a single-figure wake. Indeed single digit. I was on my own.'

I watched her dry her hands, then she turned, leaned back against the sink and folded her arms. 'You've got a pretty weird attitude about this. It's almost like, I don't know, like you're enjoying it.'

She was definitely interested, or at least morbidly intrigued, which can often lead to passion, so I slithered up into a half-erect slouch on the bed which, despite my attempt at insouci-

36

ance, caused me to wince. But I was now pretty close to her. Never go out with an intuitive woman, I counselled myself half a lifetime too late. 'Not at all,' I answered, 'it's just an act, a plucky demeanour; inside I'm a conflagration of guilt and regret, a mess of fizzing and short-circuiting wires.'

'Wrong image in the recent circumstances. Nerves is better.'

'Right,' I tried my most saleable smile, 'that's why you're the doctor and I'm the patient.'

'Anyway,' she pushed away from the sink and moved towards the curtain, 'I'll think about it. The invitation. If that's what it was.' And she went out.

Well, one thing I had said was true, I realized as I waited for the curtain to open again, it *was* an act. Not my apparent enjoyment – although there was some kind of vicarious thrill, because the truth was that I felt enlivened in a way I hadn't felt for at least five years – but the chat-up routine, the plucky wisecracks, the attempted seduction. It was just a part I was playing. Another one. And then the curtain went back and I was on for real.

'It's a simple story,' I said once more, the exasperation burning in my voice, 'and no matter how many ways you come at it, it isn't going to change. Here we go. I hired the car, I went to my folks' old house to a wake, to pay my final respects to my father; a couple of kids had been messin' with the car – I'd seen them hovering around a number of times from the window – when I came out they were in it, the car moved, bang! Blizzard of bits, glass, metal and human. That's it. So what more you lookin' for here? Mmm?' My insulting cold grin was purely to wind them up.

There were, of course, two of them. Not quite the hard and soft cops, more the strident and the silent. To me they were Deaf and Dumb. I suspected that the second one, mid-thirties, razor-cut hair, impeccable suit, was not your normal beat cop, criminal intelligence, probably. He was the silent one. Dumb.

37

He leaned against the wall, occasionally writing notes in a small leather-bound notebook with a silver pen.

'You!' I jerked my head at Dumb. 'What did you say your name was? And can I see your badge?'

The corner of his mouth twitched; he probably thought it passed for a smile, but it was more like a tic of contempt. 'I didn't and you can't.'

'We know all about you,' Deaf said. He called himself Detective Bray, and he did, when he laughed, which he only did when he thought my story was derisive. He did a lot of it.

'So? Doesn't alter what happened.'

'You know about handling explosives.'

'Yeah. Absolutely. Always with *respect*.' I sat up on the couch again. The pain in my leg was pretty intense but I wasn't going to let them see. 'So? I know which end to hold a paintbrush, but that doesn't make me Rembrandt.'

'You were in the Special Forces.'

'I was?'

'We've seen your record. You tried to frag an officer.'

'Well, well. Frag? You must have been in Vietnam – sorry, 'Nam.' I laid heavy emphasis on the Vetspeak. So they had been checking. It was inevitable, of course. 'If you read it – past the groundless allegations – you'll see I didn't—'

'Get caught! Sure.'

Bray had one of those faces you would never get tired of slapping, mean and twisted, with a wretched mouth and piggy eyes. I clasped my hands together, just in case I was tempted, then put them behind my head and slid back on the bed. 'You know, if you were really serious about catching whoever did this you'd be out looking, rather than jazzing me up. You know and I know I had nothing to do with it. You probably know who did. And you know that I know enough about explosives to ensure that if I had done something like this I wouldn't now be lying here nursing a shrapnel wound.

38

Unless, of course, you think I'm so deuced clever with Semtex,' I put my right hand up in the air, 'no, I don't know if it was Semtex, maybe home-made – that I'm so clever I can blow a car into tiny fragments while ensuring that just one sliver of metal will slice my thigh, thus creating the impression that I'm only an innocent bystander caught in the blast.

'Now, I'm going to take a walk—' that was rich, as I didn't have any trousers to put on, '—and you can either arrest me,' I paused, 'or fuck off out of my face!' I sat up with a suppressed grunt and gingerly swung both legs off the bed, letting them dangle while the pain pulsed.

'Where will you be staying, Downe?' Deaf said.

'No idea. A hostel probably.'

'Oh, a hostel,' came in Dumb, 'with all that money in your account?'

I hopped down on to the good left leg. 'Fuck, you're so predictable. You've searched my stuff without due process and proper cause. Well, well, well. I'm shocked. Wait till I tell the ACLU and my senator.'

'Sure. Where did it come from?'

'You mean, was it from gambling, or a prudent investment? Or was that my take for blowing up the car and icing the two ne'er-do-wells? Or, mostly – it has nothing whatever to do with you.'

'Ne'er-do-wells?' said Deaf.

'Forget it,' Dumb said to him. Then to me, 'You're not going to answer?'

'Know what?' I tried to smile but it was more of a grimace. 'If you two identi-cops don't get out of here right now I'm gonna start screaming that you're beating me, then I'm going to open my stitches on the edge of the bed here and watch you smart-ass your way out of that one.'

Deaf looked at Dumb, who nodded, and they both slouched out. The air felt corrosive.

The real smart-ass was me, of course. I was insisting on checking myself out of the hospital, despite the medical protestations that delayed shock would set in, that I'd be a quivering jelly before the cock crew, although I realized that was probably more of a pro forma, to enable them to avoid a lawsuit if I cracked up just badly enough to gibber pitifully and file a damages action. But in the end, after I had signed a waiver, and begged a pair of green theatre pants I promised to wash and return, I was free to go, with my torn and bloodied jeans in a plastic bag. Everything I had in the world was either on me, or under my arm, or had recently gone up in smoke and shards. America, I thought, land of opportunity, here I come again!

Still, there was the bank book, which might even turn out to be more than a chimera. I tried whistling. It's the thing to do in those circumstances. But I stopped as soon as I limped out into the night air. Deaf and Dumb were waiting, both unwinding out of a car parked in an ambulance bay, leaving a thickset driver behind the wheel. Clearly, judging by the way they had come on to me, neither was capable of passing the driving test.

Deaf pushed me in the chest, knocking my weight on to the bad leg, causing me to wince. He smiled at that. 'Here's the script, Downe. You do not leave town. You check in with me every day.' He snatched up my left hand and slapped it and when he pulled it away I was holding a business card. 'You keep me posted on your wheareabouts. Or—' He let it hang.

'Shit.' I leaned back up again, feeling the blood pulse in the wound. 'Or? Go on.'

'Or we'll take you in right now—' I didn't pick him up on having his effect and his cause ass about face, '—We can think of the charge on the drive. Or maybe it's protective custody. Clearly someone is out to get you and for your own good you should be off the streets.' I furnished him with my most sarcastic grimace. 'And don't think we're relying on trust here. We'll be watching you.' He grinned and stuck his face so close to mine I could sourly taste his last meal. 'Shouldn't be hard, the pace you're moving at.' Then he pulled back, turned and said over his shoulder as he went, 'Remember, now.'

'Got it,' I muttered at their retreating shapes. 'If I don't report in from tomorrow you'll arrest me now – fuckwit!'

I had a bad attitude and a bad leg, two cops on my case, less than fifty bucks in cash, but hell, I felt invincible and lucky, so I took a cab.

After seeking advice from the driver I checked into a ten dollars a night flophouse, still not trusting the bank book would come through for me. Anyway, I wasn't sure the Holiday Inn would give the key to the minibar to a limping gorilla without any luggage, in green theatre pants smelling of fire, iodine and sutures.

The room was more of a cubicle, containing an iron-framed bed with grey sheets and blankets I didn't trust, a metal locker next to it without a lock, dingy green walls with small explosions all over, which might have been a pattern but I suspected were squashed bugs, and one of those framed scenes of a seaside which look as if they've been painted by Grandma Moses after a serious intake of lighter fuel. There was apparently a bathroom down the hall but I didn't want to begin to imagine its state, so I decided to keep my legs firmly pressed together for the night rather than investigate it.

I could hear moaning through the walls, not the pleasurable sort accompanied by squeaking bed springs, but the pre-banshee kind, when the brain has started to wander into the thickets of infamy, ambush and outrage. Then I smiled ruefully because I had often been told that I was given to doing the same thing while I slept. Well, if that's true, this floor is going to sound like a hound dog chorus tonight.

I checked that the door locked, which it seemed to. But I

wasn't convinced that it was unbreachable, or indeed that the guy on the desk wouldn't hand over the master key at the merest financial or violent suggestion. There wasn't a window, the only way in was through the door, so I pulled the bed over until the end was jammed tight against it and then took off my shoes, lifted the back of the iron frame, what passed as the headboard, and put one shoe under each leg, before I caught myself. Habit. No one was going to sneak in to steal them. The only way in would be over my body, my dead body.

Yawning, I pulled off the mattress with all of the bedding and tipped it aside. You get used to sleeping in fields, trenches, huts or tents, pulling off leeches, lichen or sucking bugs, all manner of insects, but that routine was distracting and time consuming. And also, despite the cheapness, I was paying not to go through that. So I threw myself down on the metal cot, on the diamond patchwork of wires, and tried to sleep.

The small handful of analgesics the hospital had given me had lost their edge and I hurt badly, not just in my leg but all over, like in the early stages of flu. Perhaps it was delayed shock, or just the other chemicals evaporating in my system, so I curled up in a sore and sorrowful ball, the movement seeming to bring out a mocking moan from the springs. On the back of my eyelids a scene of fire and fizzing gobbets of flesh and metal was playing out, despite my attempts to run a comforting rural scene or some early memories of the past, both of which usually evoke a dull nothingness. Unfortunately that wasn't working.

Someone tried to kill you tonight, kept coming up in neon lettering. Which wasn't a new experience, but usually there was some presenting cause – like a declaration of war and a natural and understandable will by the other side to hold on to their own lives or their sovereign territory – and normally the opposition were easily identified, either by uniform, colour, caste or shape of eye, but this time it wasn't so. This time I knew, but did not want to admit, that the enemy was someone just like me. Indeed, probably people I knew and had shared a beer with, or at least knew of. The bed screeched in counterpoint to the mangling of connections in my head.

But it was a pretty flamboyant and intricate way of going about it. More like a mission statement or grisly warning, when a drive-by shooting, an overdose, or a push off a subway platform would have been less noticeable, and certainly more specific.

Conclusion? Well, if they weren't bothered about definitely getting me, or were doing it in such a way as to discourage others, I asked myself, *so who the fuck are the others?*

4

I didn't know her name but I made the call. From the hotel room, watching the sun flaming into a sea turned the colour of warm blood on the horizon. The phone rang for a long time and part of me was hoping there would be no answer, but after about thirty seconds a woman's voice, croaky and sleepy-sounding, yawned something.

'I probably have the wrong number,' I said.

'Depends.' I could hear her stretching and what sounded like the crinkle of bed linen. 'What you got in mind, Yank?'

I could see a few tiny moving grey dots picked out on the rose-coloured waves still, the rest of the sea inshore dark as teak. 'I don't even know your name.'

'Mmmm? Emily. And don't think about calling me Em.' I could hear what sounded like someone moving around in the background. 'What's yours?'

'Downe.' I was so used to only giving my second name that it didn't occur to me to use my first.

'As in duck down . . . or as in incoming?' I heard the chuckle in her throat. 'Much the same, really.'

'John.' Right from the beginning she had the knack of making me feel slightly foolish. It was unsettling. I was too old and experienced for embarrassment, or so I thought.

'Well?' I heard from the other end.

'Sorry!' I had caught my reflection in a wall-mirror and the look of discomfiture. 'I was wondering whether you fancied doing something? Meal, a drink, whatever?'

'Well – are you an entirely respectable man, John Downe?'
She was laughing at me and I could hear another deeper
harmonic cadence further off.

'Forget it.' I could feel the flush of anger in my face and I
began to pull the phone away from my ear, but before I did I
heard her say, 'No, don't go. Don't be so touchy. OK, when?'

'What has your friend got to say about it?' My anger still
had an edge to it.

'You want to ask him out too?' She was laughing again and
it felt friendly. 'You are not a respectable man, are you, John?
Bit of a pervert, really?' And in the same breath, but quietly,
'Tonight?'

'I was thinking that, yes.' Surprisingly I felt a wash of relief
in my gut. 'You'll have to say where and when. A stranger,
you know?' The sun had almost disappeared and the walls of
the room were slipping from rose to shadow. It was some
room, a suite actually, which I couldn't normally afford but
as I wasn't paying it felt even better to be there.

'I have ground rules, John,' she said, and now she was
whispering. 'I'll spell them out in detail later, but the most
important one is that I don't get involved.'

I sat down on the bed. 'I'm suggesting a meal, not a
wedding breakfast. Anyway, I'm just passing through. But I
like your rule.'

'Why did you say wedding, John? Is that a little Freudian?
Guilt? Are you married, perhaps?'

'Never,' I replied too quickly.

'Oh-oh. Another Freudian response. I'm seeing tortured
childhood. Warring parents. My second rule is no sad stories.
Either way.'

'You're a psychology student, are you?' I approved of my
reflection in the mirror, phone to the ear, sober blue shirt on,
button-down collar, neatly cropped hair; I could be some kind
of businessman. What kind I'd have to think. 'Sure. Where
will we meet? D'you want me to pick you up?'

'I already did that.' Her voice sounded like spooned cream. 'Where are you staying?' I told her. 'Well, well. I took you for a little lower rent than that. I'll meet you in the lobby at 8.30. And don't be late because I don't want to be mistaken for a hooker. Or persuaded it's a more profitable way of life.'

'See you,' I said, hanging up, looking at my face in the mirror again, grinning, smug. Dangerous. I shouldn't be doing this, I told myself. And I was right, as usual.

I was wearing an oatmeal-coloured linen suit I had bought in Hong Kong and a pair of hand-made brown loafers. To pass the time until she turned up I had gone downstairs to the health suite, pounded the treadmill in the gym for around half an hour, put in about forty fast lengths, then showered, so I was feeling energized and exhilarated. I asked myself why I was doing this, apart from the obvious, the possibility of sex, and when I thought about it I assumed it was also tied up with the prospect of mild danger. There I was, in a country I had never been in before, about to meet a beautiful woman I knew nothing about and would probably never see again, no common background between us so I could be anything I wanted to be, money in my pocket, going into an evening which could take an infinity of turns. I told myself, enjoy, don't analyse!

The lobby was done out in the ubiquitous trans-continental luxury hotel kitsch, a kind of jungle atrium with sprouting greenery, the ceiling about twenty storeys up and the floor a dark, polished stone which reflected the curves and lines of the plants and the glinting of the brass pots, the fitments and the polished mahogany. There were little oases of scatter rugs and leather chesterfields where well-dressed people with copper tans crouched and whispered. Reception staff in dun-coloured uniforms occasionally glided across the floor and over all was the vague hum of canned music, too low and main-stream to be decipherable. It felt like St Peter's waiting room.

I did the perimeter first, checking out who was where, whether she had turned up, and when I was satisfied she hadn't I took up a place where I could check the revolving door and picked up a glossy magazine, something touristy about wombats and Aboriginals and merchant banking oportunities, and pretended to read, the light from the carefully positioned standard lamps splashing off the pages.

She was only a couple of minutes late. She came through the revolving doors, checked as if to get her balance and orientation and I was amused and a little pleased to see, because it gave me the marginal advantage, that she looked slightly ill at ease. I had gone through a scene in my mind several times that she would arrive and I wouldn't recognize her, or worse, I would and she would not be at all like I remembered. But that evaporated. She was more than I could have imagined.

She was looking away and around when I reached her and lightly touched her arm. She was wearing a white jacket over what looked like a dark trouser-suit, cut severely at the neck. I caught her smell before the smile, something light and petalled – for some reason, I thought of poppies – and when she turned to face me a flutter of uncertainty danced in her eyes before she relaxed and gave me a rather sad and wan smile.

'You look very beautiful,' I said, and although it was true, but because I knew it was a line, I added, 'I'm supposed to say that, but you are.'

'Thank you.' She tried to smile but it wasn't happening. Something ominous seemed to have slithered between us. I dropped my hand from her arm and was waiting. 'It's not a game any more, John, and I think that you scare me.' She nodded her head.

'I'm sorry. I don't know why.' Another small lie, a pattern was forming. 'There's no need to be. How can I reassure you?' She was looking at me intently. So I laughed. 'Hey, look,

47

we're in a public place. Let's—' I looked around, '—go to the bar, have a drink and if you still feel the same way we can part, no hard feelings?'

'It's just that somehow I have this dark, scary feeling.' She leaned closer to me so that I could almost taste her scent. She was whispering. 'It's crazy, I've never felt like this before.' Then louder, 'I look at you now and I don't know what I see. You're a man – that sounds stupid. I mean, I suppose I'm used to going out with boys. Your eyes, John,' she was looking up at me, nibbling at her lips, almost, it seemed, on the point of tears, 'they seem very unforgiving.'

It's not easy to blandly brush off truth, but I tried. 'Nah, it's just contact lenses.' I tried for the multi-watt smile. 'Don't go believing all that windows of the soul stuff. Anyway, you're probably on a drug come-down. Come on.' I guided her towards the bar.

She seemed at a loss to know what to order so I went for a bottle of cold white Chardonnay. I don't know anything about Australian wine, so I went for price and the wacky name, Hickory Ridge. It kind of reminded me of illicit stills and bootleggers on back roads in the Deep South. The waiter brought it over in an ice bucket and made obeisance before disappearing. We hadn't said a word since sitting down. The bar was designed like some English tack room, or what I imagined one might look like, with leather and brass hangings, rich walnut furniture, dark, serial-killer-red walls. 'I don't know where to start.' I pushed her glass towards her and she picked it up with a marked reluctance and what could have been a mild shiver. 'Isn't this supposed to be fun?'

She took a sip and put the glass down. Her eyes, it struck me, were blazingly, interrogatively intense. 'Why are you here?'

I tried to make light of it. 'This isn't a philosophical inquiry, is it?' She didn't respond. 'Work. Working nearby.' Had been, at least. A couple of countries away.

'What do you do?' I started to reply, but she came in. 'The truth, please.'

The truth? That was a difficult one. 'I work for the government. The US government.' I took a drink from my glass, waiting. Cat and mouse. The drink had an edge of acid to it, but maybe that was just my contribution.

'Go on.'

'I'm not being coy. It's nothing very important. But nothing I can talk about.' I shook my head. 'Sorry.'

'It gets worse, John.'

'Nothing that disturbs my sleep. Pretty prosaic, really.' I took another hurried sip. 'Look, I could lie about it, spin a story, but I'm telling you it's nothing important.'

'You're in the military, aren't you?' I had deliberately taken off my dog tags and filed them under a sweater in a drawer, but I realized it was a pretty easy conclusion to come to, given the mess of my upper body.

I touched my chest. 'This? I'm just a pretty clumsy depilitator.' I felt like reaching out a hand, as if to attempt to calm her like a child, but I didn't. I wasn't very good with innocent gestures and I didn't put any trust in my touch. My hands were made to rip apart, not put together. Instead, I rubbed my eyes. 'I don't want to talk about any of it.' I looked away, took a deep slug of the wine, which now tasted like the inside of a battery. 'Do you want to forget this?' meaning the evening.

I felt the light touch of her hand on my left one. 'I'm sorry.' And the smile was one of pity. 'Maybe I should go?'

Her eyes were bright and there were touches of colour on her cheekbones. The ice bucket gave out a grumbling crackle as the bottle settled into the rearranging and diminishing ice. I tried not to think that it sounded like a dream splintering. 'I wish you wouldn't.'

She didn't. But she should have. And I should have made her.

49

5

I woke up itching and aching, but while the former was probably psychosomatic, the latter was real. The bed sighed as I got off it, and so did I. My watch said that it was 8.30 a.m. I don't know how long I had been asleep, perhaps four hours, but these were passed in a jumble of dreaming and wakening, darkness and bright explosions. The leg pulsed with pain as I tentatively put weight on it. I frisked myself for the painkillers, popped a couple and began putting the room back together, as much as was possible. I ran my hands through my hair, smoothed my clothes down roughly and mourned the powder I had emptied out on the street sluicing with water and diluting blood.

I decided still to pass on the bathroom and hobbled down the hall and then the stairs, passing the man in the glass booth at reception who gave only the merest glance as I went. Then I hit the street looking for a coffee shop and the nearest Wells Fargo bank.

The first I found quickly, a coffee shop on the corner of the next block. Norman Rockwell it wasn't. It was alive with smoke and chatter and men, mostly men, hunched over heaped plates and opened newspapers. Carefully I slung myself on to one of the vacant stools at the counter, which seemed to be covered in some sort of gingham formica, and motioned to the sole woman behind it who was vaguely waving a coffee pot. 'That'll do me,' I called. She came across, turning over a grey earthenware mug in front of me and poured. 'I'll pass on the iced water and the rest,' I said, before she could get into a recitation of the wares.

Alternately blowing and sipping on the coffee I considered the immediate future, because the longer stretch did not look too hopeful. It would be wise to assume I was being watched, or that the police at least knew where I would be heading. Deaf and Dumb had had adequate opportunity to copy out the details of the bank book and it wouldn't take even an impaired intellect long to work out that I would be going to check on whether the legacy was real, or a sick, posthumous joke. I still favoured the second.

There was, of course, the larger question to consider – who the fuck was I? – but that seemed a little weighty a philosophical consideration for so early in the day. The images of the previous night kept tumbling through my head, like fragile objects hurtling to the floor. The photograph. Why the strange names on the back? No one makes a mistake in writing a dedication on a treasured photograph . . . do they? Who was Tom? Was that me? Did I have a brother I didn't know about? Had he died, perhaps? The name Tom kept shivering and flaring in my head. *Tom.* Attached to my father, too. And the evidence apparently confirming the name was inscribed on the inside of the ring in my pocket. I ached all over, my leg pulsed with pain and I felt sick. More than that, I felt in a sort of emotional freefall where everything I knew had no underpinning.

Trying to drag my thoughts away from hopeless speculation I looked around, hoping to spot any odd faces, anyone who might be watching, but they all looked that way, weird but uninterested, so I gave up and went back to my coffee. By the time I was mid-way down the second cup I was beginning to shiver and sweat. If I hadn't known the symptoms I would have thought that I was sickening for something. My ears were still mushy from the noise of the explosion and the images of fire running in the street and the uncertainty scoring across my mind would not go away. I finished the coffee, gave another shiver and chucked a dollar on the counter, got up and went out. In the absence of the absolute there is always action.

Wells Fargo has changed just a tad since Gaby Hayes was bouncing around on top dodging injun arrows. The moment I passed through the automatic doors the huddle of security guards seemed to stiffen and their hands hovered over their holsters. I gave a quick salute like I was reviewing the guard and limped as briskly as I could into the maw of the bank, all chrome, leather and polished walnut, and security cameras which seemed to blink faster the nearer I got to the counter. I joined a queue and shuffled slowly to the front. As I did so, I believed I could see the tellers behind the armoured glass glance anxiously and shudder, no doubt each one devoutly praying they wouldn't end up with the mutilated vagrant in the hospital pants.

When I eventually made it to the head of the line, the girl facing me, looking about eighteen, was distinctly nervous, obviously expecting me to pull out a pistol – or even worse, my cock. 'How can I help you, sir?' There was a quaver in her voice.

I slapped the passbook on the counter and slid it through the aperture. 'Can you check this?'

'Check it? How do you mean?'

'Check the amount is actually there.'

She gave one of those thin smiles reserved for the terminally stupid. 'This isn't the correct branch.'

'I know that,' I was trying to be polite, 'but you must have means of checking. Computer? Phone? Carrier pigeon?' The politeness hadn't lasted past mid-sentence. I tried to smile. 'Look, I don't want to schlepp way across town. My leg, y'know.' I nodded down.

'Give me a minute.' She shot off her seat and into the

hinterland. I turned to face the audience and slumped with my back against the counter, beaming widely. The security guards were paddling around like sharks with blood in the water. A bandit could have walked in behind them and quietly helped himself, for all the attention they were paying to the rest of the place.

'Mr Downe?' Reluctantly I turned away. 'Do you have some form of identification?'

'Sure,' I said cheerily, pulling out my wallet, my driver's licence and social security pass. 'Does that mean it's all tickety-boo?' Another of my mother's expressions.

'Excuse me?'

'In order. The money's there?'

'Yes. It's in order. The money—' she glanced down at the book, '—it's all there.'

'Shit! Really?'

'Why wouldn't it be?' Her mouth was curling at my crudity. 'Is there anything else?'

'Yes, there certainly is. I'd like to make a withdrawal, please.'

'Of course. How much were you thinking about?'

'I was thinking of every single, solitary cent.' Unable to control myself, looking upwards, arms open, like a worshipper of the sun. 'Sorry,' I said out loud, then quickly looked downwards. I wanted to shout: Thank you, Father. Thank you, you miserable old bastard. But if you think this alters anything, you're wrong. Oh fuck yes. Then I looked back up at the girl – and you don't often see this – but her mouth was agape. 'In as large bills as possible, please.'

It took a little while and no amount of coded looks, but I got the cash. The manager came out, took me into a side room, clearly still not believing that I could be who I appeared to be, and tried to dissuade me. He couldn't. He went away, possibly phoning for advice or tipping off the IRS, I don't know, but after an hour, Wells Fargo, jointly, severally and corporately, decided that there was no further way they could delay, and handed over the cash in a smartly embellished wallet inside an envelope.

My demand hadn't been as impulsive as it seemed. I didn't want the money lying where it was easily traceable, or gettable, by others. The little I knew about my old man convinced me that this couldn't be kosher. And if it wasn't then I certainly wasn't going to allow the government to filch it. They owed me enough already.

I was bemused because he had hardly earned that amount of money in his life, much less saved it. And, for sure, if he had somehow acquired it, he would have spent it, gambled it, or, near the end when incapacitated, torn it up and lined the budgie's cage with it rather than pass it on to me. He didn't have a budgie, but he'd have bought one.

So, this had to have come from my mother. But that was even more unlikely. Had there been some old Scottish maiden aunt who had passed away and left it to her and then she, holding out on my old man, had kept it for me? But even accepting that, it did not explain who left the envelope for me, because she had pre-deceased him by nearly five years. Confused? I was. I shook my head, hailed a taxi, hopped in behind a black guy with his licence showing an African name, and told him to drive around while I thought things through. This was going to be a handsome fare.

I had never thought I would ever be thinking the way I now was, but the problem was what to do with the money. Banks, I knew, reported large deposits to the police, the FBI, the IRS, which can often signify drug proceeds. Presumably my legacy had passed the test, or was too low to be checked. Trouble was, I didn't know what that cut-in amount was, but it was wise to assume it was less than fifty K. So, what to do? Scoot around all day depositing small sums with different banks? I didn't think so. Keep it on me? Hazardous. Transfer it into another convertible currency? Like drugs! Now that was appealing. But I was in a strange city, at least for doing the business, and that seemed too ripe for the rip-off. Nothing wrong with risking a little, I heard myself say, but not the whole enchilada. The meter was ticking away and I was still no nearer deciding.

'Driver,' I said from the bucking back seat, 'take me to the Hyatt-Regency.'

6

Before I met Emily I had hardly touched a drug, apart from some fairly cursory juvenile exploration and the legal kind, and neither did I, much, with her. It was only after she had gone. And now that's about all of her there is to hold on to.

Slowly we drank the bottle of cold wine; the lights had gone down in the bar, and I felt a little like a battery chicken, being commanded to mate. We hadn't said a lot, nothing important, that is. She talked about herself in a fairly desultory way, how she was doing a degree in Marine Sciences at Oxford University (I couldn't tell the difference in accents between English and Ocker then), and she was spending a year in Australia studying. She laughed at this point, mentioning some kind of obscure crustacean whose Latin name has slipped through my memory skein. Except that she had become a little adrift from her vocational moorings – she laughed again here, putting her hand over her mouth as she said it – and now she didn't know what she was going to do. And how she was living with someone . . . well sort of, loosely . . . well – a deep breath – loosely to her.

I said something about how she had said she didn't want to get involved or hear sad stories. 'So what is this?'

She shrugged and smiled and touched my hand. 'Sorry,' she said, 'I'm a sucker for wine.'

'He knows you're here?' She nodded, and I imagined him twisting in torment and almost felt sorry for him. 'Let me ask you something—' she nodded again, '—what was this afternoon all about – why did you come up to me?' She started to speak but I waved her quiet. 'Don't use the drugs line. Why?'

The bar was dark now, with only dim lights meant to look like melted candles and which flickered with some electronic dissembler, and behind, in the huge picture window, the sodium streetlights and the dark ocean beyond, which I could hear tumbling, or thought I could, above the faux classical Muzak.

'You won't like this.' She seemed to be sniffing and wiping her nose – the coke or the speed lubricating it – and dabbing at her eyes. 'I saw you for a few days, always sitting in the same place, with a sort of angry aura around you, like an emotional exclusion zone. I stole a few looks at your body language, your quick, angry movements – don't get me wrong, I wasn't fixated, I didn't fancy you – and then it hit me. I felt sorry for you. I don't think I've ever seen someone so . . . so . . . so defensive and lost. So self-hateful.' She sniffed again and I could have sworn, even in the flickering fake candlelight, that she was crying. 'I'm sorry.' She waved her hand in front of her face and tried to smile, but it dissolved to water and she shook her head and reached for a napkin.

Looking at her across the table, the empty glasses, the inverted bottle in the silver bucket, the plastic menu in the holder, the basin of peanuts, the little candle-shaped light with the tiny red fluted lampshade like something you find bobbing in a sickly cocktail, I wanted to reach across the distance between us, put my hands around her neck, squeeze hard, twist and snap her spine. I heard the blood and breath roaring inside me and then something happened, a chemical epiphany probably, and all of the hatred leached out of me and I felt myself shrinking, diminishing. I felt powerless and even more alone.

'Can we maybe go for a walk?' I said eventually. 'Get a breath of air.' She nodded. I took her hand as she rose, don't even remember walking across the air-conditioned atrium,

57

and then out on to the street, the tumbling chaos of surf and motor traffic, and the dull light of a hooded moon spraying the sea the colour of a shroud. I didn't mean to kiss her so much as to cling to her. But I did. We did. Some kind of fuckin' soldier, I said to myself. I could hear laughter some- where far off, either in my mind or on the street, but I knew who it was aimed at.

We didn't rush back to the hotel, just watched the dark sea and listened to the roar of its arrival, and sat on the cold sand and drew patterns and occasionally kissed, pecked more like, almost constraining passion, as if we were afraid to do more. At some point I said, 'It looks like ground rule number one has been shattered . . . or if it hasn't, I'll look the other way while you go.' I closed my eyes, I heard her move and when I opened them she kicked a spray of sand in my face. 'Arse- hole,' she said from above, 'let's go back.'

I didn't even put my arm around her as we walked across the sand, frightened, I suppose, that if I did I would upend the equilibrium, or put my hand right through a dream.

As we got near the boardwalk, the promenade, the front or whatever it's called there, and before we walked back into reality, I asked about the lover at home, the idea of him leaden in my gut. 'I'll deal with that.' She was ahead of me slightly and out of reach, and always would be. 'So let's not bring anyone else into tonight. Anyway,' she turned, so that I bumped into her, 'I'm sure he guesses. It's not fair. But then I'm usually this unfair.'

She clasped my face in both hands and kissed me quickly on the lips. Then, she took a deep breath, looked at me, her head cocked to the side and said, 'We should stop this now because, although that's the last thing I want to do, I still feel this cold part in my heart.'

I said something stupid, like, 'Let me feel', touched her breast and kissed her back.

When we got up to the suite, the embarrassing affluence of

it, I opened the mini-bar and hoiked out the sole bottle of champagne. It seemed to be the thing to do in the surroundings. It should have foamed out suggestively, but didn't. Perhaps I should have stimulated the response, the synergy, by shaking it. Instead I poured fairly chaste measures into two glass tumblers, after first wrestling and tearing at the polythene wrappers, and then we toasted each other in quick, slight sips, occasional kisses.

'Can we have the lights out, please,' I said as we finished.

'You shouldn't be embarrassed about your body,' she whispered, putting down her empty glass on the low coffee table. But still she went round the huge room, dousing the lights.

When we were naked in bed together she began running her hands over my chest, the scars and grafts. Again I said something stupid, like 'Lost an argument with a chainsaw,' as she kept softly running her fingers, something I'd never allowed a woman to do. I said her name softly to myself. Emily. And then my teeth started to chatter and I began to shiver uncontrollably, exactly like in a malarial storm, except, this time, it wasn't.

7

I know as much about surveillance as anybody, and my number one credo is that you can never be sure you're not being tailed. If the opposition are prepared to put enough bodies on your case you'll never spot it. But why should they? I was just an insignificant bum. Well, yesterday I was, today I'm a passingly prosperous insignificance.

I told the taxi driver to pull up outside Hecht's, to wait, and I limped my way past the perfumery and the glances from the over made-up counter assistants to the ground-floor hardware section, pulled a khaki grip from the display without even checking the price tag and went on to menswear, where I bought two pairs of identical chinos – same make, different colours – without trying them on, a couple of dark shirts and a navy melton jerkin with the smallest and most tasteful decal I could find. Some fictitious English country club. Then I pulled off a thousand dollar bill, told the salesman to throw in half a dozen boxer shorts – 'but pass on Polo,' – and the same number of pairs of black socks. He punched the purchases into the till, carefully packed them into the bag and handed it and a small sheaf of bills in change to me. I limped back out past the perfumery and into the cab, feeling the salesman's eyes on my back.

'I don't really want to go to the Hyatt,' I said to the driver. 'What I'm looking for is a small hotel or an apartment that's stepped straight out of *Dragnet*.' I could tell from his reaction in the driver's mirror that he hadn't a clue what the fuck I was talking about and, truthfully, neither did I. He probably didn't understand English even, beyond the basic commands of locomotion, although I could tell he was fluent in several currencies. 'Drive,' I went on, 'west.' From a glance at the sun I guessed which way that was and pointed. 'I'll let you know when to stop.' I saw his eyes scanning me in the mirror; he shook his head and kicked into gear.

Eventually I found a small block of holiday apartments built in a U-shape round a pool, fenced off from its neighbours and the cliffs below. In a way it reminded me of a David Hockney painting, blue skies, the water, a few people on recliners around it, although none of them could be said to be pretty. My patch was on the first floor, a self-catering apartment at a little over a hundred dollars a week. It had one of those fifties American stoves you could take dynamite to and it would still come up blackened and cooking, an old cabinet fridge with a door which made a satisfying clunk, like a cell door behind you when it swung shut, a crop of vinyl and formica furniture and an old TV with early images seemingly burned into the screen. It smelled of Lysol and beeswax polish and gentle decay.

Also, it wasn't too secure. There was a corridor outside overlooking the pool, two windows in what you could call the living room and a door which wouldn't trouble even the most junior-grade housebreaker for too long. The whole complex was behind wire, with a sort of gatehouse of white-painted brick, but that only served to provide a false sense of well-being. I slung my bag on the double bed in the bedroom off an internal corridor and about the size of a pitcher's plate, went into the main room and slumped down on the couch, which gave off a crinkling sound like the tearing of a wrapping as I did so. Then I lay back to consider what to do next. Most of my life I have either been taking orders or refusing them, which doesn't leave a lot of scope for developing initiative. Well, now I was going to have to learn quickly and there wasn't going to be much growing time.

61

8

My emotional development wasn't too evolved either. I had wakened early with a cold sun coming up over Bondi and got into shorts, shirts and running shoes, tucking the plastic key card into the back hip pocket, before easing myself out of the door. I was excellent on quiet exits.

As I ran along the slow crescent of the bay, the chill slapping at me, I was a kaleidoscope of jagged, ill-fitting feelings. At some part of the evening, or perhaps earlier than that, a ripped and raw element had entered into it which now left me as angry as I was confused. It was a feeling of vulnerability, of loss. I couldn't believe how this girl had got to me. There had been a lot of girls, many odd situations and couplings, but I hadn't left anything behind.

I stepped up the pace. What had happened? Why had she got to me? And behind that there was a churning thought that she hadn't exchanged anything at all.

I pictured her slowly waking in the king-size bed, fresh sheets daily, smiling to herself, getting up, showering and getting on with her day, any thoughts of me washed off and away.

There was a stitch in my side, which simply indicated how soft I was getting physically as well, so I upped the pace a couple of notches and bit on the pain. When I reached the far end of the bay, I clambered down on to the sand and began the run back, just to make it harder, the soft, combed cushioning sucking at my shoes.

I was exhausted when I finished and flopped down, sweat

covering me as if I had just gone through a salt shower. Looking out at the ocean, I could see boys in wet suits on boards already paddling themselves out towards the perfect wave.

I don't know how long I sat there trying to ride the surging feelings inside, growing more angry with myself, trying to fix on the sea and the sky, whether for some metaphor of tranquillity or transience I don't know, but by the time I had collected enough of my thoughts to go back, the sweat had dried on me, I was shivering and the running clothes stuck to my body like chilled sheets on a fever victim.

I trailed sprinkles of sand across the hotel lobby and into the elevator, a glass box, like a dock for war criminals, which climbed to my floor without a sound. Sand scratched between my toes as I walked along the corridor, I felt it like emery paper rubbing between my buttocks. When I got to the door I paused, listening, took a deep breath, slipped in the key and went in.

I don't know what I was expecting or hoping for, certainly not silence, an empty room, a bed roughly made, nothing left behind, not even a trace of perfume. What did I feel? Angrily let down. I kicked off my shoes, checked the bathroom for a sign of her (was I expecting a lipstick message on the mirror?), wandered around, pulled off my socks in a drizzle of sand, then the matted shirt, went back into the bathroom, all black marble tiles, silver fittings, even neatly stowed towels, and looked into the shower cabinet. Droplets of water still ran down the inside. I punched the side and then jerked on the shower dial, water spluttering out in a steaming hail, not caring that most of it was falling on to the slick-shiny floor. I almost couldn't be sure that she had actually been here. Then I walked back out into the bedroom, round to the side where she had been, not even a dent in the pillow to mark it, and bent down to smell. Nothing. Only when I turned it over did I pick up the faintest of odours, something sweet and slightly salty. The displacement, I thought, that ships make as they pass in the night.

9

When I woke up I was threshing and moaning, unaware of where I was for a couple of moments. I clutched the couch hard, fingers sticking to the vinyl, mooring myself to stop falling any further. The old dream, back again. We become detached in space, falling out of the darkness from the broken plane, rushing towards the earth, five miles up; all around in utter silence are other falling bodies, some of them torn, minus limbs or bleeding hideously but somehow still conscious, looking at me as if I should know what to do. Up above, the plane is still hanging there in its exploded parts, wreathed in flame and smoke, but still aloft. This dream has nothing to do with the laws of physics. I know that we will continue to fall, that everything is utterly lost forever, I'm even welcoming the final obliteration, but slowly and reluctantly I begin to become conscious again, those around me are receding, blaming me silently for leaving them, falling inexorably towards a small Scottish Borders town.

Salty tears on my face, pulse racing, brain shooting with images too fractured and fast ever to complete, and I shift myself to sit on the edge of the settee, to take deep breaths, to focus on a far point of the room, trying to exclude everything and allow the pieces to fall together into some random order, if not to make sense, to seem sufficiently unlike reality to allow me to go on.

I sigh. Every time I pick up the blade it's a debate as to whether to cut the grains or the arteries. But I suppose I haven't quite reached the level of self-pity necessary, so I go on. Which is a pretty self-aggrandizing, as well as self-pitying, thing to say.

My head was full of smoke and wreckage and colliding thoughts as I unravelled from the couch, wincing, searched for the painkillers, dosed myself, looked at the wound, counted twelve stitches, waited till the pain was down to a bearable pulse, changed into new clothes and decided to scout the neighbourhood. A reconnoitre of the terrain is crucial. You never know when you are going to have to make an emergency retreat under fire.

I walked slowly and pretty aimlessly, glad of the freedom, but really because it seemed that something was struggling in my sub-conscious, nagging to get out. If it wasn't to do with the dream, then an element in there had set it gnawing. The houses in this area of the city were mostly low, wooden buildings shrouded in bushes and trees, lots of undergrowth and privacy. There seemed to be only two main thorough-fares, the gently curving road which ran through, snaking parallel to the ocean, and another at right angles, a jumble of shops and bars running down to it.

I stopped and sat down on a wooden bench outside a large restaurant called the Ocean Grill which had, from the sign nailed on it, provided this sponsored pedestrian resting-place. From inside the new jacket, which still smelled of the loom (or more likely some stay-new spray applied by child labour in a Far Eastern factory), I pulled out the family snapshot. Still I couldn't begin to figure it out.

I knew only what had been handed down to me, that the folks left Glasgow to seek a better life, that lo and behold and by chance, or drunken coupling in the lower decks of some tramp steamer more like, I had been conceived somewhere along the route to the New World. Or maybe just before. No other glorious little accidents were to occur, however. Whatever the circumstances of my creation, they were not to be repeated. I kept turning the picture in my hand, looking at the inscription, the mis-description on the back, and on the front the couple, however much I tried to make myself doubt it, clearly my parents.

And the baby, was it me? Couldn't be. Had to be! I stopped fidgeting with the curling photograph, the bubbling still going on in my head telling me that I knew a way out of this, a course of action, although precisely what was still lost to me. Stretching back on the seat I looked up at the sky and then down and across the street, where cars were parked in echelon and pedestrians and rollerbladers coursed along the pavement. I fixed on two guys, young men in their early twenties, soberly dressed, which is probably why I fixed on them in the jumble of raw and garish garments moving along. One wore glasses, both had neat, short hair, one had on a cream shirt, the other white, but the two of them were dressed in what looked like identical dark blue suits.

I thought Mormons, although this pair may not have been, then Salt Lake City, which made me sit up straight on the bench with a sense of excitement I couldn't place or understand. Somehow the connections seemed important to me, but I couldn't figure why.

10

'You're tracking me now.'

'What?' I looked up from my drink and the Rorschach blot of stale beer on the counter and into the mirror on the gantry. The angle of the mirror and the elongation seemed to make her look tiny and lost. When I turned, Emily was standing at my left shoulder, hair knotted in a coil, face sun-brushed and freckled. I would barely have recognized her. Probably to do with what she had on, a pair of well-scuffed and apparently dearly loved leather biker's trousers, buckled and battered boots, then, looking up, a sleeveless loose white jersey, a rolled-up red scarf caught in a silver catch at the side of her throat. She had high, clearly defined cheekbones and large, dark, trusting eyes, the kind you see on calves just before their brains are blown out.

'Just say it's a dare,' I said. 'You remember that? I thought I had to get myself hammered and follow you around for a day or so – spying on you, not speaking, before demanding you take off your clothes. Stupid, but pleasurable.' I swirled the glass. 'Unfortunately, it looks as if I didn't even make it past first base. This,' I said, taking a sip of the beer, 'is the first blow of the hammering and already I lose.'

She gave me a slow and unused smile, like a pleased morning stretch after the night before. 'So, what did you stand to win?' She had thrust her hands into her pockets. Looking past her I was vaguely aware of a couple of young men sitting at a table, watching what was happening.

'Mmm?' I put down the glass. 'I dunno – self-esteem, pride. For resisting temptation.'

Again she gave the lazy, surfeited smile. Now I noticed that she wore dark lipstick like the colour of a bruised plum, or a recent lovebite, and her teeth seemed to flare against it. It was clearly the kind of mouth which feasted.

'So you lost. And what do you get now? The collected works of Oscar Wilde?' I looked quizzical. 'You know, that line about being able to resist anything—'

'I know the line.'

'So?'

There were a few people around us at the bar, young people like her, from the glances and murmurs of welcome they had made, ones she clearly knew. 'Obviously,' I said in a loud voice, 'to sleep with you.' Then I smiled without any warmth, picked up my glass, made a toasting gesture and took a deep drink. 'Same price?'

I watched as her eyes changed, narrowed and focused; she tossed her head back, looking at the two guys at the table, then back at me. 'You take a lot for granted.' A half-step, almost a stumble away. Casually I put down my glass, knowing exactly what she would do, considering what I would. Because she clearly wasn't practised, I had a few seconds to myself before I watched her hand coming up in a wide arc, the palm open. Plenty of time to consider. And just as I had decided that I would take her shot – I deserved it for the comment – emotional and physical conditioning kicked in. Too many blows taken, too many sworn vows, and my left arm snapped up in a practised, rigid block, and her arm smacked harmlessly, but painfully for her, against it.

'Fuck!' She was bending slightly, holding the spot where the bruising would come. 'You bastard!' Like a child, she was rubbing the forearm, struggling not to cry. She was sucking in air through her teeth. 'I can't feel the fingers.'

Her two henchmen had moved off their seats and were

spilling towards me, uncoordinated, but young and fit and spoiling. I stood up quickly, aware of the silence around me and the widening space, realizing that nothing would stop them, except her call, which wasn't going to come.

Reason, I rationalized, jumping off the stool, doesn't come into it when sex and the lust for approval are bubbling and fervidly commingling in the blood. Well, that's how I would like to recall it. At the time I probably just slewed off the bar stool and screamed at the top of my voice. It's recommended for bar-room brawls, and for charging at, and over-running, timorously manned enemy redoubts.

The two stalled, then bumped into each other as they jostled to get at me. The boy on the left, who had long tangled blond hair and what looked like a chemical explosion on the front of his orange tee-shirt, was hefting a beer bottle which he swung in a roundhouse at my head. I moved easily inside the arc, stamped down hard with my right foot on his left, then followed through with a turn of the body, like a door swinging, throwing the impetus of spinning bodyweight into a rigid smash with elbow and forearm, the move you see mimed and fairly harmless on TV wrestling, but which now crashed into his nose, squashing it in an explosion of blood.

Apart from the deterrent value of seeing and feeling your most prominent feature flatten in a snotty bloody hail in front of your eyes, a substantial blow to the beak will produce floods of uncontrollable tears and render you *hors de combat*, if your heart is not truly committed.

I knew from the moment the blow landed that his wasn't, and no more was required, so I skipped over his body as it went down and saw the other guy coming at me, who was bigger, hands out in front of him like claws, trying to get to grips to tear. It was too easy. His entire midriff and pelvic area were wide open and straight on. Dipping my shoulder and spinning on my left foot, to create momentum and a counter-reaction, I fired a kick at the spot, driving all of my force into the small area of my heel, to create maximum pressure on the smallest possible area. This is a risky move for the unpractised. If you miss you are left, at best, ass-end to your opponent and defenceless. But it is a kick, expertly executed, which is capable of splintering wood, never mind bone, and mine hit truly, and with pacy venom, somewhere in his groin. In that area total precision simply isn't that important. The boy went down, was not going to get up. Might never again get it up, I thought coldly, moving in to finish him on the ground, where he was huddled in a moaning ball and preparing to be sick.

Something unexpected stopped me and I was aware that it was a screamed plea. I pulled up, turned on my heel, saw the girl babbling something keening and incoherent, her face a mess of tears and disappointment. So I checked that no one else was moving towards me. The first guy's beer bottle was spinning slowly around on the floor and I fancied that I could hear its rumbling sound above the wash of music as I started to walk to the door, looking back all the time to ensure no one was coming after me, reached it and kicked it open, and as I went out smoke followed me in the vacuum I had created, curling and snaking around. All I needed for the complete effect was the horns and a pin-on tail.

When I had taken a few steps outside I automatically turned again to see if anyone was coming for me. The door opened, and as I braced myself for the rush I saw that it was her, almost falling over her feet as she ran, coming up, then stopping and in sobbing breaths asking, 'Why?' Tears running down her face. 'I didn't do anything to you. Why?' Big gasping sobs. 'Please!'

I took a deep breath and shrugged. I couldn't say, it's because I can't do anything else. So I shrugged, turned and walked quickly away.

11

It seemed better to contact the police directly rather than wait for them to find me. And perhaps volunteering would at least suggest I was innocent which, technically, I suppose I was. After all I hadn't pitched in with the first blows. Men who lead off two-on-one on another have difficult questions to answer. Or at least they would have if they could speak, and if the rest of the bar saw it that way. If *she* saw it that way.

I asked for directions from an elderly couple who seemed neither like tourists nor bombed-out surfies, and walked away from the seafront and the hubbub of the ocean and over-wrought conversations. The cop on the desk didn't seem too interested, there hadn't been a report of any disturbance in the bar – I didn't even know the name of it, had to describe its location and he nodded as if he knew it – and he didn't want me to make a statement, just took a note of my hotel and room number and said he'd be in touch if anything came up, any complaint. 'If it's like you say, then it's cool,' he said, putting his head down, clearly terminating the conversation.

'Sure,' I said, 'it was,' and walked out.

Then I walked for a long time, watching young people in each other's arms, laughing, carrying on, in *joy*, and I kept looking intently into the faces of strangers to see if I could read anything there. Certainly there was no figuring me. Emily had called me several times at the hotel over the two days after our meeting, I hadn't called back. Why? I can only offer cheap psychology. Either I was trying to do her a favour, which was uncharacteristically generous and selfless of me, or I was trying to punish myself for wanting her and her happiness. Or again, maybe it was the virgin and whore complex, that I thought she was a slut for sleeping with me and after she did that I was better than her. I sighed, knowing it wasn't that. That I knew for sure.

'Well, you've royally fucked it now,' I told myself. And the sad part was that I felt worse now than I had before I had rejected and humiliated her. I was talking to myself. Mother, I said, you should have counselled me on the delicacies, the manners of courtship. But then, what the hell did she know about any of that? She had married my old man. Besides, emotions and sensitivity were subjects of scorn in our house.

'Hey ho,' I said out loud, looking around for a helpless beggar to bludgeon.

It was too late to feel regret, but still I did. I rationalized the incident, telling myself that I had done everything I could, that her cohorts precipitated it, but there was no escaping my initial comments to her which had invited it, the apparent and fairly public contempt. I felt bad in my gut. Why hadn't I just kept my mouth shut, when I had done that a hundred times with more just cause, taking stupidities or abuse from uniformed ass-wipes? Now there didn't seem any way to resuscitate it, particularly when I knew, more than anything, that's what I wanted to do. A line from a dumb song my old man used to play on the record player clicked on, crackling and stuttering: *You don't know what you got until you lose it/I gave you all my love and you abused it/And now I'm sorry for the things I didn't say—*. Jesus, thinking back, just what was it about him that yearned for sentimental songs and cowboy music, when there wasn't an ounce of forgiveness or romanticism in his soul? It was almost as if he became a born-again shitkicker. Fitting really, because he certainly kicked the shit out of me.

So, I should have said to her, that first night, let me take you round the topography and genealogy of this body. This one here – reaching over my shoulder and pointing down my back – is either the dog chain or the barbed wire. I'll tour you round the frontal marks and memorabilia, their histories and antecedents later. Fortunately I was always smart enough to keep my head down and my hands cupped over my balls, but if the hair gets cut real short on top – we're talking desert-style or marine basic now – you can still see a few of the scars peeping through the stubble.

Superb seduction technique, I reproached myself, the sympathy play. Look what it did for Quasimodo. I took a vicious kick at a leaking, half-empty, discarded can which spun away in a fine spray.

There had to be a way of repairing things, I tried to convince myself. There's always the 'I have an inoperable brain tumour which sometimes sends me a little wonky, hope I didn't give you a start!' line. Or, 'I have a death sentence on me from the Mob. Sorry, sometimes I get a little shirty.' No? How about, 'Let me tell you about abuse, child abuse!' Been there, been done, got the scars under the tee shirt! That was a just a little too close to home.

Home? It suddenly struck me. I'll turn up on her doorstep. Yeah, yeah – I was talking out loud to myself – clever move, she'll probably think I'm there to silence the principal witness. But I did have her address. What I had done, without even a glint of guilt, what I had done ritually, because that is what I do, was to go through her clothes and her tiny purse while she was sleeping, slithering around the floor in the half-light like some jungle beast with its prey, pulling her stuff into the bathroom and going through it all. When I thought about that now, in the gradations of my hatefulness to her, it seemed marginally worse than crudely upbraiding and beating the pus out of her pals. *Lovers?* And it came to me slowly, because I was not then wholly formed within, that this was probably the real reason I went for her verbally and then joyfully deconstructed her male companions into textbook plastic surgery illustrations. Jealousy.

But, them too. They were stupid, fuckwitted assholes out to impress her, to guard their emotional domain. After they learn to love liquidized lunch through a straw it'll be salutary for them!

I was back above the beach again, a wind had come up so that grits and grains were in the air, in my nose and in my hair and in my mouth and teeth like ground glass. I climbed on to a wall and let my legs dangle over, letting the wind blow the sand at me, a sort of masochistic and purgative shot-blasting. After a while I decided that all I could do was offer an apology, not in person but in writing, that I should go back to the hotel and just let it all pour out.

But even then, of course, I didn't tell the absolute truth. Over several sides of the hotel's embossed paper I invented a rather tragic, shattered figure, who had come from nameless horrors, the deaths of several close colleagues, who had been under medical and psychological treatment, almost pre-suicidal, that this had all come on top of the death of my mother (that bit was at least true), and who was meant to be recuperating here and spending all his saved-up cash on the last big holiday before returning to it all.

It was understated, skilfully manipulative, and kind of dry and unself-pitying. I said that I had been suffering a lot of physical pain and depression over the last few days, that I snapped, took it all out on others. Nothing like that had ever happened before, that I was shocked and ashamed of myself. That I was more deeply sorry than she could imagine, that of course I realized she would want nothing more to do with me, but that I felt I just had to tell her why what happened had done. At the end I put a thank you, writing how, in a few delightful hours which I would hold on to when I went back in a few days, she had shown me something I thought I had lost – call it hope. I winced when I wrote that. Then I signed the letter, licked the envelope, wrote the address on the front and called reception to summon a taxi to deliver it.

As I undressed for bed I told myself that there was always the possibility that she was a sadomasochist.

12

The sun was licking the street, casting soft shadows of the buildings and the people going about their business, but I was shivering. I knew what I needed. But not where to find it. Senseless sitting here any longer. I got up, my body aching mildly like in the first stages of flu, and started my limping walk towards the pier and the lip of ocean I could see at the bottom of the wide main street. I took in the shops as I went. There were book stores with dark wooden interiors, a sprinkling of expensive-looking clothes boutiques, several restaurants in the same category, but also a fair number of the more grungy establishments, a bike shop, cafés with hand-painted bilious exteriors, several second-hand stores and a music place with a large painted head on the facia, which I took to be Jimi Hendrix. And if you're near, Jimi, I told myself, hopes rising, you're never far from drugs.

Next door to it I re-focused on what I had thought was a surf shop. Natural mistake, really, because it was called Surfin' USA. But when I looked through the darkened glass I saw that it was a café of some kind, with computer bays round the walls where the juke boxes and one-armed bandits should have been. Well, I was thirsty, I needed some conversation and some guidance through the physical and moral turpitude of the neighbourhood, so I went in.

It took a few seconds for my eyes to adjust to the subdued light in which there were tiny haloes of brightness which, when my eyes adjusted, I realized were computer screens.

And the music wasn't Beach Boys but, quiet and mellow, what sounded like Mozart's Clarinet Quintet. I was hovering just inside the door, figuring this was some hang-out for nerds, when a voice asked 'Can I help?' Squinting over I saw her standing behind the bar counter, leaning over it slightly, a loose-cut shirt in a jumble of colours, hair tied back none too successfully, curls escaping on to her forehead, bony but not uncomely features, and a large mouth coloured in dark raspberry.

'Sorry?' I began shuffling towards her, wearing a loonish smile. 'Yes, probably. It's just I feel like I've stepped through a time warp.' I looked around. The place was long, high-ceilinged and fairly narrow, with a minstrel gallery half way along. It was also pretty quiet, just four or five customers who seemed to be anchored in the gravity field of their several computers. 'I'm an alien but friendly. Emm—' I looked at her and climbed on to a bar stool, '—maybe coffee? Failing that—' I shrugged my shoulders. 'Am I too old to be in here?'

She smiled. Her sleeves were rolled up and just at the fold on her right arm the bottom of a faint outline of what looked like a tattoo. 'Come closer so's I can tell,' she said over her shoulder as she reached for the Cona jug. I didn't respond, except by taking a few tentative steps. 'Your first time here? In an Internet café? Cream?'

'Oh, right.' She had pushed a mug of black coffee at me. 'Yes. No! Sorry.' I shook my head. 'Yes to the first time, no to cream.' I was floundering. 'Stupid question I know, but what goes on here?'

She gave me a friendly once-over. 'You *are* an alien. Where have you been? Don't you know about cyberspace?' I decided that telling her of my own recent five-year venture in an enclosed space wasn't the wisest of moves. She gestured towards the screens. 'These are like the pinballs of the older generation, the dating mechanisms, the entertainment centres, the voyeurs' windows, the mind candy and, just occasionally,

77

the food, the library, thesaurus, encyclopaedia and 2000-year mindstore of thought. But not often.'

'Wow.' I blew on the coffee and took a sip. 'You've had the question before. Heavy, I added rather sardonically. 'I can see most of that, but what I can't see is how you have sex with it.'

'Outmoded concept. Nowadays you get your rocks off with chips.'

'Chips? Aw, man,' I leered and shook my head, 'don't times change? In my day we used to call them chicks. Mind you, thinking about it, George Raft might have called them chippies.' I rolled the coffee cup in my hands. 'Take me back to the twenty-first century.'

'Sorry,' she said, 'we had to deconstruct it, due to the appalling habits of some of the lower lifeforms – we called them men in those days – who preyed on higher beings, shamelessly exploited them and tortured them into submission. I think it was called childbirth.'

'I'm John Downe.' I held out my hand, the thought flashing across my brain that, well, I'm almost sure I might be.

She rolled up the sleeve of the shirt on her right arm a little more, then shook my hand. 'I'm your captain for the voyage, John. Call me Stephanie.'

'This your place?' I motioned in a sweep with my left arm.

'Sadly, no. It's a friend's, a guy I went to college with. I'm just helping out.'

'So, guys just hang out here drinkin' coffee and self-indulgently playing with the Internet? Onan on.'

Slowly she shook her head. 'And maybe that's one you rehearsed, John. What you have here is surfing. We charge them for on-line time and try to make sure they don't spill best Colombian decaff over the keyboard.'

Best Colombian and decaff, in the same breath, when talking about coffee, was a blatant contradiction. Besides, that country's truly best comes in a cruet or sealed packet, not in a cup, which I almost said, but thought it was a bit premature. I noticed I was shivering slightly again. Or was it still? Putting my hand into my jacket pocket I said, 'D'you mind?' and pulled out the painkillers, uncorked the bottle, dropped two into my hand. 'Medicinal.'

'Wait.' She turned away and moved along the bar to a sink. I could see that she was wearing tight, faded jeans and that she had narrow but shapely hips. While a life of exotic travel might broaden the mind, it certainly also brings an appreciation that the girth of most American women's butts would not disgrace a Sumo, something which struck me even more forcibly after a long period of deprivation from them. She turned on the faucet, retrieved a glass, filled it and pushed it along the bar to me. 'There you go.' I swallowed the pills quickly, nodded thanks and picked up the coffee again to take the chill off me. 'The leg?' she asked. 'I saw you were limping.'

'Car accident.' Which was almost true. And, with the addict's acute sense of self-interest, it hadn't taken me more than a few seconds and syllables to realize that Stephanie would be my perfect guide to the local habitats, particularly the low-rent ones where the disreputable ply their wares. 'Do they call you Steph?'

'Only once.'

'Right.' I nodded an unspoken agreement never to abbreviate her. 'It's quiet here. Pleasant.'

'Gets busier when it gets darker. By eleven it's really heaving.'

'Yeah?' Looking back at the terminals I asked, 'So, d'you understand all this stuff?' I waved vaguely towards the screens, sort of like I was hoping to conduct them.

'Sure. My degree's in programming and computer science and I'm finishing off a doctorate.' I whistled. My slightly dated knowledge of computer technology involved communications satellites, pushing buttons and malevolently arranging laser cross-hairs. 'And you?'

At this point one of the customers, a young guy in a sloppy hooded '49ers football shirt drifted over and asked for another Coke. While she served him I wondered what to say. The truth? Almost. She came back to me. 'You were asking what I did. Truth is, not very much. Well, I was a serviceman until a little while back and now I don't know. Not a lot of what I'm qualified in is legal on the street. I've got a little bit put by—' actually it was burning in my pocket, '—and I may do a bit of travelling. That's it. Pretty unexciting really.'

She nodded across at the screens. 'Save your money, travel the world from your own doorstep. No currency problems, strange food or funny accents—' *or people with weird customs and head attire trying to waste you*, I wanted to add in, '—but no, you're right. It broadens the mind, doesn't it, whereas this tends to broaden the beam.'

I slurped at the coffee. 'I'm not keeping you away from your work, am I?'

'It's all right. I'm just filling in until this evening. Nothing to do but polish table tops, scour toilets and pour coffee. Keep me from it, please.'

'If you're sure – it's just that I'm not from here, only just arrived, actually. I don't know what's to do around here at all. So what is there? If you're not into surfing, out there—' I pointed my thumb over my shoulder towards the door, '— or in here?'

She put her elbows on the bar and leaned over. 'Depends on your particular predilection. There are some good bars, live music most nights, restaurants, a pretty decent library, watersports, some nice walks – well, you might want to pass on the last for the time being, maybe.' She gave me a nice open smile. 'Some of us stay in nights and study.'

I fixed on her face. She had a direct way of looking back that I liked. She seemed strong and pretty sure of herself. 'Not every night?'

'No.' She gave a snorting laugh. 'Some nights I wash my hair.'

'Well,' I smiled, 'it looks pretty all right to me. So, if you can put aside the books and the shampoo, what about venturing out this evening, that is—' I had already checked her fingers for any obvious signs of encumbrance, '—if there's no one else making that a problem? I could find a walking stick in the meantime.'

She looked at me for a few seconds, smiled in a way that was at least as much wary as friendly, seemed to consider it, and then nodded slowly. 'And you, there isn't someone else, somewhere else, sitting in washing her hair?'

'No. There was once, but then there was for everyone – but no—' I must have looked confused or unconvincing because she threw me a knowing, quizzical look. 'She died.' I picked up on an old line from the past. 'But no sad stories.'

There was, as ever, a sub-text. I wasn't trying to break my five year (and some weeks) sexual fast, although that would certainly not be too unpleasant. Some way into our conversation it had occurred to me – rather slower than to the rest of humanity, granted – that there was a virtual infinity of information a few informed keystrokes away, thousands of people tapping in and out of a participatory information system, libraries, papers, pages and documents accessible if you knew how to go about looking, even those secret, closed, sealed, coded and cyber-walled locations. Shit, kids had tapped into the Pentagon and defence systems, introduced graffiti, bugs and slogans to some of the most heavily guarded places; others had dipped into bank accounts, social security records, anything, really, that had been digitized and com-mited to tape, disk or chip. And knowing someone who knew about that world and could pilot smart weapons through it all could be invaluable, it seemed to me. Stephanie could be a prime asset.

I gave her all the wattage in the smile I could muster.

I met her in the café at 8 p.m. I had been back to the apartment, checked that the various tell-tales I had left around the place hadn't been violated. I had chopped off a few hairs with a kitchen knife and stuck them across the entrance door and several drawers, and lightly dusted several surfaces with pepper dust so that anyone touching them would leave an impression (not to mention snot). It was clean. Then I slept for a bit, showered, changed into one of my few choices of wardrobe and hirpled myself back to the rendezvous.

She was already there, sitting on a bar stool. For a minute I didn't recognize her, not just because her back was to me, but because her hair was down, not exactly tangled and permed, but wind-blown and unruly, as if she had just come off a fairground ride or a fairly boisterous horse. From where I was, moving towards the bar, I quickly scanned what she was wearing: a short, dark shift, with her legs crossed unconcernedly, the hem high on her thighs, a white cardigan – or what I assumed was a cardigan – rucked and knotted round her shoulders. She was drinking a tall beer, smoking a long cheroot and staring up above the bar at a TV set which was running a basketball game. In every bar, in every town, in all time-zones in each of these United States, it is a truth universally to be acknowledged that there will be a basketball game being played out on television.

The place was considerably busier than earlier (I was surprised nerds were allowed out after dark), all of the tables taken and the seats at the bar. Next to her, a middle-aged man in the middling stages of a drunk was trying to talk to himself as much as her, but she was ignoring him, fixed on the surging coloured figures framed above.

'Stephanie,' I said over her shoulder, 'I'm not late, am I?'

She gave a little jump and whirled on the stool. 'Jesus – John, did'ya used to be a footpad? My heart's gone into overdrive!'

'Sorry.' She was shaking her head. I put my hand briefly on her shoulder.

'But I'd like to claim that I usually have that effect.'

She swung down off the chair, quickly smoothing herself down. 'Right.' She touched her hand to her heart, like dutiful citizens do when Old Glory's on the move. 'It's calming. So, what's your fancy?'

I shrugged, thinking that coming out with *burying my face in a mound of powder* was probably too forward for the length of our acquaintance. 'Well, I noticed a place called Sarti's further up the street, it looked pretty tasty, a kind of Neapolitan chic, so I booked us a table for nine, if that's OK with you?'

'Now, that *is* fancy. It's kind of a buck a bite in there.'

'Hey,' I held up my hands, 'I'm paying, but if you don't want to—'

'No,' she cut in, 'I want to. I've passed it in awe and reverence often. The food's supposed to be excellent.'

'A leisurely drink elsewhere first?'

'You know, you are my kind of unexpected date, Mr Downe,' and she slipped her arm through mine. 'Let's go.' The natural spontaneity, this small gesture of partnership, threw me a little; I wasn't used to being touched by a woman, and it probably showed because she gave me a quizzical glance and started to slide her arm out, but I pressed on it with my elbow and smiled.

There was a nice breeze, warm, mellow and tangy, coming off the ocean at our backs as we walked. I felt immediately comfortable with her. Of course I was using her, or intending to, but getting round to asking her to do a little research on computer, or to guide me through, didn't seem like a gross violation. It was what else might happen because of it which troubled me. Any violence aimed at me was fairly unspecific, given the earlier attempt, and I didn't want anyone drawn into my ambit. But I didn't want it badly enough, of course, not to involve her.

As we walked, my mouth felt dry and I was vaguely nauseous, but this wasn't down to fear or date nerves, rather the stuff I was taking. I had pethidine for the pain and diazepam, supposedly for the trauma caused by the explosion, but I was using both to keep the craving at bay. So I kind of floated along the sidewalk with my partner. With the right music and some natural syncopation we could be Fred and Ginger.

Sarti's was on a corner, with an L-shaped bar and a few tables, the restaurant sprawling out behind. The bar portion had smoked glass windows and cream-coloured walls decorated with framed Italian soccer jerseys and signed photographs of teams and players. A small TV above the bar was showing what I guessed must have been RAI on cable or satellite, a soccer game between one lot in dark blue jerseys and another in black and white stripes. The waiters were in stripes too, but very understated, basically green tops with fine red and white lines through.

We sat down at one of the tables, which was covered in a white tablecloth so bright that prolonged exposure in the daylight would cause snow blindness, a jar of small-budded fragrant flowers in an off-white vase in the centre, surrounded by several dishes of olives, nuts and breadsticks. We hadn't said a word on the short walk up the street, but now I leaned over and said in a low voice, 'I've always wanted to order champagne in a place like this.'

She leaned forward, joining the conspiracy, and said, 'I've always wanted to drink champagne in a place like this.' Her right hand came across and lit gently on mine gently for a few seconds where it was holding the menu. 'But that little you said you've put by won't last long in places like this.'

'It's been earning interest,' I whispered back, caught a waiter's eye and ordered the non-local, a bottle of Heidsieck. He sneered a little, either at my choice or possibly because I hadn't gone for something fizzily Italian, or frighteningly expensive like the Krug. While we waited, I paid Stephanie the usual compliments – how nice she looked/dressed/ smelled etc. – and then the guy came back, broke into the seal, poured two glasses and battered the bottle into ice cubes in a silver bucket on spindly legs he had whisked up next to the table. We clinked glasses and I washed the champagne around my mouth. It tasted a little bitter, but, as usual, that was to do with the chemicals in me, rather than a judgment on the vintage.

'Maybe I'll open somewhere like this,' I said, making conversation, looking around to the tables in the restaurant, which looked pretty busy. 'A weekday and it seems to be doing all right.'

She shook her head slowly. 'You were in catering, then, were you? In the forces?' I shook my head quickly. 'No? Didn't think so.'

'Well, I could be on the door. I could throw people out.' I took another swig. 'Better'n that, I could throw them in.'

She wriggled in her seat and gave me a cheeky grin. 'John, I don't know you but you don't look to me like the kind of guy who's cut out to flunkey in a restaurant.'

'Tush. One thing I can do is create a pretty good *flambé*.' Truer than she knew. 'But you probably think I'm more the man of action type? Hollywood leads, that sort of thing?'

'Not really. I saw you more behind a brush and a trash can than a camera.' She took a swallow and toasted me with the glass.

Returning it I stretched my sore leg out. The feeling of

85

nausea had gone and the cramps had receded to occasional spasms. 'Seriously,' I made a toasting motion with my glass, 'I suppose I will have to get something – in a while. The trouble is I'm staggeringly unqualified for anything – anything, well, peaceful.'

'You could retrain.'

'As what? Preacher? Rocket scientist?'

'There's computers. It's the way to go.'

Sceptical glance. 'I suppose you're right, but you're getting your personal skills and obsessions in here. The problem is that I'm totally useless with numbers.' This conversation was unravelling just the way I wanted it to. 'Maybe I could pay you to give me lessons,' I sort of laughed it off, 'see if I have any aptitude?'

'Sure.' She looked around over her shoulder as someone came past, which gave me an opportunity to steal a glance at her legs, most of which were visible if I just turned a little in the chair.

'And in return I could give you lessons in identifying Soviet warplanes at night – well, it'd be Russian planes I guess, now – or surviving in hostile terrain with only a penknife, a length of string and a Mastercard.'

She was looking at me now. 'You haven't really given any thought to what you are going to do, have you? You said you might travel.'

'Yup. Maybe Scotland.'

'Why? I mean, why not? But why?'

'My folks are – were from there, and I've never been to the old country.' But as I said that, the image of the photograph flashed up and I realized that this might not be entirely true. 'I thought I might go over, see if I have any relatives – my folks weren't big on keeping in touch – try and trace the family history, the genealogy, root about in the roots, that kind of thing.'

She was giving me an oddly quizzical look, like I had

86

overlooked the obvious. 'You've tried to do it from here, have you? I mean, I'm not trying to dissuade you from going, it would probably be great, but have you done any research here?'

I looked at her, a half-smile on her lips. 'I appreciate that I'm going to appear incredibly stupid when I say this, but how would I do that? And don't look so smug.'

'As any nerd in a cyber-café would tell you, the Net.'

'It'll make you feel even more smug, but go on, tell me how?'

She leaned forward and touched my hand again, in a kind of pitying way. 'There are millions and millions of pages of information there, about every conceivable topic – and when you think about it, genealogy is self-evidently a conceivable topic – and in addition there are thousands of newsgroups, hobbyists exchanging knowledge and information about what obsesses them. There's sure to be lots on genealogy, even Scottish genealogy. Or at least some group which can point you in the direction.'

'Yeah? So will you help me?'

'Sure. Maybe I could look up my forebears, too,' she said. 'They were Poles and Latvians, brigands mostly, I think. My second name is Cross, but that was changed from Krisowoci, or something.'

'We'll use a computer in the café, just to see what's going on?'

'Hell, no. I've got my own set-up at home, megapower. Much cooler.'

I pulled the bottle in a slurp and clatter from the ice bucket and topped us both up.

Not being up to date with modern sexual manners, I had kissed her lightly on the cheek on the doorstep, saying goodnight. She lived in a small wood-slatted place, smothered in vegetation, with a wide verandah running all the way round. A light on the porch cast a gentle amber glow and I felt homesick for a life I never had. Either that or it was the melding of the pills, the champagne and the chianti.

Now I was lying in bed looking up at the ceiling as the bronze light of another sunny day began to harden in the room. It had been a superb evening, we got on well – at least the outward and disguised part of me and she hit it off – and we talked a lot. The food was on the excellent side of exquisite, the wine was superb, at least to my starved taste-buds, and we laughed a lot. Great relationships have been based on less. But I was being selfish. More than that I was probably endangering her unknowingly, which made any relationship lopsided. There could not be anything more than affection, close friendship and, now I came to consider it, lust. I was using her. I made a silent apology and pushed down a bubbling mass of memories. It's amazing, or perhaps, life-saving, what you can train your mind to admit and suppress when you spend closed days and nights locked in with yourself and only four tiled walls on which to project.

I knew what I had to do to ensure that Stephanie would be entirely safe, but then I wasn't going to make those kinds of promises ever again, to people I had willingly joined, been cast from and who clearly cared little for my life or those of others. I sighed and eased myself painfully out of bed and dressed slowly. So far, it seemed I was being left alone here in a period of peace. Just don't buy any long playing records, I reminded myself.

There had been rain overnight. The place felt fresh and renewed, vibrant with new life – I was feeling hopeful and lyrical as I walked back towards Stephanie's. Should have had a cold shower, I told myself, because I was achy and thick-headed. The pills I had swallowed with a cup of lukewarm coffee, quickly reheated in a pan from yesterday, had not yet kicked in.

I stopped at a pastry shop, set back from the road, ringed

by a stand of trees and bought half a dozen croissants. I checked my watch; it was 8.15 and I didn't want to be too early, so I bought a paper from one of the dispensing machines on the corner, and sat on a bench flicking through it until it had gone 8.30.

There were sounds of life when I got to her porch, music, something stirring and choral, as well as a bustle of human movement. I banged loudly on the planked door. It opened almost immediately; she stood with a faint smile, hair scraped back, a few twists escaping, no make-up, rosy like she had been running or just come out of a passionate encounter or a hot shower.

'Welcome,' she said, giving me a deep ushering flourish with her hand into a small hall, wood-panelled, with several doors off.

'Thanks. Oh, I brought these. Croissants. In case you hadn't eaten.'

'Oh,' she looked faintly embarrassed, 'you shouldn't have. I'll warm them and make some coffee.' She was wearing jeans again, faded and patched on both knees, and a long-sleeved, tight, crew-necked jumper. What she was quite evidently not wearing was a bra. I felt the old familiar heat in the groin and tried to think of something else. So I looked around the room, taking it all in. A lovely knotted and polished floor, lots of bookcases and books, haphazardly arranged, spilling over on to the floor and several low tables. The furniture was old, big and comfortable-looking, two settees and an armchair, all draped with bright woollen throws. The walls were plain, cinnamon-coloured, where you could see them past the framed prints and pictures, most of which looked like originals. I took a closer look. She had a fondness for bleak landscapes and strong abstracts, in blues and greys mostly, occasional figures struggling spiritedly within them. On the mantelpiece over the fireplace – which was stone, but regular, unpushy, not some kind of hunting-lodge pastiche – were two framed photographs, one of her graduation and the other I took to be her parents' wedding.

'I love your house,' I called through to her.

She came back in. 'It's small, it's rented but I like it too. I'll like it better when I can properly afford it. Did I tell you? I have sponsorship from Microsoft which helps – I'm destined to be one of Bill Gates' cyber-geishas when I finish the thesis – and the bar work just about pushes me into a situation where I don't have to steal too much coffee and cake from the café.'

I was looking around for signs of the computer, which she must have picked up on. 'The kit's in the bedroom,' she nodded towards the hallway. 'Come into the kitchen before we start, take a seat, have some coffee and we'll schmooze into it.'

I followed her. There was a big cooker, lots of wooden shelves, serious looking utensils, a stripped pine, heavily scarred kitchen table. Through the big window over the sink, leaves and branches slowly nodded in. This homeliness was disconcerting, her settled ease set my mind running.

She had three brothers, I remembered that from last night, all younger, and a sister she seemed to be estranged from, younger or older, I didn't know. Somehow we hadn't sketched out, far less coloured in, many of the previous connections; not that we were actually avoiding it, but perhaps we were both aware that going into that was like stumbling into a battlefield graveyard: just a loose covering over the past and any disturbance, any emotional digging around, would have the corpses slithering and rearing up in our faces.

I shivered as she handed me a mug of black coffee and cupped it in my hands. Then she reached for a tissue from a box on the kitchen table. 'That cut under your eye has opened up slightly.' I put my hand up and touched it. I had forgotten all about that. She pushed the tissue into my hand. 'The same accident?' The tone of her voice indicated scepticism. I got the feeling she had heard a lot of lies in her life.

I didn't want to add to the sum so I said, 'I think the croissants might be burning.'

'Yeah.' She turned to the cooker and bent down. 'Tell me about it someday.'

'It's a promise.' Really meaning it. For then.

She closed the curtains in the bedroom, switched on the computer and the printer, which were perched on the sturdy pine dresser which acted as a dressing table, next to the mirror in the rococo frame, then sat in the seat while I slumped behind her on the bed. The air smelled of lavender. I just wanted to lie back, sink into the covers and never remember.

'So.' She had swivelled round in the seat so that the colours from the screen and the distortions from the mirror stained the side of her face. 'What exactly is it you want to find?'

My story was this: my parents were dead and I believed, because of a photograph I had found and an obscure note, that I might have been adopted. I was an only child, not strange in itself but an additional and unsettling element when added in, and I thought that probably my folks had covered it up, the adoption, no doubt to protect me. And really, if this was the case, I didn't know what I felt about it, but what I knew for sure was that I did want to know what *was* true. 'All I have is two Christian names, a date of birth in Glasgow and this other child's first name – well, maybe my first name.'

I could see from the way she looked at me that she didn't quite accept it. But also that she didn't want to question me, in case she would have to refuse what I was asking. It's no big deal, I was saying to myself, no laws being broken.

'I don't know anything about genealogy,' she was saying into the screen as she typed, 'so I'll just type in a few likely headings and see where that leads us. I won't torture your head by explaining what I'm doing, about search engines and key words and the obstructions and detours on this detective trail; all I want you to do is bark out the answers in a military way when I serve up the questions. Got it?'

'Yes, ma'am,' I snapped out.

She tapped in a few characters, a hideous and pitiable wail came out from the vicinity of the computer, the lights on the screen began changing, bathing her in strobing, kaleidoscopic colours. A few minutes passed. 'OK, this is interesting, I'm being referred to a Church of Jesus Christ of Latter-Day Saints Website.' And as she said that the fuzzy feeling I had experienced in the street the day before, prompted by the two guys in blue business suits, suddenly snapped into focus. Mormons. I saw in my mind an old newspaper cutting referring to how the Mormons are constructing a database of the dead so that they could posthumously baptize them and admit them to heaven when the much postponed, but always imminent, Day of Judgement arrived. I sat up on the bed.

She tapped in a few more keystrokes, waited several seconds. 'It seems that there's a family history information section, and not just in Salt Lake City. That's fortunate. You wouldn't want to go there.' She began reading. 'It says that members of the church do their own family histories because they're motivated by love for their deceased family members and desire to serve them. "*Life does not end at death...*" dee dah, dee dah. "*Members of the church believe that the family can also continue beyond the grave, not just to death—*" it says.'

'Aw, fuck no! That's it, I've decided to live forever!'

'"*—That it is possible when parents and their children make special promises, called covenants, at temples ... that these covenants, when made with the authority of God and faithfully kept can unite families for eternity.*"' She whistled. 'And get this: the deceased ancestors can choose to accept or reject these covenants in the spirit world. "*In order to make covenants on behalf* *of their ancestors members must first identify them."* Well, that figures. Right. It goes on telling how the church has gathered genealogical records from all over the world.

'"*These records are available at the Family History Library in Salt Lake City, Utah or at Family History Centers"* – History Centers is trademarked, note – *"throughout the world."* And it says that these centres are attached to the main Mormon temples, just look them up in the phone book.'

'Does it say that—'

'Shuttup,' she came in, 'I'm reading here.' I was sitting on the edge of the bed as she scrolled and tapped and worked the computer. 'You can even get a free video,' she read, '"*enjoy your family – now and forever.* Together Forever, *a free video, explains Heavenly Father's plan for happiness."* There's all sorts of cross-references here.' She turned round in her seat and nodded towards the door. 'Why don't you make some more coffee while I snoop around and log and download it all and then we can see what we've got?'

'I vaguely remember reading a report about this.' I was sitting on the edge of the bed. 'And the way I remember it is that they've bought up records and registers from around the world to baptize the dead, so they can get them into Mormon heaven, along with Little Jimmy Osmond, John Smith and all his wives – or maybe I got those two the wrong way round? This baptism business is their ID card for the pearly gates. So when the big one goes off there'll be long queues of disappointed and crispy spirits who haven't been sprinkled with water fruitlessly queuing in Salt Lake City.'

'Did I hear the word coffee earlier?'

I had received my marching order so I saluted, got up, closed the door quietly behind me and went out to hunt in the kitchen. The cooker was next to the sink at the window; an old coffee pot, like the kind you see old-timers boil up on campfires in cowboy movies, was sitting on one of the

93

burners. I picked it up, pulled out the percolating bit inside, located the trash bin and dumped the grounds before flushing the whole contraption out and filling it with water.

The view from the kitchen looked out on to a patch of grass fringed by shrubs shrouded by trees and bushes, none of which I could identify. I noticed a few lichen-covered statues peering from the undergrowth. It looked like a little clearing in the jungle, almost like a place of worship. I could imagine it at the height of summer, blazing with colour. This whole set-up had a sense of permanence and continuity about it that I envied: my life seemed to have been marked out in transport timetables and half-emptied suitcases. It was very attractive, so I told myself to cleave to the ugly in life, which was where my expertise lay, and I started opening cupboards and jars looking for the coffee.

From the third or fourth stone pot I investigated, a strong and familiar fragrance hit me. Without looking I sniffed over it, put my fingers in and pulled out a few sprigs and dried leaves and chewed on them, like some long-deprived ruminant. The coffee was in the next jar I opened, so I poured a healthy dollop into the percolator, capped it, lit the gas and stared out of the window thoughtlessly until I heard the bubbling and the smell of the roast reached my nose.

The mugs were face-down on a wooden slatted draining board next to the sink. I switched off the gas, poured two cups (it occurred to me that I hadn't picked up on whether she took sugar or milk), and then carefully carried them through to the bedroom.

Stephanie turned from the screen, which cast a coloured aura around her. She looked like an icon come to life as she grinned and held out her hands. The printer was grinding out pages relentlessly beside her. 'Did you want sugar or cream?' She shook her head and picked one of the mugs from my fingers. I sat down on the edge of the bed facing her. 'Well?' I said at last.

94

She gave me the thumbs-up sign with the hand that wasn't holding the coffee. 'It's pretty simple. Up to a point. There's even a handy section telling you how to research from North America, together with a list of British genealogists, help groups, how to pay for commissioned research from here and a bibliography of books to read, if you really want to put together your own family tree. The main Salt Lake City history library isn't on line, but that's no big deal because all the stuff is on CD-ROMs at these local history centers. Shit, they've even got records from other countries – Germany, Hungary and Canada – there's a US social security death index, a military one too, so you can look up a list of soldiers who died in Korea or Vietnam. Seriously weird shit. They've got millions and millions and millions of names.'

'Great.' I was moving around on the bed so much the coffee was endangered.

'Yes, but—' The cranking of pages was still the backdrop to the conversation.

'But what?'

'They've got all these British records going back to before the turn of the century, from different parishes and registries. You can punch in a key word, like Smith, and get thousands of names, but – but the thing is that it seems you need the surname, that's the key. And you don't have that, right?'

The feeling of elation drained quickly away. 'No.'

'But then again—' she was grinning.

'Yes?'

'OK, see, all the Scottish records, births, marriages and deaths, are held – apart from in the individual local registry offices, I guess – in a place called New Register House in Edinburgh. And they're filed by area office and date, that's apart from surname, and these are public records – now don't interrupt – the slight glitch is that you're not supposed to browse through them. Probably concerned about privacy or something cretinous like that. But my guess is that it's not

95

difficult to get round that, especially if you're known about the place.'

'So forget Salt Lake City? You mean I have to go to Edinburgh and make friends?'

The laser printer had stopped. She looked quickly back at it, scooped a sheaf of paper from the tray and banged it into shape on her knees. 'Not necessarily. Not immediately, anyway. There are all these genealogical research services advertising on the Net – Scottish Roots, Kinhelp, Scottish Family Search, several others – and you can fill in a request on line, have your credit card debited, or e-mail them or phone up with an inquiry. These guys are in and out of this New Register House day-in, day-out, so they say in their Websites. So, what I did was send a message to them all, stating what the problem was, that we had the Christian names of the parents and child, the year of birth, the city, and a pretty narrow window around the likely date of birth. I threw in a bit of sob about how the folks who brought you up were killed in a car wreck and you were desperately trying to find out about your birth parents. Then, after the sentimental pitch, I ended up saying how we'd pay top dollar for results. Double whammy. All we got to do now is wait for the sleepyheads on the other side of the water to wake up and, answer their mail. Or we can call.'

She was looking pretty pleased with herself. She was looking pretty. I put my coffee down on the floor, stood up slightly, leaned across and kissed her lightly on the mouth, then pulled my head back a few inches so that I could see her reaction. There wasn't one. Except she, too, put down her coffee, pulled the ribbon from her hair and shook her head to free it, gave a little smile, rose slightly, hooked a leg behind mine, pushed me hard in the chest so that I went tumbling back on the bed and then launched herself on to me. 'I'm not even going to ask how you got that cut under the eye,' she said after the fever of the initial kissing went into slow burn.

Her hair was falling over my face, which was burrowing in the crook of her neck and shoulder. I nuzzled the hair out of the way with my nose and began alternately licking and kissing her neck. 'I'll make my excuses in advance,' I whispered. 'It's been a pretty long time.'

She rolled off me a little so that I could see her face and began rubbing the front of my trousers teasingly. 'And I'm almost celibate. It's – it's two weeks at least since I fucked.' Then quickly she swivelled round and straddled me, bent over so that a curtain of hair hung around our faces as she whispered, 'OK, so I'm lying about that. Just relax, I'll do the navigating.'

I ran my hands up under her jersey and began stroking her spine and rib cage as she kissed me, her tongue pushing into my mouth. I felt myself drifting into a curious but enjoyable detachment. Whether it was the pills, the past or I was tripped-out by the tensions of the last few days I couldn't work out. It was like I was a spectator, without the voyeuristic tang, as if I was outside recording it all. Even my body felt wrong, like I was a stranger in it, although my erection, squashed under her groin and several layers of cotton away from congress, proved comfortingly familiar.

Her nipples, when I reached them, were hard and her breath was coming faster as I ran my fingers around them, tenderly I hoped, as best I remembered it. I withdrew my hand, licked my fingers then returned to them, put my arms down once more behind her back and pulled the jersey over her head. As I did so she trembled slightly and smiled down with unsettling trust. She had a narrow frame with breasts large enough to spill out of my hands as I cupped them.

Remembering the moves, I began to shuffle up a little in the bed and rise but she pushed me back and leaned forward, moving her breasts across the front of my shirt, her fingers starting to pull it loose from my trousers until I put both hands on her buttocks and pushed her forwards on to my face

97

and began licking and chewing on her nipples and breasts, my face going from one to the other, left hand around her back, the right moving down her bottom to reach through to the front, stroking. I was so caught up in what I was doing that it took me a little while to realize that, with her hands, she was trying to remove my shirt, but then I mumbled, 'No. Leave it.'

Her fingers fluttered and moved away. 'Your leg?' she said deep in her throat.

'It'll be OK,' I whispered up through her tits. 'Almost healed.'

Then, gently, I rolled her over so that I was lying on top, her breasts splaying slightly to either side, she with her eyes closed, head turned to the side on the pillow. I began to move slowly down, kissing, licking and gently sucking as I went, spending a lot of time with my tongue flicking in and out of her belly-button which, surprisingly I thought, tasted not of salt but of almonds. Either the afterlife of a shower gel or the residue of unorthodox snacking.

The belt came open easily. I unbuttoned the fly and began muffling and kissing her pants before I pulled her up, slipped my hands down inside the back of the white cotton, and yanked both garments down. I could feel her feet trying to kick off her shoes as I did so.

She whispered, 'You must have been keeping up by correspondence courses,' putting her two hands round my head, pulling me down, forcing up to meet me. It would have been unfelicitous to mention that we kept in practice with mattresses or other cons.

I spent a lot of time there and gave her a lot of attention, not just a lick and a promise. My bad leg was stuck out stiff and straight behind me, like there were twin poles of different lengths in the trousers, but it still hurt. I must have winced fairly hard at one point, louder than her groans at least, because she came back, sat up and pulled me up on the bed alongside her. But I wasn't going to let her return completely, so I slipped two or three fingers inside her (I'm hopeless at counting without visual sight of the digits), as she started to carefully and very gently open my pants. I had to make a tactical withdrawal from her when she moved away to tug them off, and as they came down she lightly touched the elastic bandage I had put on over the stitches to protect them. 'I think it's bled a little,' I heard. And now a hand roamed across the front of my shorts. 'Are you sure this is all right?'

'More than,' I replied, pushing up with my shoulders on the bed so that she could easily tug down my kit. After a few tries and a bit of squirming it all spun somewhere into a dark corner of the room as she bent down, her left hand playing with my balls while the fingers of the other went round me and she began slow strokes. Then I felt it leave me and come back wet and slippery where she had licked the palm of her hand. You have to admire professionalism. As an aside, as it usually occurs in these salacious moments, I've always found it interesting that people who would reveal nothing of their innermost selves while clothed, apart from under prolonged and serious torture, will happily peel off and disport themselves in the most athletic and uninhibited revelations of the flesh, suffering spasms of profoundly unlikely indignities, while uttering at full volume their deepest and basest carnalities. And then feign afterwards, if it's ever tastelessly discussed, that it was some kind of temporary and uncontrollable condition, presumably induced by a strange brand of sexual mesmerism.

After a delightful couple of minutes, me playing with her breasts more roughly as she masturbated me, she slid up my chest, letting me go, her hands scrabbling under the pillow. I couldn't see anything except a close-up of pores. She bounced around, I heard a tearing and then she was back, her lips moving down me, slower as they got lower, over the head of my cock and further down. Slowly I realized that she had pushed on a condom as she took me in her mouth. The military would take months to teach a manoeuvre like that.

'Sorry,' she whispered, 'but I don't know you that well—' Isn't that ridiculous, if understandable? 'Now,' she plopped down beside me, head resting on her elbow, my hand going back through her pubic hair, 'I want you to fuck me as hard as you can without serious blood loss – to either of us. Afterwards we can do the slow and sensual ones.'

And, after a lifetime of orders, I did exactly as I was told. And, of course, I was saluting already.

There's a scene in Woody Allen's *Play It Again Sam* where he's on a couch, or a bed, with Diane Keaton, and he says that the way he prevents premature ejaculation is to imagine a baseball player making a frantic dash for a base. And she says, 'So that's why you always shout "slide".' Woody obviously never suffered from the effects of serious drug abuse or a war wound because I was wondering what I had to do to make myself come. Eventually, after performing every position, manoeuvre and act of deviance my brain could dredge up, I had to retreat, suffering not only from a severely bruised dick, and a throbbing leg, but also first-degree friction burns on the insides of my thighs. I sloughed back and awaited detumescence.

'Well,' she said after a few moments, 'if that's what you're like when you haven't done it for a while, if you really were in training what you do would be a capital offence. My heart's about to give out and the bits down below did a long time ago!' She patted me on the stomach through the tee shirt. 'At times back there I thought we were in some kind of competition, like sexual organ wrestling, to see who could stick out longest.'

She was covered in sweat, her hair damp and sticking to her face. My shirt was dark and sodden and when I looked down I could see, from the colour of the bandage, that at least one or two of the stitches had given out in the rough and tumble. 'Usually, for me, it's over at the first flash of ankle.'

'Usually? I thought you said it had been a long time.'

'Ah, yes, with women – not small furry rodents.'

She leaned over and lightly kissed me. I felt a droplet of perspiration plop from her chest on to mine. 'It's my turn for the coffee. I'll put it on and have a shower. If you want to think of lemmings or guinea pigs to get yourself off, be my guest.' She looked back from the doorway. 'We'll need to tidy up that leg, it's bled quite a bit.' Then she disappeared, and a second later popped her head back round the door jamb. 'Thanks. And I don't just mean for that. It was getting a little dull around here.'

I saluted and then blew her a kiss.

Over coffee in the kitchen she tried gently to probe me and I, as gently, rebuffed her. 'The mysterious stranger. Blows into town, hooks up with the barmaid, who patches him up and puts him back on his horse. The sunset beckons. Roll the credits.'

I smiled. 'You've fast-forwarded too far, we've barely passed the unhooking.' I tapped my leg and began to unroll the bandage. The wound looked angry, bloody, the middle part split open with a few black threads sticking from the gunge. I asked her, 'Can I have a shower and then put this back together?'

She was wearing a big, floppy, striped shirt over a pair of leggings. 'Of course. I'll look out the cotton wool and iodine.'

'The sewing kit might help, too.' I got up, put weight on the leg, a pulse of pain throbbing up it as I hobbled towards the door. I gave her a knowing grin. 'A joint wouldn't go amiss either.'

I left her with that as I went into the bathroom and started to run the shower.

The water stung the wound, turning the puddle around my feet the colour of rosé wine before clearing. I towelled off, dabbed toilet paper on the cut, which didn't look so bad with all of the matter and dried blood cleared away, put on my shorts and damp shirt and went back into the kitchen.

Stephanie wrinkled her nose. 'Look, you can't wear that smelly shirt again,' she said. 'I'll find you something.'

She came back with an old, torn football top, the Padres. While she was out I noticed that she had rolled a couple of joints. I took the shirt from her, hobbled out to the bathroom, changed into it and came back. I was still wearing the same shorts. 'You haven't got any fresh underwear, I suppose?'

'Nothing you'd want to get run over in.' She was lighting one big joint. 'I've got to ask you this, you know? Why don't you take your shirt off? It's a little – what, *unusual* to be so, errm, vigorous and uninhibited in bed, bare your other bits and still keep your top on. What's the problem? Three nipples? An embarrassing rash? Serial tattoos of other women? Hey, I'm not the jealous type.'

She took a few deep draws on the dope and handed it across. 'When I know you better,' I said and sucked down on the joint.

Hashish certainly gives you a finer appreciation of pain. I had considered sewing up the open bit of the cut, but doing it half-stoned didn't seem like cute suturing, so instead I told myself I could live with another ugly scar, taped some cotton wool over the injury and rolled on the elastic bandage again. We passed around and devoured the second joint and the world felt better, its noises sounding acutely. Stephanie had checked the computer but there was no e-mail message so she suggested, just for a giggle, researching the Downe family tree. I gave her my date of birth and place and my parents' name.

'Y'know, you're looking for something, a living. We could start one of these genealogy companies – nah, boring, right? What about a hi-tech detective agency? Tracing people by computer, tapping into hotel records for credit card details on errant husbands, phone companies' records, bank accounts—'

'And if there's anything in them we just help ourselves. I like that.'

'We could call ourselves Touch Downe ... Downe Home ...! Downe and Out ... Downe Fucker or You're Dead! Hey, were you an officer or an ordinary GI in the army?'

'I've heard all the Officer Downe jokes, thank you. And, latterly, I was a very underachieving captain.' No, not quite true, latterly I was a totally uncooperative prisoner.

'Bounty hunters. What about bounty hunters?'

'Finish your education,' I said, 'and then get yourself a highly paid job in a bank, or with Bill, or start your own software company designing arcade games, sell out and retire by forty. That's my advice. Get yourself a good man, unscarred in mind and body, have children, never lay a finger on them—'

'And go quietly into the good night.'

Even from my brief acquaintance with her I could see that she'd never be the type. 'Can't see you doing that.' I paused. 'You're a bit of a screamer.'

While she looked around for something to throw, I suggested going out to get some makings, of lunch or whatever meal of the day it was time for, more importantly a decent bottle of wine. It took me a little while to find my trousers and shoes but when I had done I was feeling less wrecked. Emptying an indiscriminate number of pills into my hand I stuck my mouth under the faucet and washed them down with a stream of cold water. 'Maybe we could eat outside in the garden.' I was looking out of the window now. 'Civilized.'

I felt her hands go round me from behind. 'Sure.' She nuzzled my neck. 'It's very secluded. No one to overlook us.'

'I get the picture.' I disentangled myself, kissed her a

heartbeat short of lingeringly and told her to go play with her computer. 'You working today?' I asked, moving towards the front door.

'Not till later.'

'OK, see you shortly. Check out these companies for me while I'm away, mmhh?'

'Sure. I'll be good.' She waved and began walking towards the bedroom. The kitchen smelled pleasingly of sex and marijuana.

When I opened the outside door I almost stumbled over them. It was the colours which caught my eye, I suppose. But then I stepped over, quickly closing the door behind me so that Stephanie couldn't see, then bent down.

The scent was subtle and kind of herby, no doubt accentuated by the effects of the dope. The flowers, carefully arranged and held in a cellophane collar, were lying right at the edge of the porch, almost at the first step down. I picked them up and looked around. There was no one to be seen. My heart was hammering. *At least it isn't a wreath*, I was thinking.

I drew my arm back to pitch them away, and then a better thought occurred, and I walked round the side of the house and through a small wicker gate, as silently as I could, and hid the bouquet in the shrubbery. Then another thought rose up. I walked further over the grass to one of the statues, a lichened cherub on a plinth with his stomach and willie sticking out, heaved him back on his pedestal and slipped in all of my money, save for a few low-denomination dollars, then eased him back into place.

It was a fairly shrewd guess that the flowers were a calling card, either from another suitor, which I dismissed almost immediately because there was no card attached and it wasn't Valentine's Day, or my visitors were just telling me that they knew where I was, what I was doing and with whom and, implicitly – and here I agreed wholeheartedly – that I was being stupid embroiling someone else in my business. It was an elaborate and florid warning.

They, whoever they were, must have been sneaking around the house while Stephanie and I were heaving and grunting, probably spying on us too. Obviously I had let my guard down – of course, not just that – because the place you are least likely to pay attention is when you're inside someone else.

I tried to think from their standpoint. You don't go out trailing someone with a vase of flowers stuck among the bugs, boom mikes, shotguns and electronic paraphernalia. No, the idea of the flowers – and I could almost hear the discussion – comes when you're bored shitless staking out in a car or, more likely, when the subject's doing something you'd give your left bollock for, and he's doing it blatantly and noisily within your purview, and it pisses the fuck out of you and you want to get one back at him. So that's what you come up with. And where do you get the flowers? If you're pretty dim, or if you just don't care, you go to the local flower shop.

I asked in a small local video store. There seemed to be only two florists and I struck lucky in the first one I tried. Moreover, I didn't even have to slip the young assistant any bucks. Just said that within the last few hours someone had bought flowers and delivered them to me, roses and ferns mostly, left them on the porch without a tag and I was fascinated to know who they came from. Could she describe the person who had bought them?

She probably thought it was a jealousy battle, or maybe that I had a secret gay lover, so she told me. It turned out that the shop had only made up one bouquet all morning, so it was quite easy to recall.

After that I gave up on the idea of lunch, called Stephanie's number from a payphone, made an excuse that something had come up – I could hear from the flat answers that she didn't quite believe me, that I was giving her the kiss-off – and set out walking back to my apartment where, I was almost sure, I'd find that I had been visited and looked over. The sun was warming the pavements, trees and shrubs and where they had been sprayed with rain a fine mist of condensation was rising. I spotted the car, a large dark brown sedan, as soon as I turned the corner. I wasn't meant to miss it. As I approached the gateway in the fencing I heard doors slam behind me and, turning, there were Deaf and Dumb coming across the path towards me, looking mean and purposeful.

'All right, you,' Deaf jerked his thumb at me, 'you're wanted downtown.' Dumb just motioned with his head towards the car.

'I have a choice?' Dumb simply pulled me by the arm and walked me to the back seat of the car, pushing me inside, causing me to wince.

The car took off, Dumb driving. I said, 'Next time, make it lilies, fellas,' and watched for the reaction, the body language, the glances in the driver's mirror.

Deaf looked at Dumb, they exchanged uncomprehending glances, then he turned in his seat. 'What the fuck are you talking about?' And it simply confirmed what the earlier description and my gut feeling had told me, that these guys were not involved.

'Forget it. Am I under arrest?'

'Just shut up,' Dumb said reluctantly, like the words were torn from him.

At the station I was taken into the interview room and given the customary intimidatory wait. It was the usual surroundings. Windowless, vandal-proof furniture, gangland braggadocio and street names etched into the brickwork. There wasn't anything stuck up or carved out that I could spin into a diversionary tale like in *The Usual Suspects*. During my time inside that was one of the cons' favourite movies.

106

Not only was there plenty of action but the gimp, the perennial loser, pulls the wool – and the shroud! – over everyone, which, I guess, has a redemptive message for the incarcerated.

I tried not to wonder why I had been pulled in. After about half an hour the door opened and two men slumped in, one thickset, balding and black, the other tall, very thin, wearing a three-piece dark blue suit, brown, tooled boots and fitting, well-nigh perfectly, the florist's description. I smiled. The black man threw me a surly glance and sat down in the chair opposite, the white guy leaned against the door, staring at me.

'It was a nice gesture,' I said loudly, staring back, 'but I never accept unsolicited and compromising gifts from strange men. Anyway, yellow roses don't suit my colouring.' I was hoping to get a reaction, and probably a slap in the mouth, but he just continued to stare without any detectable change in the intensity.

'We have some news for you, Downe,' the black one said. 'It's—'

'Hold up here,' I came in, turning my attention on him and leaning forward in my seat. 'You haven't even introduced yourselves. And another thing I never do is talk to strange men without introductions – or without a lawyer.'

Sighing, like he was towing a truckload of troubles, the black man looked back at his partner. They both shrugged. 'Don't be tiresome, Downe. Don't you want to be helpful?'

'Helpful?' I beamed. 'Oh, absolutely not. And I think you know why.'

'The way it is now,' the lanky one said, pushing himself off the door, 'you have a choice—'

'I know, the hard way and the easy way.'

Whitey had a very eastern voice, Boston, I'd guess, so the faux Western outfit sat ill on him. He went on, 'What you have is a certainty. Of days. Running out. You could have an indeterminacy of – well, of years, who knows?'

I ignored the white one, replying to the black. 'You obviously get taught this shit at the academy. Or is he doing evening classes in Stanislavsky?' The black one cuffed me, but without any real venom and as I was expecting it I rode my head with it. I tasted blood on my tongue. 'Fuck you,' I said pretty ritually, standing up, with less fluency and sense of purpose than I would have liked. 'Charge me with something or I'm out of here.'

Skinny moved back against the door, the black bruiser kicked his chair back and stood up. I thought about it. Perhaps achieving the second part of the threat wouldn't be that easy. But I stood my ground.

'We've had the report back on the bomb,' Whitey said, relieving the tension.

I looked from one to the other, wondering what to do next.

'Yes, it was a bomb like we all figured,' his partner took it up, perhaps trying to slide away from the confrontation. 'But it wasn't a tilt fuse which set it off, like you might expect.' And, as they clearly expected me to respond, naturally, I didn't. 'No, it seems it was a remote job, something radio-controlled. What do you think about that?'

I thought it seemed elaborate and unnecessary. With a radio-controlled fuse you are aiming to be precise and specific. You also need visual sight of your target. So why this unspecific, imprecise bodge where two innocent kids got killed? Unless, of course, I was reaching the wrong conclusion and that it had all been executed perfectly – not quite perfectly because no one could have known that two street kids would break into the car – but what if it had just been intended as a grisly demonstration, a warning? No one was meant to be in the car when it turned to overheated atoms, perhaps, but, what the fuck, who's going to miss a couple of miscreant street niggers?

But there was something else which had been bothering me about it, nagging at my sub-conscious, which now formed into an obvious question. How did they get the bomb in place? All right, so it only involves a small package, a strong magnet and a quick slide under the car, but it would be a pretty visible act in a nosy neighbourhood, particularly when the car in question must have been under surveillance for most of the time by the two deceased boosters. So, had it been stuck on earlier, had I been driving around with it, only a push-button away from eternity for hours? I let that sink in. It seemed likely, or at least not terribly unlikely.

'So? I asked you what you thought.'

'Mmmh? I think someone's either blind as a bat and should be given a white stick rather than a lever to throw, or else didn't really care very much.'

'You know how to make a radio-controlled bomb.' It was Whitey, from the door, and it wasn't a question.

I shook my head. 'Come on, here. What, you think I'm on some crazy vendetta against Avis, or street criminals? You think I went down to the toy store, bought an airplane control kit, somehow found a few pounds of high-ex, rigged it up, set it off, injuring myself in the process – hey, maybe this is an elaborate insurance scam? – and then somehow managed to crawl away and hide the lethal device in some cranny your forensic team haven't yet managed to uncover?' After pausing for a gulp of air I went on. 'And I take it you haven't found it because if you had, and it implicated me at all, I'd be sitting in cuffs considering several sides of charge sheet. No?' I looked from one to the other; they continued staring at me. 'Leave this out, fellas, this is a game and you and I know it. Difference is, you're the only ones joining in.' Still silence. 'So, can I go now?'

I was right, the apartment had been visited, but in a rather more public manner than I expected and the owner wanted me out. Now. Deaf and Dumb, after dropping me off at the station house, had gone back, either with bluster or a warrant, and demanded to look around my place. There was nothing to find, but the owner, who was elderly and middle European and had probably witnessed enough trouble in his life, wasn't interested in my protestations of innocence and police abuse. I packed my bag.

For a couple of hours I hung around the pier, even managing to score a couple of grams of speed from a threadbare Rasta, then I went for a couple of expensive drinks in an airy, slightly camp waterfront café/bar with walnut and cream fittings, modern art tastefully arranged on the walls and waiters in tight white shirts peremptorily taking orders while they waited for their acting breaks. It was the sort of place you wouldn't be in the least surprised to turn round and find David Hockney or Gore Vidal at your elbow. Not quite perhaps, but it was the kind of caboose where you expect to find arch and erudite talk and dollops of rough in their Sunday best, looking for a leg up in life, or over.

The music was something unrecognizable but baroque and I was sure they'd have string quartets playing in the evenings of high summer. I sat at the bar and drank my *déclassé* beer and munched on peanuts, rather hoping that if there were to be any kind of bombing reprise it would be mounted here just after I left. So, why didn't I go somewhere else? Part measures indolence and guilty masochism, the second clearly to do with my complicated Caledonian heritage, only feeling truly comfortable with alcohol while indulging in outward misery. But when one of the patrons tried to pick me up I decided to go. Better that than squash his nose, whose sole function on his face seemed to be to support a silver nose ring. 'See you again,' I said, grabbing most of my change from the bar and then heading towards Surfin' USA, making a slight detour past Stephanie's house to retrieve my inheritance, guarded over by the pissing cherub.

She didn't look enormously pleased to see me, but I had shoved a few lines up my beak and I wasn't going to allow that to put me off. 'Something absolutely unforeseen came up and I couldn't avoid it. Sorry, I'm not jerkin' you around.' I had on my chemical smile and my nose was runny. I felt frisky and playful.

She was pulling a draught beer and looking sideways at me. There were two others serving behind the bar, a young man with close-cropped blond hair and a girl of about twenty, high tits and a nose ring. 'You are still alive, then?'

Pulling back a bar stool I perched. 'Sarcasm's unbecoming. Honestly, it was unavoidable.'

'I wasn't being sarcastic.' She pushed the beer across the counter at the geek, said something to the lad serving with her, and pointed over to the far corner, where there were several empty tables picked out in candlelight and the faint glow of neon. 'There,' she said, 'I'm taking a quick break and we need to talk. I'll bring a drink over. My treat.'

I limped away – between the wound and friction sores I was in a raw state, but I make it a rule never to disagree with a woman offering my sort of blandishments. I picked out the darkest and quietest bit of the room. I noticed that there was a TV on bracket in the opposite corner, sound down, which seemed to be running *Star Wars*. Amazing, it wasn't basketball. The track coming over the speakers was Coltrane, 'A Love Supreme', which I thought tasty but a trifle bizarre.

From my corner seat looking down the bar, towards the door and with the gantry to my left, I had an Uzi-eyed vista of the place. Stephanie was mixing something in a pitcher, the liquid swirling around looked clear, and I wondered what it was. She came over with it on a tray, two martini glasses sparkling with frost. She was wearing a short, tight, woollen skirt and the type of loose and revealing vest favoured by stevedores and Bruce Springsteen. 'Vodka martini.' She plonked the tray down, took the glasses off and began pouring. 'The Russian tradition is to slam the vodka right back in one. I don't know what they do with martinis, but there's so little of anything else in this except vodka that you have to observe the old Russian tradition.' She slugged hers back. 'Go on. You're going to need it.'

I did. A fireball erupted in my stomach. 'Well?' I coughed out.

'I hope you're good for five hundred dollars?' I nodded. 'Because that's what I put on my Amex card to get a rapid search done at New Register House. Call it a "drop everything and get the fuck round there" payment.' I nodded again, this time expectantly. 'They said they'd let me know today.' I was nodding now like a stroke victim. 'Nothing yet.' She was filling the glasses up again. It felt like a bit of an anti-climax. 'I shouldn't be drinking on duty. I really, really hope this comes through for you.'

Now I was slowly shaking my head, pretty mystified as to what she was going on about. She filed the second vodka next to the first one. I could see she was building up to telling me something. Even so, goodbye isn't that difficult to come out with. 'When I said a little while back, "so you're alive, then?" I really wasn't being sarcastic.' She was re-filling her glass, while I hadn't even started on my second. 'Drink up. Please.' I did, but sipping this time. 'What I meant was,' she was looking into her full glass, tears rimming her eyes, 'that I checked your birth certificate. Here, in the US. And the other—' She took a deep breath, put her hand on mine which held my glass. 'I really hope this Scottish search comes through for you, John, I really do—' She took her hand away, put it to her mouth and took a deep breath. She was either stifling a cry or a giggle.

'Couldn't you just come out with it? Or is torture your other major?'

'I don't know how to say this, John. But you shouldn't be walking around. You're a dead man—'

I was slow on the uptake, despite the pumping in my veins and the raging in my stomach. I started to say, 'Oh, is that

112

all—' when it dropped. 'You didn't just check the birth certificate, you kept on looking.'

She nodded. 'It's so easy. And kind of obsessional.'

'You found a death certificate?'

She nodded again and rubbed both her eyes. 'This really frightens me, John, or whoever you are. Your death certificate. There it was, two months later, after the birth. You didn't live long enough to sit up, never mind walk around. Pneumonia and pleurisy.' I could see her hand shaking as she reached for her drink. 'I've done a lot of things, John,' she gave a little snort and took a swallow from her drink, then tried a smile, 'but I didn't ever think it would include necrophilia.'

I think I tried to smile back but it must have seemed more like a colic spasm. 'Stephanie.' She seemed to be a long way off and getting smaller by the breath. 'I don't know whether you believe this or not, but I'm even more stunned by this than you.' I seemed to be plunging into a smoky dark pit. 'Between one drink and the next I just ceased to exist.'

Part Two

1

The grave dark had stopped roaring past and now pricks of light flared and bled in the raindrops on the windscreen.

The night's always blue in the movies, Jack McCann thought, waiting for the clapper-board sounds of gunfire to open the action. It's day for night, or something, I read that. Maybe filters. Which triggered off the forgotten taste of tobacco in his mouth and he breathed deeply and grabbed the door handle. It felt wet to the touch. Even the gunfire sounds unreal in real life, in this life. Like bursting bags, the high-velocity rounds are more like mild whip-cracks. Probably sounds too fuckin' limp in wraparound stereo and Panavision.

'Right?' he said. Saying to himself, think blue. The only way he could do this, get through again, was to act reality. Then he started to smile. 'Indigo, again.'

'Yeah. Always the fuckin' same. That's funny?'

'Chromatherapy.'

'What?'

'Just ignore me, all right?'

'You been drinking?'

'Everything's monochrome at night. Y'noticed that? So, if the blood's black it can't be real. Right?'

'Jesus, Jack.'

The car had come gunning into the car park behind the block of flats, dodging the burned-out cars and spilled rubbish, laying broad-tyred trails in the wet, and the driver, McCann, misjudging the distance, or the conditions or the

117

obstacles or whatever, skidded, corrected, then dumped it half-way up the pavement, steam wisping from the tyres. He had cursed and punched the dashboard. Nerves. His colleague, strapped hard into his seat, looked at him questioningly then slapped him lightly on the thigh, and as the siren died away the two men climbed out, flicked by the rotating light on the car. Black and blue.

McCann pocketed the car keys and was now checking that his holster was unbuttoned, out on the wet, glistening tarmac. *Some fuckin' film*, he said under his breath, moving now, falling in behind the brisk step of his partner. Then, *same fuckin' film*, lips moving slightly as he silently prayed for the same, banal ending, his own warm bed, the ether of alcohol.

Ahead of him Armitage drew his gun, keeping it down long beside him, his rasping breath audible over the sucking footfalls on the concrete. Nervous, too. McCann pulled his own gun free and was surprised to feel the rough, pitted grip slippery in his grasp, keeping it concealed inside his open coat. Automatically he thumbed off the safety catch, then wiped his forehead with the back of his left hand. It never got any easier, coping with the fear.

The two men in plainclothes had reached the doorway of the end block, which swung on its hinges as if someone had recently run through. The lobby, covered in graffiti, blowing with chip papers and discarded racing sections, the glitter of needles and broken plastic, smelled powerfully of urine. There was no sign of anyone around, no street kids, no keening cries, not even a wasted junkie crouching in a corner. Silence was always a sure marker of some disaster, like an ambush.

The lift wasn't working, of course, so they inched their way up to the first landing, silent and gloomy, underlit, light bulbs long since given up on, smelling marshy, of damp and gas, all the doors locked and bolted, the crunching under foot of phials and silver paper. All around was dark muddy concrete, heavy black doors; McCann cast only the merest glance at the ceiling – it reminded him of the inside of an endless tunnel, or maybe a decaying coffin. Slowly putrefying bodies. The phosphorescent epitaphs, the gang slogans sprayed on the walls, glowed dimly.

His tongue was dry, his groin damp, he wanted a drink and the comfort of warm, soft arms. He tried to picture the frightened shadows hiding behind these walls, outside the coffin, in their rooms, clutching at night clothes, crucifixes, the security of locks. Hearts hammering, like his. Or maybe he was kidding himself, perhaps the total absence of any sign of life was merely utter disdain.

The code had blown in on the radio, a shooting, probably a robbery in progress. McCann mouthed the words to himself and concentrated on deep, even breaths as he fell in behind his partner, who had elected himself tonight's main target, then slowly began climbing the stairs, in a skating motion, feet going from side to side on the steps, hitting the outside each time, the burglar's shuffle, minimizing the creaks from wooden stairs – not that there were any but it was just a habit and, anyway, it would probably avoid most of the shite and detritus. Some day they would declare places like these a hazard to life, he thought, but they should start with the inhabitants. *As if*. He looked down at his gun.

Along the landing, light bled from a doorway, a winey, fuzzy patch, like a blotted bloodstain. Fuck, he cautioned himself, they're still there.

As they moved towards it he vaguely became aware of a rattling far-off hum and considered whether it was just the internal roar in his ventricles, his heart going like an arrhythmical drum roll. His ears buzzed and his eyelids fluttered as he tried to adjust to the changing light.

Armitage was looking back, face sheened with a nervous sweat, top teeth biting on his bottom lip. He nodded. McCann returned it. They knew exactly what they had to do. As, of course, would those inside if they were still there. He imagined darkened faces waiting, holding shotguns, Uzis, whatever, it wouldn't matter, a Kevlar flak jacket wouldn't make much difference.

Armitage moved first. McCann had never been easy calling him by his first name, Mike, because he didn't look like one, too irascible, but now he was spinning across the door opening, gun in both hands, held a few inches in front of his face, like some object of worship, or hope. McCann was crouching at the door frame, gun in the same position, waiting for the nod of the head.

And then they went in, on adrenalin jump-start, seeking the shadows, guns scouring the soft spaces in the room, waiting for the muzzle flashes. 'Police officers!' McCann shouted. Nothing.

Except the buzzing. Louder now. Separate and definitely distinct from the sound of blood in his ears. They were in a large square hall, he could see now. It looked flimsy, like a set, and had four doors off it. The walls, washed in a light amber, were studded with pasted-up cuttings from newspapers, but McCann was not looking at them closely. The carpet was a dark and plain background to the object in the middle of it, a child's teddy bear lying face down, arms spread – assuming the surrender position, McCann thought to himself.

Looking away, he caught sight of Armitage trying the handle of the first room, flattened against the wall, taking no chance of catching a round through the hardboard door. Then it inched open, squeaking in reluctance, revealing just a black upright rectangle. Armitage pulled his torch from his coat pocket and shone a long cone of light into the room and around it. McCann called out, 'Anyone there?' surprised at how timid and unassertive he sounded.

The room caught light as Armitage flicked on the switch and he shrank back against the door frame, heart hammering anew, as his eyes adjusted to the familiar objects appearing, a broken-open armchair, a couple of plastic seats, television in the corner, video below, blinking green numerals. They didn't come for that, then, he said to himself.

The two men covered the area quickly, then moved out and on to the next door. Same procedure. The nerve-jangling entry, light on, just a soft overhead glow, this time to a bedroom, a child's bedroom, cot in the far corner, a hanging jumble of animal figures above, a mobile, slowly rotating. 'Recently visited,' McCann heard himself murmur. Moving slowly, he took in the walls painted in a light pink blush, glossy, air-brushed pictures of cartoon characters looking out, Mickey, Tom and Jerry. It was a surprisingly well-kept room, as if the mother had held on to that. And then a familiar sharp smell which his brain refused to recognize. The air was heavy with it.

Moving slowly towards the cot, gun still extended like a prod, index finger tight on the trigger, McCann noticed in the fuzzy light the child asleep in the tangled bedding. His hands relaxed, the gun dropped a few inches, he felt a trickle of sweat run down his stomach, but, in spite of the tension, he gave a flitting smile. The floorboards groaned slightly, no carpet, as he moved. He was over the child now, looking down at the indistinct shape below, on its back, looking up. McCann smiled again. Then it died.

His eyes screwed up, his nose wrinkling at the powerful smell. Cordite. He recognized it now. The perfume of gun-shots. And, looking closer, he noticed that the baby had been shot in the face, a small calibre weapon (he was surprised at this professionalism in the circumstances), the wound like a ragged, charred mouth above its own, brains exploded like a lumpy, raspberry-stained porridge, in gobs and splashes and soggy whorled patterns on the white sheet with the powder-blue storks.

He turned away, acid bubbling in his throat, then he felt

his arm being pulled and he looked into Armitage's face, out of focus, as if through dewy glass. Tears coming. He felt ashamed. But Armitage was shaking his head, pulling him away, nothing to be done, barely registering that the paper shapes above the cot had finally stopped moving .

They slid into the hall again, McCann gulping for breath, feeling surprised that the fear had gone, replaced by bitter anger which felt like a hard metallic ball in his gullet. A rage for blood. If they were still here – they, formless – there were going to be no polite calls for surrender. He positively relished the harsh taste of his rage.

The humming was louder, closer, and McCann could smell something hot and rancid and, again, familiar. The two men followed the sound, threw open the door into a large kitchen. The light was low and diffuse, from a small lamp above the cooker. The woman's body was lying on the floor across from them. She had obviously struggled – a chair lay overturned and a broadening trail of blood indicated that her body had been dragged across the linoleum floor to where it lay just under the sink. Her bright blue skirt had ridden up over her buttocks – McCann felt he should pull it down, but, of course, didn't – revealing what had obviously been white pants but were now stained in death. And white, stockingless legs. Both limbs were straight, he noted.

He made a quick conclusion: it appeared that she had been dead when she was pulled across the kitchen. Her arms were also down beside her body, unnaturally acquiescent. Looking along, he noted a few flies jumping and crawling around the dark island-shaped pool of blood around her shoulders. And, still, that buzzing. But not from the flies.

Armitage was in his face, shaking his head again and McCann looked up and past him, from the body, to the battered kitchen units, and at a harsh, yellow, glowing oblong. A screen. TV? For a moment he couldn't work out what it was. And still the smell, bitingly familiar, cloying, assaulting his nose, making him pull up his left hand to wipe away the taint.

Then a puncturing scream and he jumped, heart howling, almost pulling the trigger, but it was just a bell grating and echoing, and as the yellow light gradually faded, McCann was looking back down at the body, now realizing what was wrong, taking in the black shape where the light had died, understanding instantly everything that had been done. And that smell, of broiled meat and frazzled hair. Of charred skin and boiling jelly.

Armitage flicked his torch up and, peering into the now dark window of the microwave oven, in the light beam, McCann could make out the blistered, swollen outline of a head, with a grossly bloated, bubbling and split tongue bursting out, pressing against the glass in a horribly mocking gesture.

They couldn't help it. The two men took turns throwing up in the sink. Later, both would blame it on nerves.

2

I woke when the stewardess shook my arm. She was looking at me with ill-concealed distaste. She was about forty, with a tightly set mouth in the middle of a pair of spreading dewlaps. She pointed up above me, at the *fasten seat belt* sign.

'Was I saying disgraceful things in my sleep?' My mouth was dry, my head pounded and I felt queasy. Small wonder, I had dosed myself with pills and booze before even getting on the plane and must have downed a jeroboam equivalent of champagne before taking off. I was in Club Class, the first time I had ever flown above my station, the first time I had flown since it happened. My face was wet; I rubbed my hands over it, and wondered if I had been crying in my sleep. There were five or six other passengers in the cabin, none of whom was looking my way, out of politeness or because I was an embarrassing disgrace. Either way, I felt too whacked to care. I clipped on my belt, sat up and tried not to look out of any of the windows, the blinds of which were all up apart from the one over the window next to me.

I was trying not to think about it but it was impossible. If I had had the time I would have taken the boat, anything other than fly, but here I was on an airliner, gradually descending, perhaps on the same flight path, but only a few miles, a few years and a broken lifetime away.

It's impossible not to imagine what it was like, although I would give anything to cut out that part of my brain where the memories lurk. Emily and the baby were not sitting near the baggage hold, where it would have been over quickly. Those around the seat of the explosion almost certainly died instantly. I have read all of the reports, all of the evidence, but no one will know exactly what it was like. Did the plane hold together for a few seconds, a howling vacuum sucking out its innards, before the terminal strains broke it into bits and the conscious began their plummet towards the damp fields, the bracken-covered hills and the plain, neat streets of Lockerbie? I could see her falling, Katie plucked from her arms. My hands began to shake, perspiration poured out of me, my mouth was infused with a wash of foul bile as I pictured her and the baby plunging, desperately trying to drag my mind away from it, then the rush of nausea as, too late, I scrabbled in the seat pocket for the sick bag.

I looked down at the carpet and the spreading stains. The plane began to buck as it hit air pockets on the descent, and I realized that it was never going to get any better until I, too, plunged into the end.

The immigration officer, head hunched over what looked like a music score, briefly cast his eyes over my passport, then at me, asked a couple of peremptory questions about my means and how long I intended to stay, and then motioned me through with a nod. Doubtless most of the Americans who turn up at Glasgow Airport are wild-eyed, unwashed, smelling of vomit and stale booze and clutching plastic bags of duty-free. It wasn't until I had been in the city a few days that I realized I was barely distinguishable from the locals.

I was carrying all my luggage, the same Hecht's grip, the unwashed clothes inside, as I sauntered through Customs and out. Here I was, hung-over in the land of my forefathers. I felt at home. My head continued to throb and the light seemed unnaturally bright, so I found a shop on the concourse selling sunglasses – the price seemed about forty per cent too high – and then a Menzies book shop which had trays of pills and

125

aspirin (maybe reading hurts the locals' brains, I thought), so I bought a couple of packets and retired to a coffee shop to plan and recuperate.

The coffee was large and black. I had changed money at the airport on the other side but I still wasn't making speed on currency conversion, so I offered what turned out to be ten pounds and got a handful of change in return. Then I slumped over it in the corner and wondered how long it would take me to make a drug deal. At least over here a smelly Yank in sunglasses is never going to be mistaken for a narc.

Except, and the realization came rushing back, I wasn't a Yank, despite the accent; I was as Scottish as the girl serving behind the counter. But I was also a felon, travelling on what I now knew was an illegally acquired passport, although that knowledge was less than seventy-two hours old.

I suppose I had been on a binge in those few hours since the call came through to Stephanie, and following that the confirmatory e-mail and fax kept me dedicated to it. Even then, I don't suppose I truly accepted it until I saw the copy of the birth certificate and the handwriting, the signatures, recognizably my parents', but the names totally unrecognizable. All of my past was a lie, a figment of two other people's imaginations, for what reason I couldn't begin to understand. It felt strange, but there was something else, a feeling of exhilaration. It isn't given to many of us, gone thirty, to rediscover or reinvent ourselves.

Of course, I reminded myself, sipping at the coffee, if my mother and father had changed identity once they could have done it before. But I just knew that wasn't the case. And that I really was Thomas John Bone, born in Glasgow to the former Katherine Downes Scott and Thomas McKenna Bone. It was my mother's middle name, Downes, which convinced me. It was so close to the new name they had come up with. They must have worked back from the death certificates, or death notices, looking for a child only days or weeks old. In my mind, I could see them searching records both for a dead surname easily rememberable in their rewritten history of themselves, and one which had become deceased close to the dates of their arrival in America, one which wasn't going to give education, passport or social security difficulties later. A kid close enough to my age for me to be passed off as him, for me, in a way, to live his life. Downes, Downe. The unfortunate John Downe had been only a couple of months and a consonant out.

I finished my coffee, put down the cup and leaned back in the velour seat. The questions were still moving around, albeit more sluggishly, in my head. So, why would you pitch off with a young baby from your own country and wash up in a new one? Considering it, it seemed obvious. Either seeking a better life or running away from a worse one. The change of identity, the illegal immigration and the life underground, which is what it had been, suggested that they had fled from something serious. Life-threateningly so, I thought. You don't submerge yourself in a far continent, surely, without a fairly dramatic impulsion?

As ever, I put up the counter-argument. Perhaps it really was about bettering themselves, rooting themselves in a fresh and blossoming new land while they were still young enough to take to it. Reasonable as far as it goes, I came back, but my da never appeared to be either dynamic, resourceful or adaptable. A certain graceless resilience, I'll grant you, two fast hands and an insatiable appetite for alcohol, at least until lately, but I just couldn't see him having even the imagination to say, 'Look, hen, let's make something of ourselves. Yon America seems to be the place to do it.'

Perhaps – stretching my imagination until it twanged – it was my ma behind it, back in those days, before the spark was extinguished? But why the false identities, which surely would not have survived even the mildest of inquiries? When I thought about it, the only reason could have been to intrude me, apparently legally, into the system. And now here I was – spat out. I sifted through the change in my pocket and looked for likely coins to make a trans-Atlantic call to Stephanie. I had won the first part of my compound bet with her: I'd actually managed to slip back into the old country undetected. Or at least, apparently so.

The shuttle took one bump and then clung to the runway in a howl of reverse thrust and a blizzard of spray before it stuttered, slowed to a trotting pace and equilibrium returned. Meg Carpenter watched the smeared outlines of the terminal buildings through the water shivering down the window. She stretched her legs, arched back in the seat and waited for the seat belt sign to go off and the fatuous voice to come over the intercom.

The aircraft jerked to a stop, a rat-a-tat of seat belts unclasping went off all around and passengers, almost all men in the business section, began unlatching lockers, throwing on coats, grabbing newspapers and bustling into the gangway. She took her time. *They* would wait. Her coat, navy blue cashmere from an Army and Navy sale, was on the seat beside her. She stood up, noting inwardly how the men in the passage moved aside to let her out, swung the coat around her shoulders and on, blinked a brief smile of thanks, picked up her handbag and slipped into the line as it moved through the plane.

She was tall, five-ten and a bit, and built like a basketball player, except, she liked to think, for the over-developed thighs. Narrow hips, small breasts, rangy, hands like a concert pianist's or surgeon's, depending on who was flattering her, and a long neck on which men always seemed to want to leave a calling card. Her hair was the colour of jet, another thing she was always being told, although she fancied it had dark emerald highlights, and it fell on to her shoulder blades, or would have done if it was not now in a French twist. She looked slightly oriental, there was some Malaysian filtration in her genes, with large brown eyes and a beauty spot on her right cheek. She knew that she was striking, exceptionally and intimidatingly so, almost beautiful, but, more than that, she knew she was bright, double first, etc., again exceptionally and intimidatingly so. She shook her head. That was another of the repetitive things men said about her.

Five minutes later she was walking out of the winding tunnel. She barely checked as she moved through the semi-circle of people waiting, a mix of families and men in old suits holding recognition cards, all of which she ignored. The two men waiting for her fell in beside her; she barely acknowledged them as they walked down the stairs towards the baggage retrieval. When she got there she turned, her back to the moving carousel, deigned a quick smile – it was always wise to live up to pre-existing prejudice, it allowed for the element of surprise – and held out her hand. 'Carpenter. But you already knew that. Which of you is McCauley and which Keevins?'

'McCauley.' The younger one held out his hand. It was meaty and calloused. He was about her age, around thirty, although she thought that he might be even younger, aged by the couple of extra stones he was carrying and the severe haircut which had flecks of grey in the stubble. Keevins was in his early fifties, with a toothbrush moustache, small, slight and looking professionally misplaced, like he should have been a librarian or a teacher. She took his hand. It was dry and crinkly.

'Just one bag,' she said to cover the silence as the first bags began to judder round. 'Then where to?'

'Pitt Street,' McCauley answered, looking beyond her at the baggage.

'Headquarters,' Keevins came in before she could ask the question.

*

129

'Therr's a boundary charge.'

'Charge?' I said from the back. 'You're not serious? Please, I'm tired, I don't have the legs for it. Is it OK if I just signal the advance instead, drop a handkerchief or something?'

'Right, pal. What you see oan the meter, plus the boundary charge.'

I motioned onward, rather feyly, my attempt at jet-lag humour plunging in flames. 'If you hear a noise like a jumbo jet taking off, don't worry, it'll just be me snoring.'

'Wherr to then, pal?' The taxi was spluttering and rumbling; it felt a little like what I imagine it must be like on the inside of a washing machine, which was an inner-city dare in laundromats when my parents' generation was growing up – at least according to the *National Enquirer*, it was. I remember finding a faded copy as padding under an old carpet, explaining it all.

'I've never been in a black cab before,' I said inanely. Then, trying to make a joke of it, 'Just don't think you can charge extra for the experience.' Unfortunately jokes, when there's a cultural ocean and a lake of stale alcohol between you (ignoring the body clock still tuned to Newfoundland time), can be misconstrued. 'Apart from the boundary charge,' I added in quickly, smiling at him in his driver's mirror. Then, after a little thought as the machine containing me seemed to swell and chunter, 'The city centre.'

The cab ached into gear and trundled off. The driver was a youngish man – I could tell by the letterbox view of his eyes and nose visible in his mirror and the cut of his hair – who had a bottle of a pink-coloured lemonade in a sort of home-made holster in the front, next to the windshield. 'Thirsty, huh?'

I could see his eyes switching to me in the mirror, a narrowing, then a look down at the bottle. He started to guffaw. 'Naw, no really. It's a legal weapon like, 'no. Tae clock someone if he tries tae dae a runner. 'No, makes aff

130

wae'out peying. Sorry, pal,' I could see him smiling in the mirror, 'ah forgoat yir a Sherman – sorry, Yank—'

'Sherman tank. Yank.' The translation clicked through my head like tumblers falling. 'Rhyming slang. And it's all right. My old man was from Glasgow so you don't have to translate from the native.'

'Zatright? Wherr fae? Yir auld man?'

That threw me. Govan he had said, but that didn't make it true. 'I think – Govan?'

'What's the name?'

I had to think about that for a few seconds in my befuddled state. 'Bone.'

'Christ, Bone! Mair Bones in Govan than you could shake a stick at, or rattle a ribcage. No just Bones. Skeletons, fuckin' corpses by the barrowload. Turn ower a sod'i earth in Govan – and that's difficult, by the way, because the whole place is covered in shite and concrete – and there's a great rush'i air, a flutter of murdered souls makin' for heaven.' He paused. 'Actually, no quite. It's like the noise oh ah lift gaun doon.'

I could see a licence, a picture of the driver, whose name seemed to be McGinty. Perhaps Seumas? It was difficult to read. He reminded me of American restaurants where all the waiters semed to be merely hovering around tables before their big break in showbusiness. Not that I had been in too many restaurants recently. But, don't tell me, I thought, this is just the day job, at night you're a stand-up comedian. 'Thanks for that. If I go down there I'll be sure not to take a spade. Maybe a crucifix and some garlic?'

'Take a fuckin' shotgun.' His shoulders began to move and I guessed he was laughing. 'Just jokin', by the way, just jokin'. Ah wouldnae like a foreign visitor tae get the wrong impression. Naw.' He paused and I could feel it coming. 'You won't need a shotgun at aw. Take a fuckin' Uzi.'

His shoulders were bobbing up and down and he was giggling. I shouted, so I'd be heard. 'I'll feel right at home then.' And I settled back, watching a narrow stretch of motorway unfold and a series of ludicrously boxy cars zip past. After a few minutes, just before I dropped off, I muttered, 'I'm looking for a small hotel, cheap, clean, no rip-offs, where they appreciate the privacy of their guests. Particularly for cash.'

'Nae problem, pal,' said the driver. 'Ah know a wee place where they'll no let a shadow in without a serious wedge up front and the signed approval of its owner.'

'That sounds absolutely perfect.'

'Yir auld man wis fae here, wisae?' There were a few moments of silence and then he hissed over his shoulder. 'Y'oan the lam or somethin'? Dae'n a runner?' I harrumphed, which could have been taken any way. 'Y've no kilt anybody, huv ye?' I could hear the laughter in his voice.

'Not recently.'

He laughed out loud. I don't know why.

3

The trick with jet-lag is not to become dehydrated, to observe the local time rather than your own, and jolt your reluctant body clock on to it. It won't work, but it gives you the excuse to consume lots of lag-altering substances. My life, spawned into a mixed Catholic and Calvinistic maelstrom, needs lots of excuses. I had almost run out of the drugs I had been given in hospital, and anxiety, the prospect of the plunge to come, reality rushing up to meet me, was beginning to gnaw.

The wound was a lot better. When I walked now I didn't look like the victim of Falls Road justice. I bought a packet of scalpel blades and some dressings from a chemist – the knowledge that there was a cornucopia of balming substances through the glass partition guarded only by a couple of girls in white coats taunted me – and I performed minor surgery on the stitches. It was probably unnecessary, they may have been the dissolving sort, but I couldn't remember being told, so I sliced and pulled them out anyway.

My hotel, more of a hostel, overlooked Glasgow Green, a vast expanse which seemed to have been created purely for the delectation of drunks and diarrhoeic dogs. That's unfair; junkies seemed to love it too.

It made it ridiculously easy to score. I watched the place for a couple of hours, caught on to what was happening, and then cut out a young lad with a pinched face and a pulled-down baseball cap I'd twice watched hand over small twists of something which I'm sure wasn't black pepper. 'Yo, m'man,' I said in my best NY streetese, and grabbed him by the arm. He began to cower, as if he expected me to hit him. Maybe I should have popped him one for openers, to get the relationship off on the proper footing, but instead I said, 'I'm lookin' to score.'

It was a crazy approach, but then I didn't have the time or the energy to study local street mores and assimilate myself.

'Whit?' he said, his hand sliding to his pocket which I took to be an aggressive move, looking for something sharp or deadly to extricate himself from his predicament. Which is when I hit him, just a sharp straight poke in the diaphragm with a couple of crooked fingers, only hard enough to take the wind out of him, not enough to go in through the skin and twist out his oesophagus. He collapsed forward into my arms. Embarrassing.

When he had got his breath back, between wheezes he tried to explain that he thought I was a cop – 'Oh yeah, so they talk like this around here?' – and that he was just trying to palm the stuff he had left on him, that he wasn't carrying a weapon. And when I had nodded at that, which was the nearest he would get to an apology, he said that all he had left was smack. 'Nae eggs or jellies.'

'I've already eaten,' I said. He looked at me strangely. 'And heroin's a bit strong for my palate. I'm looking for a bit of coke, some dope, too. What d'ya say?'

He shook his head. He was gasping for breath, tears in his eyes, nose running – he wiped at it with the back of his hand – and just for a moment I stepped outside myself, seeing this grown hulk that I was beating-up on this wasted child, and I was ashamed of myself, sickened. He was just a harmless junkie trying to make enough for the next fix, with, I suppose, a family who either loved him, or might have abandoned him, but had never, even though they might have longed to, forgotten him.

I was becoming sentimental.

134

When I was younger I thought of the family as some kind of prison, a structure of emotional debt, deprivation, bitter memories and longing you carried around with you. Now I realized that it wasn't a prison I was carrying around, but a tomb.

I let him go, almost ready to say sorry. 'There's a pub called McCready's in the West End,' he was babbling, rubbing his chest and vainly trying to modulate his speech. 'Ask around for a bloke called Eddie McColl. He'll sort you.'

'OK ... thanks.' I nodded my head. 'Thought you were pulling something on me. Like a blade.' I had got out of the way of saying sorry.

Walking away, my head spinning from multiple deprivations of the central nervous system, I slowly realized that it was still mid-afternoon, and I had a few hours to kill and other business to do. In my experience serious dope-dealers, either up-market or gutter, are like bed bugs. They cleave to the comfort of darkness.

I rubbed the inside of my left arm, thinking of the messy scars, and vowed to myself that I would walk off a bridge before I went back on the needle. I had to kill time, or at least give it a severe bruising, so I decided to discover this city about which I had such fixed views and imparted memories, none of which seemed to match the reality. What I had been expecting was a kind of smoke-stained grimness, sooty crumbling tenements, people in dark clothes, women in headscarves. Ridiculous, given that anywhere you go in the world today you'll see much the same fashions, the latest-but-one US icon on the tee-shirt, even if the wording is misspelt. But, even so, I was looking for the kind of place circumscribed in the past of my parents. And what I had seen so far was a sort of lightly scuffed decentness, cleaned-up honey and grey stone buildings, well-dressed people and a lot of greenery, no sign of the belching smoke from factories, the grey washed-out clothing and the whey-coloured faces. So I went looking

135

for the memories of Mum and Dad. Not theirs, but whether anything of them remained in the streets and minds of other people.

The past may well be another country, and here I was smack in the middle of it, without a map or a passport.

4

Carpenter looked around the room. It was small, dark and almost featureless. A desk with nothing on it except a telephone, a bunch of ochre-coloured files in a neat pile and an empty edifice of wire trays. There were two chairs, covered in dun-coloured fabric and the walls, painted the colour of jaundice, were naked apart from chips and smears here and there. She sighed, thinking of her own room overlooking the river, and the view. This one was windowless, lit by a tired fluorescent light and it smelled, she thought, of damp clothing.

Resignedly she took a deep breath, shook her head, looked round once again and crossed her legs, making sure she did not spill the coffee – instant, naturally – which she was holding in a plastic contraption, inside which was a polystyrene cup full to overflowing with the mud-coloured liquid. It looked exactly like a river sample. Again, she thought of her own office, the plants, the light, the views of the Thames. She felt a lurch in her stomach but, no, she said to herself, concentrate on this.

After a couple of minutes, while she sipped at her coffee, filtering the sludge through her teeth and trying not to become depressed, the door swung open and the detective she had been introduced to earlier – Brown? DS Brown? – came in, smiled, mumbled something which was probably an apology and sat down behind the desk. He was wearing a tie, in clashing, cutting, migraine colours, which had to have been a present. You wouldn't face the world with something so biliously patterned if there was not some moral obligation attached. And a light-coloured suit with a lemon tinge – it was either that or the cast from the dusty light – underneath which was a striped, white and brown shirt. The once over made her feel better. Stupid, assessing people by their dress and regalia, but it gave her a higher ground to be operating from.

So, he was evidently colour blind. As his left hand reached to the stacked files she noticed he was wearing a wedding ring. Damn it, she said to herself, a half-smile playing on her lips, chance gone.

He picked up on it, although he misinterpreted. 'You seem to be in a good mood anyway.' And now she was most certainly smiling.

'Oh, just something I was thinking about,' she said, giving one of those ritual nods and mild obeisances which seemed to be required. She uncrossed her legs, acutely aware and deliberately so, as he was, of the crackling of static from her stockings, noticing his eyes flick to her legs as she did so. She had to put her hand over her face, as if she were gently coughing, trying to avoid bursting out laughing. 'Anyway,' a dropping of the hand and a bright and businesslike grin, 'let's get on.'

A shuffle and stirring of papers and Brown was opening a file. He was in his late forties, she guessed, dark gelled hair which seemed to have a plastic patina, going to fat a bit, the face and the body below definitely were, but he looked as if he might have been passingly attractive about twenty years before, if looks were how you gauged attraction. Then his eyes swooped up, the file open and spread facing him, and he seemed slightly perplexed or bewildered. His brow was furrowed; he clearly wanted to say something and was ticking off the ways he might do it.

'Something troubling you, Detective Superintendent?' She put a smile around the words to take the chill off their edge.

'Sorry. It's just – I don't know, this all seems a bit – I don't know, unusual. A bit – a bit uncomfortable?'

His confusion allowed her to dredge up a little authority, ludicrous, given that he was about twenty years older. 'There's no need for it to be.' A crossing of the legs now, to exacerbate the confusion. 'It's pretty simple. We both, what? Obey? Follow orders? Like me, I'm sure, you've had your instructions.' A phoney sigh, a bright smile. 'So, let's get on with it.' She was aware how stilted she had sounded, but it fitted the environment.

'I know, it's just—' he ran out of words and looked at her, appealing for her to come in.

Already she felt that the question of the relativity of power, and their relationship, was clear. 'Can we speak frankly here, Mr – Mr Brown?' she asked, not intending to for a moment.

'Absolutely. And it's Angus.' He looked eager and rescued.

Another small step to higher ground above him. Deliberately she didn't offer informality back. 'You're thinking – ehhm, Angus – that somehow you've been ridden over, or subsumed—' His mouth was open to reply. '—No, let me go on. I can understand that you might feel that none of this accords with what you've been brought up with and you feel uneasy about it. Really, I can understand that.'

She took a moment while they both agreed, or at least appeared to, that this was the case. She had rehearsed, at least in outline, what she was going to say. 'You're probably looking at me thinking, "What the hell does she know about crime, criminals, this place – she's barely out of acne?". No, let me go on. And perhaps you're right. But I'm not here to give orders—' a calculated pause, knowing that the Home Office and Chief Constable's instructions gave her all the powers she might need. '—My job is to make the pattern, knit it together – pardon the pre-feminist pun! – and look at, well, the weft and weave of it all. I don't have to justify it. It's just my job. You know the gobbledegook, the overview, the trans-departmental, trans-national approach, but I really do believe that if we can coordinate the various agencies, offer a concerted approach, that it's the best way.'

She waited for him to say something. It hadn't quite come out the way she intended, but, transparently untrue as it sounded to her, seemingly it was convincing nonetheless, because now he was nodding. 'Look, Angus, I know it's not traditional policing, but this isn't traditional crime, well, except the only common tradition about it is greed. And the methods of satisfying it have changed enormously since – well, I suppose, since you started out. There are no frontiers to it any more, you know this, and it doesn't recognize conventional force or national boundaries.' She leaned forward slightly for emphasis. 'You may not like it that way, but there it is. I need to do my job. And I need your assistance.' A co-operative smile. 'And I know I'll get it.'

To herself she said: *Got that? Fuckwit!*

He seemed to have, because he began slowly to pull pictures from the file. Now that she had reiterated the ground rules he appeared better about it, as if he had made the mild ritual protest and, that satisfied, it was time to get on. He spun the pictures round for her. 'The flat belonged to a minor pusher called Andy McIntyre. He's disappeared, by the way, and you would, wouldn't you?' The pictures were in a curling mound. 'This is what's left of his common-law wife, his "bidie-in" in the slang, who's a user – or, was a user. We don't know exactly what happened, only who did it. Who ordered it. The word is McIntyre owed a lot more than he could ever repay, except physically. That he had been ripping-off, adulterating the adulterators, cutting a few more corners. To be fair, maybe it was her, chopping bits out of the supply to keep herself high.'

140

Misfortune seemed to please Brown, because he gave a grimly satisfied look to Carpenter. 'Anyway, they probably came looking for him and decided to make an example. And these guys are from the agricultural school of chastisement. Reduce matters to butcher cuts.'

Carpenter studied the shots of the carnage, the headless torso, the head in the microwave, and she had to stifle a grin. There was a certain warped, over-cooked creativity to it. Only when she came to the prints of the slaughtered child did she harden, her mouth tightened, she shook her head. 'No need, no need at all.'

'No,' Brown was biting on his jaw. 'Totally unnecessary. Background like that I don't suppose he'd have come to much, but – Christ, he was only a baby. Wasn't even a witness. Hideous. I've got kids myself. Older, of course.' It came out in a rush.

Not me, she said to herself, not ever.

'This is what happens, I suppose,' he said more evenly, 'when you tool-up junkies and send them out on a job.'

'Knowledge, Angus, experience or prejudice?' Feeling superior enough to keep him on his Christian name.

'Mmm? Experience and gut instinct.' He shook his head, the professional looking at the results of amateur night. 'This is perverse. Your normal criminal, assassin, doesn't get into this.'

Perverse? Normal? Two words, total inversion. Images of Bosnia, Rwanda came flashing up in her mind. 'Well—' pause for another perusal of the photographic evidence. 'Suppose not. But,' trying to check out if he knew more than he was saying, 'surely it must also have taken some time. What do you think? Two of them at least, you reckon?'

'Probably. A third as look-out, maybe. Not that anyone is going to interfere, in their right mind anyway.'

'What did they do the head with? Cleaver?'

'No sign of one. The initial response from the police surgeon

141

was probably not. A butcher's knife, it could be, and a lot of effort. The cut looked fairly clean, no real smashing through the bones. We haven't found it, though, the weapon. Naturally.' They silently agreed, over the spread-open file, about the cunning perversity of the criminal mind, however addled by drug cocktails. 'We'll get the pathology report tomorrow, probably. But I doubt if it'll tell us much.' He paused weightily, as if reviewing the long march of his experience. 'Also, no prints, hairs or fibres. The lab boys guess they dressed for the part. Hoods, overalls maybe.'

'What, they got changed in the car or the lift or somewhere?'

'Lifts? Here, the lifts never work. Never in housing schemes, anyway. They probably came dressed for it. Put the oilskins on over the Armani, or the catalogue clothes. But it wasn't exactly spontaneous. They certainly weren't going round to collect the dues, even if they were there. And careful preparation is not usually the MO for whacked-out killers, if that's what they were, so they were clearly working to precise instructions. Also, it obviously took some time, so they must have been oozing with confidence, chemical induced or not.'

He turned up his palms, a gesture of helplessness, but also an artful way of letting her know that, unlike her, he knew the crack here. 'Half the folk on that scheme are on smack, everyone knows the score. The dogs in the street know the dealers and the dealt, but there's a communal myopia. And by now they all know who did it, or ordered it, and they're going to talk about it. But not to us. Never to us.'

'Actually,' she was thinking about it, 'I suppose it doesn't take that long to get through a neck if the blade's sharp enough and you put enough meat behind it.' She pursed her lips and nodded. 'Messy, though.'

'Another reason the lab boys think they were wearing overclothes.'

She pushed the pictures back at him. 'So, they went there for a decapitation? Just got the wrong head?'

'Looks like it. Imagine it, you're wound up, nerves singing, you barge in, *shite!*, your man's missing. Well, fuck it. We've come all this way with the plan. So, may as well take the wife's off at the neck.'

'So it was an *idée fixe*, to unfix the head?'

'Mmm? I suppose so. If you're getting off on the idea of taking someone away at the gullet, there's probably a certain let-down when the target's not there, so you busk it and go for what's available. I remember a similar one a few years back. The boys turned up on the doorstep of a second floor flat looking for their money, the lad wasn't in but his brother was, so they hung him by the neck from from the banister down the stairwell.'

'It's not exactly professional, is it? Most pros would shadow the target, ensure his location precisely, before the hit.'

Brown shrugged. 'Maybe the message was more important than getting the right messenger. That you're the master, no one ever crosses you.' He leaned back in his seat, convinced that the killers, or their hirer, felt the example was at least as important as the result. 'But the baby?' That took a certain psychosis.

'If you're right,' she said, 'what could provide a more noticeable underscoring of it? I'd like to see the place, talk to a few of the neighbours.'

'Won't do any good.'

'Perhaps. But it'll give me a feel of it. Make it better for me.'

5

If there were any traces of my folks I was failing to find them. I took a bus which crossed the river, meandered through the increasingly empty and scorched lands where they used to build ships, past the sandstone bones of former tenement blocks, abandoned and crumbling docks covered in broken glass and reclaiming vegetation, then a lip around a serrated block of seemingly expensive flats cordoned off behind a security fence from the next-door reality. Further along, past more cleared land and dereliction and into what seemed like a grey sandstone redoubt, a tightly packed grid of tenements huddled under economic siege.

When I got off the bus the rain was beginning to get up behind a cruel wind. I walked down to the river through more roughly cleared sites and the remains of old shipbuilding sheds. The place seemed by-passed, the wide dull expanse of the Clyde on one flank, and another tributary, what looked like a fairly new road, on the other. Some kids, four or five of them, were throwing stones at other larger stones, or into puddles a couple of hundred yards further away up-river. The rain was becoming quite heavy now, gusting in dense clouds, but the skinny children in tee shirts and light trousers were paying no attention. I started to shiver, but for me the rain was welcome, for me it seemed somehow purgative.

Of course the street address given on the birth certificate (my birth certificate, I now had to accept), wasn't there, cleared away no doubt in some unspecific fit of civic zeal, leaving just a rocky expanse of nothingness behind. I poked around over the ground where the tenements had been – an old man in a collarless grey shirt and flat cap directed me – or at least I think I was in the right place, the instructions weren't that precise, but no artefacts were visible in the earth. No *bones* . . . I allowed myself a damp smile.

The rain had soaked through to my skin, sending me into a continuous shiver. Or perhaps it was deeply psychological, to do with walking over a heritage grave, or one's own beginning. But, the hell with it, I was cold. So I wandered back into the tenement stockade, looking for something hot to drink.

I found a small café which looked as if it had been there since my father's time, and so did some of the pies keeping warm inside a heated glass cabinet. I ordered tea, not trusting anything else. My shivering was becoming manageable and, when I thought about it, realized it was surely caused by one of several afflictions, or a cocktail of all of them: withdrawal, jet lag and, of course, the cold and wet.

The café was completely empty, apart from me. The woman serving – very obviously dyed hair, I put her in her late forties – gave me a smile as I picked up the cup and saucer, the latter about a quarter inch deep in slopped tea. She seemed a good place to start. 'Did you ever hear of a family called Bone from around here?' I asked. 'Thirty years ago, maybe?'

She gave me a long look. 'Don't think so. Nobody of that name around here I can think of. Bone, you said?'

I gave her the little information I had. She shook her head. 'I only moved in about twenty years ago. My husband's from here, see. He's no here, or I'd ask him.' She thought about it for a moment. 'Actually, ah widnae. It'd be a waste of breath. Yir best bet's to go along to the Pearce Institute doon the road, they've got a sort of – what d'ye cry it – an archive, a sort of history of the area. Pictures, newspaper cuttings, old books, pamphlets and that sort of thing. They'd be able to help you there or naebody would.'

'Right,' I said, feeling a jolt of warm excitement, aided by the warm tea, 'thanks.' Not even finishing the cup and leaving a fifty pence tip.

Carpenter had visited the crime scene, the violated cot, the kitchen with the dark indelible stain of death on the floorboards, and she conceded that Brown was right, that it had been almost completely pointless. As were the visits to the neighbours. She'd had more response out of pot plants. But what it had given her was a depressing realization that this was what it would be like in the future, no arcane analysing of politics and motive, just a bitter slog through dead ends, resistances, tribal alliances and muted insolence. And that was just with the people on her side.

She moaned to herself in the back of the police car as it moved along the motorway to the city centre, past the recently painted high rises, the deflated gasometers and the jumble of blocks of flats on the inclines around the road. Brown was sitting beside her, staring out of the window, probably simmering in resentment, she thought. Well, we can always add to that. 'Angus,' she said, 'do you think you could ask the driver to do a detour past McGurk's house? I'd just like to get a fix on that. Yes? Anyway, it won't do him any harm to see a police car at the bottom of his drive, will it? It'll indicate that we've marked him and his territory. Like a dog pissing.'

Brown continued to look out of the window as he said, 'Sadly, Meg, it's not quite that way. We're the territory he's been pissing over for years.' Then he leaned forward slightly and ordered the driver to re-route.

Carpenter was rather disappointed by the house; it did not bespeak highly successful villainy, but, then again, that was probably the point. It was a large and much-altered bungalow, tricked out in stucco and washed colours, vaguely Spanish, in a quiet avenue; but what marked it out was the

146

evident array of security devices, lights, cameras and, no doubt, sensors, and the his and hers BMWs in the driveway, a cherry-red 325i convertible, which she presumed was hers, and an olive-green 7-series. Both probably armour-plated.

She had read all the intelligence on McGurk and still couldn't quite believe it, the irresistible rise, the fortuitous breaks, the steady aggrandizement of a crime estate. None of which could have happened, she told herself, without the cooperation, tacit or otherwise, of at least some elements of the local plod. Which was one of the main reasons she was here. She shook her head. 'I can't quite believe this,' she said as the marked car stood ticking-over outside McGurk's casa. 'He owns a pub which has been a landmark for years, busy every night, making a legitimate fortune – even if he plans the overthrow of ordered society as we know it in the snug – and then one day the faithful patrons turn up and it isn't there any more. Gone. Didn't anyone notice the lorries making off with it?'

'Could hardly fail to, could they?'

'All right, you might not expect them to ring you lot at the time to point it out, but didn't anyone call the council and remark that it seemed a little odd that a profitable and apparently stable pub was rapidly being reduced to brick and cinder in a few hours?'

'It was the weekend.'

She snorted out loud. 'None of your beat guys thought it seemed strange that they were missing a familiar landmark, or that a large wrecking ball and a fleet of unmarked lorries were hoovering it up?'

'Apparently not.'

'And you've sifted through all of the rubble, of course.'

Brown turned away from the window. 'We couldn't trace it. The best guess is that it ended up as hardcore for the new M77 extension.'

Carpenter shook her head. 'So, any guesses why?'

147

He sighed. 'Probably because they're still waiting on planning permission to extend the M74.' Droll, she thought, perhaps he is not entirely without stuffing. He continued slowly, 'Well, you know that one of his former cronies and enforcers, McArdle, his former right hand man, has been coughing to us? Fanciful stuff, most of it – or at least unprovable.'

'He's in jail?' She remembered that from the file. 'Armed robbery?'

'Yeah, if you could call it that. Probably the most inept bank job in the history of this city. Chummie ended up in a get-away taxi with a mask over his head, gun in his hand, claiming it was all a fit-up.'

'You surrounded him, didn't you? You should just have dropped him.'

'I don't think our lads could aim properly for the tears of laughter running down their faces. Anyway, once he's inside the Bar-L – Barlinnie Prison, that is – he says he's going to give up everything and everyone he knows, claiming that he's motivated purely by hatred of McGurk—'

'But, of course, he's looking for a deal.'

'Naturally. Claims he has documents, tapes, a list of our men on his payroll, none of which checks out. Or, at least, there's a believable premise but no hard evidence. While this is going on he leaks, through his brief, a stream of allegations to a Sunday paper journalist, who duly goes to see him and out comes the tale, except, of course, in the piece they don't actually name McGurk because of the libel laws, and they call him the Licensee. The nickname's not to do with the pub – anyway, it was in his wife's name, naturally – but because he's supposed to have an immunity licence.'

'From you.'

'From us.'

'And then someone inside terminates McArdle before all of

the allegations could be thoroughly checked out?' Convenient, she noted. 'So, hadn't he asked for isolation?'

Brown shook his head. 'Couldn't. He's a hard man, isn't he – ruin his reputation. Dead vain. If you see what I mean. So, anyway, it was a contract, 30k we hear, although we haven't quite got the man who stuck the knife repeatedly between his ribs.'

'So, which particular bit of this seems to have convinced McGurk to liquidate his asset? The pub, I mean, not McArdle.'

'Shall we drive on?' Brown was motioning vaguely with his hand. 'This seems a little like empty posturing.' Carpenter nodded and the car moved off. 'When the story began to leak out that McArdle was talking, McGurk probably thought that we were going to get a warrant and pay him a visit. He claimed that two of the three who shot old Archie Thorburn's boy were done there, in a back room of The Mistral, a couple of years back.'

'So McGurk figures that you'll turn up with microscopes, tweezers and DNA kits five years on and, if you don't find the smoking pistol, you might just get a mite-sized piece of cranium or tissue?'

'It's a theory.'

The car was back on a wide boulevard leading into the city. Carpenter was amused, and slightly impressed, that McGurk would just tear down a pub worth, what, at least a quarter of a million, as well as providing a legitimate profit stream, after a few words in print pointed, codedly, in his direction. 'Did you ever search the pub around that time?' Brown shook his head. 'And no doubt he didn't have permission to erase the place from the topography?' Brown snorted with derision. 'So he'll get a hundred pound fine for demolishing it without a building warrant?'

'That's about it.'

'Well, at least he'll have been brought to justice,' she said sardonically.

'Actually,' Brown said after a moment, 'not so. It'll be his wife who gets the fine because, in this case, she's the licensee – boom! boom! – and he, officially, has no connection to it.'

'Curses,' Carpenter was smiling at Brown. 'And did anyone ever ask him – or her, of course – why they did it?'

'It wasn't anything to do with us. Apparently the line she's putting out is that she just got bored with it, just too much work. Couldn't get proper insurance. Renovations to do, staff to manage, money to bank . . . Hey ho!'

Their car, Carpenter noticed absently through the window, was having a remarkable calming effect on the traffic which was moving sedately like a funeral cortège. 'I don't quite understand,' she said, 'why just two were shot at the pub if there were three killers of Thorburn junior?'

'Theories abound.' Brown used the sleeve of his jacket to clean a smear from the side window. 'But I prefer two. You know, don't you, that in Scotland, unlike in England, you need corroboration on all evidence, essentially a second witness, which is why we have two cops on everything.'

'Right, I had forgotten about that. I just thought you were a lot of scaredy-cats.'

'So, three on the job, reduce the survivors to one and you have, in extremis, the other man's word against yours.'

'Cold. But efficient.'

'That's McGurk.'

'So, Thorburn. Remind me.'

'He was the previous top dog, the Godfather. McGurk, McArdle and the rest of their crew grew up under his tutelage. He sort of went into retirement when all the hard drugs started coming in, turned over the family business to his boy, Young Archie, who, unfortunately for him, was not a chip off the old block. As inhumane, but without the brain. He got caught and banged up for an incredibly stupid heroin

150

deal a few years back, which gave the former gofers the opportunity they needed to take over, led, of course, by our friend McGurk, who is nothing if not devious and clever.

'So, on Young Archie's first weekend out on licence, he comes to an unfortunate end on a pavement outside the family home, the Ponderosa, leaking curry from the belly he's just been shot in. Fatally. Two guys, Hampson and Grogan, the two who were stiffed – probably – in The Mistral, did it, with another gunman, but we've never been able to prove it. If Hampson and Grogan were actually shot in McGurk's pub, they ended up being discovered tucked up in rigor mortis in a car outside a pub, very dramatically, on the morning of Young Archie's funeral. Which, if nothing else, would lead the uninitiated to believe that Old Archie was responsible. They had been dead for at least six hours, and they weren't shot *in situ*, which opens up a wonderfully gruesome vignette of someone, probably Lewis, driving them propped up in passenger seats through the city to their discovery point. Talk about callous.

'What's more likely is that the three fell out with their new mentor, over another drugs deal. All of them, or maybe just the two victims, had ripped McGurk off for over a hundred grand. He was not best pleased. So he decided to get even and tidy up at the same time.'

'What's the other theory?'

'It's a continuation of the same one, really. That it was all part of the plan from the beginning. The third man, John Lewis, was McGurk's number two – they came out of the same streets, the same apprenticeship with Thorburn – and it was him who actually pulled the trigger on Junior.'

'He was lifted on that, wasn't he, but the jury,' Carpenter reminded him, 'didn't see it that way.'

'No. Combination of a fucked-up prosecution and subtle pressures on the jury, no doubt. But he did it, Lewis. And the second theory also holds that he did Hampson and Grogan as well, although they were his closest mates. This theory, of course, had exactly the same effect as in the first scenario, but this time McGurk is not the only one insuring himself against the possibility of damning testimony. Lewis has already done that for himself by taking out his two co-assassins, probably under McGurk's aegis, at The Mistral.'

'Excellent. An unbreakable bond. A community of bloody interest!'

'That, certainly, is what the dead men's families believe. Not that they're saying it to us, naturally. Now it would appear that Lewis and McGurk have fallen out, although reflecting mirrors could be at work here in an attempt to confuse us. But it *looks* as if they have. And that Lewis is intent on taking over from McGurk, or at least building up his own action.'

I don't quite know what I was expecting at McCready's, perhaps a dour, smoke-filled dive packed with elderly men throwing back pints against a deadline, or even some sort of continental wine bar, the waitresses in short skirts and severe blouses, the waiters putting on French accents, but what I got was a severe jolt to the perceptions: I stepped into what looked like a downtown American bar, minus the barrels of lard in baseball caps jostling at the bar. It even had a baseball game playing on the TV above the counter. But here the verisimilitude was seriously awry. It was a Sony. No self-respecting, God-fearing American bar owner would put up a Nip TV on the gantry. No, nothing but a bleary, bulky, home-grown version would do.

The place was full of young people. I guessed I was probably five years older than the next old codger, most of them drinking that pale-coloured insipid beer which looks the shade of what you pass after drinking five gallons of water. I've always favoured the darker, damaged kidneys hue myself.

152

I ordered a large whisky. It came minus ice without me even asking and I shot it down in one. 'Excuse me,' I caught the attention of one of the barmaids who, like the rest of them, was wearing a rough approximation of an extemporization of someone's idea of what a baseball uniform looked like, except it was abbreviated well above the knee. More babe than Babe Ruth. Which set my mind off on a mad tangent, to the tourist's lobby of the FBI headquarters in Washington where they have a range of dangerous criminal implements and paraphernalia, including a fake Babe Ruth suit which some conman tried to pass off as the real thing for a serious amount of money. What a twisted and devious organism is the criminal mind.

'Yes,' she said, looking slightly petulant, giving me the impression this wasn't the first time she had posed it.

'Got any beers other than Bud and Miller and Michelob? European, maybe?' Quite forgetting that in Europe what you don't do is refer to Europe.

'There's Budvar, that's Czech, and Grolsch – I don't know, that might be German; there's a new Hungarian beer, there's Bohemia and one that's—'

'Could I just have something,' I cut her off, 'that hasn't been conquered, annexed, seceded or made using expropriated spoils? And definitely not with a lime in the neck. Maybe something British?'

This clearly struck her as a pretty radical concept. 'Not a lot of call for it,' she said, and kind of reeled around the shelves looking for something that might satisfy. 'There's a real ale, here, it's called,' she peered at the pump, 'Old Fartpants,' and she began giggling. 'Sorry. It's not really.'

'Whatever, it'll do.'

She put her hand round the pump and began giving it sharp tugs, which I must admit felt mildly arousing, and the stuff, like long-brewed tea stewed in soap, came rushing and spurting, bubbling and vomiting into the upright glass. I

153

wasn't sure I wanted it now. It smelled like the odours from a Havana drain in high season. I clenched my nostrils internally and had a tentative swig. It tasted warm and bitter, like I imagined liquefied iron filings might taste. Odd, I thought, that something so initially repellent had seen England through the Reformation, the Corn Laws, the Hundred Years War and other bloody altercations too numerous and unfathomable to mention. It was probably, I thought, universal suffrage and allowing women in the bar which did for real ale and the Empire.

'Thank you,' I said a little uncertainly.

'Just don't let your nearest and dearest downwind of you later,' she said, turning to serve another customer.

The inside of the place had been done out in post-Prohibition chic, a series of wooden booths along one wall, suitable for clinches or for delivering the black spot in complete privacy, with framed US theatre posters and historical front pages, no doubt run-off to order, like the famous Dewey landslide whopper. Most of the action was happening on the large central floor, between knots of animated people holding beer bottles (I wondered, for a moment, if this was merely the prelude to a pitched battle) where the shouted conversations came to me in snatches above the sound of dance music. So, being a man of sensitive age, I scurried to a booth to chill and check out what was unfolding on the floor. In particular I was looking for furtive handshakes, or people rather unnecessarily and prolongedly making trips to the john.

I took the last remaining empty booth and considered. I had only a name to go on and I didn't want to go blundering around like a fool in blind man's buff shouting it out everywhere. Mind you, a couple more pints of Old Sump-oil and I might just do that, I cautioned myself. I wondered if I looked out of place enough to be considered dangerous by the other clientele, but I concluded that the accent was undoubtedly the best cover. Shit, here I was, an American in a fucking

154

American bar! How well can you fit in? Not at all in this case, actually.

Then I mulled over the disappointing convergence of British and American culture – I re-concluded and summed it up not as a melding but as a total whitewash by the Yanks – while I did the best I could with the beer. Which wasn't much. Eventually, having swirled it around my mouth and then swallowed it like medicine I decided I had suffered enough in this world and gave up on it. I went back to the bar and waited until the same waitress hove past. She looked to be in her early twenties, rather over made-up and a touch broad in the beam for my taste, but then I wasn't nibbling. 'Same again?' she smiled at me.

'God, anything but. Large whisky'll do. Have one yourself.' When you want to drain someone of information it helps to top them up first.

'Thanks. I'll have it later.' She turned away to fill a glass from the optic. I brandished a five pound note at her when she plopped it on the bar in front of me.

'I'm looking for someone.' I tried to grin slightly embarrassedly. 'The thing is I don't know him or what he looks like.' She looked quizzical; I gave the name. The way I figured it, there was nothing to lose: if she knew him she would know my mission, if she didn't, then nothing lost. When you are strung-out, your body and mind out of kilter, you make foolish mistakes.

'What's your name?' I told her Bone; it seemed strange in my mouth, or perhaps that was the after effects of the beer. I was encouraged because you don't ask for a name from someone who's asking about another someone you don't know. 'No, never heard of him,' she said, but I could tell by a betraying flicker in her eyes this was not true. At least, this is what I came to believe when I replayed the scene later. But at the time it seemed that it was all right, because I assumed that she was just being careful and would check with him and

155

he'd make his own introduction. Which is what he did, but much later.

I drank my whisky, made a few peremptory inquiries with a couple of people, had another whisky, small this time, and by now I was feeling woozy, tired and with a desperate craving that wasn't going to get any better sitting here. Eventually, as there wasn't much point in prolonging this outing, I took one last look around, did not see anyone who looked remotely like the local dealer in happiness, and went out into the night.

The pub was at the top of a cobbled lane, in an area of what had clearly been stables a century or more ago, but now was a mix of cafés, restaurants and obscure fashion shops. I imagined it was probably quite busy in the summer, with people drinking in the lane or sitting at tables, but now it was ill-lit, puddled and quiet. My feet kept slipping on the cobbles, which is probably what saved me.

I heard a sound to my left, a shadow moving quickly in my peripheral vision, and as I turned sharply towards it, alarm washing out the dopey lethargy, my right foot slipped, I tilted in that direction, scrambled to regain my footing as the knife passed through my almost new jacket and scored a searing line across my ribs under my left arm. Instinctively my hand came down on his arm as he pulled back the knife; I pushed it out wide, opening him up, and punched him to the head with two rapid shots with the heel of the hand, aiming either venomously to implant his jawbone or his nose into his skull. I couldn't see where they hit but it was enough to send him stumbling back groaning.

Still holding on to his knife hand I hooked three short kicks with the sole of my boot into his abdomen, hearing ribs go, then as he sank to the ground, me still holding on, I broke the knife arm over my knee. By then he was past crying out in complaint.

I was breathing hard, he wasn't. The knife was lying,

156

glinting dully, on the cobbles. It was one of those curved, wicked numbers with a serrated edge, making it almost impossible to pull out without bringing half the guts with it. 'Less than twenty-four hours in town,' I said over him, 'and they're trying to kill me.' Whoever they were, I had certainly made a sizeable impression.

I bent down, peering at his dark and bloody face, which I didn't recognize. I looked up and around, but there was no one to be seen, and I was tempted to tidy matters up by just breaking his neck. Then a better idea occurred and I began frisking through his pockets where, on the third attempt, I came up with the haul, what felt, satisfyingly familiarly, like small packets and tiny blocks. I transferred them to the pocket on the good side of my jacket, put my right hand inside its flaps, touched the wound and came out with blood, then quickly trotted out into the street, hailing a taxi.

'Nearest hospital,' I said, getting in.

'It's only a couple of hundred yards down the road. You could walk.'

'You don't want the fuckin' business?' He shrugged and put the cab into gear. 'Take me to ER – casualty,' I replied, 'quick as you like. Or you'll have a major refurbishment to do to your back seat.'

Carpenter had washed and changed into a long, flowing grey dress which clung where it touched her. Her room was excellent; she was quite surprised it was so luxurious, that she was being put up in such understated splendour – fresh flowers, a chocolate on the down-turned sheet, soft, luxuriant furnishings, she was almost expecting a freshly ironed evening paper – which only served to impress on her the expectation being placed on her. Then she had gone down to dinner, stopping on the way at the bar to order and slowly drink a large gin and tonic, conscious that, discreetly, heads turned towards her.

157

The meal didn't quite live up to the surroundings, a dining room done in cool lemon shades, like a variety of sorbets; heavy yellow curtains masked the windows, comfortable dining chairs were positioned around clustered tables which were far enough apart to ensure privacy, but not so much so that the diners were isolated, like an archipelago of islands, with a lazy stream of waiters and trolleys passing between them. She had a half-bottle of an exceptionally good Australian red with the meal, which seemed to carry a hint of raspberry, and then, afterwards, a brandy, generously measured.

Now, pleasantly mellow, full, and re-infused with confidence she took off her dress, hung it up and stretched out in the bed wearing only pants. She could feel the crisp sheets and pillows against her bare back and fancied that she could smell ozone from them, dried in a flapping breeze, which she conceded was unlikely, more probably the result of some chemical additive in the washing powder. She felt vaguely aroused and began to play gently with her nipples, until they became hard. She closed her eyes and began to drift into a mildly erotic trance, feeling herself sinking into a warm abandoned happiness.

The telephone rang. She sat bolt upright on the bed and grabbed it.

'It's Angus Brown. You'd better come in right away.'

The wound wasn't so deep, the knife had glanced off my ribs and perforated and stained a perfectly good set of clothes. I looked at it briefly in the hospital reception, waiting to be called for examination. It seemed a good idea to tell the receptionist, a world-weary lady of about fifty-five, what had happened, and where, and suggested that maybe she ought to tell the police. 'I don't want to be accused of running away from a crime scene or anything like that.'

Casualty wasn't too busy. I only had a few minutes to wait and just as I was being ushered into a cubicle for the cursory once-over by a resigned-looking nurse who had clearly passed this way before, a couple of cops turned up, young guys, one with a moustache and dark pocked complexion, the other blond.

'You're the victim? Downe, is it?' Is it? The moustache was waiting for a response as the nurse helped me out of my top clothing and bent to look at the cut. He had obviously taken my details from the receptionist.

I didn't think I was the victim, given the superficial nature of the cut, but certainly I was the intended. 'Yeah,' I nodded. 'Did you find the guy with the knife?'

'Someone tripped over him in the lane. He was moaning, barely conscious. What did you do to him?'

'Hurt him as bad as I could – almost. It seemed the right thing to do in the circumstances.' The blond one had a notebook out and was writing in it. I thought that I had better expand. 'It happened very quickly. All I saw was someone coming at me out of the corner of my eye. He really should have speared me properly, he had time enough. I guess I just got lucky.'

'You interested in how he is?' moustache asked. I sensed an undercurrent of hostility or disbelief. The sub-text seemed to be that entirely innocent people don't get stabbed, which is a sound rule, except that if I was guilty I didn't know what I had been sentenced for.

'Not really. But I can guess.' The nurse was dabbing something fierce on the wound, asking if it hurt. I shook my head, wincing. 'Know who he is?'

'That was going to be my next question.' I shook my head again. 'He's called McColl, Eddie McColl. A small-time drug pusher. Mean anything?'

'Mean anything? Mean fucker, don't you mean?' That went down like a British heavyweight. 'Can't say it does.' I was keeping my forearms, with their tell-tale markings, well out of close scrutiny.

159

'You've never met?'

'I only got here a few hours ago. You can check.' I gave them the flight number and the address of the grubby hotel where I was staying. My mind was figuring this way: the barmaid must have tipped off my potential assassin that I was looking for him, but she was hardly going to admit to that, to entrap herself. I was also banking on the cops being sufficiently uninterested in a local bad guy, in what seemed like a pretty straightforward case, not to trawl round bar customers checking out if I had been asking after him. I cursed my stupidity, flapping my mouth like that.

Also, I couldn't work out what the knife man was up to, trying to stick me. Surely it couldn't be because I had mildly roughed-up one of his associates, that was just too unlikely, wasn't it? Why court a life stretch over one of your dealers who has had his dignity ruffled? It seemed a little extreme. But maybe the rules were different here.

After the taxi had dropped me at the hospital I had planted the gear inside a wastebin, wrapped in an old newspaper, and prayed they didn't do evening garbage rounds. No matter how unlikely it was – and it was pretty likely in these particular circumstnces – I wasn't going to take the chance of being searched.

'What were you doing in the lane at the time?' The blond one spoke for the first time, looking up from his notes.

'Leaving. I'd gone to the bar for a drink. I was leaving.'

'Why McCready's?'

A mild display of anger seemed called for. 'Look,' I shuffled off the couch. The nurse had disappeared, presumably to find a doctor, leaving me to hold a swab to the cut. 'What's with all this? I'm the one who got fucking attacked. Shouldn't you be asking him why he wanted to skewer me with his Bowie?'

'Not unless he knows sign language – the one-handed version,' the moustache came in again. 'His face and jaw are apparently smashed into a pretty difficult jigsaw. The shooting-up arm's gone as well. Never mind talking, he'll be liquidizing his smack and suckin' it through a straw for the next few months. You did a good job. They brought him in a few minutes ago, you could check out your handiwork.'

'Thanks,' I replied, ignoring the sarcasm.

'Where'd you learn that?

'Tough neighbourhood,' I said. Then, realizing that they would probably check out my army record, 'I did a couple of tours. US army.'

'And you definitely didn't know this guy?'

'Definitely. Not. I told you that already.' There was a certain circularity to their questions which I didn't want to break into in case it set them off on a new and homing course I didn't want them to pursue. And then the curtain went back, a young male doctor came in and asked them to wait outside while he did his job.

The cut needed just four stitches, at the deepest part, and after he had finished he taped a large pad over it and told me to come back in a week, if I didn't have a family doctor, and he'd whip them out. He seemed tired and bored. Obviously he saw a lot of mysterious knife wounds and injured innocents.

After I thanked him and silently blessed the NHS I wandered back out into reception, intent on retrieving my haul, but naturally the two officers were there, obviously waiting for me. In the last week I seemed to have talked to almost no one other than cops of different hues.

'We've had a request for the pleasure of your company from our betters,' said the blond. 'The car's on its way.'

'I have a choice in this?'

'Sure,' replied the moustache, 'you could be arrested.'

'Well, as long as I've got a choice,' I shrugged, 'let's go meet them.'

She laid her briefcase on the table, connected the coded tumblers on the lock and unlatched it. The file was a large one, more than two inches thick, with several recent photographs as well as a whole batch of others, including relatives and friends. There were biographical details, medical and social security information, witness reports and a great mass of surveillance notes, comment and speculation, reams of speculation. Some of the more sensitive material, either paragraphs, sentences or pages, was blank, all of that held on the mainframe computers in London, in case the file should be lost. But she had memorized most of the omissions.

She picked up the file, flicked through it quickly, as much for reassurance as anything. But most of it was ingrained in her brain anyway.

'Ready?' asked Brown.

She nodded, considering whether to put the file away, hold it or leave it on the desk where he could see it, as another tool of the process. She decided to do that. There was another officer there, a Sergeant Warriston – she hadn't caught his first name – and she wondered the purpose of his being around. Additional intimidation, some bizarre insistence of Scottish law or police procedure? Well, they could forget about that. The law she carried about with her superseded any statute: total secrecy and ultimate force. Dramatic, but it gave her strength and immunity.

'Uh, gentlemen,' they looked at her, both standing hovering at the door, 'at some point I'll probably want to come in,' – she deliberately didn't say, *take over* – 'and I'll clearly signal that. Something like, "Can I just have a word?". Mmhh?' Both men shrugged. 'Good. I'll stand at the back to begin with, get him wondering just exactly who I am.'

And who the fuck are you, exactly? Brown thought, shrugged and nodded, then opened the door. 'Bring him in now,' he shouted.

The two men took the two metal chairs on one side of the table. There was a twin deck tape machine on it and nothing else. On the other side of the table was one battered wooden seat, deliberately rickety she was sure, just to create another tiny element of disconcertion, and that was it. Apart from a tannoy speaker on the shit-coloured wall above the metal door. A minimalist room intended for maximum effect. She had seen more comfortable caves, or bus shelters. It was, she knew, somewhere in the bowels of the building, the geography of which she still hadn't quite worked out. She imagined that if you stayed in here long enough you could miss the big one and walk out to find yourself alone in a nuclear winter. But somehow she didn't think the intimidatory ambience was going to work here.

'Sit down there,' Brown said.

He took his time looking around, checking out the room and the people. She felt him run her up and down with contempt before he unstitched his eyes and sat down. Also, she thought she saw the hint of a sardonic smile on his face, before his jaw tightened, and a small nerve twitched. It was the nearest he would come to a break in composure, she figured.

She kept looking. Attractive, she told herself, or was that the compelling allure of danger? Like the hypnotic attraction of rocks far below seen from a ledge. His eyes, she noticed, were the colour of silt, or slate, and his nose, slightly thick at the bridge where it had been broken, she knew that, seemed damp. He sniffed. Nasal passages gone, probably. Still, he looked fit. No, that wasn't the word. Tuned. He was a thing of cold interlocking parts. She wondered what it would be like to go to bed with him. Cruel, undoubtedly.

She leaned back against the wall, her head slightly thick from the alcohol, and watched. He had seen the file on the table, but she could discern no reaction in him. The two Jocks had sat opposite him and were trying the tortured silence routine, but she knew he wouldn't be the first to speak.

'So, Downe is it?' Brown started.

'Mister,' he replied, without any edge. 'So what?'

163

'Your pal. He's in intensive care. He might die.'

'Wrong tense. Might have died. I spared him. I'm not up with your local laws but I'm sure that would have been justified. Self-defence. He was trying to kill me.' His accent was not as broad as she had expected. Perhaps he was putting it on? Scottish parents, he could probably tune into the local dialect quickly. 'If he dies now it'll be of hypothermia or because the medics don't know how to deal with fairly simple fractures. Which seems unlikely. I've no complaints.'

'Smoke?' Warriston asked, pulling a packet of cigarettes and a box of matches from his pocket and putting them on the table. 'Forgot,' he went on, pushing them aside, 'you don't normally, do you? Not this stuff anyway.'

Downe did smile now but said nothing. If that little piece of dropped-in information had been meant to phase him, it hadn't.

'You knew him, didn't you?'

He shook his head.

'You were looking for him,' Brown came in, 'weren't you?'

He leaned back in the seat. 'They say that jet-lag can be like being stoned, you know, dizzy and fanciful, the mind out for a promenade?' An entirely humourless grin. 'And I thought I was the only one who had been flying.'

'Answer the question.'

'So, ask me a sensible one.'

'What are you doing here?'

'Ah, a philosophical one, I love those—'

'Please,' Brown came in, 'we have better things to do than piss around. I want to know your relationship with McColl, why you say he tried to kill you.'

He shook his head and slowly looked round everyone. 'Who gives a fuck for motive? I don't. Robbery? Maybe he doesn't like Yanks? Or my devil-may-care demeanour? You've got him, ask him, when they wire his face back together.' Downe leaned back and then came forward so

164

quickly that his face was only inches from Brown's. 'Stab me vitals,' he said quietly, patting his side where his coat hung, slashed, 'he nearly did. And I don't know if you've noticed but there's a tall, slender and leggy woman behind you. I'm almost certain she's not a figment of my imagination – they usually come a little more down-home and dirty – so she's either from yours, or she's serving some purpose not immediately apparent, unless it's to add a third element to the old hard cop-soft cop concerto. Softest maybe?' He smiled, turning away from Brown and licking his gaze over her.

'You just keep thinking that,' she pushed herself off the wall. 'I'd like a little time with Mr Downe, please. One-on-one.'

Brown looked round at her quickly and angrily, paused, then slowly dragged his chair back, got up and touched Warriston's hand. She could see the knots in his neck muscles. And the door slammed just too noisily.

'We'll start again, shall we?' Smiling, pulling Brown's still warm chair under her and sitting down opposite him.

6

'Therr he is now.'

'All right, get the cunt.'

The BMW was sitting directly opposite the pub, the engine turning over, four men inside, two of whom – one from the front passenger seat, the other from the back on the side nearest the road – quickly opened their doors, climbed out and, checking that there was no moving traffic, walked swiftly across to the far pavement where four men in their early twenties were laughing and pushing each other around. They were drunk, but not overly so. The tallest one, Sammy McSwegan, was wearing a knocked-off, dark blue Armani suit he had bought from another taxi driver; his white shirt was from the same source, although he had actually bought the shoes from a shop, which had made him a little miffed at the time.

'Yer arse,' McSwegan was saying, 'ten in a row—' when he felt a hand on each shoulder and he was pulled around, into the faces of two men he had never seen before. Out of the corner of his eye he saw that Shug, Danny and Glinchy had moved away. 'What the fuck—' He felt a sharp jab in his stomach, involuntarily grunted and made a half-bow, stumbling back against the wall of the pub, the two men closing in around him. The pain was now tearing at his entrails; he put his hands down, felt an arm and a hand and the sharp edge of a knife. He did not dare move but, when he glanced down, he could see that it had gone into his stomach by an inch or so.

The pain was raging, like a hot poker in his gut, his back was against the wall, one of the two was leaning on his shoulder, face against his, hissing in his ear. 'Move a fuckin' inch and ah'll gut ye, ya cunt.'

He couldn't look at the blade, his legs were beginning to tremble, he could see past the shoulder to his three mates and the other man, immaculately dressed, three-piece suit, jacket open. Jesus, why weren't they helping him? Then he saw that the other man, bullet-crop hair, the line of a scar on his jaw, had one hand inside the open jacket and was holding something which glinted in the streetlights as he moved. A hand gun. 'Please,' he said, 'fur fuck's sake, please!'

The man leaned off him and he felt the knife come out. Instinctively he put his hand down to hold his stomach, feeling heat and dampness, the blood beginning to ooze. Sickness was rising in his craw, his legs were beginning to go; he slumped back against the wall, stumbled into a crouch, holding his stomach and moaning.

'Now remember, lads,' the second man was saying, 'yiz urnae seein' nothin'. Yiz urnae sayin' nothin', or goin' nae-where except hame, know what ah mean? This didnae happen, by the way.' The three men nodded, easing away from the man with the gun. 'Not a fuckin' word tae naebody. Or yi'll aw huv second fuckin' mooths in yir heids. OK?' They all nodded again. 'Take care then, lads.' He motioned them away with his free left hand and they bumped off, still looking back, afraid to turn from him in case he shot them in the back, until they were round the corner and then they began to break into frantic, rubber-legged runs.

The two men dragged McSwegan across the pavement as the BMW did a screeching U-turn and drew up at the kerb, then pushed him through the open back door, where he fell across the seat, next to another man, who punched him away, then the guy with the gun pushed in on his other side and held the pistol to his temple as the other slipped into the front

167

passenger seat and the car pulled fiercely away. McSwegan closed his eyes, his teeth were chattering and he had broken out in shivers. Also his crotch was wet, whether from the blood or because he had pissed himself he didn't know. The gun came away from his head, he opened his eyes, then he felt a dig in his side, where the pistol had been repositioned.

'This is Mr McGurk. Ah think ye know his boay.'

Realization hit him almost physically. McSwegan began to cry, and shake, he was muttering, 'Oh JesusMary-MotheruvGod – oh Jesus—' and what was still in his bowels definitively gave way. He bent over holding his stomach, clutching both hands to the gash. 'Ah'm sorry, ah'm sorry, ah didnae know—'

McGurk was looking out of the window, trying not to recognize the quaking wretch next to him. The dark shapes of buildings zipped past, blurring lights from pubs and shop windows. They crossed over the motorway and headed for the Round Toll, the man in the seat beside him still doubled up and pleading for his life.

'Yi chibbed him,' he said softly and calmly.

'Ah'm sorry, ah'm sorry – ah didnae know he wis yir boay. Ah'm sorry, Mmm-Mister McGurk. He came efter me wae a cleaver.'

'You insulted his girlfriend.'

McSwegan could feel his life slipping through his fingers. 'Ah never, it wis a mistake. Honest.' He was pleading to the floor, hunched over, the car bumping along, McGurk to his right above him. 'Please, please, ah didnae know. Please—'

'Jesus,' McGurk said, 'you're stinking up the car. Just shut the fuck up.'

The BMW headed up towards the canal complex, past Firhill and along Maryhill Road, then under the viaduct and uphill until it reached the broken down lock system and the basin. They bumped over waste ground for a few yards, nosing past discarded supermarket trolleys and broken glass, until the car pulled up, the engine still running. The two minders sprang out, McSwegan following, dragged by the hair and the arms, kicked a couple of times in the ribs as he fell.

'Put the full beam on,' McGurk said, getting out, 'so I can see what I'm doing.'

His two men, his *associates*, John Toner and Andrew Walsh, both took another turn at kicking the moaning, foetal ball lying beside the car, then dragged McSwegan round to the front where he lay, casting a shadow like a boulder in the headlight beam. McGurk motioned to Toner and he handed over the knife. The lights were playing on the boss, as if he was on stage, and his shadow seemed to flare away and reach out over all Glasgow.

McGurk nodded to the men, who each took one of McSwegan's arms and yanked them back so that he came up, unwillingly, to his knees, then both rammed down a foot on the backs of his calves, so that he was pinioned, head hanging forward, in a penitential position.

He kept terribly still, knowing that McGurk was going to put the gun to his head and pull the trigger. He closed his eyes and began praying.

'This is personal,' McGurk was saying, 'which is why I'm here, why I'm dealing with you. Personally. No one touches my boy. No one. He's marked for life, you know that?'

McSwegan tried to speak but his jaw had locked and his mouth dried up.

'He wanted to do you, but I wouldn't let him. *I* want you.'

McSwegan was shivering, his legs ached where the boots held him down, his stomach was oozing burning blood, he could feel it, and it was made worse by the arched position he was being forced into.

'You're gonnae be an example,' McGurk went on. 'You're unlucky, because I'm not gonnae kill you.'

McSwegan felt an arm lock around his head and involuntarily he opened his eyes. He was looking down, and saw a pair of shiny black shoes, the light dancing off the bright leather. McGurk's gleaming, hand-made, slightly mud-splattered shoes were the last sight he ever saw.

With McSwegan's head held at his waist, locked under his arm, McGurk jerked him back into the full beam, his face the colour of chalk in the brilliance, and carefully he brought the knife across, first to the left eye, where he slashed into the eyelid, ball and socket, blood spurting over the knife which glowed like a jewel in the bouncing light and then, although McSwegan screamed and tried to shake himself free, to the right eye, where he jabbed in the bloody blade and scored upwards, before stepping back and releasing him.

The blind man brought both hands up to his ruined eyes as he fell forward, the blood pumping between his fingers, writhing and roaring with the insufferable pain.

McGurk kicked him in the ribs, trying to silence the piercing howl, then shook his head, bent forward and wiped the knife on the back of the Armani jacket, so that when he stood up and turned into the headlights the blade flared once more.

The three walked back to the car and climbed in. McGurk pressed the electric window button, the glass hummed down as the car moved into a bumpy turn. 'Hoi, Blind Sammy,' he shouted, 'you can always get a job at Remploy down the road making bendy toys.'

All four men rocked with laughter as the car stuttered off.

7

She sat on the other side of the table and put her right arm down on it. Here we go, I thought, intellectual arm wrestling. Her accent was English, smooth and dark and deep, reassuring, like one of those plummy announcers on the World Service before they tell you that a storm has just claimed an ocean liner in the Bay of Biscay. That, together with her peremptory dismissal of the locals and her youth, indicated to me that she was not one of them, but of the political police, or the military.

'It's all clear to me now,' I leaned back, 'but you didn't have to go to such elaborate and dramatic lengths; you could just have asked me out.' She shook her head. I thought she looked eminently fanciable, in a haughty sort of way. She, on the other hand, gave me the kind of blank stare the serving classes have been dismissed with for generations. But, hell, it worked for Mellors.

'I'm not interested in any of the artifice,' she said, 'the fake concern over a dealer. For all I care he could have bled to death in the street, or contracted terminal pneumonia. The last few minutes have been a fairly unsubtle attempt at intimidation, as you obviously noticed. Because you've been there before. Tawdry and rather pathetic, wasn't it?'

'So you thought you'd try flattery. I always think it's much better to have it come at you with style and subtlety, so lead away Mizz – mmmhh?'

'Carpenter.'

'Really?' I gave her a wide grin. 'Well, I'll just call you Karen.' The blank stare was removed for a quizzical instant. 'But I guess it's a complete waste of time asking you out for dinner.'

'What?'

'Nothing. Anorexia joke.' I cupped my brow with my hand. 'Love the stage prop.' I nodded at what was clearly my file. 'And can we just stop fuckin' around here and role playing, or I'm gonna give the cue for the lawyer to walk on, stage left, and the fire curtain comes down.'

'They said you were full of shit—'

'They,' I cut in, 'they being the ones who force fed it?' I moved my hand as if to grab for the file and as she reached protectively for it I switched and grabbed her wrist. 'Just don't think of going for the shovel again, lady, because I'm not digesting any more.' I gave her wrist a tight squeeze, smiled as hatefully as I could and then released her. 'That's what it's all about, isn't it? So, let's have the tape on now, eh.' I pointed to the tape decks. 'So we've got a record of all this.'

I was pleased to see now that there was anger in her face, her eyes alive. I pressed one of the record buttons, futilely, for there were no tapes in the decks.

'You just love confrontation, don't you?'

'That's what they used to pay me for.'

'And now?'

'Now? Heavens.' What was this really all about and who was she? I shrugged. 'I never think of the future. Maybe I'll go into business for myself. Private detective, who knows?'

She reached tentatively for the file, pulled it towards her and gave me an arch and withering look. 'Sure, call yourself Downe and Out.'

'You said it, lady. That's where I am, shortly. Out.' But from the moment I walked into the room and saw the file I knew that despite all the bluster I couldn't, and wouldn't, walk out.

'There's no need to go through all of this,' she tapped the file, anxious that the slight shaking in her hand should not be noticed. 'Let's start with the last part. You travelled over here on a passport which you knew belonged – should have belonged – to someone else, didn't you? You know that, we know that. You're an illegal immigrant.'

'My parents were Brits.'

'You have no passport and no automatic right of abode here. I repeat, you knowingly arrived here on a phoney passport. That is a criminal offence.'

'I've got the feeling that this isn't about a passport and you're not from immigration.'

'We're looking for your help.'

'We? Who? And what kind of help?'

She toyed with the edges of the file. 'I'm sure you'd like to help the British government in any way you could, Mr Downe – or is it Bone?' I shook my head slowly, smiling to myself in some private amusement.

'What bit of British government are we talking here? The shrouded bit, I guess.'

'Let me ask you something. How much do you really know about your father?'

'A few days ago I would have said nothing. Now, I know a little more. I've done some research.'

'Go on.'

'Why?'

She sighed and slowly ran her eyes over me. 'Let's just stop playing games. If you want to lie in a cell for a few days that's fine by me, but you'll still end up falling into line. So cut it, eh?'

My eyes stared into hers, searing, then after a few seconds, after considering my options, I began. 'I went to Govan today, which is a distinctly depressing little island of poverty along the river, if you don't know it. The house where he – we, I suppose – lived is gone. But there were a few spoors of him

173

in a local history vault and some anecdotal stuff, together with some cuttings. Someone there very kindly looked up old election details and local tax ledgers – and, what do they call them? valuation rolls? – and nailed him and his family down. They were pretty well known in the area, since the 1920s really, generations of drunks, streetfighters and criminals, I'd put it. My father, it seems, was born out of wedlock to a schoolgirl and the local gangleader, Willie Bone. Bone Senior, commonly known as 'Square Go' because he liked to get into fights with a certain decency and then batter people around. This seems to have been a recreation from when he wasn't stabbing or slashing, sinking whisky or stealing the poor box. He died in prison. Sadly not by the rope or at the hands of another inmate, but from what was probably a brain tumour, brought on by a bash on the head he got slipping on a swabbed floor, or maybe from the residue of those square goes. For some reason there was a massive local turn-out for the funeral. Perhaps the expression of a communal wish to dance on the grave.' I eased myself around in my seat, still holding her with my stare.

'Then comes my father. I suppose his own background partially explains why he took such pains to pain me. He was certainly inventive there.' I bit on a muscle in my cheek. 'But it's far too late to make excuses for him. He seems almost to have stepped into the family business. A string of early convictions, usually involving violence, borstal, prison, and then in the late fifties, early sixties, the record dries up. Not, I think, through redemption but because he finally realized that it was safer getting others to do his nasty stuff. By all accounts he ran money-lending in the place, prostitution, shebeens – the whole Clyde was covered in shipyards then, and on Fridays and the weekends the men who had been working in them during the week liked to push the boat out. The company of women, strong drink, the kind of induce-

174

ments you'd know about, that the secret services like to use to encourage compliance.'

I paused, waiting for a response, then went on. 'He got bigger. His lien ran over most of the city. So then he shacks up with a rather respectable if pretty feckless, or at least unworldly, girl from outside the city. It's my hope that she stayed with him out of fear all of those years, and my dim memories certainly support that. Then I come along. And then – then, he disappears. No visible reason. He seems just to have downed tools – knife and shotgun – and gone, shortly after I was born. As I now know, to the States. With me and my mother.'

She rubbed the side of her nose, which struck me as such an innocent gesture, as if it was an unconscious nervous response when she was ill at ease. 'And naturally you'd like to know more.'

'The file has got more than just my stuff in it then?'

She caught her breath and wriggled slightly in the chair. These chairs were made for lumpy, cushioned, civil service bottoms and her bones were probably grinding uncomfortably on the wood. 'He surfaced in America a few months ago, presumably when he knew he was dying from cancer. Just walked into the FBI building in Washington in his best suit, through the tourist entrance, among the guided tours, and said that he had some important information to deliver. Well, of course, at first he was given the slow brush-off, the shuffle from agent to agent, but I suppose that gradually they were becoming more senior, until, finally, the lightbulb went off and he was hurried upstairs to see one of the deputy directors.

'It's a remarkable tale. It seems that for more than twenty years he was the fixer, the arranger, the conduit for one of the major supply routes of narcotics into Europe, into Manchester, into London and Glasgow. That was his job. He was trusted by the Italians, he brokered the deals, hired the boats, the lorries, came up with the mules, the scams and dodges. His was the hand on the tap – faucet. And, now, he had just decided to turn it off. And also to give up the people he dealt with. Which was partially – no, very – successful, but not entirely so, because right from the start he made it clear he wasn't going to testify. He probably knew he wouldn't be around for that. Either that or it was fear, or pride, whatever.' She paused. 'For the first time I seem to have shaken you; you're looking bleak.'

I shook my head. 'It just seems so, I don't know, unlikely? He was violent, sure, but he wasn't stunningly bright.'

'Maybe just focused, with native cunning. And a good slice of luck.'

'So he ratted on his associates and the Bureau paid him.'

'He talked freely, in many sessions, about the US end. Less so about here. And yes, he was paid. I don't know how much.'

Now I know how he happened to put by the legacy, I thought. 'So does that bring us up to the present?'

'No, but it brings us to you.'

I was trying to gauge how I felt about it all. The visit to Govan had taken me to the graveside, lifted the edge of the box, and I hadn't liked the smell which wafted out. I was prepared to learn more of my father's serial deficiencies and deceits but now I was considering how I felt about his US government blood money, and when I did for just a few seconds I felt that it was fine, that accepting it wasn't a lot different from what I had unquestioningly done for years. It didn't bother me that he was a fink, and that some of the mobsters had been taken down, but it made me doubtful. When I separated out the hatred I felt from a clear-headed appreciation of him, difficult as that was, he did not strike me as the kind of person who, faced with an imminent appointment with his creator and destroyer, would attempt to clear the slate as much as he could. Neither could I see him selflessly deciding that the only worthwhile legacy he could pass on to his son came in the trade of information. As far as I could see he had always hated and resented me, the evidence was imprinted on me, and he would be more likely to leave something sick, dangerous or destructive. Which, perhaps, was what all this was about.

I was sitting with an attractive spook less than two hours after a total stranger had tried to kill me and she was clearly about to try to ensnare me in something dangerous and doubtful.

'So, go on,' I said.

Carpenter felt a knot in her stomach. This wasn't going the way she had rehearsed it to herself. She did not feel in control. She was uncomfortably aware of the presence of his legs next to hers under the desk although, as far as she could tell, he was indifferent to the propinquity. Somehow she hadn't expected him to be so – not bright, because she had known that he was at least sharp – intense, burning, giving off waves of energy, hatred mostly, but it was unsettling. What had she expected? Some defeated, morose, whacked-out loser. Which wouldn't have been right for the project but would certainly have smoothed the opening.

'Your service record—'

'What do you know about that?' he cut in, sitting up and leaning across the desk, mild distaste on his face. 'The boys in Langley or Washington or Hoovertown have been in touch?' He banged the desk with the palm of his hand. 'Why don't you just come out with what the fuck it is you want instead of pissin' around with the metaphysics?'

'I thought that was clear. Your help.'

'No chance. Tried that, didn't work.' He slumped back, the chair creaked and yawed.

'Bear with me. I think I may be able to convince you,' she carried on, he, arms in a tight fold, head shaking fiercely. 'Your record was very good—'

'Good, Jesus. Is this your typical English understatement? Lady, I would need a large stick up my ass to walk upright on a veterans' parade because of the weight of fuckin' medals on my tits. So don't give me that.'

'And then your wife died. And child.'

He hunched tighter in a ball. 'Killed,' he said quietly.

'You were in Nicaragua, Cyprus, Germany—'

'Spare me the heritage trail. I was there. I've got the tee shirts and the blisters and bullet holes.'

'And then Lockerbie. And it all came apart.'

Pieces of that dream again, those images, the slow atomization of the plane, falling away from them. Slowly, 'As you say.'

'From then on you've been obsessed with the idea that the US government had some part in it.' She waited for a response but he did nothing but glare at her. 'You're doing your own investigation, causing upset, alarm, abusing people, threatening them.'

'I was a little out of control for a while.'

That, my boy, she thought, is precisely your use to us. 'You went to military prison—'

He pushed back in the chair so that it scraped and squeaked. 'Listen up!' Involuntarily she sat back in her chair as he hissed at her, the air seeming foul between them. 'I don't give a fuck for you, your little pieces of paper and what it is you want from me. I'm going my own way. I've done more than my bit for my country, its freedom and flag. I wrapped myself in that fucking flag, bled nearly dry for it, and eventually got hung by it. However, fortunately, I suppose, it didn't end with having it folded into a neat bundle and handed to someone close to me by a spotty marine over an open grave. And I didn't end up in a body bag. So it goes on. That's it.'

'Really? It's interesting how idiomatic you become when you're angry, how your accent changes. To start with, it was very soft, almost with a trace of Scottish in it, now it's like a San Diego docker's. They still have docks in San Diego, do they?' He said nothing and the silence hardened. 'So it's Lockerbie still?'

'That's it. Still. Again.' He sighed it out after a few seconds, as if it really were not a choice, but an obligation.

'You still think your government had something to do with it?'

'I fucking *know* my government had something to do with it. That senile old dingbat Reagan, that clean-cut cur, that lying bastard North. The whole fucking nasty, sleazy, duplicitous, murdering, lying, slandering, foully corrupt former administration and their military crazies.' He took breath and came back again. 'You know, a lot of them didn't die when the plane exploded. They just plunged to earth. For days afterwards there were bodies on the hillsides, bodies in the street. Some people couldn't get out of their front doors for two days because there were corpses blocking them – some were even cut in half, looking like they were buried up to the waist in concrete – and nothing could be done until they were tagged and removed.

'But, d'you know what? While the firefighters, the doctors, the ambulance crews, the volunteers, the priests, the psychiatrists, the bereavement counsellors, the social workers – and of course the undertakers – were going about their jobs, or maybe even before most of them got there, people like you arrived. Two Boeing 727s of them, but men, almost all men, in plainclothes, and with just one coffin. One local farmer found a case-load of drugs, another was warned to stay indoors while people like you went around removing the evidence. There's lots more, of course, but you probably know more about it than I do. So don't tell me my government wasn't involved, don't tell me it was just two Libyans from Malta with a bomb. Crap. I don't know exactly where it starts and stops but I'll keep trying. Nothing you can do will stop me, nothing they can. Except kill me.' He breathed out and sat back in the chair. 'Which would prove my case. Posthumously, of course.'

'And they've already tried that,' I went on, 'or sent a bloody botched warning. Did you know that two kids died in the car? Blown to shredded beef. Or mince. My old man's great love. He used to bitch that it wasn't as good in the States as at home; now I'm not quite sure what he meant.' I paused, brain spinning wildly away. 'Anyway, next time you tuck into a bolognese or a burger just bear in mind your responsibility for the death of two kids.'

'I don't know what you're talking about.'

'No, of course you don't. Mind you, the two of them were already *well done*, black, so that probably doesn't count with you. But you'll be a vegetarian, I suppose.'

'You're rambling, Mr Downe – Bone – it'll be the drugs, I suppose.'

I looked at this pretty woman, who clearly had some foreign blood in her somewhere, no matter how distant or how much she tried to ignore it, and I just soughed with the hopelessness of human development. 'A bomb was strapped to my hire car, so it's a reasonable assumption that someone either wanted to kill me or has a vendetta against rental companies. Two kids trying to break into it were killed. Thing is, it wasn't a trip device or a timer, it was remote controlled, almost certainly within sight. And it must have been clear, although it was getting dark, that I was not in the car, but in the driveway. Nevertheless, it was triggered. Which surely indicates gross incompetence, or a callous disregard for innocent lives. And in both of these assumptions there is the same conclusion: the people who did it are scum. Anything they believe in is debased and, courtesy of the trickle-down theory much admired and adhered to by old Reagan and his buddies, their associates, their trans-Atlantic cousins, the issue of their fucking loins, are all stained by the same bloody piss.'

I guess the diatribe was an over-reaction to reality, or more likely the absence of hard and soothing drugs.

'I amend my earlier conclusion,' she said, 'not just drugs but post-traumatic stress disorder.'

I thought about blowing her an ironic kiss but shook my head instead and looked round the shit-coloured room. 'What is it you want? Just spell it out.'

'We want to get to the parts your father's warrant didn't reach. Those he wouldn't indict. We want to finish it off. At this end.'

'So why ask me? I don't know anything about it. I'm just off the plane.'

'Not so much asking, Mr Downe, Mr – what shall I call you?'

'It doesn't matter. Don't bother calling me anything because I ain't comin'.'

'Oh dear. Obviously I'm not making myself too clear. At college my tutors said that I had a tendency to circumlocution,' she smiled, in a practised way, 'and there I go again. Here are the simple truths – Downe, or Bone. You've clearly pissed off a lot of people back home, digging into what is long buried. Patience is exhausted. You've had your last warning. I really don't think you can return to the United States again with any safety.' She smiled again. 'There I go, beating round the bush again. Actually, I'm as certain of that as I am that the sun will go down.'

The things that crawl out then, I thought, the bestiary, after the light goes. It was now as clear as a signed confession that the bomb was, indeed, a simple, grotesque and callous

181

message. 'You'll never have heard of John Maclean, will you?' My side was now throbbing and I had a severe headache, cramps in my bones. 'Local political philosopher, not celluloid action hero. So the question of how you square your conscience with your intellect doesn't arise, does it?' I shook my head. 'New world order, same old methods.'

'Don't get smug and self-righteous on me, Downe. Your moral high ground is a few thousand feet below Holland's. So let's get on.'

I knew from past experience what getting on meant, and it usually had nothing to do with improvement, but more often de-construction and death. 'You're wasting your time.'

She bent down and came back up with a briefcase, out of which she pulled yet another file, more paper. My past, I thought, had evidently been despoiling large tracts of forestry. But this time, this one wasn't really about me. 'I want you to look at this,' and she spun it across the desk and around so that its contents splayed out in front of me. There were several A4 colour pictures and a few sheets of NCR paper on which reports had been typed out. Police reports. I shook my head, but natural curiosity kicked in. The pictures were of a headless torso which, when I looked closer, was female. One showed a grotesque close-up of a head in a microwave, flesh split and cooked, the sockets eyeless, presumably exploded in the heat, the tongue bloated, swollen and cooked like a sheep's. Others were of a baby with its brains exploded on the pillow like infant food. I had seen worse.

'We think they came looking for her partner, but either he was out selling or scoring, or he knew something was about to come down. Anyway, she got unlucky. The time scale was probably that they shot the baby first, in front of her, then they raped her and smacked her about for a bit, and when they got tired of that one of them choked her to death. Couldn't even finish her quickly with one to the brain. Then they sawed her head off. Her name was Shirley McNeice, she was twenty-three. The head in the microwave was an after-thought, probably, a message to her man when he got back. He was a fairly small-time dealer, called 'Wingie' McLeod, Wingie on account of how half of his arm was amputated after the veins and arteries became junked up and gangrene set in. There was no need for it. McLeod had ripped off a bit of smack to make an extra few bob. He's a junkie, what the hell else would he do?'

She paused, clearly expecting something from me. 'The gravity of the times appals me,' I said. 'I'll try to lead a better life.'

'You're a facetious bastard, Downe. Doesn't anything move you at all?'

'You're thinking sunsets, new-mown hay, that kind of thing? A baby's chuckle.' I felt my stomach cant. 'Not any more, sweetheart, you've taken it all, people like you. Now I'm the original immovable object. And what happened to the *Mr*?'

For a few seconds we sat looking grimly into each other's faces. 'I'm asking for your help.' I shook my head once more. She rubbed her mouth slowly as if she were trying to caution her words. 'People like me? That's crap. What about people like you? More than that, what about flesh and blood? What about your dear old dad, for instance? A person like him. No, not a person like him. Him! The same one who put his semen into your dear old mum – for you – effectively put the junk in the veins of most of the crash-cases in this city.' She pulled the gory pictures from the desk where I had put them down. 'Directly or indirectly he's responsible for this—'

'Balls.'

'Oh yeah? For the last fifteen years he's been orchestrating the supply from over there, the results of which are here,' she jabbed her fingers at the pictures. 'His partner, Thomas McGurk, is the one who set these psychopaths on this kid, these *kids*. He's the quartermaster, he is the one who turned

183

on the heroin. Did you know there were more injecting addicts in this city, per capita, than anywhere else in the world?'

'I'll lock that one away for Trivial Pursuit.'

'Most of the crime is drug-related, the prostitution, the majority of the premature deaths of young people.'

I pushed the chair back. 'Wrap it up, for fuck's sake. I am not responsible for anything my father did or didn't do. I'm not responsible for any of this,' I pointed to the pictures, 'and just because he recanted, ratted on his old chums, don't think it's in the blood. Don't think I'm going to do willingly anything your kind request.'

'My kind? What do you know about me?'

'Enough to know that you haven't the guts to do your own nastiness, or you wouldn't be talking to me. You'd be playing squash, riding your ponies or out at a cocktail party.'

She snorted, then began to laugh, so infectiously that I felt my lips begin to curl in response. 'No, you know nothing whatever about me, do you? But I know about you.' She had put the pictures down and was reaching for her briefcase once more. 'But not willingly. All right then. Whatever has to be.' Out came another file. She threw it down on top of the spilled papers on the desk. 'Your life is your life to throw away. What about hers? Or don't you care, again?' She nodded down at the file. 'Go on.'

I picked it up, knowing before I opened it what was inside. There were several long-range shots of Stephanie, a series of pretty well-composed shots of the front of her house, and what seemed like a tourist photograph of her in the bar, smiling at the camera, as if the person on the other end had asked her to pose for a little memento. A slow avalanche of self-disgust and despair choked me. It was the closest I had come to emotional capitulation in years. It was my blind selfishness which had implicated her. Slowly I said, 'OK.' And then, 'You must love your work.'

'I hoped that you might have wanted to clear up what your father started. I'm sorry.'

I looked hard at her face and I thought I detected just a glint of rapidly dying remorse in her eyes. Give her a year or two, she'd be over that. 'Just tell me what the fuck it is you want.'

Burns was high. He had snorted some speed, thrown back a tab with a long swallow of lager and then smoked some dope just to chill out a bit. Then he had played a couple of frames of pool until he had become convinced that the balls were made of eggshell and he kept putting his cue through them. He couldn't stop laughing. Balls were turning to dust every shot he made. And the noise in his ears was like clucking, the noise of displeased hens, and that set him off again, roaring, until tears ran freely down his face. 'C'moan,' he said to his opponent eventually, wheezing with the effort of suppressing the giggles, 'ah'll buy ye a Chinkie.'

'Y'owe me a tenner fur the gemme as well.' The other man had short-cropped, gelled, black hair, a narrow face and a prominent red weal running from his mouth along the side of his cheek. His name was John Traynor, he had drunk very little, only five bottles of Bud, which had helped to wash down a couple of Es. He wanted to go dancing; most of all he wanted to fuck, but what he wanted had little to do with it. What the Poet wanted would happen.

'Fuck'n tenner, what fuck'n tenner? Ah just hammered ye, didna!' Burns had slung his arm round him and was guiding him towards the door of the snooker hall, bumping as they went, the other punters clearing a way long before they arrived bouncing, like a multiple cushion shot, from the edges of the lines of tables. As they reached the last table before the door Burns stopped, swirled away from Traynor and, while the two men at the table watched, cues in hand, he drew his forearm across the table, scattering the balls and cackling like

185

a pantomime villain. The two men at the table tried vainly to smile.

'Ah'm starvin,' Burns was pushing Traynor out of the door, 'must be the fuck'n Bob Hope. I could really murder a Chinkie.' He began a coughing laugh again, pushing Traynor. 'An' mebbe ah wull.'

'Ah'll no huv anythin,' Traynor said as they walked along the alley towards the street. 'Ah'm no hungry. Ah'll just keep ye company. Wherr wi gaunnie go?'

'Mmhh?' Burns was having trouble keeping in mind the swirling objects of his desire. A blazing sun seemed to have come out overhead, so close he could almost touch it. When he looked round at Traynor he noticed his face was melting, like a lump of lard over a hotplate, yet somehow he knew that this seemed a little unlikely and that the acid was responsible.

'Fancy a bit o'fanny later, Shug?' Traynor asked. 'Uh've no hud it since we fucked thon heidless junkie.'

The Poet tried to remember, but it seemed to have become strangely convoluted and out of sequence in his head. 'Did we no take her heid aff efter?'

'We could go up the Tunnel and pull a coupla tarts. Or just go up the squerr and drag a coupla pros in. Therr's a new yin ah noticed, looks aboot fourteen, gies a great gammy, so've heard.'

'Fuck, naw. Aids, man.' Burns was concentrating on his footfalls because it was quite evident that the cobbles were melting and he didn't want daubs of sticky stone attaching to the legs of his Armani trousers.

'Naw, she's no shootin' up.'

'Like fuck she's no.'

'Naw, naw. Only been therr a couple weeks.'

'So is she a fuckin' student or sum'hin, toppin' up her grant like? Or maybe she's a fuckin' social worker. Heh watch—' he pushed Traynor out of the way of a puddle of hot liquid stone, he knew it was deep, would turn him into a living statue. A fucking ugly one right enough.

'We'll werr johnies, like the last time. In case, like.'

'Ah don'know. Christ!' He stopped. 'Jesus!' What was Tony Blair doing blocking the way, holding out a book to him like it was *This is Your Life*? 'Tony!' he said, holding out his hand, not sure now whether he was going to take the book or shake the man's hand. He tried to nudge Traynor, alerting him to the presence of the PM, but he wasn't there all of a sudden and when he looked around and down he noticed that he must have fallen over on his back, into all that melted stone, which was bubbling and heaving. And when he peered closer he saw that it was too late, that Traynor's face had already melted into a dripping, raw, red mess. He looked up. 'Tony,' he said again, ''fuck ur y'daen' here, man?'

'You know, meeting the people. Here, take the book. It's a present.'

'Staunin'in fur Michael, eh? Hope yir gettin' a good wedge.'

'Can you just open it and hold it up in front of your face, like you were reading it? That's it.'

'Cannae quite see wha' it's aboot. It's aw – it's aw meat, man.'

The man in the Tony Blair mask brought up the silenced .22 and as the Poet posed behind the book, *Microwave Cookery For Beginners*, he slapped a couple of rounds into it. Burns staggered briefly and then collapsed slowly in a tangle of limbs, like an old drunk.

The blood had stopped pumping from Traynor's forehead. Just to make sure, the politician stepped closer, and then over each in turn. First the Poet and then Traynor, firing the final rounds through their open mouths.

Carpenter was dreaming of brain damage, of something burrowing into her head. She remembered as a kid being told that earwigs ate their way into your cerebellum if you let

187

them into your ear. And then she sat up in bed, her whole body slick with sweat, the sheets falling away; she ran her two hands down her naked breasts and across her stomach and they came away wet. Her head pounded and vibrated, she opened her eyes, until she slowly recognized where she was. And then she realized that the door was being banged, like dull chops on wood.

'Madam,' she heard in a hissing low voice, 'therr's an urgent message. You've tae reply right away.'

'A minute.' She ran her hands through her hair, tied it behind her head in a rough knot, put both feet on the carpet, shivering as she did so, the wisps of the dream still swirling, then she inched her way in remembered steps to the bathroom, pulled open the door, fumbled for the dressing gown and swung it on. 'Coming,' she yawned as she moved towards the milky sliver of light under the door. Before she unlocked it she ran her hands over her face, then pulled the collar of the gown tight around her throat. Her right hand fumbled with the doorknob and the small switch which unlocked the door, then she turned the handle.

There was a brief burst of light, someone flung themselves at her, a leg kicked hers away and she landed face down on the carpet in a brutal armlock which made her wince, before a hand came over her mouth forcing her head back against a solid body, thumb and forefinger pinching her nostrils shut. Oddly, she was aware of a loud mechanical clunk as the door shut. He must have kicked it with his foot, she thought abstractedly, and then panic began to bubble in her.

'Quiet. Not a word and nothing will happen.' The Glasgow accent had gone, smoothed out and mellowed, and she knew immediately who it was. Slowly the hand came away from her mouth. 'That's good.'

'Downe,' she said softly, thinking, *how did he find me?*

*

I told her to sit down in the chair, opened the minibar and pulled out a half-bottle of champagne, watching her all the while, but believing she would at least be too professional to make a scene. I plonked the bottle on top of the cabinet next to the fridge and tore open the wrappings on two glasses. She sat in a hunched bundle of anger on a chair, legs crossed, holding the robe shut with her right hand at the neck. I smiled without warmth, tore the foil from the bottle, unwired the cork and popped it.

'I waited outside Pitt Street in a taxi,' I said, pouring two glasses of champagne. 'If you're wondering how I found you.' I offered her one of the glasses but she shook her head. I put it down on the bedside table. 'You're pretty distinctive anyway. It wouldn't have been difficult. If you're thinking of moving,' I went on, sipping at the drink, 'don't bother. I'll find you. I'm starting to get contacts in this town. Cheers.'

'What is this about?'

'I thought you'd want a report back.'

'Fuck you, Downe, you're trying to intimidate me.'

'Nah. Just standard military practice. Immediate debriefing by senior officer.'

'Are you stoned?'

'Fuckin' avalanched.' I drained the glass and poured another. 'I had a bit put by that I managed to dig up.' Which caused me to giggle, my mind spinning back to me up to my elbows in garbage outside the hospital. 'I'll be all right for a few days.' The bed looked warm and inviting, kind of rumpled and pouting, so I sat down on it.

'Well?'

'Mmhh?'

'So what happened?'

'You *do* want to know?'

'Next time, not in the middle of the night.'

'Next time?'

189

'Slip of the tongue.'

'I think not.' The champagne wasn't having much success cutting through the layer of iron filings in my mouth and nose. 'I think not.' Sticking a finger in the glass I sucked and then said to her, 'Drink, or I'm not telling. You *do* drink?'

'Not in the middle of the night.'

'Go on. If you don't I'm not telling. And then you won't be able to finger fuck later.'

She tossed her head, gritted her teeth and clenched her gown tighter. 'Fuck you, Downe,' she said again with more feeling.

'Maybe later.' But she picked up her glass and took a sip. 'And you're becoming repetitious. Didn't you have a university education?'

'Please. Proceed.'

'That's better. Remind me to stick to the point if I stray. I'm a bit woolly round the edges.'

'Go on.'

'OK, OK. Remember the file you showed me, on – on – what were their names?'

'Burns and Traynor.'

'Right, Burns and Traynor. Well, the surveillance said they tended to hang out during the day in a pool hall off Candleriggs. I went in, played a few frames, waited for them to turn up and then collected my new coat and went outside. By the way, d'you like the coat? It's got lots of pockets, real handy for hiding things inside.' It was a navy, inconspicuous Goretex number, without the usual flashes and lurid colours visible from the moon.

'Lovely. Get on.'

I described how earlier, when I had been walking about in the centre of Glasgow, I had come across a joke shop where I picked up the Blair mask. 'You have to add a bit of wit and style to these things,' I said, 'that's what's been sadly lacking from assassinations, in my view. Then I picked up a book of

190

microwave cooking from a book shop up the road. I decided that a clear message should be left. What do you think?'

'Good idea, if you're off your face.'

'The silenced Webley.'

'Wasn't it a Walther?'

'That's right, you're right, it was. Your armourer said it was just the ticket.' I chuckled, slurped the rest of the champagne. 'One-way ticket, right enough. I was a bit worried about it jamming, but it didn't. Your man was right.' I considered the empty glass.

'Then?'

'Mmmhh? Simple. Double-tap each. They were clearly not in control of many of their faculties. Wasted. Didn't know what happened. I handed over the microwave book, told Burns to open it, got a nice grouping with a large broiled chicken on the cover. Then another tap each, just to be sure.'

'No one saw you?'

'If they did, the Prime Minister'll be in leg irons by now.'

'What about the gun?'

'I brought it back for you, thought you could hand it back in.'

'You are joking!' She stood up, the dressing gown falling open at the neck and crotch, giving me a quick, vivid flash.

'I was, yeah. But it was worth it for the peep show.' Sadly, the curtains quickly came down. 'Where I junked it, it'll never be found. D'you wanna know where?'

'No. Of course not. Are you finished?'

'You're not going to invite me to stay, Carpenter?'

'Hardly.'

'Right. I'll go.' I looked back at her and moved towards the door. 'I came in through the car park. I'll go back that way.'

'Fine.'

'Just one thing. If this all gets cleared up – I'm looking for reassurance here – the slate's clean. I get to go back, like you said. No unfortunate little accidents. I see a retirement, new

191

career, a humble little house somewhere, a car I'm paying up. No repercussions?'

'No repercussions?'

'No repercussions. I have your word on that, Karen.'

'You do.'

I had my hand on the doorknob. 'Just one thing more.'

'Downe, I'm tired.'

'If anything happens to my friend abroad, Carpenter,' I took a sighing breath, 'be very sure, I will find you and I will kill you.'

In the dull rosy electric light it was difficult to see her expression but I could tell by the way her body involuntarily stiffened that she believed me.

'Leave me,' she said quietly.

I turned the handle and went out into the hall. When I had walked to the end of the corridor, to the stairs, I put my hand inside the jacket to a deep pocket and, fumbling, switched off the tape recorder.

8

She punched a couple more degrees of pain into the machine and grimaced as the track shuddered and sped faster under her shoes. Her shirt, a dark blue Oxford University sweater, stuck to her stomach, her grey shorts were damp in the usual embarrassing places and her legs, she could see with each pace on the revolving rubber roadway, were shining with the effort. The backs of her calves and ankles and the inside of her thighs ached, her breath was coming in unseemly gasps and her hair, tied in a loose knot, was beginning to unravel with her bouncing run, strands already dangling hypnotically in front of her eyes.

The trouble with this city, she told herself, was that it was big enough to convince yourself you could be anonymous, but small enough to quickly disprove it. It was really only a small Victorian town centre set among the raging badlands, hundreds of acres and square miles of high rises, or feature-less grey housing blocks filled with hostiles. All the decent hotels and restaurants were within either a short walk or ten-minute cab ride. It was difficult to disappear.

She cursed her metropolitan mindset. Somehow she had imagined it would be like London, well, not quite of course, but on the same scale. Now what could she do? Check out of this hotel? Yes, and with the *Yellow Pages* and a handful of spare change he could probably trace her in half an hour. And was it so bad that he knew where she was? She nodded, sprayed out an aching breath and admitted that it could be.

What options did she have? The one which loomed up, the only real one, the one she wasn't prepared to countenance, was to give herself up, call in and admit that she had been traced to home. 'You've come too far,' she hissed at the digital counters on the running machine, 'done too much to do that.'

She would have to tell Brown that Bone had smoked her out. Or would she? That would be an admission of fallibility. The local plod hated people like her, she knew that, swanning in with their privileges, unencumbered by police acts, watch committees, overseers, complaints authorities, rule books and multiple-copy incident forms.

The electronic numbers were telling her that she was nearing three miles. The limit. As it bleeped and went into slowdown mode she felt her taut muscles ease slightly. A trickle of warm water slithered down between her buttocks, a rivulet of sweat from her back. And then she was walking along the easily moving rubber.

There wasn't any need to panic or go into purdah. He knew where she was and he, similarly, wasn't going to be difficult to find. Although she felt a twist of uneasiness at how easily he had fooled her with the accent.

All right, so she was not completely attuned to it, but it seemed entirely authentic to her ears. I suppose, she said to herself, if you grow up in a house where it's coming at you all the time, in stereo, it's easy to slip into. She had done almost the same thing, in reverse. The Midlands inflections had gone, deliberately smoothed over at school and at college so that she now had the RP indistinguishable from any other educated Home Counties oik, but she could still slip into her natural patois.

The machine groaned to a standstill. She stumbled off, reaching down to massage the muscles in her legs, before walking over to the bench press where she had hung her towel. She was the only person in the small gym. The hotel was not busy and for the travelling salesmen types who made up most of the other guests, she guessed early morning exercise did not head the hotel's attractions. Flinging the towel over her shoulder she pushed open the door into the short corridor and the women's changing rooms, pulled the damp shirt off and threw it at a bench seat, followed by her ribbed training vest, then stumbled out of her pants. She caught sight of herself in a full-length mirror and admired her physique. Her body was not classically beautiful, she was too rangy and lean in the wrong places, but it pleased her. She bent down and untied her shoes, pulled them off along with her wet socks, chucked them on the bench and stood back up. Perhaps there was another way to play Downe. It needn't be secretive and confrontational; her training told her that need and dependency were crucially important in establishing the relationship. So far, in this case, it was entirely based on coercion, which wasn't the strongest cement when pressure was applied. It would never develop into approval or loyalty, but enlightened mutuality of interest, even respect, was a much firmer base when tempests blew up.

She nodded at herself. Nothing to be lost by trying to introduce a human element into it. Then she considered Downe and wondered, what exactly were the manners involved in dealing with a semi-deranged, junked-out psycho case? All right, an exaggeration. He had clearly once been straight, what he might call a stand-up guy, but was evidently now badly damaged. The question was, irrevocably so? Disposably so?

She turned away and walked the few paces to the shower cubicle, pulled back the nylon curtain and pushed the button for the hot water, cooling it to tepid before standing inside. The needle points of water felt scourging and oddly redemptive. Carpenter pushed her face up to the jets, her skin tingling in the spray. Regular contact with the case officer was the way to do it; she would try and establish some kind of connection with Downe, and do it this time in surroundings more relaxed and conducive than a police interview room.

As the water flowed over her, she tried to let her mind go blank until all she could hear and think about was the rushing of water. Then an odd and unsettling grainy little scene began to play in her mind, the shower scene from *Psycho*.

9

I had re-invented myself in a city centre bar which seemed to have been designed by an architect who had experienced a bad acid trip in the Mojave desert. There were plastic ferns and cacti, strands of wood, colours the range of a Tequila Sunrise – about the only thing missing was the sand, and most of that seemed to be in my head. Somehow I had got talking to a well-spoken, bespoke-dressed film producer, light entertainment he said, and I told him that I was an actor, that I had just finished a tediously awful independent film in London, the details of which gave me cramps to recall but seemed to involve a young woman's sexual obsession with a teddy bear, and I was just spending some time in Scotland, tracing my family tree (although I was almost tempted to mention that I had recently buried, or at least lopped off, a couple of branches).

The bar was called the Max, or something like that, and in the course of the increasingly drunken tryst between me and Seumas, or whatever his name was, there had been periodic trips to the toilet, with a vomit-inducing decor involving purples and magentas, and the mysterious collection of two women called Etta and Loretta, or maybe they were Netta and The Sweater, I couldn't be sure. Most of the time, except when, periodically, the mist cleared, I couldn't be entirely sure that there wasn't just the one of them, so similarly blonde, buxom and enshrouded in wool, and mystery, or gelatin, had they become in my vision that I had to peer fixedly, when one or both would giggle in stereo.

'You do little to contradict men's stereotypes,' I had said, I was almost sure.

'You get what you expect,' came back, followed by a giggle, which sounded pretty profound to me in my soaked and snotted state.

'I don't usually drink a lot. In fact, once I went five alcohol-free years.'

'Could have fooled me.' A hand was massaging the inside of my right leg, and I hoped desperately it wasn't Seumas's. Despite the focus problem, my head felt remarkably clear – obviously some sort of chemical reaction caused by the drugs and booze – and I considered that I was definitely going to be fit for what was to come. I thought about condoms, wondered whether I was armed, slipped my hand inside my jacket and bumped up against the gun, which caused me to snigger. And I also thought, from the rearrangements going on in my groin, I was definitely pleased to see Etta, or The Sweater.

My behaviour, of course, was irresponsibly dangerous and unprofessional. And I didn't care. I was supposed to dump the gun and I hadn't, because, vaguely, I felt I should collect all the evidence I could put together against my governors. It was a direct link to the killings – the pistol wasn't smoking but it was still mildly warm – but then I didn't think the police would be looking for me, given my apparent licence. But if they were, if I was simply the patsy in an elaborate set-up, I wanted a measure of protection and, not knowing my way around the local criminal infrastructure well enough to get another one, hanging on to this gun seemed the best option.

There was a strong chance, it seemed to me, that I was being used as the catalyst for a local criminal conflagration, that I would be sold out by the lovely Carpenter, so it seemed to make eminent sense to hold on to the gun for protection when the shit-storm hit. And anyway, there was no way I was going back to prison after that last time. I would rather die.

This wasn't the fluids and additives speaking, it was a decision taken in sobriety a long time ago. What better way to ensure a quick exit than popping at the polis, or the bad guys, with a handgun.

I shivered a little, and Etta or Sweater asked what was wrong (I was now entirely convinced that the hand was not Seumas's, as he was presently over at the bar). I don't know what I muttered but what was assailing my doomed soul was the scene in the alley. I had not killed anyone who was not directly endangering me – in truth, I had never been so close to it before – and it troubled me, which I found disturbing and surprising. I kept tripping over emotions I had thought long petrified.

Carpenter had convinced me that the two were responsible for the beheading, or at least, if there wasn't proof positive, that these two had a history of brutality and depravity that the world would be better without. She showed me their form, the intelligence on them, the witness statements later retracted (the retractors had a subsequent habit of disappearing) and the whole nasty picture of psychotic violence, which is a lot more justification than you get before going into battle, but I was still deeply unsettled.

Seumas had collected the new round of drinks and was carefully transporting them to the table. 'There's waitress service,' I heard the barman say pointedly. It was still early in the evening and reasonably quiet. The barman was a young man with a trimmed goatee and slicked-back hair.

'No problem,' said Seumas, carrying the last drink to the table with the apparent reverence of the Holy Grail. 'Line 'em up and I'll service them.' That caused him to heave with laughter and send waves across the drink as he negotiated the floor.

'So it's homicide now?' he said, slouching down heavily into the green leatherette-padded booth.

I felt a jolt of panic, then remembered that I had said that I had some part fixed up in a cop show in the States. 'Correct,' I agreed.

The girls looked puzzled, individually, and then at each other. 'You guys are actors?' one of them asked.

'Correct,' I agreed again.

'I've seen you on TV, I'm sure,' the other one said.

'Both of us,' Seumas said. 'In the same show. It's on later tonight.' Looking first at me, then the girls, then bursting into a fit of giggles.

'Shit,' I said angrily into my glass as a flashback careered at me. 'It was working, too.'

'What was?' Seumas asked.

'Drinking . . . to forget.'

'Sorry. Anyway,' he went on, 'is it a good part?'

'Haven't read the script properly, but I think it involves grunting a lot and putting John and Jane Doe labels on big toes in the morgue.'

'Do they really do that?' Etta said.

'No,' I assured her, placing her hand, or perhaps her friend's, but certainly not Seumas's, a couple of inches higher on my thigh. 'Just in the script.'

'I'm sure I've seen you in a movie, right?'

'Ah,' I said, 'you mean that small part when I punch Keanu's lights out and run off with the girl on the motorbike with the whole of Los Angeles exploding behind me like one gigantic, seismic orgasm.' I paused. 'And when you come home with me tonight I will show you—' I smiled lasciviously, '—I will show you scripts in abundance.' My mind was extrapolating like an Ornette Coleman solo. 'Floor to ceiling. Stem to stern. A to Z. From Abbott and Costello to, uhh, Zenda, Prisoner of. Except, of course, they're all in San Diego and we'd have a bit of a push getting there this evening.'

'What are you going on about?' one of the two asked.

'Quite,' said Seumas.

200

I decided that it was actually quite a good idea to collect scripts, and wondered if there was a market in them. There seemed to be for even more weird stuff than that, like old soccer programmes or hundred-year-old wine that had probably turned to vinegar, so why not? I buried my head in the new glass and ingested. 'I collect 'em. Film scripts. I've got more good parts buried in my house than Ted Bundy.' I had been waiting to get that one in.

'You're serious,' Seumas slurred.

'Hundreds. Famous and failed. All with a beginning, a muddle and an end, but not necessarily in that order.' I was laughing and tears began to roll down my cheeks, which could probably be siphoned and used as a chemical propulsion. I wiped my chin, fearing I was beginning to drool. 'Marx Brothers and Godard. And, in that order.'

'Just as long as you don't expect me to play the Linda Lovelace part,' said The Sweater. 'I haven't had my tonsils out.'

'Is any of this true?' Seumas was waving his finger and beaming.

'It might be,' I replied, 'and if it isn't it could be. Just now, I'm not quite sure. I can barely hold on to the script for this evening's pleasantries.' And the hand moved further up my leg, which indicated to me that there were considerably more to come.

The dawn came up with a pounding of drums. I thought I was dreaming a Tarzan movie, but when I opened my eyes, I realized it was just the hangover headache hammering through my unconscious.

If I just lie still enough, I thought, my brains will not start dribbling down my nose. Gingerly I raised my left arm, glad that there was no neurological damage, but seeking in the grey light the time on my watch. Six a.m. I was in a strange room, what looked like a hotel room at which I had no

201

remembrance of arriving. I imagined a couple of rubber-encased bodies in bags in a morgue. Then I let my arm drop slowly and as I did heard a grunt next to me, causing me to jump up into a sitting position, sending waves of pain coursing across my eyes. Think, I thought, think.

Slowly I turned my head and saw a light brown shape and, above it, a Gorgon's nest of tangled snakes which, when the explosions in my eyes died down, I realized was a woman's hair in disarray. At least she's alive, I told myself, for the obvious reason. Then, carefully, I lowered myself back on to the bed and gradually turned my head towards my companion.

You could get smothered by a hairstyle like that, I mused, taking in the mass of curled hair. It took me a few seconds to realize that she was lying face down, nuzzling the pillows. What did you say your name was again? I tried to remember. There was a taxi ride, that much was certain, and an entanglement in the back which was caused equally by libido and the lurching of the cab as it skidded round corners. I remembered getting out, struggling for my wallet and then it all faded to black.

And now, up come the house lights. I sighed. Still no sign of her waking, whatever she was called. OK, I had been drinking with Seumas Floyd – I called him Pretty Boy and he had grimaced, so we must have been well on – and we had noticed the two girls at the bar, occasionally looking over, the old sexual semaphore going back and forth. The two of them could have been sisters, I recalled, tall, blonde, similar clothes, tee shirts, short skirts and, now I remembered, both had silver ankle bracelets which was later a subject of lewd speculation. The Barbie Twins, Floyd called them. Me, being even more cynical than the TV producer, had opined that they probably did a lesbian sandwich in porn movies, or were a high-cost hooker double act, and perhaps we should interview them.

'Maybe it's their night off,' Floyd had sniggered.

'I'll ask them.' I had got up and skated across the wooden floor. But before I could come out with anything, one of them had said, 'We were trying to figure out where we've seen you before – the movies?' Which had led into the whole acting schmooze. Then I had flashed my melting smile and said, 'There are only two categories of people, aren't there? Those who are in the movies and those who are trying to be. Shall we join you, or you us?'

'You're American,' the other one said. 'I knew you were in a film.'

So, what had happened after the fade to black? Did we have sex? Was it good? Did I come? Did she? Perhaps I had fallen asleep *in flagrante*? Or watched helplessly as, despite her ministering efforts, I hadn't been able to rise to it? No, that had never happened. Had it? What a terrible thing, I thought, is this male vanity. The easiest way was to ask her. Excuse me, Miss – Umm, did I have as good a time last night as I hope you had?

I moved my head back so that I was staring at the ceiling. The headache had become rhythmical now, steady sore pulses alternating with the heavy heartbeats in my chest. The Barbie sister groaned again and I heard a rustling, felt an arm come over my chest and then a tickle on my neck as her head got in close.

Worse, I thought, and now I was really worried, what if I told her about me, you know, ambitions, growing up, truth, for God's sake? No, I checked myself, I could never get that stoned.

Her breath was on the side of my face, I couldn't smell alcohol on it and I wondered how mine smelled. Like a peat bog, I would bet, whatever that was like. Damp and methane-suffused, most likely. Dank vegetation and long-dead animals. It would probably be judicious to brush my teeth before she woke.

Carefully I slipped out from under her arm, swung my feet

off the bed and down on to the floor. In the dull light I could see discarded clothes, tangled and coupled, all over the rug. The movement, or the disequilibrium, my heart pushing the blood uphill, brought a renewed pounding in my head and a wave of nausea. When I stood up I felt dizzy and far from earth. The body in the bed snuffled and muttered and was silent.

My heart had begun to steady and I carefully picked my way towards the door, noting a small pair of white cotton pants draping what looked like a menu for room service on the phone table. Vaguely I remembered the giggling struggle to remove them, before tossing them over my shoulder and then sloppily nuzzling her. I shivered at the memory. As I reached the bathroom door I stumbled over something, caught myself, then looked down at a huge bag which, by its size, must, in a previous role, have held together the organs of one of the larger leathern beasts, like a hippo. It was the kind of tote bag models carry, with changes of clothing, or drug dealers with their stash, the bounty and belt-loaded automatics. For a second I considered looking inside it, then decided that was unforgivable.

Because it certainly wouldn't be doing to be caught in the act.

So I grabbed it by the handles and pulled it out of the door after me, like slain booty. Chances were she wouldn't remember – if she woke and it was the unlikely first thing that occurred – where she had dropped it in the sexual feeding frenzy.

I locked the bathroom door behind me and unzipped the bag. A woollen cardigan was bunched at the top, which I pulled out, finding first a neatly folded and skimpy-looking black dress, then a pair of high-heeled shoes – my hand burrowed further – what was either hair spray or a can of Mace, a bulky make-up bag (I could feel the sharp objects of beauty inside), a purse, a bikini wrapped in a towel, a pair of handcuffs, and something that was either a nightstick or a large dildo.

Shit, I said, from my seat on the toilet, imagine getting embroiled with a cop. Or a hooker. I wasn't sure which was worse. She was probably a girl of some pretty coarse and lively sexual habits. Which was fine, except that I couldn't remember any of them. I pulled out the purse and unzipped it. A few hundred pounds in cash, some photographs of her and other girls, her driver's licence and a passport. I flicked it open. From the picture she was unrecognizable, not that I was in the least bit confident that I could pick her from an identity parade if called upon to do so immediately, looking about sixteen. Blonde, though. So, she was either natural or an early adherent to the peroxide.

Her name was Siobhan Hope – that name didn't register at all, wasn't she supposed to be called Etta or something? – and she was born in June 1970 (I made a mental note of the date), in Bellshill. I kept delving though her purse but there was no sign of any other ID, just a few business cards for a club called The Break. Evidently she had some connection, either that or was an enthusiastic fan.

Very carefully I tucked everything back into her purse, put her bag back together and stood up, catching sight of my face in the mirror, which looked puffy as though shot full of steroids. Then I began to run the water and wondered where, firstly, I was going to get some aspirins, prayed that that was the worst of it and I wouldn't be needing penicillin shots, then whether I had paid the bill for the room. Suddenly I felt the pit of my stomach heave. What the fuck had I done with the gun? Was it still in my jacket?

I tiptoed back into the room, past the comatose body in the bed, and searched for the coat. No sign. I felt like throwing up. Then a brief flash of consciousness from the night before came back to me. Tentatively I opened the cupboard door; it was hanging up and when I patted it I could feel the rough outline of the pistol. A huge surge of relief washed through me and I sat, rather too heavily, back on the bed. Siobhan grunted and turned behind me.

I'll need to get you checked out, Siobhan, Barbie Sister, I said to myself, and then, well, it's still early and I could snuggle back inside the covers for a little while, see if I can reawaken any memories. I shuffled round the bed and gently pulled the covers back, taking in her narrow back and the blonde down at the base of her spine. By the time I had slithered in behind her and put my hands round on to her breasts I had an erection you could bunt with in the World Series. And my hangover was getting better already.

10

Yet another video company with a storefront and three floors on top, just off Sydney Street, in a boulevard which went nowhere, abruptly terminating at a breakers' yard where dogs howled at night in frustration because they had run out of rats and intruders. The windows of the store had been painted out, in a deep cerise, and inside them an alarmed metal window screen deterred entry. The steel security entrance was monitored by closed circuit cameras and was only opened in response to a push on the bell, or a four figure code on the computer alarm entry panel. The company's name, in gold filigreed lettering, was embossed on a plaque over the door, reachable only by graffiti artists with stepladders or abseiling equipment. There was no welcome mat.

Glen Lodge closed the door behind him as he came out and heard the electronics hum as the locks went home. Most of the day had gone, an unaccustomed sunset was breaking out, the sky looked scorched, filaments of grey-black cloud hung like smoke, a blood orange beyond, and a haze of exhaust pollution spread like a stain above the overpass. Lodge was dressed in code – an easy one to tap into, or break – burgundy Doc Martens boots, faded jeans, a blue and black check shirt over a white tee shirt. His hair, what was left of it in a crescent surrounding a bald dome, was cut military-close and he had a grey-flecked moustache with just a trace of a twirl at the ends. His face was whey-white, his eyes piercingly blue and

207

he wore a gold stud in his right ear. And although he looked forty-five, he was ten years younger.

Glancing around him, staying close to the edge of the pavement, he walked quickly to his car, a thirty-year-old Volvo with column change, which he had had re-sprayed from the original dried blood colour to aubergine. The interior had also been re-done, in tan and kid leather. It smelled to him of chastisement. Inside, the car was overpoweringly scented – he had several different and contrasting ersatz natural air fresheners hanging from knobs and buttons. He wound down the windows before turning the key in the ignition. The engine coughed and shuddered, then caught, and the gearbox gave a satisfactory clunk as he engaged it; as it took off, the old bus seemed to sigh gently.

As he drove, Lodge thought of the shower he was going to have when he got home, then a glass or two of wine and a meal later, a take-away, Japanese perhaps, then – well, anything but watch more TV. He yawned, his eyes were tired, still full of pictures; he searched for the tinted glasses in the glove compartment and fumbled them on. Anyway, he told himself, the traffic at this time was light and he would be home shortly, to the shower, the needle jets – he could almost taste the cold wine – it was just a pity that there was no one, for now, to share it all with.

As he turned into Mead Street, which rippled up the hill for almost a mile, he was aware of the smell first. It took a few seconds to register as his nose crinkled. Like ashes, burned-out timber, the acrid smell of smoke coming off sodden branches.

The car tipped over another small hill and the first thing he noticed was the knot of bulky vehicles, the blinking blue lights, then the barriers across the street. His eyes swung across left, to the trees, which were blackened and leafless and petrified, and then to his house, the smoking tangled ruins of it, through the showers of hose water the firefighters were casually raining down. He felt a giddy rush, his eyes filled with tears and he started sobbing and banging his head on the steering wheel as the big car slewed to a halt.

'Get the dirt track racer a Largactyl and get him the fuck out of here,' Hamish Hennessy was telling his partner, Carl Rae. 'I have no time for it.'

'Aw, come on Ham. I can't do that. I need to take a statement and he keeps crying and bawling and grabbing at my lapels.'

'Barbie dolls,' Hennessy said once more, shaking his head. He was a touch over six foot, a scowling black man, almost the only one on the force, with a sour disposition which only became sunny, according to his partner, at the sight of blood.

'That's what he says.' Rae was fingering his lapels thoughtfully. He was wearing a brown suit and a navy tie with a gold pin through it, all of which he wore every day. Only the shirts differed, and usually the underwear. He had five years left before he collected his pension and he was not going to let anything – neither shot nor shell, nor his partner's demeanour and certainly not unnecessary expenditure on working clothes – get in the way of a smooth passage to it.

'Five thousand of them?'

'Nearer six.'

'All in the pyre.'

'He reckons they're worth over a million. Seriously. He says, between choking into the Kleenex and fiddling with his moustache, that he has the finest collection in the world. Everything. Dating back to the 1950s. Barbie as a Braniff Airline stewardess, Barbie in Jackie Kennedy pillbox hat, Barbie—'

'Jesus, Carl,' Hennessy screeched, grabbing at his hair.

'And they're not insured.'

'Well, my God. And what a fuckin' loss to popular cultural history.' Hennessy was smiling one of his thin, misfortune

209

enjoying smiles. 'All of that burned plastic, too. There's probably a new hole in the ozone layer a thousand miles over his house by now. Look out for the rocketing skin cancer rate in the neighbourhood. The lucky ones, the survivors'll end up lookin' like me. Mind you,' he smiled even more crookedly, 'in the case of the fuckin' toe-toucher, the arse bandit, it'll not be melanoma that'll get him, but the Big A.'

'You're a bigot, Ham.'

'I'm allowed to be. I'm black.'

Rae was going through his pockets, looking for some of that nicotine chewing gum. 'What the fuck am I supposed to do here? You know, we're meant to be partners. No one'd dare carpet you, the PC-DC, but they'd chew ma balls like Wrigleys.'

Intuitively, Hennessy took out a pack of Silk Cut and began waving them in front of his partner's eyes, smiling the torturing smile again. 'Christ, Carl,' he sneered, 'I don't know. Take him down to Toys 'R' Us or something. Who cares?'

Three hours later Glen Lodge had calmed down and made a statement, which only ran to one side of paper. The reason he had calmed down was because the initial verbal report from the fire officer, listing arson as the certain cause of the fire, had come in and he seemed in no doubt that the entire family tree of Barbies had not perished horribly in the flames. It looked likely that they had been removed prior to the fire being set.

Lodge's account amounted to little more than that he had got up, gone to work and come back. The dolls were still there when he left, he was sure of that. Now Lodge was clutching a paper cup of coffee and attempting a watery smile. 'Where there is life there is hope,' he said to Hennessy and Rae.

'Sure,' Hennessy said, between his teeth. 'They probably all eloped with Ken and set up a commune.' And with the next breath, 'You're quite sure they weren't insured?' Thinking, if they were, well, a person might just want to cash in, particularly if he had a limited lifetime, as this one probably had.

'I couldn't afford the premiums,' Lodge replied.

'A million quid, you say? I can hardly believe it.' Rae came in. 'The value. Wish I had hung on to my Rupert the Bear.'

'Or Little Black Sambo,' Hennessy came in.

'A million, more or less. Sure. Easily.' Lodge was focusing on Rae.

'Where would you sell them, these Barbies?'

'I'd never sell them,' Lodge replied, shaking his head quickly, looking on the verge of tears again.

'No, sure,' Rae said. He was leaning against a wall, looking down at Lodge sitting at the desk. 'I'm thinking, if someone steals them, where'd he sell them?'

'Easy. To other collectors. There are magazines, newsletters, the Internet. Most of the serious collectors know each other.'

'And they don't have a serial number or something?' Hennessy asked.

'No, of course not.'

'What d'ye mean "of course not"? So how should I know? In our mud-hut scheme we played with the white man's beads and matches and packets of salt.'

'It's rarity value?' Rae asked quickly, trying to smooth over his partner's insults.

'Exactly.'

'And yours are the rarest?'

'Well, I've got the largest collection and, yes, probably – certainly! Every generation.'

'Generation?' Hennessy said. 'I don't believe this. You got genealogy charts or something?' getting up from his seat facing Lodge and starting to pace impatiently.

'Well, to each their own, Officer,' Lodge said archly.

Hennessy thought about saying, kiss my arse, cunt, then thought that in the circumstances this was probably unwise.

211

'Absolutely and wholeheartedly,' he said, vigorously nodding his head in agreement.

'Look, whoever took these would have to know where to sell them, right? He'd have to know who to go to? Unless—' Lodge tailed off.

'Unless what?' Hennessy asked.

'If he was holding them hostage or something.'

'What?' Hennessy was holding his head in both hands, mouth wide open. 'Fuck this,' he said, grabbing the door handle. 'I'm going for a coffee. Get an APB out on Ken.'

'I'm entitled to proper police invest—' Lodge was saying to the disappearing back and then the slamming door.

'It's OK,' Rae said, sliding into his partner's still warm seat. 'He gets a little fractious sometimes. Someone probably stole the doll from his pram when he was a kid. Nothing personal.' He tried a smile, but it looked a little like he was passing wind. 'Now look, someone obviously had to have known about your collection. Other collectors, of course – but, anybody else?'

Lodge was fiddling with a button on his plaid shirt. 'I didn't make any secret of it.' He turned his palms upwards and shrugged. 'Most people who know me know about them.'

'Terrific. Neighbours? Friends? Workmates—' Lodge was nodding vigorously. '—Look, I huvtae say this, what about a lover or lovers? Anyone spurned, maybe trying to get, eh, *his* or *her* own back?'

Lodge smiled. 'Come on,' he said knowingly, with a conspiratorial curled smile. 'But no, I'm quite sure not, Officer.'

Rae ran a hand over his head. 'I'm going to need a list, sir. I know that's gonnae take for ever. So what I'm gonnae do is take a run over to your house, talk to your neighbours, see if they saw anything. You know, it must have taken a pretty big bus to move all those dolls, yeah? In daylight too. Must have been seen.'

212

Lodge was nodding again, more slowly, biting down on his lower lip. 'Officer Rae, my house . . . ? Where am I going to stay tonight?'

Rae paused, looking back over his shoulder. Fucking far away from me buddy, he thought, trying to put on a concerned expression as he shrugged and once more made for the door.

Carpenter idly stirred her cup of sugarless black coffee. She was thinking about how, when she was a kid at table, if her grandfather was visiting and her hands were visible above the edge of it, he would let his teaspoon heat up in the cup, then press it on the back of her hand. It was meant to teach her table manners. All it taught her was to keep her hands below deck when he was there and hate him when he wasn't. Now she took the spoon out, let the coffee drip off it and then held it against the back of her left hand, biting on the pain until it died away. Pointless. What did it prove? Even today she didn't have very good table manners.

She looked up and motioned to the waiter who hovered around the hotplates, where great sliding metal domes like Jodrell Bank telescopes were keeping the earlier prepared food hot. He arrived soundlessly. 'Madam?'

'I've decided that I would like a croissant, just the one. Heated, if you can manage it.'

'Jam? Cheese?'

'No, just the croissant.' She hadn't been in the city for a week and she had already worked out that the dietary choices were not what she was used to, and were often deadly. Before she came, she'd thought that the deep-fried Mars bar in batter was one of those tabloid inventions, or perhaps a local fish and chip shop trying to bring some free publicity, but now she wasn't at all sure.

The morning paper, *The Herald*, was lying folded beside her plate. She could see, even from the half of the headline on the splash, that the killings were the main story. Unfolding the broadsheet she quickly scanned the main piece.

Not a lot of sympathy for the victims. A reprise of their criminal records, informed speculation – undoubtedly a police leak – that the two had been principal suspects in the Microwave Murder, as they were calling it (there were pictures of the murdered girl and baby), and had been interviewed, fruitlessly of course, by detectives. There was more speculation that the shootings were the first seasonal indication of yet another drugs war breaking out – there was a long inside history, complete with police mug-shots and scene of crime stuff, of previous victims – and a panel piece, an interview with the Chief Constable centring on just how armed crime and lawlessness would be driven from the streets. Yeah, yeah, Carpenter muttered to herself.

Well, well!' She started at the voice coming from over her shoulder. 'Fancy meeting you here.'

He was standing over her, grinning, looking blearyeyed and almost engaging, with a bottle-blonde, over made-up, tartily dressed girl in a tight jersey and short leather skirt under a leather biker's jacket, but extremely pretty for all that. She felt irked not, she told herself, about the girl but by Downe, bloody Downe, pushing her, needling her. 'What's all this about? Can't you just leave me alone?'

'Sorry,' Downe was talking to the girl, 'she's always crabby in the morning. That's why I left her and sent back the wedding presents.' A flicker of confusion ran over the girl's face.

'Grow up,' Carpenter said crossly. 'We barely know each other. And that's the way I'd like to keep it,' vehemently, almost hissing at him.

'We're in business together,' Downe was talking to the girl. 'Tell Siobhan what it is we do.'

'Go away. Just leave me alone. Or I'll call the manager.'

214

'About what? That a fellow guest was just exchanging pleasantries?'

'Christ,' she said under her breath

'What is the business?' the girl, Siobhan, asked. And then, looking at Downe, 'I thought you were an actor?'

'An extraordinarily bad and one-dimensional one.' Carpenter was looking around for the waiter, hoping that he would arrive with the croissant and break this up, but he had disappeared. Probably outside having a fag, she thought crossly.

'She's my agent,' Downe was smiling down at her, 'so you can see why I only ever get the worst parts. I'm the permanent spear-chucker in the chorus.'

Siobhan looked from one to the other, confused about what was going on. 'Er, right. Nice to meet you—?'

'Karen,' Downe came in, 'Carpenter. Your mother's probably got her records, Princess Di got the diet plan.'

'Sorry?' Siobhan now looked puzzled and embarrassed.

'It's a bad joke,' Carpenter gave her a brief smile, 'and it's not Karen. It's Meg. I'm sorry about him.' She threw Downe a look. 'You're probably only just getting to be. What is it you do, Siobhan?'

'Nothing much, really. Work in a nightclub.'

'Yes? Called?'

'It's called The Break. Dunno why. It was called something else, but friends of mine took it over recently and asked if I wanted a job. So,' she smiled and shrugged, 'why not?'

'What did you do before?'

'Bit of modelling, you know.'

Carpenter thought that, indeed, she did know. 'Well, it's nice meeting you.' She got up from the table and turned to Downe, who was grinning broadly behind the girl. 'You! I need to talk to you later.'

'Your room or mine?'

Carpenter stretched down under the table, rummaged in a

215

handbag and came out with a purse and a pen. From inside the folds of the purse she pulled a small notebook and jotted a number on the first sheet, tore it off and handed it to Downe. 'A mobile. Call me this afternoon.' She stood up and pointed to the folded newspaper on the table. 'You've got excellent reviews for once.'

'But no curtain calls,' Downe said to her back as she walked away.

'Just call me,' without even looking back.

It wasn't until I was actually in the lobby of the hotel that I even realized it was the same one she was staying in. Some mischief must have come over me the previous night to decide to come here, either that or it was the only one I could name in my stoned state, but when I walked into the dining-room I couldn't resist the wind-up. After a life mainly of circumscription and blind obedience it felt liberating to be anarchic and challenging. A part of me also thought that if I could wrong-foot and embarrass her, rail and disconcert her, it might compromise her. I didn't really believe that, but doing it made me feel better. And anyway, I knew that someone older, more devious and less humane would only replace her. 'She doesn't show it,' I said to Siobhan, 'but she adores and respects me.'

'Well,' said the bubblehead on my arm, 'she definitely can't have screwed you, then.'

Rae had dropped his partner at a café, which was against regulations but it was worth the risk not to have him around, and now he was outside the video company, staring at the door, looking for a bell to press. There was something about this case which fascinated him. Not the gay trappings, although maybe that was part of it, but just finding a satisfactory end to the tale. It was compulsive. So, what did *he*, Lodge, do with these fucking dolls? Rae asked himself.

Did he take them out to play, change their clothes, cuddle them, put them down to sleep for the night? And what attracted him to these plastic confections to begin with? Some aberrant gene? It couldn't have been prescience. You didn't naturally seize on a Barbie doll thinking, this would be a good investment for the future. There was definitely something warped and misbegotten involved, and decidedly sexual.

He found the bell and began pressing it.

And what about the guy who stole them? Or guys. Gays! It had to be males, he was sure of that. This wasn't just a commercial job. Who in the world knew these fuckin' things were valuable? It was personal, it had to be. Someone who knew Lodge, knew how it would tear him up, someone trying to get back at him. A lover, maybe, or former lover? A rival, perhaps? Rae didn't want to speculate too closely about that. So, what if he was homophobic? All cops were, he just kept it hidden better than Hennessy.

A rasping near the door, what sounded like a metallic voice, alerted Rae to a tiny speaker. 'Police,' he said to the serrated grille. And why burn down the place? The fire officer was absolutely sure it was arson, and a crude one. A few gallons of petrol and a box of matches, hardly sophisticated. Which all added up to more evidence of malice.

The door buzzed again, but in a different key. Rae pushed it and it swung open. He stepped inside, looking up a flight of stairs, at the top of which a man stood; he looked to be in his early thirties, slim, bulbous nose, gelled hair, moustache, with faded jeans held up by suspenders. Jesus, Rae thought, mechanically going inside his jacket to retrieve his ID, another bender.

'Detective Rae,' he said, starting to climb the stairs, 'Strathclyde police. I'm here about . . .' he paused, thinking, I can't say about the kidnapping of six thousand Barbie dolls. 'I understand,' he readjusted as he reached the landing, 'that Glen Lodge works here.'

217

'A terrible thing,' the man said, holding out his right hand in greeting and motioning with his other for Rae to follow him, 'they were the love of his life.'

'Mister, eh?' Rae asked, puzzled.

'Call me Arnaud.' The other man had finished enthusiastically shaking Rae's hand and was leading him into a small office, done out in a squashed tomato coloured decor with lots of movie posters, mostly of Stallone it seemed, a pair of oxblood leather chesterfields, at least three computer screens and a massive flat screen TV and video player, notably larger than your normal household model. There was music playing somewhere. Rae recognized Edith Piaf. Arnaud (what kind of name was that?) was motioning to a seat on a chesterfield, which he took, spreading himself, hoping that the other man was not going to sit next to him. Evidently noting his defensive body language, he didn't.

'What were, Arnaud?' he said. 'The love of his life? Glen Lodge's?'

'His collection, of course.'

'A terrible thing, you said.' Rae felt the leather squeak under him as he moved in his seat. 'What did you mean?'

Arnaud – Rae made a mental note to find out whether this was a first or second name – had perched on the arm of the settee opposite, with his hands on his knees. Rae noticed that his fingers were long and thin, the nails neatly clipped and buffed and that he wore what looked like a white gold ring on his wedding finger. Arnaud shook his head slowly, as if he couldn't believe the cop could be so slow on the uptake, or maybe because that was exactly what he expected. 'The fire . . . the theft of those stupid dolls.'

'You knew about that?'

Arnaud got up and walked over to one of the computer desks and picked up a tabloid newspaper. 'I take it you haven't seen the paper, Detective?' Emphasizing the last word, like Rae couldn't really be much of one. He held the

218

paper up like an exhibit, a wanted poster, or a crib sheet for a child. Even from his seat Rae could make out a fuzzy colour picture of Lodge, at least, he assumed that it was him from the bold check shirt and the bald dome above.

'Sorry, Mr Arnaud—'

'No, it's Arnaud – Arnaud Weston.'

'I didn't read it. I didn't realize, Mr Weston. Arnaud.' What kind of fucking name was that? Weston put down the paper and returned to his perch on the settee. 'They say these dolls are worth more than a million pounds; is that the case?'

'I don't really know, but I doubt it.'

Rae sorely wanted to move the conversation on. 'Tell me, what is it that you do here?'

Weston put his right hand against his chest. 'Me, personally? I'm the manager.'

Rae nodded. 'And the company?'

Weston attempted a brief smile. 'We make and distribute videos. You know.'

Rae played with his own smile. 'No. Tell me.'

'Oh, import and export. Tape duplication, mostly. Some adult stuff.'

Ah, Rae thought, of course. 'Porn.'

Weston smiled that hasty smile again. 'Nothing illegal. Tasteful, arty.'

'Aren't they all? And Lodge, what did he do here? Was he the taste or the art?' The tart?

'Detective Rae, this is a small company. Only four of us. So we all do a bit of everything. Editing, duping, producing, even shooting.'

A bit of everything, Rae said to himself. Sure. 'But, of course, you handle the money and the paperwork.'

'Of course, Mr Rae.' The smile was wider now.

'Did everyone here know about Lodge's collection?'

'Sure. It was one of his few topics of conversation.' The edge of sarcasm was clear.

'You didn't like him?'

'Oh, is he dead, then?' Weston said disingenuously. 'That's strange, he called in an hour ago to say he wasn't coming in today.'

Rae bit back a retort. 'You wouldn't call yourself close friends?'

'He was my employee, not a friend, Detective.'

This was going nowhere. 'I'm going to have to talk to all the others here—'

'Of course.'

'Just one more thing – two more actually, for now. Don't get me wrong here, Mr Weston, but were you around here all day yesterday? Did you go out at all?'

'You don't—'

'I have to ask, Mr Weston. Arnaud.' Trying a reassuring look.

'Well,' he paused longer than seemed necessary, 'I had to go out a few times, of course. Deliveries, meetings, that kind of thing.'

'And you can account for the times and places, the people you saw?'

'You mean, do I have an alibi?' Weston was on his feet, hands thrust in his pockets. Rae leaned back and crossed his legs. Mock relaxed. 'Do you think I would be interested in a bunch of tawdry little knick-knacks in frocks?'

Frocks? Not ordinarily, he thought. 'I have to ask these questions, Mr Weston, you must know that.'

Weston turned his back, and Rae could see a hand worrying at his lip or moustache, then he turned back. 'Sure. I'm sorry. Maybe I could jot down the approximate times I was out, who I saw.'

'That would be very helpful.'

'You said there were two things, Detective.'

Rae uncrossed his legs and stood up. 'Do you have a van here, Mr Weston, something like that?'

'Yes. Why?'

'I'll need to get a look at it, after I talk to your other staff.'

'Sure,' said Weston, motioning with his hand towards the door, looking, Rae was sure, just the slightest bit ruffled.

When I was about eleven I started to go to the fights. There was a Friday night fistic emporium a few streets away in what I think used to be an old Catholic church hall. It wasn't usually much of a bill, a few young kids, mostly black, and a few gnarled old pugs on their way to the welfare line, to double vision and hearing bells ring and crowds roar in their heads in the middle of the sidewalk. The shows were put on by an old pro called Lonnie Maxwell who had a gym a couple of blocks away, amazingly enough called Lonnie's. I began to hang out there. I figured, one day I'm going to be big enough to dig my old man back and I ought to have the pugilistic wherewithal to go with the bravado.

The fighters at the gym sort of took me under their wing, as did old Lonnie. He must have been in his sixties then, a shock of white hair, a face that showed the effect of several good years in the ring and a lot of bad, with a remarkable belly which looked like he had a medicine ball stuffed up his sweater. He let me bang around on the bags and the speedballs and when he saw that I had a measure of dedication and aptitude, that it wasn't just a passing fancy, he began to coach me. He was better at teaching than I was at listening – my instinct was always to tear into the other guy and damn the consequences – but gradually caution and artifice were dinned into me and I became a pretty good scrapper. If I had taken wider messages from the lessons I wouldn't be where I am now, but somehow I've always been open to the chin-punch and never been able to live my life behind a defensive left jab.

Call me an old sentimentalist, but I've always liked fighters. Most of them have a brutal honour and decency and a code of ethics which might not sit well in the dining-room but gives examples to follow in the wider reaches of the moral landscape. Which is how I came to Alex Morrison's gym in the East End, just past the Barrowland, where the fighters inside are a mix of amateurs and pros still banging their hopes into a misshapen leather bag.

Morrison's gym is above his garage, through a narrow door and up a flight of stairs, where heavy bags and speed balls hang from the ceiling and young men punish them, and themselves, under yellow electric light. The floors are at odd angles, the gym is all mismatching planes, unfolding room and nooks and crannies. It looks like a historic throwback; you expect the fighters pummelling leather to be Kid Gavilan or Willie Pep, but it is exactly where the serious business of inducing insensibility in another should be learned. Boxing is dying, and probably rightly, but there are a few here raging and swinging against the light going out.

I had heard about it from Barbie over breakfast. She mentioned it in passing as a place where some of the bouncers from her club went. I had established that she was a hostess, and occasional exotic dancer, which probably meant expensively wining the customers, showing her wares and then charging highly for them, but I didn't enquire too deeply. Well, it seemed churlish. And she might have told me, which should have demanded reciprocity, and I was too hung-over and taffeta-headed to come up with a decent lie.

So here I was at Morrison's, in the late afternoon, looking for intelligence and a suitable man to track a particular lady.

'How's it gaun?' The man asking was in his fifties, carrying the signs of leather gloves all over his face. He looked like he might have been a middleweight but had blown-up substantially. He was wearing an old, grey, hooded sweater which pressed around his ample belly, the lettering on the front of which was almost washed away. He was holding out his hand. 'Wullie Peters.'

222

'Downe—' I shook his hand. 'John.'

'States?' I nodded. 'Hope you've no come to steal ma boys away.'

'Me? Nah. Just looking around.'

'D'ye do a bit yersel? Scrappin'?'

'A bit. But Marquis of Queensberry it ain't.' I noticed a large ring set at the back of the room, a young Asian guy in headgear taking swings at a punching pad held by a trainer; another white boy, looking like a lightweight, also with head protection, was climbing into the ring. There was a large sign on the wall behind the ring saying, 'if in doubt stick the left hand out'.

'There's a few here who'd huv trouble wae the rule book as well. Unless they were hittin' ye wae it.' The white and the Asian boy in the ring were now ladling into each other, with the trainer acting as referee.

'If I got some kit could I maybe come back later for a workout?'

'Sure. Nae problem. Y'could batter some bags or ah'm sure we could find someone your size to gie ye a squerr go.'

'Good. I haven't done a proper workout—' I was thinking, since prison, '—I dunno, for months. Too much indulgence since.' As I watched, the white lad sat smartly on his pants, caught by a left-hand bolo punch under his guard. The Asian boy was prancing around, arms in the air, feet doing a shuffle, like the young Muhammad. I smiled. 'That lad looks pretty neat,' I nodded towards the ring.

'Limited technique, but he's got a good dig and a heart the size of a house. Totally fearless.'

'He's a pro?'

'Just starting out. Only twenty, three fights, all blood and snotters. Stopped them all.'

'What's he do during the day?'

'Not a lot, except train. Occasionally helps a cousin out in a shop. His parents have retired and gone back to Pakistan.

223

Says he's not going to see them until he's carryin' a title belt.'

'D'you think he could do with a little extra cash over a few days? It's nothing crooked. It's more in the line of being a watchman.'

'Sure. Ah'll introduce you. His name's Naddy Ahmed, Nadeem.' He walked a few paces closer to the ring. 'Naddy! Hey, showboat! Get your arse ower here, therr's a man wants to hire you tae guard his property, or his life, or somethin'. Even pey ye in pounds and no rupees.'

Naddy jumped out of the ring, thumbed off the catch of his head guard with a gloved hand and then held out the right glove, palm up, which I slapped. 'An' whit dae they ca' ye, big man?' The smile was about as long as his reach and it got to you just the same.

11

It wasn't so much a crime as a cry for help. By the time Rae had interviewed Weston's staff, two surly middle-aged men who seemed to be a couple – Rae deduced this by the way they kept bickering and disagreeing – and the secretary, a young and efficient woman in her twenties, he had a fairly good picture of Weston's movements. Which barely coincided with the account of his itinerary the manager had given him. All of the staff were convinced that Weston had been out for most of the afternoon as Lodge worked away in the editing suite, while Weston claimed to have been in his office hitting the telephone and poring over accounts.

Rae was deeply pissed off now at Hennessy, because nothing he had been told was admissable, due to the lack of a corroborative witness to it. Who should have been Hennessy. He had also picked up in his conversations – more by what had been glossed-over rather than confirmed – that Weston and Lodge had, until recently, been more than workmates. He had also checked out the van, a small 15 cwt. Escort, but could find nothing during a cursory once-over. He considered calling in the forensic lab, to scare Weston more than in the hope of coming up with anything (by now Rae was virtually convinced that this fire was to do with the extinguishing of the flames of passion) but decided this would almost certainly be a waste of time.

Now he was standing leaning over the unmarked car, a neutral-coloured Cavalier, punching into his car phone the number of Hennessy's mobile. 'I need you now.' He could hear chatter in the background and the thump of a jukebox. 'We're going to lift someone.' He gave Hennessy the address and hung up, then went back inside and asked for Weston. When he arrived, a too-bright smile on his face, Rae said, 'Get your coat please, sir, we're going to make a visit when my partner arrives in a couple of minutes. He's been checking out a lead in the case.'

Rae watched Weston's smile waver and plummet; he looked as if he was about to say something, then shook his head and turned away.

When he came back, wearing a dark brown leather jacket with a fur collar, Rae led him to the car, opened the nearside back door, allowed Weston to climb in, then slammed it and slipped into the driver's seat. He adjusted the mirror so that he could see Weston, or at least his eyes, in it.

'Where – where are we going?' Weston seemed on the edge of tears. Clearly he felt that it was going to be the station.

'Your place,' Rae said into the windscreen, his eyes focused on the mirror.

'Why?'

'For a look around. Any objections?'

'Objections?' Rae could see Weston's pupils flitting around worriedly. 'No. I don't think so. But shouldn't I – shouldn't you—'

'Look, I can get a warrant with just one call. But that would indicate hostility on your part. And let me tell you,' he sighed and smacked the steering wheel, 'my partner can get pretty—' he let it hang, '—pretty unreasonable in the face of hostility. I should warn you,' he paused again, 'he's got what you might call a biblical aversion to homosexuality. Just cannot get his head round it, tends to rant and rave. But don't worry about it too much. It takes a lot to really get him going.'

'R-r-really going?' Weston's eyelids were doing a rapid dance.

'Believe me, as a police officer he's the best kind of partner. I mean, look at me, I haven't too long to go and I'm not exactly built for streetfighting. I'm careful, too. I've got a pension coming up that I want to have a decent pop at enjoying.' He shook his head. 'Sorry, I'm rambling. Anyway, Hennessy just steams right in. Merest hint of trouble and he just pours in on top of it. Like a half-ton of nutty slack. Actually, that's probably not the best simile. He's black. And sensitive. And of course if you pour a half-ton of coal on a combustible situation you've got a major conflagration on your hands.' He laughed and shook his head, eyes still searching out Weston's. 'Yup, that's my Hamish all right. A roar and a rumble and he's straight down the chute on top of it.' He chuckled again and rubbed the wheel. 'He'll be here any minute now. I'd just play down the camp thing.'

Rae heard a strangled cough behind him and the rustling of clothes followed by the sounds of a nose being blown heavily. Weston had slipped out of his view. He looked back over his shoulder and saw him concentrating on the expectorant in his handkerchief, biting his lip.

'Can – eh, can I m-make a call?' Weston's voice was trembling.

'Telephone or nature?' Rae eased himself back into the driving position. 'Why d'you want a lawyer, Mr Weston?' He shook his head again. 'God, there's nothing Hennessy hates worse than a lawyer. Except, of course, a gay lawyer.' He turned back to Weston again. 'We have all these awareness tutorials on the force, you know, race, creed, sexual orientation, but I don't think much of it gets through to many of the polis.' He turned his head, hearing a car approach. 'Good. That'll be him now. And then we can really get moving.'

Weston shrivelled back into the seat.

He lived in a large sandstone villa on the south side. It was hidden behind a waist-high wall and a mass of rhododendrons, a gravel-chip drive ran up to it and to a wooden garage built alongside. The main storm doors were shut. They were painted a heaving shade of vermilion, and there was a closed-circuit camera over them. It struck Rae as off, as well as ostentatious. How much did a manager of a video house make? Less than thirty, he imagined and yet here was this place, in the best part of King's Park, which couldn't have left change out of three hundred thousand. So, maybe he had wealthy parents? But why the camera? Hey, he thought, maybe he likes to perform unseemly acts on the front lawn for it.

The two policemen slammed the doors of the car and began taking in the house and the gardens, leaving Weston still locked in the back seat. He hadn't said a word on the journey, just clung to himself in the back seat behind Rae, and Hennessy hadn't uttered a syllable either, just grunted and mumbled to himself as they cut through the streets to the house.

'Thinkin' what I'm thinkin'?' Rae said.

'I doubt it.'

'That all of this didn't come from that video company?'

'Either he's got money in the family or he's won the lottery recently. Or—'

'I was thinking that maybe there's more to the company than there appears at first sight.'

'Fuck movies?'

'For sure.'

'Drugs?'

'Worth turning the place over.'

'Absolutely. After we've done this one.'

Hennessy walked over to the front doors of the garage, breathed on one of the glass panes, rubbed it with the sleeve of his jacket, and peered in. Then whistled.

'Ham?'

228

'Two-car garage. Looks like a brand new Shogun and a beautiful old Jag, XK150, looks like.'

'More conspicuous wealth.'

'Let's roust the fag.'

'Just keep your hands off him, Ham.'

'Absolutely. I left the plastic gloves at home.'

Inside, the house was, of course, immaculate. Not your distempered walls and plain and tasteful carpeting, but rooms done out in bold and warm colours – the colour combinations were unimaginable to the two detectives – but they worked. The walls of the huge living room (Rae thought, entirely with malice, that it was bigger than the whole ground floor of his house), were painted a deep red which ought to have induced catalepsy but instead suffused the room with energy. The effect was muted, Rae noted, by the collection of oils and watercolours, all of which looked original, all of which suggested expense. He noted also the tastefully positioned sculptures and carvings and the furnishings, huge plump sofas, antique table and cabinets, which must have cost more than his house.

Weston slumped into a sofa. 'Well?' he said.

'The family home?' Rae was looking around, deliberately trying to imply that he was impressed, which wasn't hard.

'What?' Weston came out with an insulted choking laugh. 'Hardly. My parents live in an insufferably dreary upstairs flat in a four-in-a-block in Arden.

'Really?' Hennessy was cocking his head like a parrot gazing at an abstract. 'Bet when you were growing up you got a lot of doings.'

'Because I'm gay?'

'Did I say that?'

Weston, probably because he was in his own surroundings, seemed to have recovered a little of his confidence. 'What is it you want?'

229

'I want the key to the garage, if it's locked,' Rae smiled at him.

Weston thought about it, then dug in his pocket and threw a bunch of keys which Rae snagged. 'It's the Yale, the silver one.'

'I'll leave you with DC Hennessy. Be on your best behaviour.' The fragile patina of self-confidence crumpled and he seemed to sag and burrow into the sofa. 'Do I need other keys to open the cars?' Weston shook his head and pointed at the key-ring Rae was holding.

The garage was immaculately clean, tools were neatly hung up round the walls and the two cars looked spotless. The garage smelled of beeswax, Rae thought, as he opened the Jag, got behind the wheel, taking in the smell of polish and leather and his own fantasies, then uncurled and climbed out to open the Shogun. Immediately he was aware of a faint odour of petrol. He leaned over the back seat and traced it to a petrol can in the storage space behind, which looked to have been opened recently. To get a better look he climbed out of the car, went round to the tail and opened the door.

The container was moulded red plastic, it looked very new, although there was a stain of petrol down the front of it and when Rae leaned down to sniff the carpeting he could detect traces there too. Was there a way of tracing purchases of these petrol containers, he wondered? Because if there was he was damn sure that it had been bought in the last seventy-two hours expressly for one purpose, and probably bought in a garage near Lodge's place.

Time to put a squib up the queer, he thought to himself.

When he got back into the house, Hennessy was sitting on the edge of a chair glowering full beam at Weston, who seemed hypnotized.

'There's a can of petrol in the back of the four-by-four.'

Weston nodded.

'Why?'

230

'What do you mean?'

'The Shogun's diesel.'

Weston looked quickly from one to the other. 'I don't have to say anything.'

'True,' Rae nodded. 'Ham, I didn't give the Jag a proper search. Can you give it the once-over? You know the form.'

Hennessy winked. 'Happy to.'

'It would be much better if you just told me all about it,' Rae said when Hennessy had left. 'Getting your own back, were you? Did he walk out on you, is that how it was? Decided to teach him a lesson?' Weston did not respond, just hugged himself and sank lower. 'What did you do with all his toys? Are they here somewhere? Mmhh?' He walked over to the large bookcase in an alcove behind the television. 'How did you do it? You left work while he was still there, but decided that the van with the name of the company splattered all over it was a bit of a give-away, so you came back here, picked up the Shogun and went on in that? I'll bet we can get a witness placing it there at the time. Also someone who remembers you buying a plastic petrol can or filling it up round about the same time. What do you think?'

He looked up at the hundreds of cased videotapes. 'Fair collection. Anything good?' He waved his finger like a diviner's tool and then picked one at random, grabbed the remote, switched on the TV and the video, then rammed the tape in. 'Really, you should come clean because we're going to put it all together now and if we could tell the judge that you were co-operative – contrite and co-operative – it would probably knock a couple of years off the sentence.'

'I want to speak to my lawyer. Now.'

'Sure, sure. Later. Where are the Barbies, Arnaud? Were you planning to sell them? Or just ransom them? Mmmhh?' He was looking at Weston, trying to drill him with his gaze but his victim was averting his eyes.

231

He heard the door open and looked up to see Hennessy come in. He held what looked like a bundle of envelopes and documents in his hand. 'Check these, will you,' he said to Weston. 'Just confirm that these are the correct papers relating to the car before we check to see if it's stolen or anything like that.'

He handed the bundle to Weston who began to sift through them then stopped, in apparent puzzlement, over a long, thick manila envelope. He held it for a minute, gazing at it, unsure. 'I don't recog—' then he shook his head, peeled back the flap and put his hand inside. And out it came holding a small see-through plastic envelope. 'This isn't—'

'Well, fuckin' hell, Ham,' Rae said, 'and what do you think that is?'

'Jesus, Rae—'

'You planted it, you planted it!' Weston was screaming. 'I've never seen it before!' Throwing the packet away.

'Jesus, Jesus,' Hennessy was looking perplexed and thunderous.

'D'you reckon coke or smack, Ham?' Rae was smiling broadly. 'Class A for sure. Tut-tut-tut, Mr Weston, you are going down for a doubly long stretch—'

'For fuck's sake, look behind you!' Hennessy was pointing and grimacing as he did so. 'Jesus Christ!'

Rae turned round and for a second or two didn't know what he was supposed to be looking at, and then when he figured it out he still couldn't quite distinguish what was going on. It looked like a human macrame puzzle. The TV screen was playing back what was clearly – because of the high production values, the pin-sharp focus, the glowing, vibrant colour – one of Weston's company videos. As far as Rae could make it out one love-handled white guy was dog-knotted to a young Asian boy, no more than twelve, while another lumpy white slob tried to give him oral abuse from the front.

He looked away from the screen and to Weston and drew

him a wide smile. 'We can probably forget all about the drugs,' he said. 'Although where you're going, you'll need a lot of painkilling pessaries and AZT because, believe me, your arse will be ragged for about the next ten years.'

'How's your friend?'

'No need to get jealous, Karen.' I had moved alongside her as she stood against the railing beside the walkway at Clyde Street, just down from St Enoch Square. I could remember my mother telling me that there used to be a railway station here, but it had clearly been demolished and some glassed-in shopping mall thrown up in its place.

'Don't call me that,' she said, turning to look at me. 'And don't be stupid. I'm simply against this getting any more complicated than it is already.' A four-man rowing team were sculling in the cold waters below us, warmly wrapped in leggings and, no doubt, thermals. A watery sun sprinkled tiny sparkling beads of light where the oars hit the water.

'It's not complicated. It's just a pastime. You should try it. Want me to show you the ropes, the clinches, the knock-out manoeuvres?' I was hoping that Naddy was checking us out, imprinting her face on his brain, so that he would never forget it.

'Just leave it out, Bone.'

'I prefer Downe. It's softer, less brutal. You might even call me John, after what we've done together.' The wind was light, but it was just enough to ruffle a few of the strands of hair escaping over her forehead.

She had it tied back with a scarf, and was wearing a long, dark, military-style coat – that's if Farhi ever designed for the MoD – which came down below the knee, with black boots disappearing up under it. I could just detect a faint perfume, which had strands of camomile through it. Her face was taut, her eyes huge and fixed on me and I thought, in another life, Downe.

'You and me,' I went on, 'we create death. Another couple, just like us, might make love, or life, but not us. Death. How does that make you feel, Carpenter? It makes me feel depressed, hopeless. I have no innocence left in me. I'm cynical, knowing, I have nothing joyful in me at all. That's why I do the nose and arm stuff, I guess. To forget.'

'To forget what exactly?'

'Dunno. I forget.' I grabbed her face in both my hands and kissed her forehead. She struggled away, pushing. 'Thank you, W. C. Fields, for that one. I've been waiting half my life for just that exchange. Thank you, Carpenter.'

In spite of herself she smiled, then after a few seconds she asked, 'What was your wife like, Downe? Did you treat her well?'

'Odd questions.' The familiar feeling in my stomach, falling, then steadying. 'Isn't it all in my file?' She shook her head. I looked out at the water and the faraway skiff rowing down river. 'I don't know what to say about her. She was pretty, she was bright, she was—' I saw the falling wreckage again and I shivered '—she had her faults but I suppose what I can't really get over is that she seemed so permanently alive—' A young girl laughed somewhere nearby. 'It just shows you how wrong you can be. Have you ever felt that something is entirely meant to be, kismet, and then it's torn away and trashed?' I looked round at her; she shook her head. 'I think that when I got over loathing myself I was good to her. I did something pretty terrible at the start, probably because I was emotionally fucked up, or undeveloped, maybe jealous, but we got over that. Hey,' I tried a smile, 'the drugs helped.' She shook her head and smiled back. 'Did you ever love someone?'

'Maybe. But I don't think so.'

'Then don't, is my advice.' I leaned back against the railing and caught sight of Naddy sitting on a step in the tiny amphitheatre above the walkway. 'There's bound to be a country song to sum it up succinctly, there always is, but right now nothing comes to mind. 'Cept "Get The Biscuits In The Oven And Your Buns In The Bed". Not terribly apt or PC.'

I looked around at her. She, like me, had her back to the river. 'I shared a cell for two years with a good ole boy who sang country songs constantly, usually with a Walkman strapped to his head. And we came to an understanding. I wouldn't kill him if he either chewed Red Man or gum, given that it's difficult to sing with a mouth full of elastic or tobacco juice. Mind you, he often managed it just the same. I came into the cell one day to find him hanging by his shredded, plaited and knotted shirt from a cell bar.' I could still see it plainly. 'Yup, there's probably a country song for that too.' I rubbed my hands together and blew on them. 'I fuckin' hate country music. Anyway, what's this all about, Carpenter? Why'd you choose here anyway, this particular place? Is it something you were taught, or was there a similar scene, perhaps, in one of Le Carré's books?'

'I just like rivers. I came past here yesterday and it seemed, well, normal.'

I breathed in deeply. 'That's cool. The killer and his cohort have a normal day out.' I took her by the elbow. 'Let's walk. It's chilly. And tell me about yourself, the bits that aren't covered by the Official Secrets Act.'

It was beginning to get dark and the street lights came on as we passed the strange sandstone gateway to the underground in the square, and as we dodged across Argyll Street I caught sight of a sign advertising a pub and restaurant, Sloan's. 'This way. There's nothing in the Act about drinking on duty, is there? Or taking a coffee break?'

Sloan's was through a covered alleyway (I seemed to have spent a good part of my time in this city in alleys), and across a cobbled courtyard.

The bar was quiet. I shuffled Carpenter into one of the

velour-padded booths and ordered a mineral water for her and a large whisky for me. The atmosphere was warm and smoky, my nose began running like a faucet, but I knew that the temperature had little to do with it. I pushed the water across to her and sat down opposite. She had taken off her coat and underneath she had on a tight, brown jumper over which the edge of a white silk blouse peeped. A tiny silver pendant with the glitter of diamond hung just below her throat, which gave me an excuse to take in her breasts, which seemed more than adequate to me.

'Right,' I said, 'enough of the pleasantries. Who do you want me to kill now?'

She paused in the tiny sip she was taking from the glass, shook her head. 'It's not that at all. This is more of a warning. You know the dealer you hospitalized, McColl? Well, he's been getting visitors. A couple in particular are leg-men for McGurk. So he'll know all about you by now, if he didn't before.'

I took a deep swig of the whisky, played its fire around my mouth before gulping it down. 'Why don't we just cut to the chase? Why don't I just pay McGurk a visit and then I could be out of here by the weekend.'

'No. That's not how I want it.'

'So, how?'

'This is not just about bringing *him* down, but the whole bloody involved, impenetrable, indestructible operation. As it is just now, if we got rid of him, anyone could step in. His wife's sharp, and hard—'

'We have scruples about stiffing women, do we?'

'And there's a son, in his early twenties. Used to be a junkie, but not any more.'

'So?'

'We've got to make him think that you're acting for someone, that there's a take-over bid going on. There are a couple of smaller operations in town, tolerated so far because

236

it doesn't do to have all the attention on one exclusively, and headed by very ambitious young people. McGurk's in his forties now, and maybe they think he could be mellowing. All right, fat chance, but right now he doesn't know what's going on, except that a couple of his trusties have been taken out. And that an unknown Yank has arrived and busted-up one of his street salesmen. We have to put more questions in his head.'

Someone had stuck money into the jukebox and a disconcertingly familiar song was playing which I couldn't place. When I hummed a few bars to myself I realized that while I couldn't remember the title, it was by Frankie Miller. 'You don't mean there's a price on my head?'

'It would probably be wise if you changed address.'

I looked at her; perhaps I was deluding myself, but there seemed to be just the slightest fuzzy outline of softness in her attitude to me. She seemed less defensive in her posture too, more open.

'I'm sure you've considered this,' I said, 'but McGurk couldn't have risen so successfully and stayed out of trouble for so long without some assistance. From Big Foot.' She looked at me quizzically. 'Your colleagues in uniform. He has to have some employees on the state payroll, or no matter how careful he's become he would have tripped over something along the way.'

'Not lately, not even a parking fine.' She took a sip of her water.

'You agree?'

'I think it's possible.'

Superb, I thought to myself, so if internal corruption was part of the plot then my presence in it must surely be known. 'Look,' I said, pointing at her glass, 'fancy something a bit stronger?'

She gave what I would call a wistful smile. 'Why not. But I'll get them.'

I looked around the bar again, checking the faces, in passing noticing Naddy clutching an orange juice, good Muslim lad, and then at her back as she moved to the counter, and down. She was wearing a tight skirt which skimmed her knees. And she had fine and lengthy legs. Uneasiness struck me cold in the heart.

12

Rae peeled off the Post-it messages stuck to his desk and slumped into the lumpy chair. Hennessy had disappeared again, so he would have to write up the arrest and the confession. He didn't mind. It wasn't often you got such a succinct result. Often? Never. Once they had stuck Weston in the interview room, with just artificial light, the blinking warning from the tape recorder and two hard-eyed, unsympathetic coppers to talk to, it had all come gushing out, tears and the truth.

According to Weston he had meant it all as a frightener – a reprise of the past but this time with vengeance – and it had spun rapidly out of control. What he had intended to do, he maintained, was go round to the house, remove the dolls for a few days (he still had a key to get in, Lodge hadn't bothered to change the locks), just long enough for his ex-boyfriend to have come apart, and then he was going to return them anonymously. He had envisaged the enjoyment he would get out of Lodge's distress, watching him break down a little day by day at work, perhaps he even saw his former partner throwing himself at him for help, but when he let himself in by the front door, leaving the four-wheel drive tucked in under the rowan tree, it had all fragmented. What he saw, so he said, was the spoor of his replacement (although Lodge maintained that that this, too, had been over for ages – well, the sheets were cold and washed), a strange aftershave, perhaps alien handwriting, he couldn't quite recall, and he had gone into meltdown, diving out of the house to the Shogun where there was an emergency can of petrol, splashing it all over the place and then striking the match. Having first removed the dolls, naturally.

Rae didn't believe much of it. To him it had all been planned – carting out the Barbies must have taken ages, and probably more than one trip – but the details didn't matter. Whatever the sequence of intent, he had coughed for it. Had to be worth five years, plus what he would get for the hardcore porn. Rae smiled to himself. There were elements to this he would miss in retirement. But not, he reminded himself, the writing-up of it all.

He stretched back in the chair, then decided to scan his messages before he began. They all said the same thing, see Hovis urgently. 'Urgently' progressively more fiercely underlined. Fuck, he muttered under his breath, and went looking for him.

The DS was in his office. Rae knocked and went in. Hovis was on the phone. He waited, standing, for Brown to motion to a seat before he sat down. His superior was clearly pissed off, he could detect it in his crabbed body language and the short sentences and grunts he was making into the phone. He hung up, slamming the receiver down and swinging round to take in Rae.

'You wanted me, sir?'

'Yes. Oh, yes. Good work by the way. The fiery sodomizer.'

Rae adjusted himself in the seat. 'Easy, sir. I think he wanted to be caught. Remorse, maybe. We found all the dolls in a lock-up garage he has in one of those railway arches on the south side of the Jamaica Bridge. Loads more porn, too. Of all kinds. Not just the single sex variety. It'll take the vice squad about a year to review it all – and, of course, make the copies.' He tried smiling but Brown wasn't responding.

'Look, Rae, I won't mislead you here. There's a problem. We're probably going to have to bail him.'

'You're joking?'

'Sir!'

'You're joking – sir.' He was leaning forward now. 'Bail – probably? Why?'

Brown cast his eyes upwards. 'Orders from on high. I'm no more happy about it than you are. There seems to be a deal going on, at least the bones of one. ' Brown picked up a pencil from the desk and began jabbing it aimlessly at a pile of files next to his trays. 'You're probably aware of this organized crime initiative—?'

Rae shook his head. He was going to let his governor spell it out precisely.

'This all goes way above my head. We have company here, some Home Office-installed spook who's giving the commands. It turns out that Weston's little video project is owned by our friend McGurk. Through nominees, naturally. Just another one of his slimy tentacles. Filming and pirating all kinds of porn – gay, hetero, paedophile, some that probably hasn't been labelled yet – and flogging it through magazines, the Internet, personal contacts, wherever.' He paused, Rae giving him no help by saying anything. 'The feeling is that Weston can perhaps be prevailed on to tell everything he knows about the set-up in return for – for—'

'Immunity? Re-location? That, with respect, sir, is a load of shite. One, he probably doesn't know much and two, he doesn't have the guts to do it. Whatever he might agree to here, with the cells giving him a foretaste of what's to come, when he's out, when he realizes how easy it is for McGurk to reach him wherever he is, he's going to bottle it. We're not talking about someone who's been in the front line, who's had a bit of experience of being under threat; what we've got is some poor, sad wee poof who's involved in something so hideously beyond his experience that he cannae begin to understand it.' He knotted both hands together. 'Jesus, sir, he disnae huv the gumption to keep his mouth shut.' Rae's

241

accent was broadening the more worked-up he became. 'He'll say and do anythin' in here tae get out. He's shitein' himself. But once he's back out in reality, he'll realize he's a dead man. Christ, just bailin' him's enough sign that he's talkin'.'

Brown put down the pencil. 'I don't disagree. But it's not my call, as I said.'

Rae sighed deeply, all of the argument and resistance hissing out of him. 'It's a rotten one, sir.'

Brown shrugged. 'I'll let you know. For the time being we'll just keep him in a cell, lightly decomposing.'

'How did you get into this, Carpenter? You seem otherwise pretty sane and decent.'

'Long story.'

I had bought another round and some nibbles which purported to be of Spanish provenance, bits of roast chicken, vegetables, sauces frisky and tame. It seemed to be some kind of intelligence test, to keep your fingers clean while at the same time avoiding dropping gobbets of chilli on your clothes. When I was at the bar ordering – I threw in a chilled bottle of Chablis, which might not have been the appropriate accompaniment, but my knowledge of Spanish wines is even more hazy than of French – I had a few words with Naddy, like I was being sociable. 'Follow her back to wherever she goes,' I said, as if I was offering a comment about football. I had dropped him fifty quid earlier as expenses.

'It looks like you already know the destination.' He was grinning.

'What?' Involuntarily I had looked back at her in the booth. 'Me? Fat chance.' It was a fine thought, nonetheless.

When I sat down I told her, 'I've read the books,' a little jab with the finger, 'the dependency theory—'

''You mean it wasn't just Marvel comics in the prison library?'

242

'How, when you people turn someone, develop a relationship of some sort, they become slavishly dependent. I'll probably end up sending you valentines or knitting revolting cardigans.' I splashed a measure of the wine into a new glass.

'You should live so long.'

'There is that, of course. How long do you give me?'

'Forget the pension payments. And I wouldn't bother starting on *War and Peace*. Cheers.'

I clinked her glass. 'Try that brown sauce,' I pointed at the tray of dips and bits, 'it's supposed to be eccentric. I think that's what the barmaid said. Or ethnic.'

She carefully picked a piece of chicken, dipped it in the sauce and swallowed. 'Mmhh. Not bad. You?'

I shook my head. 'Go ahead. You could do with a bit of feeding up.'

'What's wrong with me?'

'I'd need closer examination to answer definitively.'

'Get real, Downe.'

I smirked. 'You mean, get real Downe and dirty.'

She dipped another piece of chicken in the sauce and slipped it into her mouth. 'In another life.'

'When you think about it, Carpenter, what better combination could you get? Both of us without illusions, no need for lame explanations, excuses, pretence. You wouldn't be coming in from the office kissing some sad dupe on the forehead and pretending to be a bond trader with a headache. We could exchange useful *aperçus*, you know, the quickest and most effective way of peeling off a fingernail, the finer points of carving off the bone. Bone! A little Freudian there, what?' She reached into her discarded jacket and pulled out a mobile phone. 'No, I insist,' I put my hand on hers which was holding the phone, 'really. I'll book the hotel room.'

'It's still getting a signal,' she said.

'More than I'm getting.'

She put the phone on the table and casually licked a couple of fingers on her right hand. 'Why are you doing this – this, this game?'

I gulped down my glass of wine and re-filled the glass. 'Mind-altering substances. I recommend them, if you're interested.' I took a sip from the new glass. 'I don't know. It beats dreary reality. Truth. We could pretend we were two ordinary, relatively unsoiled people, for instance. Rather than a couple of killers conspiring.' I leaned across the table and whispered. 'It was the way I grew up. I always treated it like it was a play, or a movie, when my old man was hammering me round the room, or whipping me. Trying to keep it outside myself, not letting him humble me, searching for wise lines, spitting out the comebacks with the blood and teeth. Very Jimmy Cagney, it was.'

I leaned back slightly. 'D'you think it's too late for me? Maybe I could go to drama school. What do you think, an actor? The heavy who gets shot in the second reel, the loser who sometimes gets the girl. As long as we can use a body double for the steamy bits.' She looked at me over her glass, and shook her head, slightly puzzled. I leaned closer again. 'Have you ever shot somebody? No? Well, if you have to I recommend acting every time.'

'You're a poor damaged soul, Downe.'

'Forever damned.' I toasted her with the glass and took another swallow. 'Hum it and I'll join in.'

I was just about to suggest that I order a cab, a bottle of champagne and a hot bed – didn't that old Scottish war hero and patriot Robert Bruce counsel that one should repeatedly press one's case, even if the spider, or the state, enmeshed you in its web? – when her phone rang. Saved by the bell. She did a lot of nodding, and ah-ha-ing, then pressed the off button.

'I have to go. Something's come up.' She retrieved the coat from beside her, eased out of the seat and threw it on like a

cape. 'There are things we still need to discuss. Call me later.'
She put the phone into her coat pocket. And then her hand
came out with what seemed to be a folded couple of sheets of
lined paper. 'Read this quickly. I don't want it lost.'

'What is it?' I was distrustful of taking it.

'It's from criminal intelligence. A run-down on McGurk's
businesses, what he owns, his wife, all of it, and the names of
the surrogates running them, of course. You'll be interested
in some of the later additions.'

I did not reach for the paper. 'Come to the point, Carpenter.'

'Seems he's recently taken over somewhere employing that
friend of yours. Siobhan, was it? That club. The Break. Not in
his name, naturally, but it's his. I suppose it cuts the length of
the supply lines if you own a club. Gets the stuff into the
system quicker, saves hawking it about the streets when
you've got a captive audience of young people inside your
own four walls gagging for the product.' I could see she was
enjoying imparting this. 'And if you're insulated from the
consequences, if no one can prove you're behind it and your
ciphers would prefer ten years rather than admitting to it, it's
cosy. What did you say your girlfriend did at the club?' She
threw me a sarcastic smile.

'Carpenter,' I said, refreshing my glass, 'you're jealous!
Such emotional exposure.' I smiled back just as falsely. 'So I
feel I should be honest in return. I've done something disgust-
ing and deceitful. Forgive me.' I was enjoying this.

'I'm waiting,' she stood there, grinning uncertainly now,
looking down at me, the smile fading to a distinct glower. 'Go
on.'

'I don't know if they had this at university when you were
there, or whether you were the kind of girl to indulge, but
you know you can get cannabis oil, in a little tube? A couple
of drops on the skins – that's the cigarette papers in the drug
argot, if you didn't know – is highly recommended. Well, see
that sauce you enjoyed—' I nodded at the tray. 'When I was

245

at the bar getting it, the old sleight of hand trick, abracadabra, the dope bottle down the sleeve and sloshed over the sauce. I should think in an hour from now you'll be seeing more than rabbits coming out of hats.'

13

The Range Rover's sidelights were on. It was the only vehicle parked on the edge of the car park on the brae where the city, through the wet windscreen, was spread out in the darkness below, just a million bleary points of light. Eddie MacIntosh thought that it looked like a shroud shot through by buckshot. But then he was feeling uneasy, with trembling twinges of panic in his stomach. He checked once more the locks were down, not wanting to be caught unawares, the doors torn open and him pulled out and bludgeoned, mugged or raped. Stabbed. Shot. It was stupid but he was almost convinced that there was a severed head in the back of the car. There had been a rolling sound when he drove up there and while he knew that it was almost certainly a can of Wet Start or something, the doubt was growing stronger that he was kidding himself, that in fact it was the missing top piece of some unmourned corpse.

This scary fantasy had probably come from covering the head in the microwave story; but shite, if even lightning could strike twice, so could fucking microwave killers.

Behind the unease, the problem, he knew, was that he wasn't used to the sounds of nature in the night. Put him in a haunted graveyard overnight and he would be fine, providing it was overlooked by multi-storeys or had sounds of humanity breaking in, like belching and brawling, from nearby. Out here he felt vulnerable and, more than anything, incredibly stupid.

He had been sitting in the car for twenty minutes, with the sidelights and the radio on. But somehow that just made it worse, because he knew that the voices were coming from even farther away than where he had come from. He turned the engine over, just to check it wasn't going to fail if he really needed it; it grumbled and shivered and then settled into a deep rumble.

Five more minutes, he vowed to himself.

It was nearing ten when he saw a glittering flash in his driver's mirror and then the bright white-out as the headlights flooded the car then swung away, scouring the ground alongside before going out. He observed a shape getting out of the other car and then coming alongside the passenger window. He checked in the dim light from the dashboard that it was the right person, then breathed out relievedly and pulled up the lock trigger. The door opened and the man got in. About all that MacIntosh could make out was a glowing crescent of shirt round the neck which reminded him of a dog collar.

'Sorry I'm late. It was difficult to get away.'

'No problem. I've been doing a bit of off-roading while I waited.'

The passenger chuckled, looking round the gleaming interior. 'Why do you want to keep a four-wheel drive in the centre of the city, then?'

'Easy.' MacIntosh looked round. 'Because I can.' He switched off the engine and the lights. 'Look, I'm a bit pushed. I have to get back to the paper. You go missing and they automatically assume you're in the pub. Which used to be a point of reference, and a mark of pride, but now it's a sacking offence. I don't want to have to go through the breathalyser bit and pissing in a jar just to get through the front door.' He noticed the firefly lights of a plane inching across the black sky. 'You had something, you said.'

His man shuffled in the seat, so that the leather squealed. 'I can't give you it all. Some of it you'll have to get by yourself. It's too sensitive, easily traceable. I'm taking a huge fucking risk.'

Yeah, yeah. 'So, why? Apart from the need to get the truth out there, somewhere.' MacIntosh was pointing out into the darkness and thinking: *and most of all, the money*!

'Because this is all going way beyond the law. Out of control. Unmonitored.' MacIntosh waited for him to go on. 'It's like – you remember a few months back all that fuss about the Yardies and the Yard? How they were letting these Jamaican gangsters come and go, getting them off charges, even paying them wages and for flights and rent on the basis that they were giving information on crack deals. And, naturally, the scum were robbing and shooting and scoring and raping—'

'Sure. I remember. The only difference between the Yard and the Yardies was the dreads and the large woolly hats. And those were just the undercover guys.'

'This is a lot worse. I think there's a shoot to kill policy going on.'

MacIntosh couldn't help himself; he gave out a spluttering laugh, recalling the dozens of shootings and gun-related incidents he'd been on in the last months. 'We're fuckin' doomed if the polis have only just noticed.'

'You know what I'm talking about.'

'Not really. That is, I don't see any evidence.'

'All I can do is lead you.'

'At this point I'm not sure if I'm Redford or Hoffman.'

'Sorry?'

'Nothing. Just a journo-reference. Deep Throat. Here, Deep Thrapple'd be more appropriate.'

'Jesus, Ed, what are you on about?'

'I'm sorry, why don't you just tell me what you're able to and then I'll ask the questions.'

'It can't get back. Not to your editor, not to your confessor, not to—'

'It won't. Trust me. And if not that, well, you're too valuable to lose, for another. It'd be self-destructive. So, go on.'

'Well, I don't know where all this comes from. The Home Secretary almost certainly, dreamed up in some brandy-fumed drawing room somewhere. It's supposed to be about justifying expenditure, finding a peacetime role for the SIS, now they still have hundreds of millions of pounds to consume but no Iron Curtain to piss it up against.' He paused and let his next sentence out with a sigh. 'Anyway, a week or so ago I'm dragged in before a Deputy Chief Constable and told I'm to work alongside one of the nation's finest and most anonymous. It's a girl, a fucking girl!'

'Name?'

'I can't give you that.' MacIntosh could see him shaking his head, an internal debate going on. He wanted to, that was clear. 'Let me go on, ask questions later. This is all about what they term organized crime. Obviously it must have been totally disorganized before. And, apparently, us swedes here, we don't know too much about this, or individual forces don't talk to each other too much about it; whatever the reason, or the pretence, MI5 has this operation – and we have this girl! – to sort it out. And no, I don't know what the operation's called, if anything. "Doll's House" probably. So, basically I become the pen-pusher and local guide to this lassie. The strategy seems to be this: since we haven't been able to do it the legal way, bust up the drug cartels, bang-up the major villains, we'll do it the other way. Bang-bang. Box them and plant them.'

'Specifics?'

'You did the story the other day, just got the wrong conclusion.'

MacIntosh flicked back to the two bodies under sheets in the lane, the police line, the forensic bods. 'Yes? Well, no doubt that was because you weren't around to provide it.' He wasn't normally too big on conspiracy theories but this one, sourced as it was, was intriguing. More than that, if even just a grain of it was true – and his man was a rock-solid, reliable source – he had a huge story. 'You're talking about the double shooting. But the word was that it was an inter-gang thing and your lot weren't too unhappy about it.'

'Come on. Who's going to take out a couple of McGurk's trusted foot soldiers? And if that's what happened, why no comeback? Why no profligate retribution? Naw, that line's pish. McGurk knows where everyone with any attitude shites in this city, never mind stores their weapons or stash. Therefore you can assume, because of the lack of reciprocity, that he doesn't know what the fuck is going on here. And if he doesn't, then it's clearly nothing to do with the locals.'

'Wait a minute, here, you're not telling me that the "lassie", as you're calling her, is cruising about the city selecting targets and levelling them?'

'Cruising about, no. Selecting them, yes. It's all done with files and computer screens and surrogates. So clean. It's assassination by software. I suppose it helps to distance you from the moral responsibility.'

'Surrogates? What do you mean? Who? You're saying that Huey and Louie were shot by someone commissioned by the agency?'

'Commissioned? Not exactly. Coerced? Yes. Oh, certainly.'

'I just want to be absolutely sure of what you're saying here, before we go on. That there is some state-sanctioned operation, a conspiracy, to wipe out all the crime overlords, the head villains, and that the shooters are hired, or bribed or plea-bargained into co-operation?' His passenger nodded. 'Come on now!'

'Absolutely. And it's more than that. It doesn't seem to be just selective culling but a policy to also set the teams at each other's throats so they'll mutually liquidate themselves.'

'So that crime eats itself!'

251

'Aye, well put.'

'Christ. This is either fantastic or fantastical.' MacIntosh smacked the steering wheel. 'I can't just write a story based on this one chat, that the government has declared open season on hoods, that hitmen are stalking the mean streets taking out the major players. Fuck, it could win them an election. You're going to have to give me more than that, Angus.'

MacIntosh waited, staring at the shifting lights of the city in the silence as the internal debate went on. 'I can give you a little more—'

'Names, Angus.'

'Not that much. Only three or four people know them. It'd be too easily traced.'

'Look, if I run a story just based on what you've said, there'll be questions in Parliament, the whole thing will be rubbished and I'll be a laughing stock. Sacked and fucking ruined. I can't do that. You'll have to get me something tangible.'

'All right, all right.'

'What then?'

'I was thinking, can you get an artist to do an Identikit picture?'

'Sure, why?'

'I can give you a picture, a copy of a photograph. You get your artist to a room somewhere, locked in. I'll get the picture there for him to do the mock-up from it. Keep it close enough to be recognizable but not identical. And then I destroy the copy. OK?'

'Sure, but where's this leading? Who's the Identikit of?'

'The guy who did the hits. What you do is say that the drawing is a reasonable likeness of the killer based on talking to witnesses – there weren't any that I know of, but no one can disprove what you're saying – keep it vague and ephemeral on detail. You know, a guy like this was seen loitering in

252

the vicinity beforehand, making off quickly after, that sort of thing. And then you put it to us that this is the number one suspect. We will neither confirm nor deny it. But the shit will hit the fuckin' fan inside our place. And I'll let you know exactly how it's playing. Right? And another thing. You say that these mythical witnesses describe the man as having a strange accent, possibly North American. That'll bring the fucking house down.'

'Who is this guy, Angus?'

'Not yet. In due course, Ed, in due course. You break this in bits, you hear me? The first story is simply about the suspect. You don't get into the agency, or any of that. We'll approach that from a different direction, how there's discord in the local force about power being handed over to the newcomers. How there's a major push on drug-related crimi- nals and the local plod's being kept largely out of it. Lack of accountability, tame dial-a-quote councillors and MPs expressing disquiet, then gradually over days the two lines meld into one. OK?'

'It makes sense. Sure. I like it.'

'So you come up with our man on day one and you stress how the polis are convinced he's an import and not connected with the local scene. Who hired him? We don't know. Or maybe he's a vigilante? That'll make good copy. Speculate how you like. But, officially, no one's going to deny it. And it'll send the top brass into paroxysms.'

'Good. Excellent. But we still need a more direct link to our avenging spooks.'

'It'll come. Let me work on it. There's something, but you're going to have to give me time to think about how I go about covering the leak. You can't mention this to begin with, OK?

'Sure, whatever you say, Angus.'

'Well, the forensic report is probably going to discover that the bullets which killed our justly deceased had an official history, one that when traced, will lead directly to their door.'

'Whose door? What do you mean?'

'I'm saying that the gun was used in a previous killing, that it was recovered and was an exhibit in a murder trial, and that it could only have come from within. So, how's that going to be explained?'

MacIntosh whistled. 'Brilliant, absolutely beautiful.' But he was puzzled. 'So, how are you going to give me that?'

'I don't know. Not now. You're going to have to let me find a way to orchestrate this so it doesn't lead to me.'

'Sure.' MacIntosh was thinking, I can see professional jealousy, being miffed at being trampled all over by the guys in grey suits, but why all this? This destruction? And why put your career on the line? Not only that, putting out the suspect's likeness – might as well put target rings all over it because McGurk would be buying up all the available copies of the paper and issuing them to his underlings with the promise of a substantial reward attached. It was a death sentence. But to the policeman he said, 'I'll play it like you say, Angus. None of it will attach to you.'

Now he could not wait to get him out of the car and get on with it, but first there was the indelicacy of the reward. He reached for his inside jacket pocket.

Sadly, I hadn't really had the wit or the deviousness to come up with the dope ploy on Carpenter. Saying it had only occurred to me on the spur of the moment, to wipe the smile off her face and spoil her evening, leave her expecting that at any minute the colours were going to go all soft and mellow, conversation would ebb and flow with the tidal pattern of the drug and even Fleetwood Mac elevator Muzak would seem awesome on a turned-down stereo.

But The Break and Siobhan seemed worth checking out. I didn't know if she would welcome me, or even remember me, but I was heading there. On the way, walking through the puddled streets, I stopped at a phone box to call Naddy's

254

mobile. It was switched off, but I left a message on his answer function telling him where he could catch me later, and to meet up once he had checked out that Carpenter hadn't moved hotels, or caught a late flight south.

Actually, I thought as I hung up, the second part, the going, would be the best for all. Except, I let the door close behind me, she wasn't too unsightly on the eye and I was sure that if I trawled for long enough, and went deep enough, I could find the faint murmurings of a human heart. My darker, more pragmatic side sneered at the softer, libidinous part of me. I kicked a squashed Coke can and cast a fearsomely dismissive glance at a *Big Issue* salesman.

I had a couple of hours to kill, so I started walking, which I've always found conducive to thinking. Or it might just be conditioning from trying to keep relatively fit and passing sane by doing repeated laps of a prison cell. I climbed the hill past the Art School and when I hit the plateau, turned left and down towards Charing Cross, negotiated the traffic, moving aimlessly to a background of passing cars, when the café seemed to rear up in front of me, like some omen of good fortune. It was a cyber place, with electric ladyland writing on the inside of the windows, down which condensation was starting to dribble. I pushed open the door and went in. It smelled of good coffee, fresh baking and wet anoraks. A guy behind the counter, mid-twenties, dark hair tied back in a ponytail, greeted me.

'Coffee. Black and in a mug if you have it.'

'Sure. Anything else?'

'Now you mention it, there is. Could you help me set up on one of these computers so's I could e-mail a friend in the States?'

'No problem.'

He poured the coffee and led me to a corner under a garish painting of Timothy Leary. I put the coffee down on a ledge next to it while he punched a few characters into the machine.

255

'This is idiot proof, right?'

'Virtually. What it is exactly you want to do?' I told him that I had a long message to send, but that I needed to compose it. He hit a few more keys. 'If you write it here, off line, it won't be costing telephone charges. Keep saving it—' he showed me the buttons to press, '—and when you're ready to send, just give me a shout.'

'Great.' I dug into my pocket for money, he waved it away saying 'later', and I rooted around some more to find Stephanie's e-mail address. I figured it this way: I had been less than totally honest with her, she had been drawn into danger, or at least under threat, and she needed to know about it; and to take her own decision about what she should do, whether to hang in with me (she didn't have many other options that I could see), or make her own way. Slowly I started to type in the story, about who I was and what was happening. I tried to keep it concise and relevant but even then it took me an hour to write it all. I added that I was also going to send her a tape, the one of me and Carpenter in her hotel room, which didn't amount to evidence but which might be useful. I finished off by saying that if anything happened to me – I was going to call or e-mail her every forty-eight hours, so, if I didn't, she'd know I had been hit – then she should publish all of this on the Web, together with the voice recording, and find a far corner of a very large country for herself. I hoped that we'd enjoy babies together and signed off.

The Break was up a flight of stairs – and past a couple of Neanderthals – on Sauchiehall Street, as the road falls towards Charing Cross. I thought that I might get the chilly rebuff, on the grounds that I was insufficiently cool, but as Dylan should have put it, money doesn't talk, it squares! A tenner did it. The place wasn't too busy but it throbbed with that brand of techno which convinces your heart it's in spasm, particularly when combined with those migraine shades of dark fluorescent lighting. The punters were not that much younger than me, late twenties, most of them looking furtive, I thought, as if they actually had a partner elsewhere they were deceiving, but then I always put too much of my own experience into damning judgements of others. On the other hand, the place did hold out the strong possibility of adult drugs.

I made my way to the bar and bought a bottle of American beer, which seemed to be all they served except for lurid cocktails of the kind you'd expect to see in an episode of *The Addams Family*. I took a swig. It might be American, I thought, but it's been handled in the traditional British way. It tasted warm and soapy. I took it to a dark corner of the main bar, which had what looked like an artery feeding off, a corridor painted the colour of a main internal organ, to where I supposed the dance floor was. It seemed like the best location to check out the room.

My eyes were slowly adjusting to the light level as I scanned the knots of people at tables and standing around. There seemed to be no sign of Siobhan, although there were a few fine impersonators, with the same build and hairstyle. It was only an off-chance. There was no reason she should be working tonight, or even telling the truth about herself to me. I took another slurp of the beer, looked round again, and then caught sight of her coming out of the bile duct, towing a man. She was wearing a skimpy, light-coloured dress which would make a cummerbund on me. The man looked Asian or Arab, it was difficult to tell in the distance and light, and he was about twice her age. They were making straight for a table about ten feet from me. I felt distinctly uncomfortable and began casting around for dignified exit routes, when she spotted me, I don't know how, perhaps I was giving out distress or homing signals. She said something to the other guy, who detached himself and sat down, and she moved across to me, then said something I couldn't catch above the electronic thrum. I bent down and gave her my right ear.

'I wasn't expecting to see you.'

Again? 'Just thought I'd update my paltry knowledge of popular culture,' which came out even more flat and pompous than I intended.

'I'm working.'

She smelled smoky and musky. Incredibly sexy. The top of her dress was low and loose-cut and from my superior altitude and the way my head was cocked I could see that she had nothing underneath holding her together. 'Don't let me interrupt,' I screamed in her left ear, 'I'm just a lonely guy in a strange town, so don't feel guilty in the slightest.'

She gave a half-shake of her head. 'You know what's going on here?' she said after a little while.

'Oh, I think so.'

'Sorry.'

'Why? It beats nursing the terminally ill. Probably.' There didn't seem to be much to say about the situation we found ourselves in.

She looked back over her shoulder, where the Arab sat waiting, then back at me. 'Fuck it,' she said, 'life's too short for regrets. Give me a second and then we'll get out of here.'

I started to say 'forget it', but she was moving away. I saw her say something to her new friend, who seemed pretty exercised by the conversation, then she cut through the smoke and the perspiration to the bar, where she beckoned over one of the barmaids, had an animated few seconds with her, complete with glances back at me and hand signals, then she slid behind the bar and disappeared for a couple of minutes before reappearing holding a jacket and the large hand-grip. She nodded her head at me and then towards the door; I deposited my half-drunk beer on the nearest table and navigated towards her, catching her just before the pay booth immediately inside the exit.

'I think I just quit,' she said, 'I hope you're worth it.'

'I'm not offering anything,' I said too quickly.

'I know, but even that's got to be better than this shite.' She looked back, then at me. 'Fancy something to eat?'

'I'm not too hungry.' These appetite suppressing drugs. 'But I could nibble and watch you.'

We went out through the knot of gorillas and waiting punters and slipped down the stairs. About a dozen steps from the bottom she stopped, pulled my arm around her shoulders and nestled into me, kissing my neck and chin. She was trembling. 'I'm scared.' Her voice resonated in the hollow of my cheek.

14

The driver dropped Carpenter at the bottom of the driveway.
She climbed out, fished in her handbag for her wallet, pulled
out the warrant card she had been given, flashed it in the
faces of the two cops guarding the tape, ducked under it and
began walking up the path, the gravel crunching under her
feet.

She eased around the police caravan and as she came past
it she could see the open garage. The air seemed laden with
diesel fumes, but she knew that this was partly her imagination. Brown was talking to a woman, late thirties, early
forties, who had a mop of long blond curls and was not
sympathetically dressed for the occasion. She was wearing
stilettos and what looked like an opera cape. Brown noticed
Carpenter as she arrived and nodded his head in recognition.
'This is Angela Joseph, the pathologist. Angela, Meg Carpenter, who's working with us on this one.' They shook hands.
'Angela was having a late supper after the theatre when we
caught up with her.'

Joseph smiled warmly at Carpenter. 'I've got a doggie bag
in the car. I'll finish it at home.'

Carpenter looked around. Policemen in overalls and boots
were moving past, observing the traffic ways marked by tape
and small flags in the ground. 'So, what's the script, d'you
think?'

'Well, we'll do the PM first thing in the morning. Some of
my colleagues like to poke around the site and the deceased;

I'm more one for the evidence of the scalpel.' She grinned. 'Particularly when I've a grousing husband at home and a cold chow mein in the passenger seat.' Carpenter could see that the body had been bagged. It lay just in front of the open doorway of the garage.

'A neighbour noticed the lights on in the garage,' Brown came in. 'He heard an engine running after he switched off his TV for the night and was getting ready for bed. Looked out, spotted the light show, called it in. When our lads got there they had to force the door open. When they pulled him out it was clear he had been dead for some time.'

'Suicide?'

'Assisted, I'd guess,' Joseph said, ramming her hands into her pockets. 'Probably never be able to prove it, unless the PM reveals some evidence of trauma. But it's not normal MO to strap yourself by the neck with a choke chain to a beam while the engine rumbles on and Radio Clyde pumps out of the speakers.'

'More of a Radio 3 man, I'd have said,' Brown was grinning.

'You think someone strapped him up there and turned on the engine?'

'I should think so. The DS's got a reasonable point – rather sickly put if I may say so, Angus – but if you look around his house, his tastes, his record collection, there's not a lot of evidence that he was pop music fan. It's all long-dead, long-haired composers. And we're not talking Jimi Hendrix here.'

'Any evidence of resistance, bruising, cuts, torn nails?'

Joseph shook her head. 'Not from a cursory glance. Looks as if he went pretty quietly.'

'Doesn't that tend to indicate suicide, then?'

'Not to us conspiracy theorists,' Joseph was grinning. 'Maybe. But, you know, you get hunches, don't you Angus?' He nodded. 'Sometimes, under enormous stress, people will do the most unlikely things. From selfless bravado to queuing up for slaughter.'

'Be particularly careful with this one, Angela. Watch the blood. He was an arse puncher, so be warned.'

Joseph shook her head, looking at Carpenter, sharing a communality of distaste. 'I'm always careful. But was there any evidence of HIV?' Carpenter and Brown looked at each other without offering an opinion. 'So it's just the usual polis prejudice, Angus? To be on the safe side I won't go poking around in the head unless I absolutely have to. Are you coming to the PM, Angus, or one of your underlings?' Brown made a shrugging, don't know gesture. 'What about you, Ms Carpenter?'

Carpenter couldn't discern whether it was a challenge. 'Can't see the point really. I won't be giving evidence. I'm sure the report will be fine.' She turned to Brown. 'Well, Detective Chief Superintendent, so much for your theory of benign liberty encouraging candour in Weston.'

'I can't believe it,' Brown was looking mildly puzzled, 'his first name couldn't really have been Arnaud. Probably changed it from Arnold.'

15

'What is it that you do? Really?' Siobhan was curled up on a large, cream-coloured leather sofa, sipping a healthy shot of brandy. She was wearing a dark-blue towelling robe and her hair was pulled back in a twist from her face, which was free of make-up and remarkably pretty. I was sprawled face-down on a matching settee opposite, a towel knotted round my lower body, an old, faded olive green Israeli Special Forces tee shirt on top.

'I don't want to lie,' although I was thinking that it was the post-coital norm. 'So let's talk about something else. I came into some money recently and I decided to travel. Here I am.'

'Right. *Vene, vidi, vici.*' She tilted the glass at me and smiled. I groped with my left hand for mine which was on the floor, stretched up, returned the salute and sipped, with difficulty, at the brandy.

'You don't give much away.'

'All I can. There just isn't much. And I don't find talking about myself too interesting. I could ask you what you do. Really do.' It was rhetorical; I wasn't expecting an answer, both of us knew the score. Men. I didn't make moral judgements any more, I'd be a hypocrite to do so. Whether or not it was prostitution, men gave her money and presents. And she wasn't doing too badly on it, at least outwardly. Her apartment was at the top of a converted West End mansion. We were in her huge living-room, the floor of which was wood-panelled, leading across to what seemed to be a low-level stage, on top of which was the heftiest array of hi-tech hi-fi and TV equipment I had ever seen. It was about the only area of the room our buttocks hadn't bounced earlier. One side of it was almost entirely glass, a large, bevelled window which looked out on to the Botanic Gardens and the sky above.

'It's a lovely place. Your apartment.'

'Apartment?' She played with the word. 'Thanks. It suits me. I think this level used to be the ballroom of the house. That's what one of the people in the flats – apartments – below said. And, judging by this floor, who can say they're wrong?'

The wood was dark, highly varnished and smooth as glass. I put down my drink and ran my fingers over it. 'Amazing finish.'

'It was, wasn't it?' She was chuckling. 'Great floor, too. No friction burns or nasty skelfs.'

'Should I be saying sorry, because I don't feel it?'

'Not at all. It was fully participatory.' She finished her brandy and got up. 'I'm sore,' she said, moving across the floor towards me, 'but not as sore as I expect to be.' She knelt down beside me and began pulling at the towel. 'You know,' she went on, 'it's very ungentlemanly not to remove your shirt when having sex. It's nearly as bad as keeping your socks on.'

'Ah,' I put down my glass, 'but I have lovely feet.'

She ran her hands up under the shirt and began massaging my back.

'Strange. Most men worry about size. But not you. You don't mind wavin' your cock in my face for microscopic inspec—'

'Less of the microscopic.'

'But I can't get a glimpse of your pecs.'

'Drool on my buns instead.' I began fussing with the knot of her dressing gown and when I had it open I slid my left arm inside and pulled her closer to me.

'Don't you think we know each other well enough to have it off?' She giggled. 'I mean, of course, to dispense with it, the remaining layer.'

'It's horrible.'

'It doesn't matter.'

'To me it does.'

She pushed me away and face down and began to roll the shirt up my back. I surrendered. 'It looks like what the topography of Vietnam must have been like after we carpet-bombed it.'

She began kissing my back. 'I can see a few scars—'

'And skin grafts.'

'Is this one,' I felt a finger run over a spot on my left shoulder blade, 'a bullet wound?'

I nodded and squirmed round to face her. 'Check the latest,' I said, rolling up the front of the shirt to show the fresh stitching. 'Some people collect postcards, or badges, tattoos, stamps on their passports. These are my reminders of difficulties at home and in foreign climes. Sort of snapshots – no pun intended – of a life.' The towel seemed to be levitating, but it was simply the urgency of my erection. 'Now can we forget about all this and just fuck?'

She shucked her robe off, whipped away the towel with a fierce tug which left a warm glow in my buttocks, grabbed me in her left hand and, almost as if she were holding on to a saddle, vaulted on top of me where, astride, she began to rub my cock up against herself slowly as she and I gradually became wet. I closed my eyes. 'What about the condoms?' I breathed.

'Listen, who's in the driving seat? I'm coming to that. Just shut up and do as I tell you.'

She was moving all over me. 'That's what they used to say to me in the army. That's exactly what got me into this – heh! You're hurting me.' My eyes snapped open and I looked down to see that she had her teeth attached pretty firmly.

265

She relaxed and looked at me, her hair now falling from its arrangment and across my stomach. 'You were going to say trouble, or mess.'

I pulled her gently towards me. 'I'll shut up and follow orders,' I said. No escape. I'd been here before. And it had its pleasantness.

I woke feeling more tired than when I had gone to bed. So I stumbled into the bathroom, showered, retrieved my clothes from various parts of the apartment, dug a sharp knife out of a kitchen drawer and retired with my twist of coke to the bathroom where I laboriously cut four thick lines on a shaving mirror. After the inhalations I felt charged and on top of it.

When I looked in the smeared mirror I had to admit I looked like shit. My eyes resembled prime oysters with a Tabasco garnish, my skin had that grey rubbery look bodies have when they're pulled out of water after a week or so, and my chin and cheeks, with several days of growth, had that eighties butch fashion look which went out with rolled up jacket sleeves and shades stuck into hair gel. When I stuck out my tongue it looked like the original Alexander Fleming penicillin experiment.

I poked my head round the door where Siobhan was sleeping, bent down over her, noticing that, alarmingly, she looked wholesome and rested, kissed her lightly on the cheek, whispered that I would call her (telling myself to note the phone number on the way out), then quietly let myself out.

The day was alive with colours and possibilities. I felt that now, in two nights on both sides of the sea, I had almost caught up on the interactive sex I had missed in five years (there had been, I was forced to admit, occasional onanistic bouts and other stuff I didn't want to recall). I walked along the gardens, where the first burst of spring was coming out, turned down a cobbled mews lined with cars and dustbins, the warm air turning the overnight slick of rain to mottled camouflage on the stones. My mind was racing – thankfully forward, and not back like it usually did – and I could almost convince myself there was a way out of this, a future that did not shortly lead to a funeral where the grave-diggers outnumbered the mourner: I was banking on Carpenter turning up out of grim satisfaction.

It was around 8 a.m., the workers were beginning to come out of their houses to pick up the papers or turn over their cars, the students were reeling their way back home, those who hadn't already turned over other cars. I was a little shivery, but that went with the previous hours and the recent imbibing. My nose dribbled like a faucet, so I wiped it on the back of my sleeve as I went, conscious that I probably looked like a hobo, regretful that I couldn't remember any Woody Guthrie songs.

The T-junction loomed up in front of me. I looked left, then right, decided with my scant knowledge of the geography of the place that it looked busier if I hung a right, so I did, vaguely imagining that I would collide with some rescuing mode of public transport if I kept marching, then slowed up alongside a newsagents, inside which I could see a large, glass-fronted fridge full of cold, and allegedly energizing, drinks. Pushing into the shop I collected two bottles, the names alien to me, which I chose purely on the basis of the appeal of their colours, orange and fiery red (why do you never get a navy blue drink? I wondered). And a paper. I scooped the nearest tabloid from a pile, paid, giving the assistant a beaming smile (only later did I remember that I had not cleaned my teeth), then set off south again.

There were several benches alongside a wall next to a bank on a crossroads, I was thirsty and hopeful, so I sat down and unscrewed the top of the first bottle, took a long swallow and unfolded the newspaper.

The gas raged in my throat and fizzed in my nose, I

spluttered and coughed and hugged the paper to me, my eyes darting around. Carefully I looked again. There, dominating the front page, was an unmistakable photofit likeness of me. The headline was direct and accurate enough. It said, 'The face of a killer'. I slunk down on the bench.

Carpenter re-read the inside piece and flicked, once more, to the front page. The likeness to Downe was unmistakable, the similarity to the file picture of him too close to be coincidental. Someone had put together the artist's impression from it. There was no other conclusion. Surely? She compared the picture on file to the tabloid rendition again. Apart from a few, probably deliberate, differences, like a slightly longer hairstyle, it could have been copied directly from it. Had to have been, she told herself. Couldn't have been. Surely?

She looked around the dingy room and at the grey filing cabinet, which she hadn't bothered to lock. That was stupid, irresponsibly so. She felt a flush of anger and embarrassment flood her face. It was Brown's room, Brown's filing cabinet, natural that he would be using it, she had seen him go in and out of it dozens of times in the last few days, so how could she lock it? Who else knew about the picture, where it had come from and where it was stored? Slowly, she shook her head. It wasn't possible that a senior detective would leak a picture to the press which could only help damage, or kill, her operation. Was it? All right, the local plod's nose was being rubbed in its own excrescence, but to criminally leak sensitive information to the media? She pushed back the chair and took two steps over to the cabinet. That was fantastical.

She mulled that over, then whirled round to face the door. Why was it so? What did he stand to lose? A job and pension? Hardly. It would never be made public, simply hushed up out of embarrassment and he'd be quietly told to go. Criminal charges? That caused her to smile. The last thing her bosses would do was pursue a case against him, given the public ordure he could spray from the witness box. So he stood a more than reasonable chance of no sanction at all, other than marginally premature retirement, which he was probably angling for anyway.

She stopped herself. There wasn't a smidgeon of evidence to support her conviction. Just general prejudice against career coppers, particularly ones in the sticks. Dozens of people could have had access to the file. Maybe, but, she argued with herself, how many knew it was there? Well? She couldn't answer. It came back to Brown. Again she tried to shake off the sureness. People talk, gossip, lots of them could have known who I was, what I was up to and where I was billeted. Maybe it was just a lucky fishing trip? A sigh and shake of the head. Bugger the prejudice, it still all came back to Brown. He was trying to fuck her over.

How did he do it? Take a photocopy of the picture and hand it over to his stooge in the press? Almost certainly. She thought about that. Was there any record kept of photocopier use or any way of telling, from the photograph, if it had been copied? Again she shook her head and grimaced. And then, like a shutter clicking open, they occurred to her. A print. From the photo. He hadn't handled the picture at all – she could remember that much – so his prints shouldn't be on it. It was a pretty long chance that they would be, but worth punting on. Even if they were, it still wasn't a smoking gun, he could have been compelled and nosy enough to rifle through the file when she wasn't around. But it would be enough for her.

She took in the room and his desk. There had to be a print of his for comparison somewhere, assuming that there was anything at all liftable on the picture. What was there? She walked over to his desk and looked for something conclusive and dispensable, which wouldn't be missed if it walked. There was a calculator, a picture of a group she presumed to be the wife and two offspring, a leather-bound blotter, a couple of pens off which they'd only be able to pull a partial, a key in a drawer (too obvious) and then she leaned over and noticed the half-full wastebin.

All of the items in here, she said to herself, were deposited by him. There were torn envelopes, several polystyrene cups, a few glossy advertising flyers and lots of shredded paper. Taking one of the pens from the desk she slipped it inside an old coffee cup and lifted it out, putting it down on the desk; then she picked up a second pen, used the two like twin prongs or chopsticks, and pulled out several leaves of the shiny advertising offers. Discarding one of the pens, she swung up her bag from under the desk, flicked the catch and knocked in the potential print stock with the other pen. Then, from the file she eased out the photograph with the fingers of her right hand gingerly on its edges, then hunted around for an old A4 envelope, which she found in her own bin, slipped the photograph inside and into her bag.

Her heart was pumping too hard and she heard herself breathing too loudly. Clearly, she could not trust anyone or anything in here, so the post was out, and from now on candour on the telephone was unacceptably risky. She would have to find a courier, a safe phone and even a place of refuge, chosen by her, where she could be reasonably sure the walls did not have listening devices.

As she walked out into the dark and gloomy day towards Bath Street her bag began chirruping, which caused momentary panic that her exhibits had triggered alarms, until she realized it was her mobile phone.

'What the fuck is going on?' I was screaming in a hiss, if that's possible, trying to keep my voice down so as not to attract attention. I was in the dark lobby of another snooker club and even at this unseemly hour most of the tables were taken; it used to be boxing or football but now for the poor and fearful the baize offers an escape route. 'Was it you?' I went on, hunched over the phone, sticking coins into the relentless machine. 'You're trying to get me slotted!'

'Of course it wasn't me.' I could hear the rush of traffic around her. 'Look, where are you?'

'I'd be a fucking idiot to tell you that, wouldn't I?'

'Downe, believe me, I had nothing to do with it.' But I could detect an edge of uncertainty. 'Not directly, anyway. But you're right, it is an inside job.' I felt my stomach tilt and slide away, pulled the phone away from my ear. I could hear her saying, 'Don't hang up, please! Don't hang up. We can put it right.' I looked at the phone, across at the office booth and the dark hall with tents of light over the tables, back at the phone, hearing her tense appeals, and I realized whatever decision I made it would not be the right one. For a few seconds I swithered, until the pips came in, which seemed to make the decision for me because I responded mechanically, shovelling in a few more coins.

'I've had enough of all this. You'd better listen very carefully and do exactly what I tell you or, when I hang up, I'll be coming after you.' The bright lights of flames and bodies falling through the darkness blotted out my vision.

'You've seen this, have you?' Carpenter pushed the tabloid across the table. She was standing over the desk, anger roaring in her.

Brown glanced at it, then up at her. He nodded.

'Where did it come from?'

'What do you mean?'

She kicked back the chair on the opposite side of the desk and sat down. 'It's a leak. Obviously. From here. And who else knew, Angus?'

'It's crap. The story's rubbish, barely a scintilla of sense in it. As far as we know there were no witnesses, as far as we—'

'Fuck the story, Detective Superintendent. The drawing. Downe could have posed for it, it's so accurate. But you know exactly where it came from, where it was copied from, don't you? From the file. In your filing cabinet.'

Brown studied her; the heat was in her cheeks and she was breathing slowly and deeply, clearly to keep control of herself. He smiled briefly. 'My filing cabinet. Your file. You're the one responsible for it, so if anything has leaked – and I very much doubt it – then it happened under your stewardship. Your responsibility.'

Carpenter eased her chair back, feeling an almost irresistible urge to leap across the desk and claw at him. 'What I don't understand, Brown, is why? I can see how you must hate us coming in and taking over your job, I can understand the resentment, but not deliberately undermining, putting everything at risk, putting lives at risk.'

'Lives at risk? That's interesting. I wonder who exactly put lives at risk, concocted this crazy, lawless, odious, utterly hopeless fucking scenario? Who is it exactly who is responsible for two recent deaths, assassinations – I'm not wrong in assuming that it was you who pointed the finger, signed on a deranged, psychopathic junkie and chucked him out on the streets. Tell me, Carpenter, what kind of warped system of justice do they teach you down there?' He paused, shifted a layer of papers into perfect order, and gave her another cold smile. 'And of course I deny having anything to do with this.' He picked up the outside edge of the newspaper, then pushed it away. 'If something went astray it happened on your watch. And if you want to start throwing allegations around, then why don't you start with the Chief Constable, see what he has to say about it and what he believes?'

Carpenter leaned back in the chair, sighed and looked up at the ceiling, then stood up. 'You're a worm, Brown. Your view of the world is strictly low-level, slow-witted, circumscribed by shit and darkness. You're fucking here with powers you don't begin to understand. Justice? Don't give me that self-serving pap. If you had honoured it a bit more, if you had been even half-way diligent in its defence, we wouldn't be having this conversation. You sit there, a sanctimonious, fat-arsed form-filler, when outside the window kids are shooting up in schools, the place is being taken over by the people pushing it, they're shooting each other, buying up taxi companies, bars, clubs, legitimizing themselves. They're not even being very secretive about it. Everyone knows who they are, the players, and have done for years. And what have you done about it? How many have you caught?' She made a zero sign with her right hand.

'So stick to your traffic management and school patrols. Don't talk to me about justice. Justice is about being able to send your kids to school without having some pusher at the gates selling them heroin, or watching them growing up healthy, not missing fingers, because the veins have clogged up and gangrene set in, not having to ID them when they've died amongst faeces and sickness in a public toilet with a needle in their groin. Justice is about being able to live quietly without a junkie breaking in through the back door to steal your TV for skag. And it's about removing the vermin who cause it from the place.' She paused for breath. 'This is a city without justice, Brown, and you're sitting on the fucking sidelines making notes about jurisprudence! You're a disgrace, Detective Superintendent!' Leaning forward she put both hands on the desk. 'So, fuck you, Brown and fuck your opinions. Just get your head down and go back to making your tiny casts and residues.'

She smiled sarcastically, leaned back, kicked the chair so that it fell over behind her and walked away. She thought she heard him chuckle.

16

I came out of the snooker club expecting that it would be like stepping into a spotlight on stage, that everyone would be looking at me, pointing and running for the phones; but it was raining heavily, most people seemed to have sought shelter and those that hadn't were scurrying intently, too busy avoiding puddles and splashes to look out for a passing killer. I prayed that the rain would continue until dark.

Holding the paper over my head, my visage folded inside, I carried it as if it were sheltering me from the rain, rather than the true purpose, which was to obscure as much of my head as possible, as I trotted towards the expressway and river. The plan, such as I had one, was to stay out of sight during the day, adopt some kind of rudimentary disguise if necessary, and hope that the public memory of sketches of the wanted was passing or amnesiac. The river, I knew, was lined with old warehouses and gap sites, which I hoped might offer some sort of hiding place until the light went. Now I had nowhere to stay and once I got off the street and out of sight I would need to think about a bivouac for the night. There was also my new batman, Naddy, to consider. Would he go to the police or the papers? I decided that the risk of phoning him was too great. I had stood him down on the Carpenter surveillance, he had no way of contacting me, so that seemed a closed avenue.

The rain was falling considerably harder as I reached Dumbarton Road, so I kicked into a run, head down and still covered by the sodden paper against the gusts until I reached the road running along the waterfront. About half a mile along I slipped through a broken railing and across a muddy site to the broken shell of a large shed, probably some relic of the days when ships were built on the river. As I splashed past piles of stone and sand and into the shed, which was completely open to the river, I could see across it to one of the few remaining yards, in Govan, I was sure, where it had all started out for me.

I was cold and wet. I considered dragging together some elements to start a fire but when I thought about it I decided that, rather than send smoke signals advertising my presence, it would be simpler just to walk into a police station and sign a confession. So I found the most protected corner of the building, dragged some abandoned oil cans and spars of wood into a semi-circle, which I could hide behind if anyone else turned up, and burrowed down, feeling exactly how the early pioneers must have felt, encircled, behind the covered wagons.

Carpenter had phoned home, on the digital mobile, to the scrambled line on her superior's desk. Jonathan McAuliffe was of the old school, waiting out retirement and the honours list, now lost in the upheaval and tumult as the agency strove for a new role in the changed world order. His instinct was for caution, always for caution, and when she had briefed him he reacted as she expected he would. 'Oh dear,' he said – she could almost feel the despair seeping out of him – 'I'll need a report on this, Meg.' Which meant four or five days, at least, of inaction and machinations.

'With respect, Jonathan, I think we need to act quickly here, before it all fragments.'

'What are you suggesting?' She was standing in a terrace, in the gathering darkness, on Great Western Road. What *was* she suggesting? 'Are you asking for back-up?'

She was certainly not asking for that! She could just imagine what that would mean, an admission that she wasn't up to it, knowing, patronizing nods over the MCC ties, a check on her career, a relegation to computer fraud or Sig. Int. Because, despite there having been a woman director in the past, women – or girls, as the senior men insisted on calling them – were few, and lowly in the organization. 'No – no, I don't think that's necessary yet.' The traffic was moving slowly along the road, the traffic lights at the corner seemed to be out of order and the rain was beginning again. 'I just thought you should know the state of play.'

'Good, good. Well done. A watching brief then, Meg, eh? And the report . . . in the morning?'

'Absolutely, Jonathan. Thanks.'

She switched the phone off and put it in her coat pocket. A watching brief? What exactly was a fucking watching brief? And she started to walk towards the park.

The water coursed beside her, gravel crunched under foot, setting up echoes and aural confusion so that she imagined someone was always behind her. Or perhaps that was just her anxiety about all of this, the rapidly spiralling problems here, the inaction back there. Water dripped from the trees and in the occasional wan puddles of light from the moon as it broke through the cloud cover, the vegetation had a yellow cast; it looked acidic, as if the trees and shrubs were poisoned and dying.

The path lay alongside the river, meandering through the park alongside the bank. It might have made a fine walk or running track in daylight; at night, it was just a narrow murky ravine in the darkness. She stopped. And now she was sure she could hear footsteps, which then also stopped. Or was she imagining it? Her heart began to speed. *Don't think about it!* she told herself. Not about the muggings, the rapist on the loose – she had noticed stories in the papers over the last few days – the alcoholics and buggerers in the undergrowth. A couple of days back she had overheard a conversation in Pitt Street between two policemen, one obviously attached to the helicopter team. 'Sometimes,' he had said, 'when it gets really boring, we fly over the park area and shine the searchlight in the bushes and catch the poofs at it.' At least, she presumed, she would be safe from them. The other part of the conversation had been about the rapist, who had carried out more than a dozen attacks in less than a square mile of this part of the city. 'He'll probably top the next one.'

And then there was Downe. He was erratic – she checked her step – *erratic*? That was wrong. Emotionally, perhaps, feelings fizzing and darting like phosphorus. She checked herself again. Phosphorus was apt. As in bomb. She could feel her heart rapping for escape in her rib cage. Erratic was not what you could say about Downe, about the way he did things. Unfortunately. He was entirely focused, uni-directional. The original smart weapon. And she was walking straight towards the warhead. Alone, on an unlit path beside the river, no one in sight or nearby, apart from the phantom in her head. It wouldn't take him more than a few seconds to – to? Throttle her, break her neck, knock her unconscious and throw her into the river?

She stopped again. And this time she was sure someone was following her. The footsteps did not stop, she heard them crunching louder and coming towards her. Was it Downe, playing games, or someone else? She started to walk more quickly now and as she did she heard the crunching echoes behind break into a run. She gulped, feeling tears prick her eyes, and she, too, started to run. Looking over her shoulder as she went, she thought she caught sight of a dark shape, which she lost as she turned a bend, the figure blotted out by the shrubbery. Almost without thinking she plunged between two huge rhododendrons and squatted down in a small dark clearing, her legs jellied, stomach clenching, the breath hard

277

in her chest. Her hands fluttered over the ground, looking for a weapon.

'Wherr are yi, hen?' The voice was slurred, sing-song, definitely not Downe's. 'Ah just wantae talk tae yi.'

Her right hand had found a round stone, slightly larger than a cricket ball. She clutched it to her.

She could see him now through the branches; he seemed to be swaying on the path. Drunk, she thought. Had she over-reacted? The clutching panic in her chest told her not. But now there was another feeling: anger. Why the fuck was she cowering like an animal in the bush when this arsehole was striding the walkway? Was he innocent? Was he fuck. Only some kind of pervert would be mooching around in a park, on an unlit path, following women in the night.

'Hoi!' She came out of cover in a roaring crash. 'You!' He looked round – he seemed to be in his fifties with long, lank, grey hair – 'FUCK OFF!' She screamed it out, so that he stumbled back, his coat flapping open, and then she hurled the stone as hard as she could at his midriff, aiming for the largest part of the target, from less than two yards. It caught him in the chest, knocking him back and down against the fence nearest the riverbank. She heard a moaning wheeze as she took off.

A couple of hundred yards along she stopped, listening for any sounds of pursuit, but there were none. Her heart was tripping, she was surprised to feel tears on her cheeks, but she felt a sort of soaring redemption. And when she thought about it she wasn't sure whether the blow she had struck was entirely against the flasher, or potential rapist, whatever he was, or whether it also had something to do with what she felt about her earlier conversation with McAuliffe.

Taking a deep breath, the panic down to a manageable terror, she walked on, seeing the bridge swing into view in the distance, the spots of light and the sounds of the passing cars, their roofs just visible above the parapet. She wiped her face, snuffled, felt a sour sickness in her stomach, but walked on.

Downe was terrorizing her, she knew that. For fun.

A few more yards and she saw the bench he had told her about, enveloped on three sides by dark, dense vegetation. Narrowing her eyes, blinking back the tears, she could see herself sitting there and him behind, a length of cheese wire and—. Somewhere high above her and to her left she heard a high tinkling laugh, a girl, uninhibitedly letting go, the resonances floating around her. She shivered again and wiped at the tears. The bench was beside her now, but instead of sitting on it she stood leaning against the railing over the Kelvin, keeping the seat and both approaches along the path in view.

A quick look at the watch. Two minutes late. A glance up at the bridge, but no one was looking down, looking after her. A shuffling and stamping of her feet, hands thrust deep into the pockets of her coat, then a rummage for a tissue, a wipe at her nose and eyes, head going from side to side, then behind her and down to the darkness and the black river. Feeling inside her pockets she found some coins and a set of metal nail clippers. She slipped the coins between the knuckles of her right hand, holding the clippers in the palm against them, so that they formed an impromptu knuckleduster. She wasn't going to take any more chances.

Now, as she looked back and to her left, a cyclist was coming along the path towards her, no light, slowly, seemingly ill at ease, the bicycle weaving slightly, the rider just a shaded grey outline against the inky backdrop. Drunk again, she thought. The bell tinkled. Definitely drunk. And then a skid and crunch of brakes. She shrank back as the bike pulled up in front of her, her hand grasping the metal in her right-hand coat pocket.

'Sorry I'm late.'

The voice. Downe. Having to swallow and keep swallowing

to avoid throwing up. Then gasping for air, swallowing, swallowing, nose running, eyes filling again. Just a nod of recognition.

'It's a few years since I've been on one.'

A nod of the head. Agreeing, going for the tissue again. Blowing her nose. *Try and make a conversation*, her head said. 'Where did you get it?'

'Shop. Obvious, really. Went in. Took them a bit of time to understand what I was on about – the accent, you know. Then gave them a credit card. Simple.'

She nodded her head rapidly. His face was still between her and the washed-out source of light, lost in the blotches of shade. 'Right. I see. Right.'

His head moved closer to hers and when he began to speak she could see clarity form around his mouth and the ivory glow of his teeth. And what seemed like far-off and hopeless lights in his eyes. 'Carpenter? Are you all right?' His head came even closer and now she could see the face dully, as if it had just surfaced from underwater. 'I wasn't being serious, you know. I mean I'd hardly disport myself for security cameras, Mastercard officials, alert fucking shop assistants, would I? Where'd I get the bike? Where d'you think I got the fucker? I stole it, naturally. The wheeze came to me as I was huddled down shivering in an old warehouse on the river – your chic New York loft this was not – and I thought, no one ever looks at someone on a bike, they're just a passing inconvenience, you don't exactly study and record their physiognomy. A motorbike would be even better, of course, but then I'd have to work out how to beat the locking system and the electrics – and it isn't easy to steal a tin lid.'

He came even closer, so that now she could see all of his face, the colours, grey and pitch, sallow, looking as if he had been recently disinterred. And she couldn't help herself: her teeth began to chatter and the tears welled and ran, the heel of her left hand grinding at her eyes trying to stop them.

'Carpenter?' His hands grasped her shoulders and she heard a crunch and clatter, presumably where the bike had fallen. 'What is it? Time of the month, I suppose?'

She saw the white of his teeth, the open smile, and she swung at it with all of her power, the right hand coming up and across venomously. The shock going up through her shoulder, her knuckles crumpling and her wrist jarring, the coins breaking out of her grip under the impact. 'Time of the month? You bastard! You think this is funny? You make me walk through a park, a fucking wildlife park, like my sex was raw fucking meat. You think this is a game, you sick, twisted shit! Trying to frighten me. You are finished – it's over. You are—'

'Don't tell me,' he was holding his mouth, swaying slightly and trying to spit out what she hoped was blood and teeth, 'dead meat?'

And she hit at him again, this time with her open palm, not quite as hard, and as he was expecting it he slipped it, her trying not to laugh, aching with relief as well, but on the edge of hysteria, great bulbous tears rolling down her cheeks. Then she started howling like a defeated ten-year-old.

'Jeez, Carpenter,' his face now just a few inches from hers, 'you're potentially human.' Shifting into a neat side-shimmy as her knee came up towards his groin and then grabbing her in a rough bear hug, blood oozing from his nose and lips. 'And what a right hook.'

She relaxed for a moment, then stiffened again. 'What – what is that?' she asked between sobs. 'In your pocket?'

'I'm just pleased to see you,' into her left ear.

She pushed him back and away. 'It's a gun? Isn't it? It's not *the* fucking gun? Tell me it isn't, you witless fucking pea-brain. You were meant to dump it, for Christ's sake!'

Downe shrugged, bent over, picked up the bicycle and wheeled it over to the bench, where he parked it alongside in the foliage. 'Sit down and we'll talk,' he said, pointing to the bench, then peered over to inspect it. 'It's wet.' He unbuttoned his coat, took it off and spread it over the seat. 'It isn't much drier, but there you go.'

Carpenter stood, her arms folded, shaking her head, sniffing. 'I'll stand, thanks.' Downe shrugged and sat down on the bench. 'Why here, the great bloody outdoors?'

'Why not? You'd have preferred a posh restaurant?' He crossed his legs and patted the jacket beside him. 'I suppose it's because I couldn't quite see your guys in grey suits crouching among the rhododendrons like a shooting party. But I scouted the terrain very carefully, just to make sure there wasn't an SAS hit squad buried in leaves and branches squinting along night sights.'

'Are you serious?'

'No. Well, only partly. But it's one of the reasons I held on to the gun.' He nodded his head towards the jacket.

'You thought what, that I was going to arrange to have you removed?' Only a few minutes ago she had been thinking the same of him.

'Where could I have got such a thought? Ridiculous, huh?'

She snuffled and wiped at her nose, then crunched across the path and sat down beside him. 'We have troubles, Downe, big time.'

'Really?' He put an arm round her shoulders. She flinched. 'Yours, compared to mine, seem a mere trifle, Carpenter. And this—' he nodded at his arm, '—don't think this is a display of affection. It has a double purpose. Disguise. Persuading casual onlookers that we could be lovers – sort of flawed ones, but tender. But also, if there are any more purposeful watchers, if your cavalry should suddenly come clattering in, all I need to do is firmly hook you in with my left hand while reaching into the jacket with my right and blowing the top of your head off.'

Carpenter sighed and sniffed. 'I wish that I thought you were joking.'

'Fuck, I'm a bundle of laughs.'

'So, what now?'

He craned round to look at her face, which was resolutely staring out towards the river bank. 'Sorry? I thought the deal was, I did the action, you had the grand scheme.'

'It was a leak, I know that. I even know who. I just can't prove it for sure.'

'I see. So what you're saying is that there's no grand scheme. We're going to have to extemporize. You blackmail me, you embroil me, you have me on a wanted poster for every hood to shoot, and there's no tail man or exit route. You should have been a Marine Corps officer, Carpenter. Don't they teach you lateral thinking in spy school?'

'I tend not to think my best when I'm scared witless, Downe. You didn't need to do this.' She didn't want to tell him about the earlier encounter, although it now brought her reassurance.

His left hand reached round and tickled under her chin. 'No? Listen. We're going to do it my way now, Carpenter. It's my life being paddled around in this mad pinball game and I made my mind up a few years back that I wasn't giving it up lightly. This is what we're going to do. I've had plenty of time in a wet, cold shed to think about this. It may not be very good, but it's the best I can come up with. You're going to hire a car and we're going to check into some out of town, discreet hotel. You're going to book a double room in assumed names and pay cash. You'll say that your husband will be arriving later. I'll be waiting in the car, you'll let me know the room number and I'll sneak in when no one's looking, even if I have to scale the back wall.

'Now the car is a problem because you'll have to show your licence and your real name but we'll only be holding on to it for twenty-four hours or so and anyone checking on rental cars will know you have it but not where it is, even if they phone to check every hotel in the country, which they won't, and anyway you won't be giving the proper registration in reception. With me so far?'

Carpenter nodded. 'So, where does that get us?'

'It gets us cover for a while, time to think and plan, and it gets me off the street.'

'I'll need to report back about all this.'

He gripped her shoulder and shook his head quickly. 'Oh no. There's been enough leakage already. This way, if anything slips out, I know where it's coming from.' He stood up. A thin watery moon had broken through the cloud cover. 'Let's find a friendly nearby Hertz.'

'Hello, this is Room 297.' I was putting on my local accent. 'Mr Richard. I arrived a little while ago. I wonder if we could order some room service? Sandwiches for two? It doesn't matter what. Just whatever you have—'

'Except tongue or veal,' Carpenter came in. 'Or corned beef, beef, not beef—'

'Sorry,' I said down the line, 'my wife is just going through a food fad. Maybe some chicken? Cheese and tomato? Fine. Do you have any soup? Yeah? Cock-a-leekie would be fine.' Whatever the fuck *that* is. 'How long? Fifteen minutes is good. Oh, and also a nicely chilled bottle of Chablis or something like that to enjoy when I get out of the bath? Superb.' I hung up.

I figured that a reasonably busy, expensive hotel was the best place to be assured of discretion. We had picked up the car, hit the city motorway system and ended up being spewed across the bridge and heading south. There was a small AA book in the glove compartment, so I looked at where we were heading, the coast basically, and the places and hotels, checking the stars and ignoring the prices. I used Carpenter's mobile to phone round, discovered there was an amateur golf tournament on in Troon, and pulled us a double room in the course hotel, one of the few left. I thought that if golfers are oblivious to the elements they'd hardly pick up on a flitting fugitive in the corridors. Anyway, sportsmen only read the back pages.

It was a rather nice room, spacious, well-furnished with an oblique view of the golf course. Well, that's what I'd been told. All you could see now was wall-to-wall darkness. I had wanted a suite – each one named, apparently, after a famous golfer – but they were all taken. I had come up with the Mr Richard monicker easily. Carpenter, Karen and *Richard*. She had grimaced.

Now she was sitting glaring at me from one of the tweed armchairs. 'What's the problem?' I asked. 'Worried that because the bill's in a different name you won't be able to claim it on expenses?'

'What really gets me about you,' she was wearing a long skirt, her legs crossed and showing a long swathe of stock-inged leg, 'is your insufferable ebullience.'

'Really?'

'I put it down to intrinsic stupidity.'

'It'll be the genes.'

'There you go again.'

'Again what?'

'Fucking glib quips. Can't you act seriously for once?'

'I'll try it. I thought derring-do, freeze-dried upper lip, was the appropriate act here?'

'Cut it out, Downe. I'm unsettled enough.'

I was sitting on the edge of the bed, with the mattress and what seemed like an acre of carpet between us. I got up and went over to the minibar and pulled it open, rummaged around inside and came out with a box of nuts and a bottle of chilled champagne. 'I'm having some, you can do what you want. If you want to join me I can also act the sommelier, if that wouldn't offend you.' She shrugged, I popped the cork and poured two glasses, put down the bottle, handed her one. I drained my glass in a long slurp and filled it up again. 'Cheers,' I said. Hers stood untouched. 'Let me tell you something. Let me tell you what this beats, because it beats just about everything I know. It beats crawling through jungles eating roots and insects, it beats slipping in and out of Iran or Muslim Beirut with only a hand-drawn map and a short-arm, it beats parachuting into the fuckin' desert behind the Republican Guard looking for mischief to cause, and most of all it beats slops and a cell and the black brothers and the alien brethren and the sadists in uniform and freedom circumscribed in stone and metal.

'Look out the window, there's a fuckin' world out there that doesn't stop at a high wall, barbed wire and watch towers. We're sitting here in a fancy hotel, drinking champagne – at least, one of us is – waiting for the flunkey to appear with the neatly cut and arranged sandwiches. All in all, it doesn't seem like too bad an act to me.' I took a gulp from my second glass. 'Joining me?'

She gave a tentative nod and a shrug of her shoulders and picked up the glass. 'I'm sorry, Downe, I suppose I'm just not used to things going wrong. I must have missed the classes in managing defeat. Cheers.' She raised her glass. 'To us.' I returned the gesture, then leaned over and touched my glass to hers, as she added, 'To survival.'

'I'll try not to act so cheerful – and gormless.'

She reached out with her left hand and gently touched my right. 'I'm sorry for what I said. I was feeling depressed. Sorry. It's been some day.'

'Heh, look on the bright side. It's nearly ten and we haven't killed anyone yet.'

'There you go again.'

I drained the glass. 'I may as well have that bath. If I don't lock the door, no peepin' now.'

'Have your bath, Downe.'

'Put the door on the chain, check out the waiter before you open it. The gun's under the pillow, my side.'

'Your side! You don't think we're sharing a bed, do you?'

286

I opened the door to the bathroom. 'I know where I'm sleeping, sister, the rest is up to you.'

I soaked in the bath, sipping champagne long past hearing the waiter's knock on the door and the mumbled conversation, probably a complaint about the size of the tip. The water was warm, soapy, endless and comforting, probably evoking some pre-birth memory of the amniotic fluid.

'Carpenter,' I yelled, 'is there a sharp knife there?'

'Don't tempt me,' came back to me.

'Just slide it under the door.'

After a few seconds I heard scrabbling at the door. 'Won't go. What do you want it for?' And then the door swung open and she stood there, steam drifting around her, holding what looked like a steak knife. It happened too suddenly to be embarrassing, although reflexively I pulled up a shielding right leg. She stared at me. 'Didn't grow up on a farm did you, Downe?'

'What?'

'Looks like you came out second best to a threshing machine.' She was grinning, holding the knife and tapping it on the back of her left hand. 'Move your knee a bit, Downe, can't quite tell if you've been circumcised.' She pointed the knife at my groin. '*Yet.*'

'Just pass me the knife, will you, and get out.'

'I hope you're going to donate your body to medical science. It looks like the kind of thing Buffalo Bill would have been proud to put together.' I must have looked puzzled, wondering what a medicine show and stage Indians had to do with each other. '*Silence of the Lambs?* Didn't they show you films in that prison of yours?'

I nodded. 'All the time. I was just thinking arrows, and outrageous fortune, rather than movie villains. For weeks after they showed that one the bad guys were going around carving ears and lips off. Only difference to the usual was that they were doing it with phoney English accents.'

'Welsh.'

'Pedant. Anyway, you've cheered up. The misfortune of others does that to you, does it? The knife, please.' I held out my hand.

She shook her head. 'Not until you tell me why.'

It seemed pointless to prolong it, so I said, 'To take out the stitches from my side.'

'Yuch. Show me.' I shook my head. 'It's down under your arm, isn't it? Awkward. I'll do it. I should have a small pair of scissors in my bag. And tweezers, too,' she smiled without warmth, '—in case I have to deal with your cock.'

And she was away before the empty glass hit the door.

From behind the door I grabbed and put on the white dressing gown with the golfing emblem and went out into the bedroom. Carpenter was sitting on the bed toying with a sandwich, the wine was open and up to its neck in ice and water in a bucket on a small table next to her; and the pistol was lying, as if casually discarded, on the bedspread.

'Mmhhm,' wiping crumbs from her mouth, 'the salmon's good.'

'The champagne's finished, I see.'

'Go out in style is my motto.'

'You seem better.'

'You know how it is, having a man about the house makes us gals feel good.' She swallowed the last of the daintily cut sandwich. 'Even if he is a psychopathic dope-fiend.' I didn't respond. 'That trick in the park was really shitty, Downe.'

'You can talk to me about shitty? All I was doing was attempting to protect myself, save my life.'

'And you couldn't have made the meeting in a subway station or a dark cinema?'

I shook my head. 'Exactly.'

'So can I take it that I passed the test and you now trust me?'

'Absolutely.'

She reached for the bucket on the table, pulled out the wine in a grumble of breaking ice, and sloshed two clean glasses full. 'Which is why you felt able to leave the gun with me?' I smiled agreement. 'That's due a toast.'

'Thanks.' She handed me my glass across the bed. 'Cheers.'

'So, what about this?' She had a glass in her right hand and picked up the pistol in her left by the trigger guard, letting it swing between her first and index fingers.

'Better put it away. In the bedside drawer beside the Gideon.' Carefully she set the glass back on the table and swung round to open it. I dug deep into the left-hand pocket of the towelling gown. 'Mind you, Carpenter,' I was pulling my hand out, 'it'd be useful if you slipped these back in the clip first.' And I threw the handful of bullets down on to the rumpled indentation where her bum had just been.

She looked back, and down. 'You shit. So much for trust.'

'It's there,' I said. 'It's qualified.'

'I'll get the results tomorrow,' Carpenter was saying, with minor problems of enunciation.

'A matching print on a photograph and cup don't amount to a heap of evidence.'

'He did it, all right.'

'Sure. But if you hope to pin it on him you need more than that.'

'I just want to be certain. Unequivocally.'

'And then?'

'Report it upstairs, I suppose, let my superiors deal with it.'

'That won't go down well for you.'

'Don't I know it. I fucked up.'

'Too trusting, Carpenter.'

'Unlike you.'

'Exactly. I found out several years ago that those you could trust least were those closest to you.'

289

She was lying against the headboard, shoeless feet up on the bed, her skirt unbuttoned to the knee, musing over a glass of Chablis. She had, with a few pokes and tugs, taken out the stitches from my side, the dressing gown rolled down and bundled around my waist, which helped to conceal my erection (sick bastard!) as she put her hands all over me. Sexual frisson is nothing without interludes of mild pain, ask any masochist.

I had remained in the dressing gown as my sole suit of clothes (with the underpants washed) dried out over the central heating radiators. Then I had cut a few lines of what was left of my stash (she had turned down the offer of shared imbibement). Now I was sitting opposite her in one of the armchairs in the window alcove.

'Tell me more about your wife,' she said suddenly. I shook my head. 'But you're going to continue with your Lockerbie conspiracy theory?' *'Til the day I die*, I said inwardly. 'You are, aren't you?'

Easing myself out of the chair, making sure my gown covered my groin, I took the couple of steps across the carpet and refreshed my glass, then sat back down. 'Change the subject.'

She dipped her finger in her wine and ran it round the rim of the glass until it began to moan. 'I'm really sorry, Downe. All of it. It all seemed so easy, clear-cut and uninvolving back in London. You were just a fuck-up in a file, a characterless summation of facts and foibles. And now – now you're a fucking person.' She slurped her drink. 'You fucker.'

'Alcohol certainly brings out the articulacy in you.'

'D'you know what we call people like you—'

'Down in your excrescence on the Thames, you mean? I've seen pictures of that building in *Time*. Now that is truly one ugly building. Interesting, that the heir to the throne didn't add that to his carbuncular list, isn't it?'

'That's because it doesn't officially exist, you see; like me, it's a figment of the communal imagination. Anyway, shut up. I was telling you what you are. You're a leper, in agency-speak. One of the untouchables who do the dirty deeds, the lost, the unaccountable, the damned, the deniable.'

'So there are more of us, then?' She nodded. 'I don't suppose we get a club tie or anything? But maybe we could hold a survivors' ball? It'd have to be a one-off, wouldn't it? Because I don't imagine the Treasury need be concerned about budgeting for pension payments.'

'What are we going to do, Downe?'

'Us lepers? Well, retiring to a clearing in the jungle doesn't seem an option.' I sipped on my drink. I was high and hopeless and I didn't give a damn. 'Infect as many of our carers as possible.'

'There's something else that's been nagging and bothering me. Not just the leak to the paper, something worse—'

'You're kidding!'

'No, listen. The manager of one of McGurk's interests, a glorified porn shop, he was a gay guy, had a stupid tiff with his ex—' she motioned airily with her free hand, '—details don't matter. Got himself into serious trouble, we pulled him in, he confessed. He was facing five in the place where the homosexual sex is rarely consensual and the boys aren't too sophisticated in their sexual manners, and we tried to pressure him into doing a deal, telling us what he knew about McGurk, in return for the soft solution. My friend Brown was so insistent that he would do his thinking and talking best outside the nick he even managed to convince the Fiscal, too, it seems – fucking odd legal system they have here! – and guess what? He ends up swinging from a gibbet in his garage, not Brown, unfortunately, the gay guy, in a cloud of carbon monoxide from an exhaust pipe.'

'Suicide – you don't think.'

She shook her head. 'Exactly. Waiting on the pathology report for confirmation. Of doubt.'

'And you think our friend had him topped.'

'Are you thinking McGurk or Brown?'

'Exactly.'

I explained about Nadeem and how it was important that Carpenter square him. My plan was rudimentary and hedged around with difficulties, but it was the only one I had. I told her that she would have to call him from Pitt Street, so that he could check back that she was for real, and then she had to see him and persuade him.

'You mean it was him! You had him following me around, like a stalker?'

'Not quite like that. But he was checking you out, just keeping in touch so that I could reach you in a hurry if I needed to.'

'And not because you were missing me.' Carpenter was more than half-cut, her cheeks rosy, her eyes alight and her enunciation of sentences was done with the utmost care and attempted clarity. 'Do you think we should have more wine?'

'Probably not. I'll ring room service.'

She waved an arm exaggeratedly. 'No, leave it a while. It's early yet anyway.' She rubbed her nose and shuffled on the bed. I was still on the sofa, legs now firmly crossed, feeling as if I had an aura of electricity around me, even the hairs on my legs seemed to be crackling, my nose was running – I kept wiping it very undignifiedly on the sleeve of the gown – and, despite the wine, my mouth still tasted as if I had been licking a metal post. 'Downe? What does it do for you, cocaine?'

I shrugged. How to answer? 'Not much, but enough. I don't know. Chills the soul, provides enough of a sense of purpose to keep going – or maybe it just blots out the bad bits. It's no big deal. Makes you talk a lot—'

'Not you, not about personal stuff.'

I rubbed my nose again. 'Believe me, 'til I had a coke habit I used to talk in sign language.'

'You know, if you keep pursuing what happened to your wife they'll do for you.'

'I know. But I can't stop. It's a promise I made.'

'Fuck promises. You have to stop. Let the past go. You have to live. Just give up, there's nothing you can do.'

'Maybe not. But it doesn't matter.'

'You're being stupid and pig-headed, Downe. She wouldn't want you to kill yourself for her. I – no one would want that. It's such a waste.'

'It's not for her, it's for me.' I didn't want to think about it. There was a smell of burning in my nostrils, and I was sure it wasn't coming from the cocaine after-burn. 'It's for me.' And now the room was going bleary.

'If it's for you, save yourself. Don't just throw yourself away.'

'It's a bit late for that, don't you think?' I tried to laugh. 'Here's the one who made it impossible for me, now telling me that it could be all right. It can't ever be, and you know it.'

'There's a way out. Give up your stupid quest. If we can get through this you can walk away, start again. Whatever happened to your wife, and your baby, you weren't responsible, you don't have to carry this to an early grave.'

'I was.'

'Sorry?'

'I was responsible. Culpable, anyway. Morally.'

She sat up on the bed and swung her legs off so that her feet were on the ground. 'How do you mean? That's not possible.'

'It's possible. I am.' I stood up and turned away, opening the curtains to the darkness.

'Explain, Downe. I don't understand.'

'Mmhh? I can't talk about it.' Tears of condensation were making their way down the inside of the window; I was fighting to stop my own.

'Please. It might help. I want to understand.'

I drew a glum little face in the glass. 'So do I.' Then I brutally wiped my arm down the window. 'I saw them off at the airport. Frankfurt. We had rented a house north of Boston for Christmas. My leave started a couple of days later. She had been going to stop off in London but at the last moment decided to travel all the way through, to get started on making our Christmas perfect. She had changed since the baby – I can't even say her name, or the child's, not any more – no drugs, clean living, healthy, hopeful. I kissed her goodbye. She was tearful but really happy. Exhilarated. A natural high. Then she walked through the barrier, pushing the baby chair, stopped, looked back and blew me a kiss. That was it.'

I turned back to the room and Carpenter. 'I was out of there and running. Didn't even look back. At the time the bomb went off I was rolling around in bed with the wife of a colleague. I was probably having an orgasm when their bodies hit the ground. *Petit mort*? Hardly. Sex for me now is about death and guilt. Fucking me must be like banging the Grim Reaper. Except when I'm off my face. And when am I not? Then it must be like fucking an agricultural implement. So,' I pulled open the front of the towelling gown, 'your earlier comment wasn't too far off.'

She started to rise, like perhaps she was going to come to me, to comfort me, but the distance between us was too difficult to traverse and slowly she sat down. 'Jesus, Downe,' she said. 'Jesus.'

No hope there either, I thought.

I woke howling, in my head rather than out loud, and when I wiped the sweat from my face and stopped shivering and gibbering I began to pick out a milky shape against the darkness. 'Carpenter?' There was a murmur back at me; I turned to the part of the bed beside me which looked smooth and untouched. Even in the half-light I could see that there was no indentation in the pillow, no faint tell-tale smell of cologne. 'Carpenter? Look, I'm sorry. Get into bed and I'll sleep in the chair. I must have passed out.' I noticed that I still had on the towelling dressing gown, which I might have kidded myself was causing the film of sweat all over me, if there was any part of me left to fool. 'What time is it?'

'Around two.' My eyes were becoming accustomed to the murk and I could pick out the outline of a face on the ghost. Her hair was down, making her look very young and entirely vulnerable. 'Downe?' I could hear tears in her voice. 'You know what? You really scare me. You do. I imagined you would, but not in this way. I can't cope with it. I don't think it would frighten me as much if you were obviously – I don't know ... fuck! I *don't* know – bad, evil, threatening, mono-maniacal. I don't know what I'm saying. Someone *constant*, for Christ's sake. But you're not. You can be funny and self-deprecating, fanciable – what am I saying here, what's that say about me? – and then, like in the park tonight, you just seem to enjoy hating, terrorizing. You scare the lifeblood out of me.'

She took a deep breath and walked nearer, paused, then sat down on the end of the bed. For some reason I imagined golfers' dreams, perfect shots, difficult lies (whenever were they problematic for me!) and simple, geometric answers. 'And then the drugs ... I don't know how you're going to be, what they do. I don't know if they promote one part of you, subjugate another, I don't understand the chemicals, the imbalances, or – I suppose what I'm saying is that I shouldn't want to, but I do want to – to know you.'

She put up a filmy hand at me, I thought of the Lady of the Lake and a shining, brandished sword. 'Just don't try to make a fucking joke now, Downe.' And she was scrambling up the bed and throwing herself on my wet and ravaged chest. 'Just hold me, Downe, nothing else. It's a fantasy, that's all. I just

295

want to believe in love and kindness, innocence undefiled, until the dawn at least.'

I kissed the top of her head, which I fancied smelled of heather and herbs but was probably some concoction from Harrods, fiddled with the tie of her dressing gown and she scuttled hot and long and naked into the bed and around me.

'I fancied I heard you say innocence,' I said softly, 'or was it some kind of chemical flashback?' My groin ached, my head pounded and my mouth felt like the bottom of a spitoon. It seemed churlish to ease her over to grab, from the side table, the infallible way of shutting out the night and the circling bats.

17

I spent the early part of the morning walking along the beach, beating against the wind, the westerly whipping the sea to breakers and froth. Squally rain kept coming in, splattering the coast, then disappearing, leaving the sky the colour of old underwear. The sand was covered in driftwood, seaweed, plastic, and what seemed like the entire contents of a small town's bowels. I guess it was too early in the season to bring out the tractors to scour the beach clean for the tourists. There weren't even any treasure hunters with metal detectors, just the occasional man or woman and dog adding to the general defecation.

Carpenter had visited a thrift shop for me. I had on a dark blue knitted woollen hat, a large serge overcoat and underneath, dark baggy trousers with a hooded tracksuit top. Also a pair of wire-rimmed, slightly cracked glasses which, with the hat and stubble, were meant to effect a dramatic change in my appearance. It worked for me. I had been transformed from a dangerous villain to a dangerous and villainous flasher.

I walked on towards the distant, misty and rain-battered shape of Ailsa Craig. My nose was runny, but when wasn't it? And then I remembered the golf competition. Even in this half-hearted gale it would be going ahead – I had seen the troops of brightly-adorned, oil-skinned spectators leaving the hotel earlier – and I thought that on a golf course one more odd gink among the many would not be too noticeable. At least I could check it out, walk round the roads on the perimeter of the course, as I imagined the golfers, like twigs bent against the season, straight out of some primitive, figurative painting. The coke and the uppers were kicking in.

I walked over the dunes and the scrubby grass, over a hill and into a large and virtually empty car park. There was a camper van with a sail board on top but the owner, sitting inside reading a newspaper, clearly didn't feel like assailing the elements. One miscalculation on the board and, if he was lucky, he would touch land in Newfoundland. There was another car there, a red saloon, and then I became aware of a buzzing sound, turned around and saw a small airplane, battling the currents and thermals; then, on the far side of the football field-size concrete apron, I spotted a man and a young boy, the man holding the box which was clearly controlling the plane.

The model took a bit of a buffeting, then seemed to duck under the wind into the quiet air below the dune and skimmed the perimeter of the park before landing with perfect precision and taxiing up to the couple. I felt like applauding. The man put his arm round the boy, who was about half his height, and gave him a cuddle. I would have done anything to change places.

Then the rain started again, droplets pattering against my cheek and the glasses. I drew my collar up again and headed for the course.

The message on the mobile was from Brown. All it said was, 'Your boy's been at it again,' and a number to call him back. He hadn't put a time to the message and the phone had been off for at least fifteen hours. She slammed the car door, locked it, fished in her purse for change for the meter and forced in five twenty pence coins. She decided not to call Brown back.

There was a note stuck to the desk she shared with him, saying that he would be back around 3 p.m. and that it was important that they talked. She sat down in the chair on the opposite side of the desk to his, taking in the neatness, the blotter, the paper knife, the empty wire filing trays, the quill of pens and pencils in a red holder, the two telephones, one of which she pulled towards her by the cable. From the number in the small plastic window she saw that it was a direct line. She was about to lift the receiver when it began to ring. She let it go on for three or four bleeps then picked it up, saying nothing.

'Angus? Is that you – Angus?' Male voice. Local.

For a second or two she even considered trying to pass herself off as a Glasgow male, doubly ridiculous. 'Sorry. He's not here right now. Who's calling?'

'Doesn't matter. I'll call back later.'

'He'll be here about three,' she said just before he hung up.

Grabbing for a pencil she punched in 1471 and jotted down the number played back on the note he had left her. Then she punched three on the array of buttons. The voice she had spoken to thirty seconds before said, 'MacIntosh . . . Hello? Ed MacIntosh.'

Gently she pressed her finger down to disconnect the call, then released it, heard the dialling tone and punched in 100. 'I'm calling from Strathclyde police,' she said when the operator answered. 'I need to talk to someone there who can provide me with the name and address corresponding to a particular telephone number. Local, yes. Sure, I'll hold. Oh, and before you go, I need complete itemized phone records for another number. Should I talk to your supervisor about that too? OK, that's fine. I'll hang on.'

Brown was sitting at his desk when she came in. It was almost 3.30.

He looked up and smiled. She knew little enough about him, but that curl of the lip always seemed to indicate pleasure in misfortune. She nodded, pulled the other chair away from the desk and sat down at a decent distance, so that he was not dominating her vision. 'I left a message,' he was opening a file on the desk, 'on your mobile.'

'Just got it.' She crossed her legs, allowing her skirt to ride up quite deliberately. She had been back to her room in the hotel and changed into fresh clothes, a dark suit with a faint chalk pinstripe and a skirt which was several inches above the knee when she was standing. 'I've been away. Out of range. Sorry.' Her fingers tugged at her skirt, deliberately drawing his attention to it, which slid back up when she took them away. 'Anything important?'

He nodded. 'Your man, Downe. Done it again. Have a look.' He pushed the file towards her, inviting her to get up, which she did, to lean across and pick it up. She sat down, crossed her left leg over her right, balancing the file in her lap, opening it up. A glossy colour photograph looked up at her. A woman, blonde, naked. She picked it up, then noticed there were several different prints. She took the file in both hands, dumped it open on her part of the desk and pulled in the chair, then spread the contents out, making a loose fan of the photographs.

The first photograph again. The woman was lying almost as if sated, her head turned away from the camera so that a long hank of hair fell across her left shoulder just above her left breast, her left leg pulled up slightly and pointing away from the camera. She looked as if she might be sleeping, but Carpenter knew, of course, that she wasn't. Then she caught sight of a pool of blood between her legs. She said nothing, lifted the next picture. She could see more of the face and lower body in the second shot. Her body was beautiful, *had been* beautiful she corrected herself. In this one she could see a dribble of blood from her lips. And, in the next, that she had been shot with a small calibre weapon in the middle of the forehead. Her expression looked resigned.

'I know—' Carpenter began to say, then pushed aside the

photographs and looked at the report. The victim's name was Siobhan Hope, and now she remembered why she was familiar. 'I mean, I don't understand? What this has to do with me?'

'Not you exactly, Downe, or whatever his name is.'

He waited for her to ask. 'Why don't you just tell me everything, Brown, and we can stop this little game?'

'Until a few days ago Siobhan here was a hostess, or whatever you'd call a high-class hooker in a club. One of McGurk's places. According to some of the other staff there she walked out a couple of days ago, probably for good, with someone bearing a strong resemblance to your man. Several of the staff are sure of it—'

'Presumably from the newspaper picture you pushed in front of them?'

He ignored her bait. 'She left the place with him, or his twin brother, and wasn't seen again till this morning, early, when her cleaner let herself in and found her employer splayed over the bedroom carpet. Shot with a .22, although she seems to have been dead when it happened, or near enough, because she didn't struggle and our chaps think that he probably suffocated her with a pillow first. There's a post mortem going on now. She was most likely drugged first, there's a lot of evidence of recreational gear around. In a post-coital slumber perhaps. Probably been at it for thirty-six hours.'

She shook her head slowly and with distaste. 'The really nice bit,' he continued, 'is that he seems to have dragged her from the bed, arranged her neatly on the floor as you see, then put one through her head and one up – errm, inside her. Obviously we'll be checking for semen and DNA.'

'There are a whole parcel of assumptions neatly wrapped up there, Detective Superintendent. She leaves the club with someone who looks like Downe and,' she snapped her fingers, 'you've got him convicted.'

Brown leaned back in the chair. 'Didn't I tell you? His prints are all over the place.'

'I'm really sorry, Downe.' The engine was running, a Carpenters tape was playing (bored of skulking around and watching young and old men batter the cover off balls, I had bought it in a music shop as a stupid joke for the other Carpenter), drowning out with its hum and confusion – although it seemed unnecessarily cautious – any hyperbolic listening devices, in the ludicrous event of them being aimed at us. We were in the same car park where I had watched the man and boy fly the remote-controlled plane earlier; the wind had gained focus and was beating breakers against the sea wall and driving heavy, foamy flecks of spray over the top of the embankment. It was almost romantic, but for the circumstances, and when I looked up at the night sky it looked not so much like a darkness sprayed with stars as a riddled blackout curtain bleeding light.

Everything I touched turned to blood and coldness. I tried not to think of her end, the fear and the pain. 'Yeah,' I said, punching the eject button on the tape. *Siobhan ... Hope*, I whispered to myself. 'Hope would be hope of the wrong thing,' I said quietly to myself.

'I didn't say that I could vouch for your alibi, because—' she paused. I said nothing. 'A couple of reasons. Not because I was embarrassed or ashamed, but because I knew he'd be straight down here on the hunt.'

'And the other's obvious.' I rolled down the window, pulled the tape from the machine and spun it backhanded out into the wet car park. 'He's leaking, not just to the press but to the opposition.'

'We don't know that for sure.'

'So, it's three coincidences. I'm hung out to dry all over the front page, the video shop gay is stretched from the rafters and now—' I paused on Siobhan's name, '—someone else who just might have been able to sketch in a little of McGurk's background is taken down. Of course—' the windscreen wipers were on intermittent, sweeping away the sea water every few seconds, '—it could just have been a warning, a grisly game, a challenge to me. Two of his to one of mine. By that reckoning, I guess—' a shiver and twist in the gut, '—I guess we're still ahead.' I tried to make it sound like a hard and bitter aside, but it came out flat and distasteful.

'There's no definite proof.'

'You might need that. I don't.'

She banged on the steering wheel with both hands, turned round and hissed at me. 'Listen, I did something stupid and unprofessional last night. I'm not going to do it again. Just give me some time. I've had the result of the fingerprinting on the stuff I sent for analysis. Brown's prints are there – there's a match, not enough to use definitively in evidence, there was only a usable partial on the picture – but enough for me. But that still only proves that he handled the photograph—'

'You know and I know that he gave me up to the newspaper.'

'Will you stop interrupting, Downe? Just hear me out. Someone called today on his direct line when he was out. Wouldn't give a name. I checked it back through BT and it turns out to be a direct line into the newsroom of this reporter MacIntosh's paper.'

'There you go.'

'Shut up, I said. Also, I'm having the phone records from the last eighteen months on his private line delivered to me by BT and I've also set up a tap on it.'

'You got permission?'

She gave a dry chuckle. 'You mean, did the Home Secretary sign on the dotted line? Hardly. There's a small internal bug installed, down the line to a voice-activated tape recorder, which will be reviewed every couple of hours.' I nodded. 'I

303

was thinking about getting a warrant for a tap on his house phone, but I decided not. The local engineers and even the supervisors can be a bit bolshie about it, things can leak. It may be unlikely, but I didn't want to take the chance.'

'I get the feeling that he'd probably feel more secure inside the bowels of the beast than at home. So I don't think it matters. If he says anything, it'll be from there.' The thrum of the engine was in counterpoint to the rhythmic pulses of the crashing sea. 'My mother,' I said, 'she always wanted me to be a priest.' I grinned. 'Pretty unlikely, mmhm? But celibacy would have saved at least three people, wouldn't it?'

'Don't be maudlin, Downe, it doesn't suit.'

'I wasn't being. Just an observation.' I dug deep into an inside pocket of my coat, my fingers moving past the cold stock of the gun to the ring. 'Are you superstitious, Carpenter?'

'I don't think so. No, not at all.'

'Good, because I am.' I took her left hand in my right and dropped the ring into it. 'My hideous inheritance to squander as you may.'

She peered at it in the dark. 'It's a ring. I can't take this.'

'Cool down, Carpenter, it's not a proposal, nothing at all meaningful even. I just want rid of it.' I put my hand on the door lever. 'You're right. I'll ditch it.' I put my hand out.

'You're not serious?'

'It served its purpose. I don't need it any more.'

'I don't understand.'

'I don't think I do myself. Maybe I was just holding on to hatred to avoid blaming too much on me.'

I pushed the lever down and strained to open the door against the wind. Her hand grabbed my arm and pulled me back. 'You *are* serious. Close the door. I'll hold on to it for the time being, until this crap is finished.'

Sitting down in the seat again I pulled the door closed behind me. 'Do you know if she had any family. Siobhan?'

304

'I'll find out.'

'I suppose the ring must be worth a couple of hundred bucks. Will you get it to her family?'

'If that's really what you want, sure. But you shouldn't blame yourself. You didn't kill her. Look – don't get me wrong here – but she wasn't entirely an innocent. I mean, she was mixing with the scum, involved there, if you see what I mean?'

'No, not entirely.' Anger was rising in me. 'What do you mean?'

'Don't lose the plot, I'm not suggesting that anything she did deserved the outcome, but she was an employee of McGurk's – OK, only indirectly. I checked her out on the computer—'

'You would, Carpenter!'

'Fuck you, Downe, there's a murder investigation going on!'

'Tell me about it. Not so much an investigation as a rush to judgment.'

'I'm trying to help you, Downe, be reasonable.' I nodded. 'There's a post mortem happening. They'll be looking for interlocked pubic hairs, semen—'

'Mine.'

'Exactly. DNA. Will they find any?'

I took a deep breath and sighed. 'No semen. We were careful. And we showered, so I doubt it. But what's the point? I have an alibi, don't I?' There was a cold clasp around my heart. I was entirely reliant on her. No one had seen me at the hotel, there were no independent witnesses to corroborate my story, so if she wanted to give me up I hadn't a hope. No one would believe me. It would be an easy clear-up, although I knew that it wouldn't come to that, that I wouldn't be given space to make embarrassing claims. The last thing anyone wanted here was a garrulous witness, however likely his tale.

'What are you talking about? Of course.'

'Keep it that way, Carpenter.'

'You should give the drugs a miss, John, they're making you paranoiac.'

I think it was the first time she had called me by first name. I felt it start in my stomach and soon it rose up and I was choking on laughter, incapable of speaking. She giggled, then she too was howling until she punched and slapped at me and eventually, panting for breath, I was able to stop. 'Sorry—' I said, wiping at my face, '—the paranoia. Just because the entire local police force is on the case and every hood who wants to earn a nest egg, or a major drug score, is looking to hunt me down like an animal, I should be more reasonable and rational. Please, I apologize.'

The engine was still running, the windows had misted up inside, and from the outside the car must have looked like the venue for a tryst, apart from, perhaps, the fact that it wasn't rocking on its axles. My head hurt, my stomach ached and I cursed my infectious, fatal leprosy. 'She was a nice girl, whatever was on the file, or the floppy disk.'

'Do you want to know?' I nodded my head. 'According to the intelligence – OK, just gossip collated by the local plod – McGurk and she had a fling a while back. That's based on them being seen out together in various clubs and him being spotted going into her place and not leaving, apparently. Maybe he regarded her as his property in some way, which is why he reacted so violently.' I said nothing, just stared at the weeping windscreen.

'What's the script, about what happened?'

'She seems to have known whoever was at the door. Opened it, no sign of a struggle – and – maybe your mind can take it from there?'

'Just tell me what you think, Carpenter. I'm not sensitive.'

'Possibly there was a small party. Drugs. They found a bit of blow, a few grains of speed or coke, maybe heroin on the mirror, it's being analysed, smeared fingerprints, hers probably, so they must have been tooting up. If there was sex, it looks like it was consensual. Maybe she fell asleep, an overdose, it could have been a lot stronger than she was used to. Perhaps he, they, deliberately doped her, fixed her drink. She's undressed, in a stupor, someone presses a pillow hard down on her face and sits on it. When she's dead, a while later, the killer lifts her down on to the floor, poses her and shoots her once in the head with a .22 and then, sorry, inserts the gun in her vagina and pulls again. Or it could have been the other way round.'

'Making a point.'

'A brutal point.'

'This is what happens to those that stray out of the fold. I shouldn't have asked her to leave the club.'

'You have a grand conceit of yourself, Downe. You think she took one look at you and decided to give it all up for love? She walked because she wanted to, because for her own reasons she had had enough.'

'I suppose.'

'Listen to a walker, Downe. It was her choice.'

'Anything more?'

'Not much. You want to hear it all?'

'Not really, but maybe there's something there to go on.'

'She had one minor conviction for passing dud cheques, no serious form. There was a deposit account paying-in book with a couple of thousand, she owned a car, a fairly new Golf GTi. And—' she took a breath.

'And, Carpenter?'

'We found a couple of videos. When I checked the inventory of the stuff at Weston's, the gay guy who was topped, the titles matched.'

'I'm not with you. He was gay, wasn't he? What was she doing with gay porn videos?'

'He was a businessman. A hired hand. It wasn't just gay stuff the company made and manufactured, there was loads of straight stuff too. If you can call that kind of thing straight.'

'Still, I'm not with you.'

She tapped my leg gently in what could have been a gesture of sympathy or mild chastisement for stupidity. 'She was in them, Downe. She was starring in them.'

I nodded and exhaled. The world was a tired, dirty and cynical place. 'Now I'm with you.' I needed something, quite a lot of something, to take away reality. 'Let's get out of here.'

She leaned over to switch the screen blower on, then wiped at the window with the back of her sleeve. The punctured blackout swam into view. 'Any ideas?'

'I want to study everything you can get me on McGurk. And Brown. I want to get inside his head.'

There was silence between us for a long while, the engine idling and the blower howling at the screen. Eventually she said, 'Anything else?'

I pursed my lips and shook my head. 'I was thinking about tombstones, about what I'd like on mine. Did'ya ever think of that?'

She put the car into gear. 'Can't say I did.'

'Of course, I'll have no say in it and there is no one to pay heed to my wishes.' I looked at her meaningfully.

She put the car into reverse. 'Here's a deal. I'll pay for the inscription – as long as it isn't too wordy and they don't charge by the letter. All right? So what is it?'

'Haven't quite decided yet. But when communal madness, nuclear waste or global warming does for everything, I've got one for this part of the planet. Hopefully, the last man alive will be an ornamental sculptor. It's by T. S. Eliot, courtesy of the prison library. Something earlier made me think of him. "And the wind shall say, 'Here were decent godless people: their only monument the asphalt road. And a thousand lost golf balls.'"'

We moved back and then forward in a sweeping circle. 'I don't know what to make of you,' she said quietly.

I turned and smiled at her profile. 'About six foot two and

a pauper's grave.' The wipers were furiously whisking at the rain and sea spray. 'I'm toying with this one, bear it in mind: "There's no such thing as bad publicity, except your own obituary."'

'What did I tell you about expensive letter count? I'll just make it RIP, unless, of course, you can think of a further abbreviation.'

I held up my fingers, British-style, in the V.

18

He put down the mug of tea on the bench and pulled across a tray of seedlings. There were still at least a couple of hours of daylight left and he wanted to pot them on.

The thermostatically controlled heater whirred softly into life and he felt a breeze of mild warm air blow around his legs. He bent down to screw the typist's chair up a couple of notches, turned on the radio, delved into the open bag of compost on the floor beside him and began to fill up a row of pots with handfuls of the dark loam. He then turned to prick out the seedlings painstakingly with the end of a pencil before plunging it into the first of the pots and, rotating it, made a planting hole in the new medium.

The greenhouse was almost at the bottom of the long rectangular garden behind the blond sandstone villa. He had insisted to Marjorie that it should be made of wood when they moved house five years before, even though it worked out more than four times as expensive as the aluminium version. She had complained about the price, how they couldn't manage it so soon after moving to a larger new house, but he had reassured her without, of course, telling her that they were never going to have to worry about money again.

'The kids are gone, Marj,' he had reassured her. 'Don't you think we both deserve some treats now? When we've got a good long while to enjoy them?'

It was funny, he had never really been interested in

gardening before; now he regretted all of the missed years, the plants he could have developed and brought to maturity, the landscapes he could have created, stage-managed. Some of the lads had got into golf – a good nature walk ruined, as they say – while he was helping to create the environment which they ignored and sclaffed through. There was something about watching fragile life bursting out and tremulously finding its course which was such a therapeutic contrast to what he did at work each day.

They had chosen the house well, or at least he had. The old couple who were selling it for something smaller (a coffin, he thought at the time), had let it run down so that it seemed grubby, full of old smells and decay, which must have helped to put others off. But he could see the possibilities in the large, flower-papered rooms, the dark varnish and the antique kitchen full of industrial artefacts. Marjorie hadn't been too keen – 'What do we need with a larger place at our time of life?' she mumped quietly – to which he quickly came back: 'We could always start a second family!' Then he had cuddled her, shaken his head and smiled.

'Well, it's somewhere that'll appreciate, something to leave the kids. And there's plenty of room if they want to come to stay, lots of space to avoid each other if they want, lots of room for our kids' kids.' She moaned about the cleaning but let him go ahead, have his own way. She usually did.

The garden was a mess, overgrown and under-managed. The former owners, the crumbly couple, were too infirm to see to it, another visual blight which, no doubt, also helped deter potential purchasers. He hadn't cared. The weather was changing, it was coming to the end of winter and he could always hack it down, cover it with weedkiller or paving slabs when the weather improved. But when the time came he was enraptured by the renewed life appearing, first the daffodils and crocuses, the buds appearing on the fruit trees (he had spent his previous life barely noticing the change in seasons), shoots of other plants he didn't know the names of pushing through the soil. It was as if he was in charge of his own benign and walled world. He started to buy gardening magazines and tuning into programmes on TV, surreptitiously at first, afraid that the new enthusiasm would either wither in his own seasonal interest, or in his wife's tolerant, laughing support, but instead it began to flourish. Whatever had happened, he had somehow implanted in himself a perennial interest, one which did not fade or fold with the seasons, but which, even in the midst of the darkest winter's day or murky job, left him hopeful of what was to come, in time.

The greenhouse arrived within a few months. The packages were unloaded from the back of a van and he carefully put the prefabricated parts together, with great ceremony and enthusiam, over a mild weekend. This was another strange and late development. He had never really used his hands before, besides the form-filling and typing and, lately, the gardening, and now he discovered that he had a real aptitude. Probably because his training had taught him to be methodical, to examine all angles.

But he began to feel, with a growing disquiet he did not want to admit to himself, that he would have been better in his life being more self-contained, that he had never really made a choice of what he wanted to be or become, that it had been an immature and pressured decision – not so much from outside but by the ill-equipped, delusional and conventional kid he then was – and that, by not allowing his personality to develop before he tucked it into uniformity along with the imparted ambitions of his parents, he might have been immeasurably happier. Not just happier, more useful. His life, he realized, had been devoted to keeping back the jungle, which he regarded as a fairly noble and important calling, but, instead of slash and burn, he realized what he had really wanted was to till and adorn the clearings.

He heard himself laughing at his pomposity. But he was happy. The radio news was sending out waves of words about the forthcoming visit of the Prime Minister to Scotland, but it washed over him. He had squared his conscience with his intelligence, he didn't have long to do and his retirement would be prosperous. He had made his own existential accommodation between the savages and the pilgrims and what it amounted to entirely was looking after his own. In just a few months he would go and if he looked back, which wasn't likely, he wouldn't see accusing or betrayed eyes in the long undergrowth. He would simply look at his family and know that he had kept them from it, that they and their offspring would prosper, not just financially, but in growing up apart from it and secure in the daylight. It really was about separating and nurturing the best strains and breeding out, or keeping out, the worst, no matter what blood, shit and bone went into the process. And, after he went, there would be no traces left of any of that.

Long before the flat boxes arrived he had decided to site the greenhouse about eight feet from the back wall, alongside the spot he planned to use for his compost heaps, where it was unimpeded by bushes or branches or shadow, where it caught the sun, when it was there, all day long. Beyond the wall was a huge open playing field, some historical bequest, apparently, which had been another attraction of the house, the knowledge that there was a grassy exclusion zone, that a rash of Wimpey homes or housing association flats would not inch up to his borders. Above the wall was a twelve-foot high wire fence which shielded the garden and the new greenhouse from any misplaced ball, bottle or divot, through which only a perfectly directed javelin descending at a forty-five degree angle could penetrate. And not only did they not allow spear-chuckers in the park, dogs were banned too.

In theory, anyway. Looking across now he could see that the wet grassland was all but deserted apart from a couple of distant groups walking – very furtively it seemed to him – a couple of small dogs. Leaning over he picked up the mug of tea, took a deep gulp and put it down. So preoccupied had he been with the therapy of seeding that it had become luke-warm. He shrugged and turned back to the infant sweet peas.

It must have been around half an hour later when his concentration was interrupted by an irritating and far-off buzzing. He turned the radio down, some endless and impen-etrable play performed in Home Counties accents again, and listened. It was the sound of a light electric saw. He turned back to the pots. But the noise seemed to rise and fall and he realized that it did not sound at all like an electric saw, it was too inconsistent. He looked over to the playing field, the direction it seemed to be coming from, but could see nothing unusual. Curiosity aroused, he opened the greenhouse door, walked the few steps to the bottom of the garden to look over the wall and through the fence.

About two hundred yards away, after focusing his eyes properly, he saw the source of it. A man, with his back to him, was hunched down, fiddling with a fairly large model aircraft. Then he stood up, still facing away but clearly holding a control panel, and the plane began racing and skipping across the grass before taking off and soaring into a wide arc and a lazy circuit around the field. Shaking his head, he turned away and went back into the greenhouse.

His back was sore and his eyes, too, but there were only a few more plants to pot on. About eight weeks from now, he thought, the garden would be a riot of colour. He leaned over and began burrowing with his right hand into the three-foot high bag of compost, aiming to take out enough to fill the remaining pots. His hand hit something hard in the bag. His fingers groped for it. It felt like metal. Curiously he pulled it out, becoming aware of what it was almost before his eyes locked on to it. A handgun. He stood looking at it lying in the palm of his hand for a few seconds, stunned, his mind slow

314

to detach from where he had been, in tender beauty, to the ugliness of his reality. Then the vague buzzing became noisier and more insistent. He looked up through the glass roof and saw the small plane diving irresistibly towards the greenhouse and him.

The wings tore off as it smashed against a cedar strut and through the glass. Brown might have been fractionally aware of the shattering before the impact cap ignited the half-pound of explosive. The three-inch nails tied around it with rubber bands blew out in a blizzard of white-hot metal, glass shards and fragments of wood, slashing, scoring, shredding, tearing and pitting. Before Brown's body slumped into the small internal bed of what was left of the young, razored tomato plants, the clothes remaining on him had been reduced to tattered ribbons, the skin on his face and the front of his torso turned into a red, meaty pulp.

For some reason the left eye survived entirely untouched, and it remained open to the sky as the blasted body and its blood mulched the earth.

19

It's pretty simple to make an extremely powerful, sophisticated and deadly bomb from common components found around the house, car or garden shed. All you need is a little know-how and strong nerves. Terrorist movements throughout the world have been relying on this method for decades, when supplies of commercial explosives are too difficult to obtain, and knowledge of how to improvise effective bombs is part of Special Forces training. It had been a long time, but I was hoping I remembered the formulae.

Explosive theory is simple – in theory. An explosive is basically any sort of material which, when ignited by heat or shock, undergoes rapid decomposition or oxidation. Energy stored in the material is released in the form of heat and light, or by breaking down into gaseous compounds which occupy a much larger volume than the original piece of material. Because the expansion is incredibly rapid, large volumes of air are displaced by the expanding gases, the expansion occurs at a speed greater than the speed of sound, hence the sonic boom of the explosion. Simple. For years kids have experimented (you can usually tell them by the missing fingers) with sodium chlorate, sugar and fuses, and the fertilizer bombs beloved of the IRA are only a small step up.

The two essential ingredients of any master-blaster's chemical cupboard are nitric and sulphuric acids. Sulphuric acid can be obtained from any uncharged car battery, and, to avoid any awkward questions at the chemist's, it's relatively easy to make nitric acid. It's wonderful stuff, the heart of nitroglycerine and dynamite, the profits of which enabled Alfred Nobel to fund his various prizes. Nitroglycerine is just nitric and sulphuric acids, sodium bicarbonate, salt, distilled water and glycerine, but it's essential to keep the materials chilled as you work, below thirty degrees, or they bury you in a shoe box. Nobel got the message about the instability of the stuff when several of his workers exploded, not exactly through spontaneous combustion, and from this he developed the more reliable dynamite, which is basically the same stuff soaked into sawdust and horse shit.

Nitroglycerine had one strong recommendation for me: it's an impact explosive, but with a vengeance – any bumping in a bus queue and it's likely to be a mass funeral. Mercury fulminate is another choice impact explosive – with five grams of mercury, thirty-five millilitres of nitric acid, 30 millilitres of ethyl alcohol and distilled water you're in business – but again it's too unstable. And as my plan depended on impact, I didn't want to use an electrically controlled fuse because I wasn't sure I would have a clear line of sight all the way. Seeing the kid flying his radio-controlled plane had given me the idea of how to deliver the bomb, and although Carpenter tried to dissuade me, there was no way she could, short of quickly raising the temperature under my nitric acid.

When I went to the model shop for the plane, part of the problem was solved for me. One of the newest hobbies is model rocketry and a model rocket's engine is composed of one single large grain of propellant which provides enormous explosive power and thrust. It's encased in heavy cardboard tubing and the way to get at the propellant is to slit the tube and unravel it like a paper towel roll. I bought a pack of three of them. I was going to break this down, roll it out like gunpowder and mix it with fuel oil and sodium chlorate, then add some home-made nitroglycerine which, in the pasty mix, would become much more stable.

Then I gave Carpenter a list of the ingredients I needed, none of which would arouse suspicion when purchased. I also needed a place to make the stuff, somewhere with fresh air and, ideally, air extraction, because the fumes given off in the process can be deadly. A hotel room was too much of a giveaway – there was also, of course, the possibility of disposing of half the guests – so, reluctanctly, it had to be back at the river hide-out. At least this time I would be getting some heat off the primus stove I asked her to buy.

It took me most of a day, and several heart scares, to complete the compound. The nitric acid I made from fertilizer, sodium nitrate, sulphuric acid, with the addition of some distilled water, fifty-eight grams of the first, thirty-two millilitres of the second. At the end of the process I had a goodly amount of pure acid sitting in a flask in my ice bath. At one point when I was making it, a dosser came into the shed and, seeing me crouched over a flame, thought I was brewing tea. It cost me a pound to get rid of him.

By the time I had my nitroglycerine, my head was splitting, and when I had finished mixing up the paste and carefully slipping it into the plastic tubing, into which I would seal the impact fuse, my stomach was heaving. Fortunately there was a reasonable through-draught in the shed, or I would probably have been overcome.

The fuse was extremely easy to make and highly sensitive. I cracked the cover on the Magicube flashbulb, revealing the four small bulbs which, in rotation, produce the red-eye in the family photographs. Each of these has a small metal rod holding it in place. Carefully I pulled out a bulb by its rod with a small pair of needle-nosed pliers, then soaked the bulb in acetone for half an hour to dissolve the plastic coating around it. As it was soaking, I stripped and crushed the heads of several dozen matches with a scalpel, smeared glue on the bulb and rolled the bulb around in the red explosive powder. I tested the other bulbs by chucking them against a wall and watching them explode and fizz gloriously.

I was packing the explosive mix and the detonator into the three-quarter inch nails, taping it up and taping the nails to it, when Carpenter came back.

'I don't like this,' she said.

'You don't have to go along with it any further, but there's no way you can stop me, other than by turning me in.'

She just looked at me and shrugged resignedly.

20

I rang the doorbell, trying to look casual and relaxed in my body language, slouching on the step, head down, studying the list on the clipboard I was holding. It was raining, the sky was black and boiling and the light was the colour of porridge. My bobble hat was pulled down over my forehead and my collar was up. I rang the door bell again. It was 7.30 a.m., and I was hoping for hangovers and early-morning lassitude. To enhance the act I hopped around a little, hunched my shoulders and leaned over the board to prevent the rain hitting the list. I rang again, an even longer burst. Which got some response: I could hear a dog barking, which was an additional problem to deal with.

After a couple of minutes, 'Yeah. Whit is it?' a sleepy male voice answered.

'Sorry to get you up so early,' I shouted at the intercom. I had my old man's best accent on. 'It's Maxi Cars. I've goat a letter fur Mr McGurk. Sanny said it was dead urgent.' Sandy McAteer was the ostensible owner of Maxi Cars, but he was only the front man for McGurk and what seemed like a legitimate business, which it was mostly, but more importantly it was a way of cleaning large amounts of drugs money. A cash business, where there are no invoices and receipts, and only punters handing over fares, is the perfect vehicle for laundering money. You can lose clean chunks of money inventing fictitious rides. So you have to pay tax on the 'profits'. Big deal. When you're making thousands of per cent on your initial investments, a sliver of the final result to the Revenue is a small price for legitimizing it all. There were several other money laundries in McGurk's operation but this one, with more than five hundred cars in the city, was the most important.

This was Carpenter's and my last throw. The word about Brown's demise would be searing its way to London, not that it needed any special scrambled communication – his death had led the news and was all over the papers. I had argued that we now had to go for McGurk, that he would soon begin to figure out that he might be connected to the bombing, or he would at least be worried that something might filter out in the aftermath which could indicate a relationship between himself and Brown.

'Put it through the door,' McGurk's voice said.

'Sorry, sir, Sanny said I hud tae hand it over personal, or ah'd huv ma jotters. Ah'm really sorry, like. Ye'll huv tae sign for it, ah'm afraid. You know Sanny, he'll huv ma knackers.' Which he would, if he knew about this, or if McGurk called him, which would be difficult, as before arriving here I'd cut the phone lines to Maxi and to McAteer's home. Now, if McGurk tried to ring him on a mobile – well, I was banking on that not happening – but if it did, I was rather hoping he'd be sufficiently sussed to realize that shooting me in the head on his own doorstep wouldn't be the wisest strategy for his future. Besides, he wasn't fool enough to keep anything that could bring him a jail sentence, like a shooter, on his own premises, or he would have gone down long ago.

'Right. Give me a minute.'

It was a long one.

Carpenter had agreed that there was no other option, apart from retreat, to going after McGurk – 'And I'll be damned, having come so far, if I'll give up now,' – but she worried that she would become identifiably embroiled in the leprous actions. 'Us lepers spread our own infection,' I said, 'there's no reason why you can't deny everything. Just tell them that I went off the rails again, that I sought my own solutions. *That* they'll believe.' She hadn't looked too convinced.

Eventually I heard various tumblers move and the door swung open. He was wearing a white dressing gown, a shade under six foot tall, with a lean face, the line of a scar across the right side of his jaw, and dark, greying close-cropped hair. 'The letter,' I said, putting my hand into the inside pocket of my coat. There was just the slightest flicker of bemused recognition before the spray was out and I had fired a long burst of Mace into his face. He screamed, clutching at his eyes, which left his lower region nicely unprotected for a fast shot with my right foot to his scrotum.

As he gagged and writhed and fell back into the hallway I jumped over him, dragged him away from the door by the back of his collar and then kicked it shut. The dog was the next problem. It was a large and rather aged and portly German Shepherd which came bounding from the back of the house, hit the polished wood flooring of the hall and then came sliding and scrabbling towards me. I crouched slightly, intending to give it a cloud of Mace as it came, but its legs seemed to give up, it buckled and slid and came to rest against a wall, completely still. For a second I couldn't work out what was happening. Then I started to giggle. 'It's had a fucking heart attack!'

I took a few quick steps back to McGurk, who had the sense not to try to move, went into the pocket of my coat again, stored the gas canister, pulled out one of the pre-cut lengths of rope, jerked his hands behind him and quickly bound and knotted them together.

'Not one word,' I said quietly in his ear, 'or I'll blow your wife's fucking head off first. Got it?' He moaned, which I took to be assent, and then I set off in a run to hit the bedroom. A door was opening at the end of the hallway. I jumped at it, jerked it open and she came tumbling out into my arms. She had a phone in her right hand. I locked her wrist, forcing her to drop it, then kicked her legs away, pulled her on to the floor and trussed her hands just like her husband's. The ties that bind!

She had a dressing gown on too – probably with his and hers on the pockets, I wasn't looking too closely – so I grabbed hers by the collar and pulled her behind me along the hall like a sack, to deposit her behind her man. She was cursing and kicking out at me, so I flipped her on to her stomach and stood with my left foot on her like a hunter with his dead trophy. 'Listen up!' I shouted. 'You've survived this far. Stay lucky. Do as I say and shut the fuck up!'

She started to shout again so I moved my foot quickly up behind her neck and pressed down hard, forcing her face into the floor. She stopped. 'Better. Now, I'm not going to kill you unless I have to. So don't make me have to. And having to involves the slightest disagreement or dissent, OK?' Both of them seemed to nod, although in McGurk's case it could still be a rictus of pain.

I did a quick run through the house, opening cupboards until I found the one I wanted in the kitchen. I hit the eject button and pocketed the closed-circuit tape, then, scanning around, I picked up a bottle of Heinz ketchup and slurped some into the innards of the recorder.

By the time I skipped back to the hall McGurk was on his knees. Brave but foolish. I clipped him hard on the jaw with a right, sending him spinning back and out. Most people wind up their punches and try to land the maximum area of knuckle, whereas the killing way is to dip the shoulder and spin in like a shot-putter, making sure that all of the force is concentrated solely into the points of the first two knuckles. A bit of training and you can punch through wood like that. I hoped I hadn't splintered his jaw.

The wife was moaning again and trying to slither towards him on her stomach. I stood on the hem of her dressing gown, stopping her. 'If you want to see him alive again,' I said loudly from above, 'you'll tell no one when we take him. Not the police, and not your pals. I'll be in touch about the ransom. Of course,' I let go with my foot, 'you may not want to save him, in which case just say the word now and I'll stiff him.'

'Fuck you!' she snarled between gritted teeth.

'I'll take that as a vow of silence, then?'

I skipped over the two splayed bodies and opened the front door. Carpenter had backed the van right up to it and the sliding rear door was open, the engine running. I gave her the thumbs-up sign, which she caught in her driver's door mirror, and then I went back for McGurk, first taping his mouth with the gaffer tape (his jaw didn't feel broken but it was certainly going to puff up). I dragged him along to the door, then pulled him up and over my shoulder before shrugging him off into the van, heaving down the steel door and locking over the hasp. Then I walked round and opened the passenger door and climbed in. The whole escapade had taken less than three minutes. I was surprised to see that my hands and legs were trembling. Out of practice.

Carpenter had the van in gear and we were off. 'I still say this is stupid and unnecessary.'

'Quiet. On this manoeuvre *I'm* the senior officer. Just drive on at a reasonable speed and make sure we don't get stopped.'

The van bumped into the road and away.

Once we were clear of the city and heading up the side of Loch Lomond I told Carpenter to pull into the first empty lay-by. McGurk had been displaying signs of consciousness. When she pulled the van up I jumped over the seats into the back, retrieved another length of cord, tied up his feet, and then pulled out the fisherman's knife Carpenter had supplied me in the list of kit I had given her. I put the razor-sharp blade to his dressing gown sleeve and scissored through it right up to the armpit. There were several boxes in the back, all marked with my code, and one large and heavy one, together with several off-cuts of old carpet. I dug into the box where I knew the medicinal gear was, pulled out a sealed pack of syringes and needles, broke into it and set one dose-master up, pulled out the sealed bottle next to it, opened it up and drew off the needful. When the syringe was full, allowing a quick blast on the plunger to blow off any air – if he had to die, I didn't want it to be prematurely of an air embolism – I pulled back his bound arms, selected a vein, jabbed in the needle and pushed. Then I tucked the works back in the box, skipped into the front seat and signalled to Carpenter to drive on.

It was one of those mornings when the early season sun comes up and slowly cooks the dew, puddles of mist hanging in hollows of the land, the loch still and polished, with the hills on the other side running into it ochre and charcoal-coloured, slashed occasionally by burns and waterfalls. I rolled down the window a quarter turn. 'Smell the day, Carpenter.' I squirmed back in the seat and put my feet up on my side of the dashboard.

'I'm surprised you can smell anything, after the stuff you've stuck up your nose.'

'Not any more Carpenter, I'm a changed man. I'm finished with drugs.' She snorted. I was wishing I could. 'Almost.'

I looked back over my shoulder, McGurk was still. The heroin and morphine fix would gave him happy slumbers for hours to come. 'You've OD'd him, I hope,' the driver said out of the corner of her mouth.

I ignored her. 'We've forgotten something crucial.'

'The Teflon overcoats?'

'Music. Walkman, CDs or whatever.'

'What's the choice of soundtrack for slow torture and murder?'

'Anything by Sting or Barry Manilow.'

She glanced round at me. 'So what's wrong with Baz?'

'We can stop on the way and pick up a Walkman and some tapes.' Although the prospect of finding a hi-fi shop or a garage with a well-equipped shop along this route was remote. 'I haven't properly listened to any music in years. The last thing I bought—' I searched the mental juke box, '—was something by John Fogerty, because Emily was a bit of a musical throwback and she got into Creedence Clearwater. So I bought this album, because I thought he must be this really cool guy. There was this quote about him, someone famous was sitting next to him on flight, Paul McCartney or someone, who goes, "Hey, John, I've always admired how you could get so much out of three chords." And Fogerty pulls the sunglasses down on to the bridge of his nose, looks round. "What the fuck you mean, man, three chords? I only know two."' We had reached Tarbet and a fork in the road. 'Anyway, the album was shit. I applied a little heat to the vinyl and shaped it into a plant pot holder.'

She changed down the gears, then swung right and up them again. 'You're just like a big kid. You're loving this.'

I considered this for a few moments as we picked up speed again. 'At least it gets me into the outdoors.'

We were retracing the route I had scouted out forty-eight hours before. And bar any unexpected eventualities, like a random police check at 8 a.m., it would be as easy. The only other real risk was that the van number plate had been noted by neighbours and relayed to his minions, but where were they going to start looking? There was no one on our tail and the van wasn't going to be hanging around anywhere looking like just another rusting and abandoned West Highland eyesore. 'Maybe the music isn't such a good idea,' I concluded. Carpenter said nothing, just swung the van around the hairpins of the Loch Lomond road.

We fell quiet until we had left the loch behind and hit the higher ground towards Crianlarich. We had barely passed another vehicle going the other way and, looking back through the rear windows of the van, there was nothing behind us. McGurk was lying in a relaxed, comatose S-shape of limbs and body. I looked closer, being vaguely concerned that he might throw up in his stupor and choke to death, but he still seemed to be breathing and the only emission was a damp patch on his dressing gown where he had evidently pissed himself. I settled back into my thoughts as we turned right towards Killin.

'I'm feeling a bit sad and depressed,' I said after a while, realizing what the feeling was, but this time unable to properly attach it to anything.

'Drug deprivation.' She was getting to know me.

Looking around at her, this stunning big woman in the driving seat, it occurred to me. 'Just a few days back, I was the one being called glib. There's some kind of strange personality exchange going on here.' I sat up sharply in the seat. 'Hoots, mon. D'ye think we could've crossed into Briga-doon yet?'

'Do these violent mood swings ever worry you, Downe?'

'Just drive the van, Carpenter. I'm bored, restless and itching.'

Past Killin I told her to take the left towards the Bridge of Balgie, piercing between two Munros, Ben Lawers and Meall nan Tarmachan, and after a mile or so I found the westerly track, shrouded by scrub and afflicted Scots pine. We nosed up it a couple of hundred yards to the caravan, which stood on a muddy plateau surrounded by rhododendrons, haw-thorn, overgrown gorse and spindly trees. As I got out of the passenger's door I could hear in the distance the mumble of falling water in a burn.

The caravan had sunk on its axles, tyres long since perished, and alongside it was a dilapidated wooden shed patched with corrugated iron, where the calor gas canisters were stored along with the rusted metal dustbin. I had seen the advertisement for the van on a postcard in a newsagents in Killin – the ad stressed the seclusion and the location for serious hill-walkers – and although the card was yellowed, and when I called the farmer who owned it he said it was out of season, my excuse of being a mad Yank with money, keen to stravaig the hills of his family's youth, did the trick. I took it for two weeks, but what I had in mind wasn't going to take nearly that long. We couldn't afford the time.

'Better get the cargo unloaded,' I shouted into the cab. 'You deal with the caravan and I'll unload this.' I chucked the keys for the door in to her.

When I had everything hefted out of the back of the van, including the last package, McGurk (I tore most of his covering off and humped him on to a single divan), I took a pan outside and found the water tap on the end of a long green hose which disappeared into the vegetation and prob-ably drained from some stagnant pool further up the glen. I filled the pan, then slapped it on the cooker and lit the gas under it. 'A nice cup of tea, eh, Carpenter?'

She gave me one of her raised eyebrows looks, I walked over to McGurk who was showing signs of life, although fairly amoebic ones, and I ripped off the gaffer tape. 'You can scream all you like now,' I said, slapping his face, 'because I'd rather enjoy it, and there's no one around to hear you.' I leaned over him. 'You're not in your own patch now, you cunt—' a few vicious swear words always impart seriousness of intent, '—this is my kind of terrain. Just consider it's like an Outward Bound course. Because if you fail it that's exactly what you'll be – from this life.'

Just to make sure he was listening – well, actually, because I rather like doing it – I slapped him with the back of my hand around his violently swollen jaw. He winced, which I took to be understanding.

When I looked back, Carpenter was standing with her arms folded against a drawer unit next to the small, hissing cooker.

She had a curious and frightened look on her face, which I tried to make light of. 'Stop looking at his cock so wistfully, Mrs Grey,' which certainly had the effect of changing her expression from fear to contempt and mystification.

'Mrs Grey?'

'Code.' I blew her a kiss. 'You can call me Captain America.'

'Like fuck.'

'What's up, haven't you got the stomach for it now that it's no longer abstract?' She turned away and began rummaging through one of the boxes I had marked 'supplies'. 'Anyway, he shouldn't get a chance to look at your face.' I partially drew the concertinaed partition between the two halves of the van. 'Make a strong black coffee for my guest because I want him to be fully aware, to have informed choices, about what's going to happen.'

Bizarrely, I was beginning to feel a troubling sense of loss, of parting. At first I couldn't quite place it. 'I'm going to miss you, Karen,' I said as much to myself as her. Then louder, 'You should be going shortly.'

I was slapping my subject's face again to rouse him when I felt a light tap on the shoulder. Carpenter was standing just behind the half-shut partition. She motioned to me. I raised my eyebrows and she motioned again, moving across to the door, opening it and slipping down the two wooded steps to the grass. After looking back at the lolling McGurk I followed her outside.

She took a deep breath. 'I hate this, Downe. It's – I don't know, so calculatedly bestial.'

I shrugged and quickly touched her cheek. 'Yeah, but what he does is a lot worse. Justify it that way or, better still, don't think about it. If that still doesn't work, get out, change your job, marry a social worker.'

Her head dropped a little so that she was staring at my feet. 'Take care of yourself, Downe.' And then she looked up, and either there were tears in her eyes or the wind was in mine, as she quickly leaned forward and kissed me on the lips and stood back.

'Carpenter, you care!' and I grabbed her in a big bear hug, which became much more tender, and then I kissed her, and loitered there. 'Just keep to the deal,' I said, pulling away. 'You'll have what I have in a few days and then I'm off. OK?'

She nodded, almost sadly, then turned away, and I watched her climb into the van, start it up, wave to me through the windscreen then turn away to concentrate on backing the van out. I stared until I lost sight of it and her in the trees and scrub, and after a couple of minutes even the sound of the exhaust had been drained out by the rushing of the burn. I felt so bad about myself that I went back into the caravan and slapped McGurk with renewed vigour.

After an hour or so and the four cups of strong coffee which I fed to him, he was awake and conscious enough to respond to questions, with nods and grunts mostly, because the side of his face was swollen like a dirigible. He hadn't tried to drop dire threats on me, he wasn't that stupid, just sat hunched up, naked, arms caught behind him (my conscience had allowed me to release his feet) throwing me murderous glances, undermined slightly by the pumped-up pupils and a tendency to nod off now and then.

When he was sufficiently recovered to take in what I was about to tell him, I sat down on the single bed opposite, clutching my own cup of coffee. 'I don't have a lot of time, McGurk, so this isn't going to be very sophisticated. You're in the middle of nowhere, there isn't a house within three miles, no one's going to come charging to the rescue. Understand?' He made no sign that he did. I shook my head, as if in sadness. 'Listen, pal, you don't know just how lucky you are to be alive. If it were up to me you wouldn't be, believe me. It may not seem like it now, but just try to regard all this—' I motioned around, '—as your lottery win. Congratulations, McGurk, you've won your life.'

He slurred and mumbled something.

'No need for thanks.'

What he said sounded like, 'I know you now.'

'That doesn't matter. I don't care. You would never find me. And if you did, well, I still wouldn't care.'

'It'd be slow,' jerking his head up, trying to focus through the junk still drifting in his system.

I sipped the coffee. 'Sorry, McGurk, I don't have time for this. I have a plane to catch and we've got a lot to do, you and me. You're going to tell me everything about your organization, about the people involved, the businesses, the bank accounts, the police, councillors, members of the church or whoever else is on your payroll. You're going to give me a complete run-down on everything, the minutiae, the list of serial numbers, account numbers, tax dodges, frauds, victims – everything.'

He shook his head and spluttered, or perhaps it was a laugh. 'I know, your guys will be after me, you're stalling for time, hoping against hope that something will turn up for you but, I assure you, it won't. You'll talk. Even if your wife breaks the old code and goes to the police, it won't do you any good.' I instanced for him. 'Your pal, Brown, did I mention? Dead. He was involved in an air disaster, an explosion, actually.

'There's something about the arrogance of power which usually leads to over-confidence. His mistake was to use his private line at work to keep in touch with you on your mobile. I'm sure he never imagined that someone would actually pull all of those phone records from BT and set up a tap on the phone. He should have known that you can't even trust your own side in these changed days.'

McGurk was sullenly staring. 'I thought his ending was

331

particularly fitting – did you know that he was one of the cops involved in investigating Lockerbie? I got that from his service record. My wife and kid died at Lockerbie. You'll bear that in mind, I know, thinking you can find out who I am that way. And you can.' I took several deep breaths. 'But all you'll find is someone I was. You won't find me. Nobody can.'

I drained my coffee. 'Enough of this existentialist tosh, McGurk. I don't want to hurt you, other than by way of teaching you a bit of a lesson. I loathe myself for all this – well, and other things – believe me. So, now I feel better about myself, just tell me everything nice and calmly over several nights and many cups of coffee or, trust me, I'll hurt you so badly you'll never recover. I'll break you. I have highly developed skills in extracting the truth under heavy manners, millions of dollars have gone into my training – doesn't it make you just the littlest bit proud that the essence, the apotheosis of American military know-how is deployed against you? No?'

He tried to spit at me, but because of the state of his jaw it ended up as a futile spray which he got most of. 'Fuck you,' he enunciated very clearly and intently. 'I know you.'

'So *that's* where your wife got her charming mouth.' I swung off the divan, grabbed him in a headlock, then dragged him across the tin floor to the door which I kicked open, and jumped out into the air with him following me, before letting him go to sprawl face down in the grass. 'Up! Or I'll drag you by the arms or the fucking hair!' He stumbled to his knees and then on to wobbling legs, completely naked, grass and mud and sheep shit sticking to him, looking white and recently disinterred, as I pulled him along by the shoulders into the trees.

About ten yards in I kicked his legs from under him and went into my trouser pocket for twine, looped his ankles to the thongs on his wrists, then trotted back to the caravan. When I came back he had slithered a few yards on his stomach, trying to get away, thinking that I must have gone back to get a knife or gun, something deadly. Which I had. I bent over and smacked the needle into his ass and pressed the plunger. 'Smack and acid,' I said down to him. 'This is your last choice. Choose the humane way.'

He roared and shook and struggled, so I bent down, grabbed the bindings and pulled him the few yards to the where I had prepared the ground a couple of days before. 'The visions will start in a while and they won't be pleasant. No change of mind?'

He was shivering and struggling, cursing and shaking his head. I threw away the syringe, grabbed the knife from my pocket, cut the ties with a couple of slashes and, before he could stretch or begin to force the circulation back, I rolled him with my right foot and he went over the lip, falling on his back into the coffin in the grave. I had the lid down and was standing on top of it, screwing it down, before he even knew where he was. Then I hopped out and eased behind a bush where I had left the spade and the plastic tubing. The sound of muffled screaming sounded like some far-off animal caught in a trap. I had drilled a two-inch diameter hole through the coffin lid and now I screwed the piping into it.

'Save your breath. Save oxygen, McGurk, you're going to need it all.' I pulled myself out of the grave again and, carefully at first so as not to dislodge the air line, began shovelling dirt into the hole, until I really got into the rhythm and worked up a sweat as I hefted the spade. It took me ten minutes. When I had finished, the tube was sticking out of the ground by about six inches. Who knew what kind of creeping insect life would find its way down during the night? 'I'll be back in the morning, McGurk,' I shouted down the tube, 'and I think you'll be in a more communicative mood!'

21

I woke next day with the first light, after a remarkably
dreamless and entirely guiltless sleep. Condensation was
washing down the insides of the metal-framed windows. I
wriggled out of the sleeping bag in my underpants and tee
shirt and lit the cooker to get some heat around the prefabricated alloy hut, shivering slightly on the linoleum. Nothing
like what McGurk was going through, of course. Did I feel
anything about that? Only that he was inconveniencing me,
stalling me in getting on with my life.

That threw me slightly. I couldn't remember when I had
last looked forward rather than back. And I hadn't had the
airplane dream for days. I shook my head and hunted for the
one saucepan and the water jug to make coffee. Gradually, a
feeling of guilt inched over me, but not about McGurk,
however. Somehow I felt ashamed of myself for my guarded
optimism, that I had let my dead ones down. No one, I told
myself, would expect their surviving partner to grieve forever, to destroy their own life in memory and regret, but it
didn't take root. I slopped water into the chipped cup and
spooned in coffee, stirring it viciously, then sat on the rumpled sleeping bag nursing it, feeling the darkness rolling back
in. I wanted to punish myself, or some excuse like that, so I
put down the cup, hunted down the medical box, broke out
another syringe and needle and put them together. Then I
retrieved the spoon from the sink, licked it, stuck it into the
open plastic bag of smack in the box, knocked most of the

stuff back off, and moved back to the cooker and the saucepan to cook up the fix.

There were enough different fixes, potions, hallucinogens, heart boosters – smack, speed, acid, even a small harvesting of the mellow herb – to have me put down for about a five-stretch for trafficking, which caused me to laugh. That would be the least of it. How was I going to explain about the premature burial in the woods? A *Guinness Book of Records* attempt? I laughed so much that I almost let the spoon bubble dry.

Sitting on the bed, syringe in my right hand, looking at the pumped up vein in my left arm, the blood caught by the belt looped and tightened round it, I told myself that I was only doing this to fight off the demons, get me through, or because I didn't care, and I recalled the last time I had shot up in prison and I knew that I was lying to myself then and now. That I was doing it because I loved it more than anything I had left in the world. I felt a shiver of revulsion and then the nip of the needle as it went in.

I rolled out of it three or four hours later, slowly recomposing in the bed. It felt like one of those cod special effects movie scenes where you watch a small cloud in a dark place gradually metamorphose into a scheming villain. It was stupid, I shouldn't have shot up, possibly fucked everything up for chemical bliss. I felt sick, unused to the smack, my system slowly devolving into another dependency, or battling against it. I found my clothes and got dressed, retched in the sink several times, then went back to the cardboard box and dug around until I saw the sealed packet of amphetamine sulphate glowing biliously at me. I cut it open with the edge of my nail, scooped out a covering on my right pinkie, blocked my left nostril with my left index finger and inhaled, repeating this action a couple of times until I felt the motor begin to sputter and turn inside me.

As my mind slowly began to glow and catch fire, I started to wonder just how much I could trust Carpenter, then dismissed the subject. What other option was there but just to keep on? But I restated one particular vow: there was no way I was going back to prison. I'd be taking the final exit route instead.

Carpenter swam back into my thoughts again as I was trying to put on my boots, and I realized that, somehow, I had become extremely fond of her – she was as much out of her depth as me and everyone else I had ever known – although the rational area of my raddled brain also hoped I would never see her again.

When I got to the grave in the clearing I shouted down the air hole. There was no reply. For a moment I considered not going through the effort of digging down, of just hoiking out the length of tubing, patting down the soil and leaving, particularly as I was having difficulty keeping concentration enough to find and wield the spade. But I shook my head to dislodge the wool and began attacking the fresh earth. If this compressed session of brainwashing hadn't worked, then the next time I put him down was going to have to be for good.

It took me a half-hour of sporadically intense digging to hit the wood. As I was doing it, flashes of scenes from every Christopher Lee movie I had ever seen scrolled through my head. One thing I had never done, and which I promised myself I would, was to see a vampire film on a huge screen with stereo sound battering me while completely off my face on acid.

I scraped most of the remaining dirt off the surface of the coffin, my sweat falling like beads of blood on to it and, with some difficulty, unfastened the screws holding the lid down. I don't know what I was expecting when I got out and hunkered down over the hole to ease up the lid – the hairs on the back of my neck were at quivering attention – but McGurk was lying there, like a long white slug, his hands almost held up in surrender, which I realized was probably a frozen poise from fruitlessly pushing up on the lid. His eyes were open, staring fixedly into the distance, but he was completely motionless. A heart attack or suffocation?

I stood up, looking down on him, naked, droplets of dirt on his chest and stomach, a ruff of scrubby, greying pubic hair around his penis and balls and I thought, 'Shit. Now I'm going to have to fill the bastard in again!' And then he blinked and took a small breath. He was probably still tripping, poor bastard. I didn't want to think about the gruesome and uncontrollable visions he must have seen. But nothing, I thought to myself, the equal of my everyday tortures.

It took me half an hour to get him out of the ground and into the caravan. He was shivering, occasionally babbling, batting at unseen things in front of his eyes. I half-carried, half-dragged him up the stairs, threw him down on the other single bunk, put my sleeping bag over him, then gave him an armful of heroin, which seemed to calm him. And waited.

Perhaps his mind would never come back. In which case not everything was lost. At least the head of the organization had been taken off, if not all of the tentacles and stringworts. It was still a fair result.

The hours passed, which I spent brewing tea and coffee, with hash, doing fitful exercise, fighting myself about shooting-up, finding a sort of chemical equilibrium in occasionally tooting speed and slurping the adulterated hot drinks. I hadn't eaten for about eighteen hours but, even then, the two drugs must have provided some sort of balance, because my stomach felt hollow rather than hungry.

I nodded off as the darkness came down, waking a couple of hours later to his mumbling, and some of the words were even intelligible. At least he seemed to have passed through catatonia, and the fearful hallucinatory phase. What I needed now was enough lucidity to debrief him, as we used to say as we held various implements to sundry enemies of varying coloration.

I brewed some more tea and shot McGurk up again, then tied his hands to his feet and retired to bed. Nothing to read, nothing to listen to, except, at best, the babbling nonsenses of a drugged captive – I had really come well prepared.

I dreamed of a clean beach and sunshine. It felt like it must be somewhere in southern California. The sky was clear, the sun seemed to bathe me and warm my soul. I looked back over my shoulder and noticed two sets of footprints, but when I looked around there was no one else there, just my own sense of someone missing. The sea seemed endlessly inviting and I felt I had the strength to swim in it forever. It lapped over my bare feet, and when I looked back once more there were two sets of footprints again, leading to where I was. And then there really was someone at my shoulder. I knew it would be Carpenter. 'Do we really have to go back?' I said as she smiled at me. And then an inky darkness, save for bright and burning objects falling through it, replaced everything. I woke with my tee shirt sticking to me.

Throughout the day there were signs of awakening in McGurk, although I kept his smack level topped up. I wanted him to be fully appreciative of the effects of what he was dealing with. As the light began to fade in the late afternoon, his eyes, huge and all-seeing as they were, at least seemed to be able to focus properly. He was looking at me, shivering, his jaw trembling. I moved closer to hear what he was saying. The voice was cracked and husky. 'Wa-wa-ter.'

I skipped over to the pot, brought it back, held up his head and dribbled water into his mouth and down his chin. His lips were cracked, with a bluish tinge all around them, but the death pallor had faded to a uniform grey. 'D'you know where you've been, McGurk? Are you beginning to remember it all?' His head shook and large tears began to form and slide down his cheeks. 'You're never going to forget it, are you?' He was shivering, drawing his knees and the sleeping bag up to his face. 'You don't want to go back, do you? No, didn't think so. I told you once before what would happen if you weren't honest with me, if you didn't tell me everything. You know what will happen to you, don't you?'

He was crying like a child now, the hard gangster buried, probably for ever, just a few feet away. I could not begin to imagine what a hallucinogen-filled experience like that would do to your mind, but it wouldn't ever be the same. I only hoped enough of it remained to remember and retrieve what I wanted.

'I'll give you something to make you feel better.' Then I stuck another needle in his arm.

Next morning, rain was battering on the roof of the van, as if it was being peppered with a shotgun. After I made some herbal tea and topped up the junk in McGurk's system, I untied him and broke out the food, confectionery mainly, bars of chocolate, nut toffee, with a few packets of emergency rations of the type favoured by climbers and astronauts – just one tear of the packet and some internal chemical reaction produces a three-course meal, complete with candles, a laid table and a gypsy violinist in the background.

I settled for chocolate and fed him a few squares as I ate. He seemed to be on a tidal wash between reality and some dark place where the demons dwelled, because he kept shivering and flinching in terror. But over a couple of hours that seemed to settle down in favour of a raw sanity.

I broke out the tape recorder and put it on the fold-down table between us. But before I switched it on I told him, 'You're going to tell me everything about your operation, aren't you, McGurk, or you know what'll happen?' He nodded frantically. 'I'm going to tape it all and then I'm going to check it out. And if everything you tell me checks out –

every single, last detail – you'll get away from here with your life. Otherwise – otherwise I'm going to throw you back in the pit, chuck the dirt on and walk away from here. You know that, don't you?' He shook his head, then nodded feverishly. 'OK. But first I'm going to tell you a story. It's about me, but you come into it, and if you listen carefully you'll see how it has saved your life. So far.'

I didn't know what his attention span was, what little chemical globules were disturbing the flow of electricity around his brain, so I kept it as short and unrevelatory as possible, sketching in how I was born of Scottish parents in the States, how I came to join the army, and a brief precis of the events leading up to and past Lockerbie. 'It began to go wrong when I started to enquire too long and too deeply into who was really behind it, you see. But that was really the catalyst which, through a sort of chain reaction, brought us here. I made enemies, I guess, and I wouldn't heed a warning.' He was staring at me, either trying to memorize my face for later, or off on some wild flight of his corrupted imagination. 'They found a load of stuff in my apartment in Frankfurt, coke mainly. And it wasn't mine. I don't say that I wasn't using, I was, and I was pretty open about it, didn't care. Even doing a little bit of friendly dealing. But none of this – and it was a serious amount – was mine. So I was court-martialled for trafficking. You might think there's some rough justice at work here—' he seemed to snarl at me, which I took to be approval of the way it was, '—prison, well—' images, increasingly more violent flooded through my brain, '—it was something I don't intend to go through again. Drugs, bribes, sodomy, the lash – get the picture?'

I got up and wandered over to the cooker. Turning my back on him was a mistake. He launched his manic last attempt at escape. I heard the noises behind my back but was too slow to react. As I turned he was flailing at me. Something hard and heavy glanced off the side of my head as I tried to duck inside the swing and for a millisecond I lost consciousness, finding myself on my knees in front of him, with him aiming another blow down at me, the small tape recorder a bludgeon in his hand. I was severely out of practice. I had badly underestimated the power of the will to live.

As I threw up my left arm the blow came down, and whether he was weak from the last few days, had expended all the nervous energy in the initial swing, or it was the result of drugged disequilibrium, the blow bounced through my defensive guard but hit my left shoulder. He must have struck a nerve because the feeling drained out of my arm. Sounds in my head were coming and going like someone was using a wah-wah pedal, and I could feel blood pumping out from above the hairline over my left eye. But instinctively I shot out my right hand, grabbed his naked balls, which were unmissable in front of my eyes, or rather the unbloody right one, and twisted and squeezed with every ounce of my strength.

He squealed like an animal, dropped both hands to mine and his dick, and his body began to close over like a knife. Hoping that I had enough strength, like a boxer coming up after a count, I launched all my effort into scrambling to my feet, still twisting his scrotum off, and smacking him under the chin with my head. He flew back with me still attached, knocking through the screen between the two parts of the van, bouncing off the edge of the bed, the back table, then against the wall on what had been my side.

The impulsion of twenty-odd stones of meat and muscle at pace must have finally unhinged the old axles of the van because it sagged over to the side, giving me another advantage. I fell on to him and kept driving my head at his face. I went on too long, long after he was still, but there wasn't much force in my punishment and eventually I slid off him.

He looked a bit like one of those Borneo mud men, except the mud was blood, and a lot of it mine. I staggered up, against the angle of the floor, and searched for the ropes in the mayhem, circulation painfully beginning to return to my left arm, and then I trussed him as tight as I could. I searched for the medical box where, along with the medicaments, I had packed bandages and plasters, and painfully I attempted to staunch the blood and tape myself up.

When he came to he was back in the grave, but this time looking at me and the sky rather than oppressive darkness. 'I'm not fucking about with you any more, McGurk.' I had neglected to pack scissors so I hadn't been able to cut the hair away around the wound, only stick a couple of plasters on to the hair – after dousing the area in water and a cocaine paste to numb it – and then bind a bandage round. I looked like a particularly careworn Swami.

I had splashed water over him and his wounds were superficial, although his face looked like it had been worked on by a special effects make-up artist. His genitals, too, because his balls looked like the kind of obscene numbers which hang down from stallions. I had shot him with smack and morphine again so he wouldn't be focusing on the pain, but rather on what I wanted. As he moaningly came to, I considered whether I should thank the army for my battlefield first aid skills, or curse it for first removing my fear of the needle.

'Please,' he was shivering in the coffin, 'no more.'

'This is it, McGurk. You either give me detailed answers to every question I ask you or I shut the fucking lid now and dance on it. You hearing me?'

'I'm shivering to death,' he croaked.

'It's not the cold that'll kill you, cunt, you'll go warmly with three foot of insulation on the lid.' I was sitting on a pile of cushions I had dragged from the van and fortunately I hadn't forgotten to bring a notebook and pens because the tape recorder, after its encounter with my skull, was reduced to its component parts. 'We're going to start with your finances. I want all of the details of all the businesses, the directors, the bank accounts, I want personal bank account numbers, sums, deposit boxes, wife's jewellery, whatever there is. In every nook, cranny and offshore account. And I'll check. And if there's any one thing wrong, or you've omitted anything, you get it! Understand?'

'Ye-yeah,' he was shivering uncontrollably. 'Can I have another fuckin' fix, man?'

'Give me all of these details, or make a good start, and you can. I'll also wrap you in the two sleeping bags. Maybe make some tea.' I opened to the first page of the shorthand notebook. 'Now let's go.'

It took three hours at least to get everything down, then another hour to cross-examine and double-check, until I was sure that there was nothing he was holding out on. There was three to four million in cash salted in various bank accounts around the world, but mostly in Dublin, and a spaghetti of conduits and money-washing filters. When I was entirely satisfied that he was honestly relieving himself of the information, I did what I had promised, shot him up with skag, heaped the sleeping bags on him and fed him herbal tea, which was deuced difficult to make at an angle in the van. Fortunately the gas line hadn't fractured in the fracas.

We got on to the names of his knaves and associates. By the time I had all that down, and tried to catch him out on errors and omissions, it was getting very late in the day. Sleeping in the caravan was going to be a little problematic, so I made a bivouac in the trees using branches as a skeleton and mats, mattresses, curtains and cushions from the van, as well as foliage, for cover. I made a fire, too, which took some time because, despite having matches and the rough makings, I was a little out of practice.

The cooker in the caravan was a four-ring portable so I

343

unhitched it from the gas, dragged it out, then coupled the canister back up to it so we could play houses in the forest. McGurk slept most of the time, mostly because I kept him chemically comatose. I wanted him hooked, I wanted him to have a habit, I wanted him to ache and know what it was like to be an addict, I wanted him on the level of those he profited from. I wanted him in the mud and shit living like a worm, or I'd put him among them.

Finally I shot him up again, dosed myself with some hash tea and we bedded down in our shelter as the rain began to spatter and fall and the fire hissed and fumed.

I had to wake him up in the morning. He had been bound all night but I wasn't going to take another chance like yesterday so I left him that way. I fed him straight tea and a couple of nut bars, then propped him up against the back of the bivvy.

'What I didn't get a chance to tell you yesterday,' I was sipping on tea, 'was that we have a connection, which, I suppose, is why you're still alive. Call me an old sentimentalist – actually, it's not that, I wanted to reserve this news for the end. This is my final revenge on my old man. I won't bore you with the angst, finally destroying all that's left of him, everything that he worked for, connived over, atonement for the lives he ruined.' I grinned. 'I was getting a little pompous there. What you don't realize is that he was your man, your father's man, in the States. What d'you think of that, then?' I was smirking but it was impossible to tell what he was thinking, past incredulity.

His mouth opened, as if he was about to say something – I fancied he was overcome because he realized that finally everything, even the remote hopes that he was harbouring, had just foundered – but then he began to laugh, more of a cackle, but he was definitely laughing.

His head bowed down on his chest and he roared to himself while I watched, and then he looked up. 'You know the name

344

Scott, don't you?' It came out in a throaty rasp. A slither of uncertainty ran through my gut and, I suppose, by the look on my face he could tell that something was falling into place. 'Your mother was Kathy Scott, wasn't she?' He snorted with laughter. 'You don't know, do you? My maw's her sister. Your mother's sister. *Cousin!*'

He was laughing and chuckling to himself and I had nothing to say. I could only look at my sole remaining blood relative. 'A piece of shit like you,' I said to myself as he smiled on.

It made sense now, why my old man had been prepared to sell out the home side, but not the Scottish connection, because it went right to the heart of his family. Loyalty or fear, I didn't know which. Not that it mattered now. I suppose I had been going to kill McGurk, although gratuitous killing doesn't sit easy with me. Now a frayed familial thread was holding me from it. What could I do? I reached for the medical box next to me and brought out the syringes and needles.

'That's great,' McGurk was mumbling, dribble on his chin, 'it'll be like it always was. You're the US end. That's right. It'll be all right. I forgive you, man.'

I looked at him, his head puffy and misshapen, eyes all but closed, a clot of dried blood on his upper lip from his nostrils, scratches and bruises all over his upper body, and I shook my head. I felt hysteria welling up in me.

I said to him, 'Shuffle round and give me your arm.'

He tried a punishing smile. 'Brilliant.' And he bounced around on his bum and held out his bound arms. I grasped an arm, puckered up a vein, stuck in the needle. But instead of pushing the plunger, I pulled it, drawing off a phial of blood, then pushed him away. 'Wha-a-at?' Struggling round to face me.

He watched as I put the other needle into a vein in my left arm and drained out the same amount of blood. I showed

345

both to him, then put them behind my back. 'Blood relatives,' I said. 'What I haven't told you about is me in prison. You've done time, haven't you? But not recently. You'll know that prisons in the States, over here too, I'm sure, are awash with hard stuff – it's the currency. You can get all you want, for a price. Apart from the drugs there's the sex – not much rock 'n' roll – which tends to be rather brutal and, more often than not, non-consensual. Gang rape for pleasure or for punishment. So, what do you get when you combine intravenous drug use, shared needles and bloody homosexuality?'

His mouth was open, either because the shock of realization was setting in, or because it was difficult to breathe. 'That's right. HIV. Aids. And who gives a fuck if there's an epidemic in the prison farms, the military jails and penitentiaries, because these are infected scum anyway?'

I reached behind me for the two syringes, shuffled them around until I didn't know which had come from which arm, and then brought them around in front of me. 'You have reasonable odds. Fifty-fifty.' I was holding the syringes by the barrels, between thumbs and forefingers, needles shining and pointing to the dome of the bivvy. 'It's your choice. You pick.' He was shaking his head, inching back on his buttocks away from me. 'Your shout. Be lucky.' His head was darting around like a cornered animal's, but there was no escape. 'If you don't choose you get both barrels.' I smiled at him. 'Cousin.' His head kept moving but he was making no choice so I began to move towards him.

'All right, all right!' He was on his back now. He nodded towards my right hand.

'Sure?'

'Yes!' he screamed and began howling like a kid. I sat on top of him, his arms between my legs, found a vein and plunged in the syringe.

I left him crying to himself in the shelter as I got what I needed together. Then I went back and cut his bonds. I was going to walk out, try and thumb a lift, which, although I had clamped the bobble hat over my bandaging, might be difficult, given that I looked like a zombie on the loose. If not, I would walk into Killin because I had several calls to make, prime among them to Carpenter's mobile, checking that she had fixed up the passport and ticket, which was the only way she was going to get the notebook. And then I would call the local police and tell them anonymously about the mad junkie in the hills sitting on a sizeable stash of Class A drugs.

I began to walk down the path. 'You can't leave me here!' I heard him screaming from behind, as I did just that.

22

I had done the last of the coke in the toilet at 35,000 feet (does this make me a member of the 'mile higher club'?) because I didn't want to risk smuggling anything through US Customs. I was in Club Class, which was a nice touch from Carpenter, and had been drinking my way pretty steadily across the Pond, with a small interlude for sleep. My new passport, again courtesy of Carpenter, was in the inside pocket of my new suede jacket. She had fulfilled her part of the bargain, as I had mine.

Except that we had a couple of days head start on her. We being me and my friend Stephanie, the computer whizz, who they had used as moral leverage, and this was the payback. I had been keeping in touch with her throughout my mission in the land of my fathers, especially since I had been given the warning that any lack of co-operation might mean danger for her. On the phone I hadn't wanted to alarm her, and also I didn't risk interception of the calls, even though I only called her on public payphones or on the digital mobile I had insisted she get.

I had also transferred the rest of my old man's blood money to her account, keeping just a couple of hundred bucks, telling her I'd explain everything when I got there. And when I did I intended grabbing her and getting lost together for a very long time. We would go to Canada or Mexico, anywhere out of reach of the demands of the new world order, or at least until they forgot about me. Which might take a very long time if the plan I had hatched with her worked.

But I had to make it up to her, for dragging her in, involving her, endangering her. Although I didn't feel too bad about myself: all she had done was to help me, which didn't warrant whatever they'd come up with, destruction of a career or, ultimately, the threat of a death sentence. Now it was payback time for us.

When I had arrived in Killin, walking all the way, I phoned her immediately and gave her the details – account numbers, codes, locations – of all McGurk's diverse stashes. I wanted her to hack into the banks' computer systems and transfer the monies to a variety of worthy causes, I left her to pick, but threw in Medécins sans Frontières, Amnesty, Greenpeace and a couple of others – or, failing that, erase all trace of them ever being there. The last thing I wanted was for the money to be recycled into government accounts where, unlike for the ordinary citizenry, it wasn't a crime to profit from the proceeds of drugs.

I smiled drunkenly to myself. She said she could do it, or at least if she couldn't she knew several others who, together, could, so I left the scale of rewards for them to her and felt good for the two-and-a-half days I hid out in a hillside bothy before handing over the notebook to Carpenter.

McGurk had been picked up not far from the caravan site. He was hopelessly lost and rather grateful to be rescued. He had been trying to find a house where he could steal clothes and a car but it wasn't just his sense of direction which had gone astray. According to Carpenter he had totally cracked. Kept going on about Aids, the grave, and having the test, demanding information about the likelihood of catching it from infected blood, when he wasn't pleading for a fix, that was.

Insanity was probably a good defence against the charges he would face over the drugs. There hadn't been enough evidence to properly pin him, despite fingerprints, mine as well, all over the scene, but there was enough to hold him for a while. So when Carpenter suggested that in exchange for the test and smack liberty he would have to sign a statement, he almost bit her hand off for the deal. He wasn't properly in control of his faculties, of course, probably never would be, but then who, with the possible exception of a Vietcong tunneller, could survive to retain sanity after being locked into a coffin and buried while tripping?

Cruel, but brilliant, I told myself. I smiled at the movie screen in the arm of my chair and settled down to sleep.

23

Carpenter parked the car on the double yellow line, ignoring the signs warning against doing so, had a word with the policeman with the Heckler & Koch at the doorway, then went inside, her heels clicking on the hard polished floor. She cut past the knots of people and children, the parked trolleys and bags, looking for the board. She checked the time, her watch, then headed for the coffee shop to wait.

Sitting down at a table which gave her a view of the arrivals board and the concourse, she sipped at her cappuccino and took a book from her bag. It was a superior Cold War thriller (it held antique fascination for her), which kept her turning the pages and, as she did so with each one, she checked the people coming through and the changing signage.

She had long finished her second coffee when it was time. With a little smile to herself she eased the chair back, stood up and walked crisply across the wide, busy floor.

Less than ten minutes later she saw him, looking dishevelled, drunk, bewildered, but most of all angry. She could see it in his clenched mouth and the muscles twitching in his face. He had a bag slung over his back and he walked slowly, in a slight stoop, as if much was weighing him down. He wasn't looking in her direction when he came through the gap in the barrier and she eased out of the crowd of waiting people and went up to him.

'Short trip, Downe,' his head shot round to take her in, 'but welcome home anyway.'

He spun round, catching sight of her in the knot of people in front of him. 'It was you!' He was biting on his words. 'You arranged it. Me being turned back. A deal—' he went on, leaning close so that she could almost taste the stale booze on his breath, '—is a fucking deal!'

'Funny, that's almost exactly what I was going to say to you, with the expletive deleted.'

'I'll sort you for this.'

She pulled her head away and tapped the end of his nose with her right index finger. 'Careful, now, one word from me and that passport of yours will be withdrawn. We had to bend the rules to get it, you know, you have no right of residency here. And if that happened you'd be stateless. You'd spend the rest of your life bouncing between one airport and another, like a tennis ball, being continually returned.'

He said nothing, just stood hunched over, glowering at her. 'People are watching, Downe,' and, just to rile him further, she bent in and gave him a quick peck on the cheek. 'There, just like a couple. Now take my arm and we'll go to the car and on to somewhere quiet I have in mind, where we can discuss our future together.'

She tugged at his arm, he looked back at where he had been, then back at her, and fell into step a pace behind her as she walked. 'Such plans,' she said over her shoulder, 'I have such plans.'